I0638306

INCURSION
The Narrows of Time Series: Book #2
Written by Jay J. Falconer
www.JayFalconer.com

ISBN-13: 978-0-9840011-0-1   ISBN-10: 0984001107
Publication Date: April 20, 2014
Published 2014 by BOOKBREEZE.COM LLC

This is a work of fiction. Names, characters, places, and incidents are the product of the author's imagination or are used fictitiously. Any resemblance to actual persons living or dead, or business establishments or organizations, actual events or locales is entirely coincidental.

BOOKS BY JAY J. FALCONER

Frozen World Series
> *Silo: Summer's End*
> *Silo: Hope's Return*
> *Silo: Nomad's Revenge*

American Prepper Series
> *Lethal Rain Book 1*
> *Lethal Rain Book 2*
> *Lethal Rain Book 3 (Coming Soon)*
(previously published as *REDFALL)*

Mission Critical Series
> *Bunker: Born to Fight*
> *Bunker: Dogs of War*
> *Bunker: Code of Honor*
> *Bunker: Lock and Load*
> *Bunker: Zero Hour*

Narrows of Time Series
> *Linkage*
> *Incursion*
> *Reversion*

Time Jumper Series
> *Shadow Games*
> *Shadow Prey*
> *Shadow Justice*
(previously published as *GLASSFORD GIRL)*

ONE

Flandreau City, Earth Outpost Eutopia-3

Heaven is waiting with a bloody meat cleaver.

That's what Lucas Ramsay figured the undertaker would write on his tombstone as he walked to the front of the mahogany chair where his latest prisoner sat bound and bleeding. He lifted the man's head, holding it firm with his left hand. He focused on the target, pulled his right arm back and let loose another punch, hammering the dark-skinned man on the jaw. The captive's head snapped to the right, sending the man's weight and a stream of blood flying as he flipped over sideways in the chair. He lay motionless on the basement floor, though his chest was still heaving.

Lucas shook his palm, flexing his fingers to dissipate the throbbing from the last blow. It worked. He bent down and grabbed the crook of the man's arm, then wedged his foot under the leg of the chair. He leaned back, pulling Jenkins and the chair back into a sitting position, thanks in part to the coil of rope still doing its job. Jenkins' head rolled and then slumped, pressing his chin into his chest.

Lucas studied the pool of blood collecting around his latest prisoner's neck as it soaked into the collar of the cotton shirt. He admired the material's absorption properties; they were almost as efficient as Lucas was with his interrogation techniques. He'd certainly had plenty of time to practice, given the string of four guests he'd entertained recently.

He was hopeful that this might be the last interrogation—the last bloodletting—the last meet and beat. He and Professor Kleezebee were close to finding the answers they needed in order to access the past and unravel their godforsaken lineage with the help of the Incursion Chamber. Their brilliant colleague, Master Fuji, was nearing completion of the revolutionary remote viewing device, but the tiny monk needed to make it operational before the veteran constable put the pieces together and figured out that Lucas was the Eastside Exterminator. If not, then the only trip Lucas would be making would be to the hoosegow.

Lucas knew how the townspeople on this remote Earth outpost would react if they knew he was responsible for the recent spree of torture. He couldn't blame them. He hated himself for what he had to do, but he didn't have a choice. There was no other way to find out what happened to his foster brother, Drew. It had been eighteen months since Drew went missing in Lucas' universe after stepping through the portal to the stolen hive ship. Each day was a struggle to breathe without Drew at his side.

Lucas was tired and exhausted, stuck in a vicious cycle of guilt and regret. His version of Earth seemed so far away, both across time and dimension. Dr. Kleezebee's version of Earth was much closer—orbiting in the nearby Milky Way Galaxy—though the Krellian invasion had left the professor's Earth in shambles. Lucas knew he wasn't going anywhere. This outpost in Kleezebee's universe was home, at least until they could crank up the Incursion Chamber and square off against his own version of history.

Despite everything that had happened in the last year and a half, he was thankful to be alive. Thankful that he could continue his search for Drew. Thankful that the stolen Krellian hive ship held together long enough for Kleezebee and their crew to walk away from the crash-landing in the desert of this remote outpost in the spiral Omega galaxy. Otherwise, his missing foster brother Drew would have been an orphan, again—destined to live his life alone and scared somewhere out there in the multi-verse.

Lucas let loose another right-handed punch, this time whacking Jenkins in the stomach. Then he nailed him with an uppercut to the chin, and finished the volley with a quick backhand for good measure.

Jenkins was still conscious. Barely.

"Unreal," Lucas mumbled, as his focus blurred into a thousand-mile-stare. Just one more answer to complete the puzzle; that's all he needed. Yet, it was the most important piece—the one needed to rescue his friends and recover the trio of confiscated E-121 power modules. But time and space stood in the way, as did his latest captive, Alfred P. Jenkins, who was one of Cyrus' Level Five operatives and a traitor to his own people. Lucas needed Jenkins to talk, *now*, and tell him where Cyrus had hidden the two dozen containers of the BioTex material that belonged to Lucas' mentor and boss, Dr. Kleezebee.

Lucas was running out of options. The morning staff would soon arrive to open the restaurant and begin preparing the daily specials. He figured there was only one way this interrogation was going to end, the same way it had with his last victim: with a pile of bloodstained fingers quivering on the floor. The most efficient method of removal was to aim just above the first set of knuckles and use one vertical swing of the razor-sharp cleaver.

The sad thing was, these *meetings* always seemed to end the same way no matter what he tried or how many chances he gave his guests. Nobody talked right away. Blood always had to be drawn first. His guests dared to defy him, holding out as if it were some type of noble cause, filled with a long list of rewards in the afterlife.

"Fools and their fingers soon part ways," Lucas mumbled.

He'd understand if they were protecting their kids or their spouse, but testing his resolve over the simplest commodity—information—didn't make any sense. But it wasn't his job to understand. His task was simple: extract the information any way he could and report it to Kleezebee. He would have gladly passed on these field assignments from the professor, but he was pinned between the narrows of time and necessity. He was on a myopic path, one filled with suffering for his guests, but yet, they were the ones who got off easy. His half of the road was hell, drowning him under a mountain of guilt and loathing for his own skin.

Jenkins grunted and moved his head slowly. He coughed a few short bursts, spurting blood into his lap. He lifted his head and opened his eyes.

Time for another punch, Lucas thought. His hand wasn't throbbing as badly now, but he wasn't sure how much more punishment his knuckles could take. He thought about skipping to the end and using his trusty meat cleaver, but he wanted to, or maybe it was that he needed to give Jenkins another chance.

He leaned forward and threw another right with the full force of his shoulder behind it. When it landed, his hand hit something sharp, tearing open the skin across his knuckles. "Fuck!" he shouted, shaking his hand to disburse the pain.

He peeled open the gash and found a jagged edge from one of Jenkins' teeth buried deep inside. He tore the chip out, tossing it into the wash sink next to the rust-covered water heater in the restaurant's basement. The tooth bounced twice, then circled around the bottom of the porcelain bowl, finally disappearing into the open drain with a click.

"Damn. I can almost see bone," he said, looking back at Jenkins, who was slumped over in the wooden chair, his chin resting against his chest.

He turned on the hot water knob and slid his knuckles under the faucet. The pipes groaned and shook violently before a rush of brown-colored water spit out, soaking the front of his shirt. He turned to scowl at Jenkins. "When's the last time you used this thing?"

Jenkins' head swayed from right to left as he mumbled something through the blood dripping from the corners of his mouth, but Lucas didn't understand the words. He couldn't read the man's lips, either, with the blanket of dreadlocks hanging in front of Jenkins' head.

Lucas shut the hot water off and tried the other knob. It worked. He waited for the cold water to run clear before rinsing off his hand. A minute later, he dabbed the wound with a red towel hanging on the bar to the right, sending a jolt of pain up his arm and into his shoulder. The bleeding stopped, but only for a few seconds, then it began to seep through the skin again.

He tore a ten-inch strip of cloth from the back of his t-shirt. He stretched the material tight across his knuckles and wrapped it around his palm, making sure there was enough pressure to stop the hemorrhage. He tied the ends together, pulling the knot tight with his teeth. He knew the injury would be tough to hide from Kleezebee, but he was too tired to care. The professor would just have to deal with it. What did it matter anyway? He was just doing his job.

He checked the angle of the mirror's reflection to that of the chair holding his prisoner: No, Jenkins couldn't see his face. He removed the makeshift hood he was wearing and draped it over the edge of the wash sink. The red-stained pillowcase reeked of perspiration and blood.

Lucas bent down and put his head under the faucet. He ran the water through his short-cropped hair and across the back of his neck, It was heaven, just what he needed. His fire cooled off.

He allowed himself another minute to enjoy the water before he stood up and looked into the cracked mirror above the sink. Water dripped from his forehead as his eyes were pulled deep into the center of the damaged reflection where an impostor was standing. He tried to look away, but couldn't; it was as if his body were frozen in time. The man in the mirror was wearing his same chin, freckles, and blue eyes, but Lucas didn't recognize the rest. The charlatan lived in his skin, consuming the same air, but he hadn't been invited in.

Lucas had tried to evict the hitchhiker for weeks, but the noisy traveler only grew stronger with each failed attempt. Its tentacles were now buried deep into the fabric of his soul, twisting his emotions and thoughts into a constrictor knot. He figured the traveler was his punishment for the crimes he had been forced to commit. God knows he deserved it.

Lucas stepped back when the mirror snarled at him, distorting and expanding to inject more of its random thoughts. The reflection's face turned a deep shade of red and snarled another one of its meaningless riddles—*Strident downhill wanderers veer east along rising inland surprises, mostly locking away your righteous earnings.*

"Leave me alone!" Lucas shouted, ripping the four-foot-wide mirror from the wall. He tossed it across the room in a direction opposite to Jenkins' back. It shattered into a dozen pieces as it skipped its way across the cement floor; it slid through the dirt and dust. Jagged fragments bounced off the base of the wall, clanking and pinging as if they were singing their death song.

He returned to the wash sink, took a deep breath, then wiped his head and face with the towel. He took out the last four aspirins he carried in his front pocket and tossed them into his mouth. The strong taste of acetylsalicylic acid flooded his tongue before he cupped his hands under the running water and washed the medicine down in one gulp.

He shut off the spigot, slipped the mostly-white hood over his head, and returned to Jenkins. "Look, I know you work for that fucking psychopath, Cyrus. So, tell me what I need to know or so help me God, I'll make you wish you were never born," he said, grabbing the front of Jenkins' shirt.

He lifted the man's head to see if his eyes were responsive. They weren't. Jenkins' left eye was bruised and swollen shut from the last round of stiff rights, but the other eye was unharmed. Yet, it was still shut.

He tapped Jenkins on the cheek, twice. "Hey, buddy? You still with me?"

Jenkins' head moved on its own, slowly looking up. His good eye opened partway, but Lucas couldn't see the pupil—only the bloodshot white.

"That's better. I need you awake."

Jenkins wriggled and twisted, apparently trying to free his arms. The rope stood firm, keeping the man secure.

Lucas thought about using the box cutter in his tool wrap to relieve the pressure in Jenkins' swollen eyelid, but decided against it after studying his own shaking hands. His adrenaline was firing on all cylinders, meaning he would probably cut too deep and puncture the man's eyeball. The queasiness in the pit of his stomach shot up to the top floor when he thought about the eye's goopy gel oozing out. He took a moment to gather himself. The nausea faded.

He leaned in close to Jenkins' right ear and whispered through the cutout in the hood for his mouth, "Come on, Jenkins. Talk to me." He waited another minute, but the man said nothing. "Okay. Fine. I tried. But remember, I really don't want to do this."

He unrolled the red tool wrap across the front edge of the sink. He shut his eyes, angled his head back slightly, and ran the tips of his fingers across each of the items inside: claw hammer, red-handled meat cleaver, needle-nose pliers, ten-inch ice pick, silver box cutter.

"Which one of you wants to come out to play?" he whispered.

He waited for one of the tools to speak to him and one did. He opened his eyes and was about to pick the trusted meat cleaver, when he noticed the electrical cord on the back of the floor lamp next to him. It gave him an idea—one that didn't involve spurting blood or severed digits. No cleanup, either. He smiled, then bent down and ripped the wire out of the base of the lamp. He split the frayed end with his pocketknife, peeling the sheathing off both wires to expose the copper.

Lucas' alter ego pounded at the inside of his skull, screaming at him in a fever pitch—*Endearing kindness never softens its stance against lonesome jesters nullifying an increasingly irregular retort.*

Lucas ignored the ramblings. "You have any family left?" he asked Jenkins, thinking about the Krellian incursion and the countless deaths that followed.

Jenkins nodded.

"If one of them was taken from you, you'd do whatever it took to get them back, wouldn't you?"

"Yeah," Jenkins answered in a weak voice. "But I don't understand. What's that have to do with BioTex?"

"That's why I'm here. I need the BioTex in order to find my little brother. He's been missing for eighteen months. He's the only family I have left. I need you to tell me."

Jenkins hesitated, then said, "I'd like to. But I can't. Cyrus will kill me if I tell you anything."

8

"Look, I know you're scared of Cyrus. Trust me, we all are. . . . But please, I beg you. You have to help me. I don't want to hurt you anymore."

Jenkins shook his head and cried silently. A single tear dripped from the corner of his still-functioning eye, ran down his cheek, and then joined forces with a glob of red-colored spit hanging from his lips. The blob swayed back and forth below his chin.

Lucas looked at the meat cleaver that was waiting patiently in the tool wrap. His hand moved closer to it, but he yanked it back. Use the electrical cord instead, he convinced himself.

"If you're not going to talk, then you leave me no choice." He unbuckled Jenkins' belt and tugged at his trousers, but they wouldn't move. He wedged his shoulder into the man's armpit and forced Jenkins' torso up a bit, allowing the pants to slip down past the chair. "Wow, didn't expect commando," he said, seeing the man's penis hanging between his legs. "You have a wife?"

Jenkins nodded quickly, sending the dollop of jaw-hanging spit into his lap.

"Then she's gonna hate this. No more kids for you, buddy." He inserted the cord's plug into an electrical outlet and held the other end in his injured hand. He put the wires in front of Jenkins' face, hoping it would persuade the half-conscious man to talk. "See these? I'm gonna' use them to cook your balls. And from the size of them, it's gonna hurt like hell."

Jenkins shut his good eye, still crying. "I can't tell you anything."

"Look at me!" Lucas shouted in a deep voice. "I know you know, so tell me. Where the fuck is Cyrus storing the BioTex containers?"

Jenkins opened his good eye, though not all the way.

Lucas touched the ends of the leads together, igniting sparks that danced off the man's cheek.

Jenkins slurred an uneven grunt, then said, "Don't. Please."

Again, Lucas touched the ends together, sending more sparks into the air. "It's gonna smell like burnt ball sack in a minute." He waited a few seconds, but still nothing from Jenkins. He touched the wires to the side of the man's neck to give him a sample of what was to come. Jenkins' face tightened and constricted, as did most of the muscles in his body. Lucas pulled the wires away from contact. "Hurts like a motherfucker, doesn't it?"

Jenkins exhaled and his head slumped to his chest. He appeared to be resolute in his defiance.

Lucas' arms grew heavy and his neck ached. Damn it, he thought, shaking his head. He's really gonna make me do this? He lowered the copper ends to within an inch of Jenkins' testicles. "Last chance before I flambé your balls."

"Okay. . . . Okay. . . . I'll tell you."

Finally, Lucas thought. He grabbed the underside of Jenkins' chin, tugging it hard. "Where the hell are they?"

The words dripped out of Jenkins' mouth slowly. "In our Clark County storage facility, along Route 9. Cyrus has them hidden in the back of the Dunn-Rite Café. " Jenkins drew in a deep, unsteady breath before he added, "But you'll need a password to get in."

Lucas released the man's jaw and pushed his head back. "What is it?"

"When the hostess greets you, tell her you heard they have the best double apple fritters in town. She'll ask you if you want anchovies on them and you must answer 'Yes, with yellow cream sauce.'"

Lucas straightened his back, returning his posture to the upright position. His muscles relaxed. He didn't have to puke after all. He tossed the electrical cord to the ground and walked to the electrical outlet. He bent down and pulled the cord from the socket before returning to Jenkins. "Now that wasn't so hard, was it? You could've saved yourself a lot of pain by just telling me what I wanted to know up front, ya dumb son of a bitch."

"Are you going to kill me now?"

Lucas never would've killed him, even if he didn't talk. "That all depends. Are you going to tell Cyrus about our little chat?"

Jenkins shook his head.

"Good. Then you'll see your wife again."

Jenkins' crying grew louder as a river of tears streamed down his cheeks, running into his lap.

"Why are you crying? I said I wasn't gonna kill you."

"Cyrus will know it was me."

"Maybe next time you'll think twice about selling out your own people to an evil son of a bitch like Cyrus."

"He's going to kill my family. My wife and daughter have nothing to do with this. Please, you have to help me."

"It's not my problem," Lucas said, as a knot swelled in his gut.

Supreme psychosis allows childish meanderings until lady heaven ends lavish eagerness, the voice in his head said. Lucas winced when a sharp twinge of pain reverberated inside his skull. He collected himself, then laughed at the traveler's nonsense. Gibberish, he thought.

"Please help me," Jenkins said again. "You have no idea what Cyrus will do to them."

Lucas turned his thoughts to Jenkins' wife and daughter. He sighed. Jenkins was right: They weren't part of this man's actions. They were innocent. Just like his missing foster brother Drew. He needed to do something or else the knot in his stomach would continue to consume him. He thought about inviting

Jenkins and his family back to Kleezebee's cabin where they would be safe. It was an obvious security risk, but what else could he do? He couldn't leave the man's family to fend for themselves. Then he thought about Kleezebee's reaction and knew it would never fly with the professor. He needed a different plan, and fast. Jenkins's kitchen staff would soon arrive to begin their work day.

Lucas searched Jenkins' pockets and found the man's sleek, nanofilm storage device in his back left pocket. He held the electronic device up to his own digital wallet, then activated and used the light-blue touchscreen interface to transfer his three remaining Mag-Lift credits to the Jenkins' account. Lucas had been saving the passes for emergency use in case he ever needed to get the professor and Drew out of town in a hurry. He had obtained the hard-to-get passes through trade at Big Betty's Barter Boutique located in the musty Narrows on the south side of Flandreau City. He made a mental note to break in again and steal more handguns and ammo from the town's gunsmith to use as trade. It worked once, it'll work again, he thought. Simple enough.

"I just transferred some Mag-Lift passes to your account. Use them to get your family as far away from here as you can. Change your names. Change your appearance. Do whatever you need to do. But for fuck's sake, get on the Mag-Lift and get the hell out of here and never tell anyone you ever spoke to me."

Jenkins finally stopped crying. "Okay. I will," he said, though it wasn't very convincing. "Thank you."

Lucas cut through the rope with the pocketknife and threw the soiled towel into Jenkins' lap to cover his privates. He gave the box cutter to Jenkins and stepped back in case Jenkins tried to take a swipe at him. "Use this to relieve the pressure in that eye. If you don't, you may never see with it again."

Lucas rolled the interrogation tools inside the wrap, then stuffed them inside his soggy, rust-stained shirt before walking to the bottom of the basement stairs. He looked back at Jenkins, adjusting the mask to allow him to see through the eye holes properly. "Count to a hundred before you leave this room. Got it?"

Jenkins nodded.

Lucas climbed the stairs, but before he made it to the top step, the basement door opened. Two people—one male and one female—stood in the opening wearing chef attire. The woman looked at Lucas. She screamed. The male cook charged with an angry fist, but Lucas ducked to slip his punch. Lucas whirled around and shoved the man, sending the chef down the stairs to the bottom.

Lucas ran past the hysterical woman, through the restaurant and out into the empty street where a chorus of long, early morning shadows covered his escape route. He sprinted to a nearby alley where his getaway vehicle was parked. He opened the overhead door and sat inside. He pulled the mask off his head and exhaled a long breath.

TWO

Overcooked

Lucas pulled alongside Kleezebee's cabin on the north face of Ghost Mountain, set the drifting brake, and got out of the skimmer truck. The gravity inversion vehicle, a *skimmer* as the public called it, used a combination of pressurized air to achieve initial lift, and a vat of Mercury plasma spinning inside a magnetic coil to generate momentum and speed by modulating ground-level gravity fields. It traveled precisely eight and a half inches off the ground and, if properly maintained, could reach a speed of a hundred and twenty miles an hour.

Kleezebee had acquired the hand-me-down vehicle a few months earlier from Crazy Larry, the local preacher in town, whose idea of proper maintenance meant simply parking it in the shade. The used skimmer's top speed was closer to eighty-eight and reminded him of his adoptive father's old Ford beater back on Earth, except this one was blue instead of red. Both of them leaked fluids faster than he could fill them up.

Lucas closed the overhead door slowly in case the professor was sleeping in, but the hinges complained loudly. "Fucking POS," he muttered as a sharp headache began to mount in the center of his forehead. He winced, looking in the skimmer's side mirror, but he didn't see his own reflection. Instead, it was the face of his missing foster brother, Drew, who had disappeared without a trace.

Drew's lips were moving at half-speed, but Lucas couldn't hear or understand the words he was saying. It was a common vision the past few weeks, one that he encountered in the occasional reflective surface. Each time Drew's face appeared, so did a sharp pain that burrowed through his ears and into the deep recesses of his skull.

The pain escalated, pounding at his eardrums from the inside. He turned, leaning his back against the driver's door of the skimmer truck. He wrapped his hands around his skull as his chest took over, sucking in a series of deep, rapid breaths while his brain temporarily disconnected to confront the pain. Eventually, the headache subsided. So did his rapid heartbeat.

It had been a year and a half since Drew had disappeared after stepping through the portal to the stolen Krellian hive ship. Many thought Drew was dead by now, but Lucas could sense that his foster brother was still alive somewhere in the multi-verse. He had to be. Life without Drew was hollow and meaningless, deepening the hole in his heart a little bit more with each passing day.

He didn't know if Drew had been transported to the distant reaches of the galaxy, kidnapped by the flesh-eating Krellian Empire, or sent across time to an alternate version of Earth. Maybe it was worse. Drew might be stranded on a distant moon, injured and alone, possibly without his wheelchair.

One thing was certain: Drew wasn't anywhere here on Eutopia-3, a distant Earth outpost in the spiral Omega galaxy. The subspace transmitter hidden in Drew's leather pouch wasn't registering on its private channel, meaning he was probably out of range in another galaxy or possibly in some remote spatial dimension.

He wondered if Abby had stayed with Drew or if they'd been separated. Perhaps she was dead. If that were the case, would Drew have given up hope without his newfound girlfriend and had cashed it in?

Lucas knew he might never know the answers, but didn't care. As long as there was a sliver of hope, he would never stop searching, even if his actions were hard to justify. This certainly wasn't what he'd signed up for when he'd enrolled at the university seven years ago. But that was on another planet in another universe, long before he and Professor Kleezebee were marooned on this fucking rock.

He untied the temporary bandage and removed it from his hand. He checked his knuckles—they were still throbbing a bit, but they weren't bleeding. A thin black scab had formed during the long drive from Jenkins' restaurant in Flandreau City. He tossed the hood, bloody wrap, and his interrogation tools into the bed of the skimmer and covered them with a torn, half-sized burlap sack. He grinned. "Play nice 'til papa gets back," he told them, before heading for the cabin.

He side-stepped to avoid the dirt path that led into the forest. A memory flashed in the back of his mind of a torn, severed foot lying sideways on the deck plate of the Krellian hive ship. He winced. "Sorry, Mom, not today," he said quietly. "Probably not tomorrow, either. But if we're lucky, maybe next week—or never, if Fuji's right."

He walked to the wooden porch in front of the cabin, went up the stairs, and opened the screen door.

Kleezebee stood bent over by the stone fireplace, poking the ashes with an iron rod. "Did you get it?" he asked without turning around. Flares of ash crackled as they shot up to Kleezebee's waist, narrowly missing the frazzled end of his twenty-year-old gray beard.

"Sure did, Professor. They're in Clark County storage, along Route 9. It's disguised as the Dunn-Rite Café." Lucas slipped his right hand into his pants' pocket. The jean material pulled at the scab, reminding him the wound was still fresh. "It took a little convincing, but I got it done."

Kleezebee hung the ash fork on a metal hook to the right of the fireplace, then turned and stared at Lucas' front pocket. "Your hand. Let me see it."

Lucas pulled his hand out, palm up, then flipped it over. He waited for the professor's reaction.

"I thought my orders were clear."

"Sorry, boss, but Jenkins wouldn't cooperate. What else was I supposed to do?"

Kleezebee grabbed a red first aid kit from under the kitchen sink. He handed it to Lucas with the cover open. "Better clean it."

Lucas nodded.

"You should have appealed to his sense of family, like I told you to do. I'm sure you could have convinced him."

"I doubt it. You're the negotiator, Professor, not me." Lucas dug around the kit for a gauze bandage. He found it buried under a red-handled pair of scissors and a spool of white medical tape.

Kleezebee exhaled loud enough for Lucas to hear. "That's what you said the last time. This whole thing's spinning out of control."

Lucas shuffled his feet and didn't respond. He wouldn't admit it to Kleezebee, but he hadn't started the interrogation as his mentor suggested. He was mentally exhausted from the endless scavenging and planning, and didn't have the patience. The first thing he did after tying Jenkins to the chair was pound him with a few rights. He hated to admit it, but at some level, taking his frustration out on Jenkins felt good, at least until his knuckles caught the edge of the man's tooth. He wondered how he could find a moment of pleasure in something that made him feel sick and ashamed. His deceased adoptive mother would never have approved.

His secret traveler spoke up to add, *Torrid rainbows always pinpoint picturesque sunsets hidden inside private daydreams of energetic nurses.*

Lucas fought hard to hide the associated head pain. He didn't want his mentor to know that the hallucinations were back and in full force. It seemed to work.

Kleezebee combed his two-foot beard from top to bottom with the two primary fingers on his liver-spotted hand. "If your mother was still alive, she wouldn't be happy with what I've made you do the past year and a half since Drew disappeared."

Lucas finished wrapping his knuckles and applying the tape. "You didn't make me do anything I didn't want to do."

"I seriously doubt that. Beating up people for information wasn't in my curriculum when you enrolled."

Lucas didn't know what else to say. It was clear that the professor knew the field assignments were eating away at his gut. He wondered if Rico's hand-to-hand combat training was at fault, transforming him from a disciplined scientist into something less human. Either way, it didn't matter. Someone had to do it and his name was the only one decorating the duty roster. Lucas hadn't told Kleezebee about the meat cleaver or the rest of his tool wrap. "Neither was a field trip to an alternate reality. Gotta do what we gotta do to get Drew back now, though."

"Yes," Kleezebee replied with a numb look on his face. "And to think, all this could've been avoided."

Lucas rubbed Kleezebee's shoulder with his hand, gently. "I know you think this is all your fault, but I'm the one who reopened the rift after Drew went missing in my universe. I'm sure that's how the other Krellian ship tracked us here. The ambush wasn't your fault. Neither was the crash landing on this outpost."

"Still, I should have factored it in. It was my job. A lot of good people died that day." Kleezebee brushed past Lucas and sat on the sofa.

"None of us would be alive if it weren't for you, Professor."

"How do you figure that?"

"You outsmarted Cyrus. You tricked him into letting us go. Otherwise, I'm sure he would have eventually had us stuffed and mounted in his trophy case along with everyone else who has dared to defy him."

"A lot of good that did," the professor said. His right ankle popped like a cork when he flexed his foot. "Your mom. Trevor. Half our crew. Hundreds of thousands of civilians. All dead because of me."

Lucas realized that the professor didn't want to listen—he was more interested in wallowing in a self-pity party. Time to shift the focus of the conversation, he decided. He slid a pillow under his boss's leg. "Ankle still bothering you?"

"Every once in a while."

"The docs must have misaligned something."

"Or I'm just getting too damn old for all this."

"Do you need something for the pain?"

"It'll be all right. Just need to rest it."

Lucas looked past Kleezebee into the kitchen ten feet beyond him. A nearly empty gallon of raspum was on the counter with its twist-cap sitting upside down next to it. Lucas had just purchased the moonshine two days earlier from Crazy Larry. Some might think Lucas was enabling the professor's drinking habit, but truth was, the old man was trying to cope with a serious bout of insomnia and rarely drank alcohol during the day. Lucas needed his mentor rested, and a handful of shots before bed seemed to be the only solution. A sleeping pill prescription was out of the question since there wasn't a drug dispensary left standing within five hundred miles.

"Did you talk to Caroline today?" Lucas asked, figuring she was the reason for the open jug of raspum—again.

"I tried, but I think her new husband is blocking my transmission; the wife-stealing asshole doesn't let my calls through—and all I want is a few photos of my son; something I can put in my digi-frame to go along with Drew's."

Lucas clenched both his fists. "If you like, I can go up north and reason with him."

"Thanks, but no. Your type of reasoning won't accomplish anything."

When Kleezebee's eyes focused on the moonshine in the kitchen, Lucas thought to distract him with some positive reinforcement. "I'm sure she'll come around, eventually. Just give her some time."

Kleezebee's voice was full of pain—the kind of pain that turns even the most emotionally-detached man into a sobbing idiot. "Why didn't she wait for me?"

"I don't know, Professor. You *were* gone an awfully long time. But at least she waited ten years. That has to count for something. I'll bet it's longer than a lot of women would have done, given the circumstances."

"But she should've known I'd find a way home. That I'd never stop trying."

That was Kleezebee, demanding excellence from everyone he knew. How the man expected his wife to wait forty-plus years for his return from an alternate universe was beyond reason. Sometimes the professor's grasp on reality was worse than his. "I'm sure you need some type of closure, Professor, but she has another life now."

"I hate that word, *closure*. There's no such thing. I'm sorry, but when a hole's been ripped into your life, it tends to stay open, wide open. And no amount of talking, or forgiveness, or self-help mumbo-jumbo will *ever* close it. When you boil it down, the best you can hope for is to avoid the wound altogether."

Lucas didn't respond. The professor obviously needed more time to deal with the pain.

Kleezebee's jaw tightened. "*Closure* is simply a pseudo-clinical term invented by an overcooked counselor who didn't have a clue what else to say to his patients."

Lucas exhaled, but didn't respond. He didn't have the words. His mind drifted as the events of the day began to soak in and take root. They mixed in with the rest of his memories, allowing him to escape into that special realm where clarity starts to form deep within your soul. Kleezebee needed help, but he was a tough man to read, let alone comfort. His thoughts turned to Drew, but that made the moment even worse.

He searched his memories for something that Kleezebee had once told him. He found it tucked under a pile of mental dust, in the forgotten section of his brain. He thought about tweaking the words to fit the situation. It might just help his boss. He ran through it in his head:

Let's face it. Loss happens. Usually, at the worst possible time. But how we respond to it defines our character and that shapes the future of our existence. We can choose to hide in suffocating darkness, drowning in the magnitude of our loss, or we can challenge ourselves to rise up from the despair and treasure the most precious gift of all: Life itself. In the meantime, we battle to survive another cold-blooded day. Yet, without allowing your heart to fill with hope and wonder, taking another breath is meaningless. When you boil it down, all we can really ask of ourselves is to get up, face the day, and take another step forward. The rest of life is pure happenstance. The only real control we have is our attitude toward life and effort for others, nothing else.

Sometimes though, in order to change the momentum of one's life and escape the gravity pinning us down, we must embrace the unknown and consider new and unexpected possibilities. Possibilities that were never on the radar before. Happiness can't be quantified, cataloged, or even planned. It's random and unpredictable—often, a complete surprise. You must have patience and wait for it to find you, not the other way around.

It sounded poignant and comforting in his head, but he decided it wasn't the right time for a speech. Besides, who was he kidding? He wasn't a patient man, and neither was Kleezebee—not with the fate of the universe sitting on their shoulders. He tossed the idea away and kept quiet. He wanted to help his boss, but sometimes what you don't say is more beneficial than trying to comfort someone with stale platitudes and misplaced sympathy. Especially when you're dealing with a brilliant, but emotionally-detached man in his late sixties.

He sat on the other end of the couch and rubbed the professor's sore ankle. Lucas drew in a long, slow breath, but couldn't smell alcohol on the professor's breath or on his clothes. Maybe the professor wasn't plastered.

After thirty minutes of silence, Kleezebee seemed to be coming out of his funk. Good thing, too, because Lucas' hands were cramping.

"Any word from Rico?" Lucas asked.

Kleezebee looked at his watch and pressed two of the orange buttons along its perimeter. "He reported in earlier. The mission's a go."

"Am I part of the assault team this time?"

"Yes. Rico says you're ready."

Lucas smiled. His heart danced a bit.

"We'll be staging operations in the safe house along Route 9 for both the BioTex recovery and the procurement of the E-121."

"You mean that old warehouse near the burnt-down sawmill?"

Kleezebee nodded.

Lucas looked at the rug covering the trap door in the center of the room. "So, I take it Fuji finished his calculations?"

"Yes. They're quite elegant."

"It's about time that wiggler cracked it."

"I had my doubts, but he proved me wrong *again*."

"He's a unique bundle, that's for sure."

The processor shook his head in disbelief. "Chance favored us that day when he found us wandering in the desert after the crash. If it weren't for him, none of us would have survived."

"We owe him big time."

"You have no idea."

"But if you hadn't convinced him to help us, the Incursion Chamber wouldn't exist." Lucas thought about heading down to the thousand-square-foot basement to visit the eighty-pound, tunic-wearing mathematician, but wasn't sure if he had the time or energy. It was getting late and he figured Fuji was busy lighting the two hundred floor candles in preparation for his daily prayer vigil. The last time he interrupted the baldheaded monk, he'd been forced to sit on the floor cross-legged for a two-hour chant-fest that was almost hypnotic.

Over time, Fuji had proven that through intense meditation and rhythmic chant, he could enter a metaphysical state, whereby his mind was free to tap into and extract scientific information from the Akashic Field—a central repository where all knowledge in the universe is said to exist. Lucas had read about similar claims of transcendent knowledge before, many of which had been touted by some of the greatest minds in history, which included Einstein, Socrates, and even Nikola Tesla, Lucas' personal hero, so Fuji's achievements were not revolutionary. At least, not on the surface.

He had tried to achieve Fuji's level of altered states, but failed miserably. He lacked the mental discipline to focus his thoughts properly and control his breathing. That left only one choice: The use of advanced technology, like the Incursion Chamber.

Fuji's experiment was based loosely on an old U.S. military project from the 1970s, called Project Stargate, in which the federal government funded years of psychic research with the hope of developing remote viewing, the ability to psychically see events, sites, and information from a great distance. However, Fuji's theories elevated those concepts to an entirely new hemisphere.

"What about the Smart Skin Suit?" Lucas asked.

"Tested and operational," the professor answered.

THREE

Extreme Possibilities

A smile found the corner of Lucas' mouth, knowing they were only days away from powering up Fuji's Incursion Chamber. "That spud can barely carry on a conversation, but he sure knows his shit. We'll have to come up with a name for his new math. I was thinking 'Fijix,' short for Fuji Physics. Got a nice ring to it, don't you think?"

Kleezebee smiled, then winced. He grabbed his ankle.

"Did you finish the new interface while I was gone, Professor? You said you were close."

Kleezebee nodded. "It's complete and I ran it through a number of simulations. All we need now is a sufficient amount of E-121, and the view screens."

"How many modules does Fuji think we'll need?"

"Two. But I'd prefer to have three spheres on hand, just in case we need to make a few runs at this." Kleezebee checked his watch again. "You've got time to go visit your mother's grave, if you like. Maybe say a prayer or two?"

Lucas shook his head. "Not until we get Drew back." He looked out the window to his right, just beyond the unpaved driveway where he parked the skimmer. At the end of the dirt trail was a flowery hillside where the empty graves of his adoptive mother, Dorothy, and former lab assistant, Trevor, were located. The video player in his head replayed the last time he saw both of them alive . . .

He was walking down one of the ship's longer corridors to meet his mother and Trevor, the mammoth Olympic wrestler-turned-lab-assistant, for breakfast outside the mess hall's entrance when a trio of Krellian guards stepped out of an inter-dimensional rift on Deck Nine of the stolen hive ship. The intruders cornered his mother, but Trevor stepped in the way to protect her. One of the alien guards impaled the Swede with a four-pronged grappling hook mounted to one of its giant claws. Lucas could hear bones cracking as Trevor squirted blood and guts as he was pulled apart and across the deck plating and all over Dorothy. Then the worst happened—the nine-foot arthropods turned their attention to his mother. Lucas was too far away to stop them before they quickly gorged themselves on her bones and tissue. Every time he shut his eyes, all he could see was Dorothy's face, crying out for him as the bugs ate her alive.

It was a memory he wished he could erase. Every time he thought about his mother, those final moments of her life were all he could see in his mind. He'd gladly use a crowbar and pry the memory out of his skull if he thought it would work. He hadn't visited the makeshift gravesite since Kleezebee began erecting the memorial when they first arrived at the colony. He planned to visit Dorothy, but not until his foster brother was at his side. He'd already decided to let Drew offer up a prayer when the time came. He'd had his fill of religion, even more so lately.

Ten days earlier, Lucas had been walking past the twenty-pew church near the center of town on his way to pick up supplies, when he'd overhead the Sunday preacher delivering his famous fire-and-brimstone sermon. Crazy Larry's voice carried far out into the street, echoing to every corner of the empty town square. His words were filled with the usual rhetoric about God, the Devil, and the glorious rewards of life after death. The self-righteous preacher went on to explain how God's manuscript is all about forgiveness and faith, that *how* we live our life is just as important as actually living it.

Lucas didn't buy any of it. Not after what he'd seen. He agreed—the devil is real, but it's not some rogue angel gone bad. It's a nine-foot-tall crustacean-like arthropod with four glowing eyes and an unquenchable thirst for human flesh. This Krellian devil eats whatever it wants, wherever it wants, and whenever it wants: man, woman, child. It didn't care. Meat was meat. Granted, the Krellian invasion had been thwarted and the non-aggression treaty would keep the foul creatures at bay for a while, but he knew the bugs would be back and with a serious case of the munchies next time.

He wondered how the marauding Krellian Empire fit into "God's Master Plan." Sure, his religious faith was nonexistent, but even if he were a Bible-thumper, he couldn't understand how anyone could cling to religious doctrine after the Sentinel Guards had rolled through town and eaten everyone in sight. He had never studied the scriptures, but figured they didn't contain any parables about giant, scorpion-like bugs tearing open men, women, and children and eating them alive. If there were a Supreme Being, how could God just sit back and let that horror show unfold? Religious dogma made about as much sense to him as the incoherent prose of the traveler squatting inside his brain.

Truth was, Lucas used to have faith, just not the religious kind. His used to be the reality of hard science, but even that conviction had faded. Everything he believed in had been twisted and mangled until nothing made sense anymore. He'd learned the hard way, after just a couple decades of breathing, that life wears on you, stripping you down one layer at a time until there's nothing left but sun-bleached bone.

He wished he could unwind the clock and go back to being a scrawny five-year-old, sitting by the front window in the state-run orphanage back on Earth, hoping his long-lost parents would show up and claim him. His puny, insignificant life made sense back then, even though he didn't know it at the time.

Lucas believed the meaning of life was simple: We exist solely to survive. That our reason for living is to be able to stand on stage at the end of our days and look back and say that we did it—that we beat the odds—that we never gave up. That this life happened to *me*, not to someone else—me—and it never beat me. He knew that he had to give to get, but that wasn't going to be easy, not with the glacier of disappointment filling his soul. He vowed to do better.

Just then, Lucas saw a vision of his dead mother standing in the forest on the lonely dirt path that led to her gravesite. She was wearing a flowing white gown, holding her arms out for him. He thought about running to her, but before he could decide, the image disappeared. So did the knot is his stomach. He decided his mind or his guilt was playing tricks on him.

"I understand why you want to wait to visit your mother," Kleezebee said, snapping Lucas back to reality. "Of course, if Fuji's correct and your incursion is successful, we can put all this behind us."

"Yeah," Lucas replied, accepting the possibility that Fuji's plan to control the flow of exotic particles in a hyper-localized containment field might ultimately fail. "But we should continue looking for Drew in other dimensions, just in case."

Kleezebee's eyelids tightened, as he ran his pock-marked hands through the thinning bundle of gray hair keeping his skull warm. He sighed. "You know the probability of ever finding Drew that way is—"

"I know, Professor. Slim and none. But we have to try. I can't just sit here and do nothing. I'm not wired that way. Besides, until we have a sufficient amount of E-121, Fuji's tech is useless. And that's not going to happen until we recover the BioTex and regenerate our crew. If you ask me, both of them are long shots, even with Rico's and Fuji's help."

Kleezebee stared at Lucas. "Regardless, it's only been a few days since your last trip. We need to let your body recover before we send you in again. You know the risks of too many successive trips."

Lucas had made almost fifty trips into other realities and, other than sore legs from searching a handful of University of Arizona campuses and seeing a few random visions of Drew in reflective surfaces along the way, he felt fine. Well, almost fine, if he discounted the jumbled mess of traveler quotations he'd had to endure in recent weeks. "I know, but the longer we wait—"

"It's already been a year and a half; another few days won't matter."

Lucas disagreed. There were an unlimited number of alternate universes to search and they had only just begun. But he couldn't operate the rift displacement equipment by himself, so he decided not to argue the point. An angry Kleezebee wouldn't do anyone any good. "Just so you know, I'm fine and ready to go whenever."

"Any more hallucinations?"

"Nope. Not a one. I'm good to go. Trust me."

Kleezebee's eyes tightened on him. He hesitated, then said, "I'm not so sure about that. But regardless, we need to give Fuji's plan a chance first. Agreed?"

"Sure," Lucas said, though he really didn't want to. Kleezebee had been trying to convince him to open his mind and his heart to extreme possibilities, but Fuji's theories were difficult to accept—perhaps, in part, because they were beyond his comprehension. He wanted to believe, but believing and achieving were two separate things.

Lucas preferred the comfort and safety of proven scientific fact, though that had become a rare commodity in recent months. He knew first hand that some speculative versions of science were the greatest of lies, even if a brilliant mathematician like Fuji claimed he had calculated and quantified every conceivable outcome.

Lucas knew the drill; he'd lived it. Every scientist is confident his theories will work, right up until the last possible moment when the unexpected happens, condemning some poor lab rat to die a horrible, mangled death. Sad thing was, Lucas was slated to *be* that lab rat, the one who would step into the Incursion Chamber wearing the Smart Skin Suit. If Fuji's calculations were off even a thousandth of a percent, his destiny would be that of a vitrified heap of cosmic goo.

He stood up from the couch and walked to the kitchen counter, his back to Kleezebee. He put the cap back on the jug of raspum, twisting it tight. "Is Rico coming back here first?"

"No, Rico wants you to meet him there."

"Just me?" Lucas turned around to face his mentor.

The professor rubbed the crux of his foot. "Yep. Looks like I'll have to sit this one out."

"What's the plan?"

"That's up to Rico. He's in charge of tactical. Now that we know about the Dunn-Rite Café, it won't take him long to devise a plan. I just need to call it into him. He'll brief you when you meet up with him. Just do me a favor: Try to keep your head down and let the man do his thing."

"Not a problem, Professor. I'm just glad that dude's on *our* side. You still gonna let him take Cyrus out?"

Kleezebee nodded. "That's the arrangement. Otherwise, he never would have helped us. But he's agreed not to make his move until after our mission's complete."

"He's a better man than me," Lucas said, admiring Rico's restraint. If Cyrus had raped and killed *his* sister, he'd never be able to hold back his revenge; not for a second. "What about the Royal Guards?"

"That's why you're going in tomorrow morning, when Cyrus and his men are at the victory party in New Robyn City. He's going to need them for crowd control and probably won't have them protecting the café."

"Good idea. Let's hope Freakshow is with him so we don't have to deal with that psychopath."

"Can't rule anything out at this point."

"I still can't believe Cyrus got re-elected."

"You really need to concentrate on things you can control."

"Yeah, but Cyrus the Virus? Come on, the guy's fucking insane."

"Why should this universe be any different? It doesn't matter where you go; public opinion is controlled by the media. I'm afraid it's just human nature. Whenever there's a vacuum in leadership, militants will rise to power and seize control. People will believe what they want to believe, especially when they fear all hope is lost."

"But still, we should have found a way to let the public know that we saved this colony from the Krellians, not him. We're the *real* reason the bugs signed the non-aggression treaty. If that asshole hadn't confiscated your technology, we could've used it to—"

Kleezebee held up his hand, palm out. "None of that matters now. We need to focus on finding what's left of our friends. And do so quietly. We'll only get one shot at this. Cyrus has spies everywhere."

Lucas agreed, though he didn't want to. He exhaled slowly to calm his temper. "You hear anything from Claude lately?"

"Not a word."

"That's good, right? No news is good news."

"Yes. His scheduled check-in is tomorrow, so we'll know for sure then."

"Do you need me for anything else? I need to take a shower."

"No, go ahead. There's food in the processor when you're done."

A last supper, Lucas thought, celebrating with a rainbow smile. "Some form of dead animal on a plate?"

Kleezebee nodded and winked. "Taku Beast."

"Seriously?"

The professor smiled.

Lucas' mind flashed an image of the semi-transparent, phase-shifting predator. The first time he had seen a Taku Beast was about a year ago, while driving at night through the Cave Creek Forest on his way back to Kleezebee's cabin. The ten-foot-tall, gorilla-like animal phased into normal space directly in front of his skimmer truck, making him slam on the grav-brakes and angle sharply to avoid smashing into it. The creature's deafening roar shook his bones to their breaking point, right before the great beast took a swipe at the skimmer's undercarriage with its seven-fingered claw. It tore a three-foot-wide hole in the metal skid plate and nearly flipped the vehicle. Lucas sped off before the beast could inflict any more damage. The town's best hunters had been tracking the slippery animal for years, but hadn't managed to kill it. "Did you shoot it?"

"No, I set a trap. Turns out, the great beast likes raspum almost as much as I do. Mixed it in with a batch of flour and butter and left the bucket out. Worked like a charm."

Lucas smiled. "Ahhh. It couldn't phase shift once it was shit-faced. Damn, why didn't I think of that?"

"Sometimes the easiest solution is the hardest to find."

"I was wondering what happened to all the booze."

"What? Did you think I went on a bender today?"

Hell, yes, he did. "Of course not. I figured you spilled it or something."

Kleezebee's lips tightened, but he didn't say anything.

"At least the locals won't have to worry about being outside at night anymore."

"I wish that were true, but I heard another growl right after I skinned and gutted the one waiting for you in the kitchen. Probably the female. If so, she's gonna be on the prowl. I'm sure she didn't like me killing her mate."

Lucas smiled. "Hell hath no fury like a woman's scorn."

"Sort of like my ex-wife," Kleezebee said, laughing. Lucas joined him.

A few seconds later, a familiar melody reverberated through the floorboards, then fell silent. "Sounds like Fuji just finished his prayer vigil. I think I'll head down for a quick visit. Wanna join me?"

"What about dinner?"

"In a bit. I want to check out the suit."

"You go ahead. I need to rest this ankle. Those steps are hell on these old bones."

FOUR

The Smart Skin Suit

Lucas walked to the middle of the Kleezebee's living room and bent down to grab the recessed handle of the trap door, swinging it open from right to left on a trio of six-inch metal hinges. The 3x6 reinforced door creaked wildly as he pulled it up and laid it over. A mist of dust particulates and odor drifted up from below, filling his nostrils with a medley of scents—smoke, candle wax, stale humidity, and what he thought was scorched meat and hair. His belly erupted in a low-pitched gurgle as he walked down the seven steps into the basement.

Kleezebee's cabin had originally been built as a mining shack during the great Tritanium Ore Rush that had occurred some fifty years earlier. Ghost Mountain was the first of many rich tritanium deposits discovered on the colony, making the elite class on Kleezebee's version of Earth extremely wealthy in the process.

When they'd first arrived at the abandoned cabin, Fuji and the professor had spent several months enlarging the existing basement by carving space out of the mineral-hardened rock with modified stunner technology in order to provide a shielded, temperature-controlled environment for Fuji's work. They'd even managed to build a secure, underground, five-hundred-foot-long escape tunnel that led into the adjacent forest. Unfortunately, in the process, they'd exhausted the energy stored in the only two E-121 spheres they had on hand. The rest of the power modules had been confiscated by Cyrus' new regime. Kleezebee needed the BioTex material in order to revive his crew of replicas, and then use their shape-shifting abilities to infiltrate Cyrus' compound and reacquire the E-121.

Lucas stepped off the last rung of the ladder. Fuji stood just three steps away, his arms folded with his hands tucked inside the oversized cuffs of his child-sized robe. His frail-looking jawline and cheekbones were stiff, as if he were paralyzed with focus. Lucas could see into the next room where the metal cage that formed the exterior to the Incursion Chamber was waiting for him. Fuji still had work to do in order to complete the device, but it wouldn't be long, assuming the team could acquire the remaining items on their to-do list.

"You having a barbecue down here?" Lucas asked him, wondering what had caused the odd smell. He sniffed twice. "Smells like KFC on steroids."

Fuji's brow pinched and his eyes flared but he said nothing. The monk pushed his middle finger at the center of his wire-rimmed glasses, sliding them up the bridge of his nose.

Lucas scanned the man's bronze-colored robe. "Get a little too close to the candles, again?"

"Today's celebration was in honor of the eleventh sacrifice," Fuji answered, spreading his arms like a priest blessing a meal.

"Okay, but what's that smell?"

Fuji peeled back the tattered cotton sleeve covering his left arm. A red, blistered area dominated the center of his skin. "Homage was paid."

"Holy shit." Lucas knelt down next to the pint-sized monk, wanting to inspect the wound. He reached for Fuji's arm, but the cleric stepped back before contact. "I know I'm not allowed to touch, but I need to take a look at that."

Fuji bowed slightly, walking closer. He held out his injured arm.

Lucas bent his torso forward to inspect the damage without touching the man. "That's a pretty significant burn. Third degree from the looks of it. Man, that's gotta hurt."

"Pain is a forgotten fruit. Without it, you wither and die."

"You better have Kleezebee treat it before it gets infected. Jesus, why would anyone do that on purpose?"

"Young Lucas, if you don't arrest the fire within, it shall consume you."

"What?"

"I speak of your recent transgression. Debts must be paid before virtue becomes all but trivial."

Lucas sifted through his recent memories. Which transgression was Fuji talking about? Jenkins' torture? His impure thoughts about the daughter of the town baker, Carrie Anne Fisher? His break-in and theft of guns and ammo from the town's gunsmith to buy Mag-Lift credits? His anger toward the Krellian Empire, Kleezebee, and the entire universe for what happened to Drew? His list of sins grew longer with each passing day. He shrugged.

"We have spoken at length before."

"Yeah, I remember. But that's not why I came down here."

"I am fully aware of your quest. But a forsaken soul is ripe to suggestion."

"You want me to stop my interrogations. Or at least how I'm doing them."

Fuji nodded.

Lucas wondered if Fuji had a crystal ball hidden somewhere in his dungeon. How else would his tiny friend always seem to know what he was feeling or doing. "I know you don't approve. But I have to find my brother."

"Torture is not a recipe for success."

"Maybe for you. But trust me, I don't care what you or anyone else thinks of me or my tactics. I'll gladly meet Lucifer himself at the gates of hell before I stop looking for my brother. I *will* find him. No matter what it takes."

"Only a penitent man shall endure."

"I'll tell you what, Fuuj, let me think about it, and get back to you on that," Lucas said with a half-smile, as he slid past Fuji. He made his way to the monk's workstation at the west end of the basement. Fuji followed two steps behind, his soft-soled sandals brushing across the cement floor of Kleezebee's basement.

Lucas opened a cardboard box stenciled with the letters SSS-2. He pulled out a body-length suit stored inside. A maze-like symmetry of orange lines flowed across the black surface of the synthetic material, much like the pattern of conductive pathways etched into the bottom of a computer circuit board.

Lucas smiled. "The micro-circuitry looks even better than it did on the schematics." He pulled at the neck seam of the body suit, inspecting the array of alternating graphene layers. The meta-fabric snapped perfectly back into place. "The buildup of nano-wires is a work of art. I'm impressed, Fuji. Damn impressed."

Fuji bowed.

"What length did you use?"

"Four hundred and forty-four nanometers."

Lucas hadn't expected a wavelength just inside the visible spectrum. The original specs called for nine hundred nanometers. Obviously, Fuji had improved the meta-material's efficiency. "Will we still achieve the proper index once it's supercharged?"

"Calculations indicate minus point eight."

"I'm not sure my code will handle a negative refraction," Lucas said, wondering if the garment would bend visible light, especially after the suit was electrified with several terajoules of pure energy. "Did you run it through the test bed of simulations I programmed for you?"

"Yes. Suit exceeded expectations."

"What about potential energy loss through absorption?"

"Conductive efficiency at one hundred percent."

Lucas smiled; Fuji may have actually solved it. He held the suit up to further inspect its elastic properties. He put his hand inside the waistband, and pushed out a section of the groundbreaking material with a five-finger spread. He wondered how well the Smart Skin Suit would fit his body. It looked a bit restrictive and uncomfortable.

"Maybe we should do a fitting? Right now, I think my boys might feel a little suffocated in this. And you know, I just might need them someday."

"As you wish," Fuji answered in a soft voice, retrieving a yellow metal tape measure from the top drawer of the work desk. Old school tech, to be sure.

Lucas removed his clothes, then slipped both legs into the split-pouch hidden in the back of the suit. He stretched open the top half of the suit and pulled it over his head and down to his shoulders. He wriggled and tugged until the suit was into position, hugging every inch of his six-foot frame. "Damn, this bitch is tight. I sure wouldn't want to run a marathon in this."

Fuji pulled the tape measure open, wrapping it around Lucas' waistline. "Twenty-eight inches exact. Perfect fit."

"Can you loosen up the crotch a bit? My balls feel like frightened turtles in this thing."

Fuji checked the inseam, then the span across Lucas' back. "No adjustments are needed. Specifications require maximum contact across your physique to protect you during the incursion process."

"Yeah, I know, but a little comfort would go a long way."

"I will recheck specifications."

"Thanks, Fuuj; I appreciate whatever you can do." Lucas turned around, putting his back to Fuji. "A little help?" Fuji helped Lucas slip out of the Smart Skin Suit. "Free at last." Lucas wiped a dozen beads of sweat from his forehead with a cotton towel.

Fuji walked ten steps to his prayer altar and wood-burning fireplace. He draped the Smart Skin Suit over the back of the wooden rocking chair sitting to the left. "Do you plan to mate with your lady friend in town?"

"Who? Carrie Anne?"

"She occupies your thoughts, yes?"

"I guess," Lucas answered, shuffling his feet. "She's a little chunky and missing a couple of teeth, but her rack is a killer. Plus, she has all her body parts, so that's a bonus. But I'm a little busy right now."

"Time may adjust to find its way."

"You're getting a little ahead of yourself, Fuuj. I haven't even asked her out yet."

"Emotions quicken without provocation. Especially for a man with limited restraint."

"More riddles?"

Fuji didn't respond.

"Hey, I have restraint. Just not your kind of restraint," Lucas said, thinking of the last time he had sat and talked with Carrie Anne, last week at the bakery. He'd learned she was preparing for the forty-day Neophan season, meaning in four days, she'd once again give up meat, make-up, and sex, leaving Lucas alone to entertain himself, again. Self-gratification wasn't the end of the world, but he'd watched all the adult material on his insta-block. Even if he could wait until after the holy season to ask her out, chances were either the police would have arrested him, or Kleezebee would have activated Fuji's incursion experiment and, assuming it worked, they'd be off to rescue Drew.

He knew he needed to acquire the courage to ask her out, and soon. His mind flashed a scene from an old Earth sci-fi movie—a klutzy, good-intentioned young man breaking through the roof of an after-hours 7-Eleven convenience store, only to fall through the drop ceiling, landing back-first on top of the chip rack below—all in the name of a stunning blonde bombshell who wanted a chicken burrito.

Lucas smiled. "Fine. I'll go see her tomorrow on my way to meet Rico and get it done. Okay?"

"The professor won't approve."

"Well, it's not up to him. He thinks he can control everything I do or say, but he's mistaken."

Fuji didn't say anything.

Lucas' original plan was to take Carrie Anne out on a romantic picnic in the forest, but realized he needed a new plan with a pissed-off Taku Beast on the loose. Maybe a romantic dinner on the Mag-Lift train? Damn, he'd just given away his only passes to Jenkins. What the hell had he been thinking?

FIVE

A Little Gamey

Lucas picked a seat at the far end of the counter in Fisher's Bakery, away from the line of weary-eyed patrons waiting to order their morning dose of caffeine and Danish. A wrinkled newspaper was lying sideways across the stool next to him as if someone were saving the seat. The headline read *East Side Exterminator Terrorizes the Narrows*. He tried not to stare at it. Just blend in, he told himself silently. Nobody knows it's you. He figured the pair of cooks that caught him leaving Jenkins' basement must have squealed to the media.

He closed his eyes and rubbed his temples. If they only knew me, the real me, he thought, they'd surely understand. He was an astrophysicist on a desperate quest to find his disabled foster brother, not the cold-blooded butcher who dominated the town's whisper mill. He didn't have a choice. Certainly, anyone of them would have done the same thing if the roles were reversed.

Lucas drew a slow breath, trying to calm his pulse. His nostrils tingled with the delicious scent of fresh pastry and finely brewed coffee. He planned to order his usual: the hungry-man Danish smothered with cherries. Even so, he flipped the handwritten menu that doubled as a place mat and pretended to read it, waiting for Carrie Anne to appear from behind the door to the kitchen. He could hear her lovely, high-pitched voice, singing and humming a pleasant tune on the other side of the back wall.

She always seemed to be in a good mood, no matter who was in the bakery, and that was true even back on the very first day he had met her. He didn't remember why he decided to first enter the bakery. He was walking along the street, minding his own business, not intending to purchase a pastry when something called out to him. It wasn't a verbal hail, more of a subconscious pull drawing his body inside the bakery. It were as if a giant magnet snagged his heart, sucking him inside the establishment against his will. Regardless of the reason, he was thankful that fortune had smiled on him that glorious day in May.

He planned to honor his promise to Fuji and ask her out today, but as usual, his best words evaded him. They were buried deep under a pool of thick mud swelling inside his brain. He feared they would once again fail to line up in proper formation, making him sound like a drooling idiot. "Get it together, dickhead," he mumbled to himself. The wetness in his throat evaporated and his chest seemed to shrink inside its own skin. He pulled his partially stuck lips apart, then wiped the stringy bead of spit from his mouth.

He felt a firm double tap on his left shoulder.

He spun around on the stool. It was Carrie Anne's old man, Stump Fisher.

"You here again, Ramsay?" the seventy-something man asked in a low-pitched, gruff voice.

Lucas ignored the old codger's tone. "Hi, Mr. Fisher. Could I get a glass of water, with a lemon in it?"

"Do I look like a goddamn waitress to you?"

Lucas didn't know what to say.

"You can't fool me, you little shit. I know why you're here. I see how you look at my daughter. Never going to happen, punk. She's only for Piston—a real man."

Who the hell is he calling a punk? Lucas clenched his fist, but didn't unleash it. "I thought they broke up a while ago. At least that's what she told me a few weeks ago."

Fisher leaned in close, sending a wash of foul breath across Lucas' face. "Forget about it, ass breath. She's not for you. Do yourself a favor and leave now before Piston gets here. He eats wimps like you for breakfast," he said, throwing up his hands. He turned and waddled away on his stubby legs, giving Lucas a clear view of a nasty, purpled-colored bruise that stretched from the man's right elbow down to his wrist before he disappeared through the kitchen door.

"What a prick," Lucas muttered.

A tall, but slender gray-haired woman removed the newspaper from the red stool next to Lucas and sat down. She put her cast-covered wrist just inches from Lucas' right arm. The cast was an odd shade of yellow and cracked near the midpoint. It looked as damaged as her arms and face—they were covered with bruises and skin sores. She must have fallen out of a skimmer recently.

"Don't let Stump intimidate you," she said in a rusty voice. "He's just looking out for his little girl."

"Yes, that may be true, but—"

"You can't blame him. She is a *very* pretty girl."

Lucas wouldn't agree that she was pretty, not in a glamorous sense. But yet, the Krellian Empire had abducted or eaten many of the age-appropriate girls during their assault, and with Rico scooping up the few remaining hotties in town, there wasn't much left to choose from. Perhaps the old bag meant she was popular by default. Not pretty.

The woman held out her hand. "My name is Tehani Fria."

"Lucas Ramsay. *Doctor* Lucas Ramsay," he said, gripping her hand for a light shake.

"A doctor?"

"Yes. With multiple post-graduate degrees in physics. Not some schmuck like Fisher thinks."

"I'm sure you're a very nice young man, but Stump is very set in his ways. Try not to judge him too harshly. He wasn't always this way."

"Have you known Mr. Fisher a long time?"

"Yes. He and I used to be married. But that was a long time ago."

"So, I take it, Carrie Anne's your daughter?"

"Step-daughter. She's from his first marriage, which didn't last long, either."

Lucas couldn't believe anyone would have agreed to marry that duck-walking jerk. Let alone two women. "Yeah, he's pretty rough around the edges."

"Life has taken its toll on him, I'm afraid," the old woman said, sipping a bit of coffee from a blue mug. Her hand tremors shook the cup front to back, clinking the porcelain against her teeth.

"What happened to your arm?" Lucas asked.

"Taku Beast," she answered after a two-beat hesitation. She put the coffee cup on the counter, then dabbed her chin with a paper napkin. "It attacked the prayer group I was with. We were walking home from last month's service in town. I wish they would capture it before it kills again."

"You know that there are two of them, right?"

Her eyes widened. "No, I hadn't heard that."

"Well, there used to be two, until recently. My boss trapped and killed one of them yesterday. We had it for dinner last night. Not bad—a little gamey."

Tehani smiled as her eyes widened. "Your boss sounds amazing. Is he single?"

"As a matter of fact, yes. But I'm not sure he's available right now, emotionally, that is. His ex-wife sort of ripped his guts out. He's a total mess over it."

"Yes. Love can do that. Especially when it ends suddenly."

"It wasn't exactly sudden for her. Just for him."

She looked confused, yet didn't respond. Instead, she seemed to be staring at his four-inch cheek scar.

Lucas rested that same cheek inside the palm of his hand, with his elbow propped against the countertop.

"I don't mean to pry, but what happened?" she asked.

"Some bully back home in the orphanage. He decided I needed some makeshift plastic surgery."

"It must have been painful."

"I really don't remember. It was a long time ago."

Carrie Anne walked through the doors from the kitchen, carrying a three-foot-wide tray full of food orders for the trio of patrons sitting to the left of Lucas. She slid the plates in front of the customers with precision; not a second wasted. She doled out the food: two plates of breakfast items to the first patron, a portly male, maybe thirty, with thick, black-rimmed glasses, and three plates to the second adult, the man's wife by the way she was futzing with his shirt collar. The plump toddler sitting between them whipped her tiny hand around to grab the closest sausage link from her father's plate. It squirted from her fingers and shot across the counter, striking Carrie Anne in the upper thigh before it dropped to the floor. The child let out a high-pitched squeal, sending Lucas' eardrums into hiding.

The sausage fumble reminded Lucas of his encounter with NASA and the U.S. President eighteen months earlier when Lucas had similar trouble controlling his fingers while unscrewing the water bottle cap during an underground meeting. Actually, it wasn't much of a meeting, more of an ambush, one orchestrated by those hell-bent to place blame for the countless deaths just prior to the Krellian incursion on his version of Earth.

Carrie Anne turned her head and made eye contact with Lucas. She smiled.

His heart raced, as the air in his lungs turned heavy, making it difficult for him to breathe. Lucas waved and nodded. He looked down at the place-mat menu, trying to play it cool.

Tehani leaned in to whisper into Lucas' ear. "She's such a lovely girl."

Lucas nodded, but kept his head down. He flipped the place mat over, running his finger down the menu, as if he were searching for something.

Seconds later, he could see Carrie Anne's chubby, stark-white legs and twin rolls of stomach fat standing in front of him, just beyond the counter. Then he saw something new: The center crease of her belly button was pulled out and held into place by a one-inch, pearl-braided stud. The skin surrounding the implement was an odd, pinkish-red color.

The number 1400 flashed in Lucas mind—the typical number of bacteria strains living inside the average human's belly button. Probably six hundred or more of them unrecognized and potentially lethal—a bio-diverse playground for the unclean, he thought quietly. At least she wasn't covered with tattoos; he hated them. It seemed like every girl he knew had desecrated her gorgeous body with the proverbial tramp-stamp above the crack of her ass.

He craned his neck to make eye contact with her.

"Hi, Lucas. Haven't seen you in a while. I thought something dreadful had happened to you."

"Been busy," he said, trying not to stare at her well-presented cleavage—it jiggled wildly with every breath she took.

She ran her index finger over the cotton-wrap protecting Lucas' punching hand. "What did you do to yourself this time?"

Lucas cleared his throat. "Oh, ah. It's nothing. Just a little accident. I'm fine."

"You really need to be more careful," she said, scooping up the newspaper sitting in front of the old women. "Can I put this away, ma'am?"

"Yes, my dear."

Lucas through it was odd that Carrie Anne called her step-mom "ma'am." Some type of local tradition, he figured—not his forte, to be sure. At least Carrie Anne did not seem to notice the front-page article. Maybe it was his lucky day.

"Did you see the headline?" the old witch asked.

Lucas felt his blood pressure spike.

Carrie Anne opened the newspaper and scanned the front page for a good minute. "That's horrible. How can anyone torture innocent people?"

"Maybe the victim wasn't so innocent?" Lucas suggested.

Carrie Anne pressed her hands to her mailbox-wide hips, newspaper still in hand. "Why would you defend a cold-blooded psychopath like that?"

"I'm not. I'm just saying, until we know all the facts, isn't it a little premature to judge him? He might have a good reason for what he's doing."

She scrunched her face and raised her voice two octaves. "There's never a good reason to hurt people. It's just wrong."

"Makes you wonder what makes a man like that tick?" the old woman asked.

"He's just a sick, twisted bastard," Carrie Anne said, contemptuously. "When he's arrested, I hope they put him into a locked room with a Taku Beast. Let the exterminator get exterminated."

Lucas didn't respond. His emotions and thoughts were competing for the same space in the front row of his mind. Probably not a good time to ask her out, he figured. She hated him with every fiber of her soul, and she didn't even know it; yet.

She turned the page. "It says here that the victim—a restaurant owner—got away."

"Plus, he stabbed the attacker," Tehani added, elbowing Lucas on the side of his ribcage.

Lucas wasn't sure if the elbow was accidental, or if the old lady was trying to tell him something. He decided to ignore it. He slid his injured hand under the counter, resting it on his lap. "I read that same article and it didn't say that he stabbed the attacker. It said the assailant was injured and bleeding, but it didn't say how."

"Either way, serves him right."

Lucas needed to change the subject without being obvious, but his mind froze. Before he could decide what to do, the restaurant door behind him banged open, smashing into the wall next to it. Four men, raunchy-looking, in their twenties, strolled in laughing and cussing.

Carrie Anne ducked behind the counter in front of Lucas. Only the tuft of her disheveled hair was visible.

"Where's my slut?" the tallest of the four men yelled, walking with his chest pushed out and a well-defined bounce to his step. A rust-colored machete hung from his beltline, the shiny tip about mid-thigh.

"Oh, not this fucking guy," Lucas mumbled.

One of the teenage boys standing in the To Go line gave the dirty-blonde loudmouth an elbow bump. "Piston, my man. You rock."

Piston pushed through the line, forcing his way to the front. "Carrie Anne! Get your fat ass out here."

"Don't tell him where I am," Carrie Anne whispered to Lucas, her eyes peeking over the edge of the countertop. "We broke up, but he just won't leave me alone."

"He'll see you down there," Lucas responded. "Maybe you need to talk to him and set him straight."

"I tried but he won't listen."

"Do you want me to handle it?" Lucas asked, spinning his legs around to get up from the stool.

"No, Lucas. He'll kill you. This is my problem," Carrie Anne said, grabbing a handful of plates from under the counter. She stood up and walked six steps toward Piston, though at a snail's pace. "I'm over here, Piston."

Piston and his gang met her halfway, slipping their bodies in between the now well-fed three-member family sitting on the swivel stools to the left.

Lucas avoided eye contact with the loud mouth, but readied his arsenal of hand-to-hand combat skills. He figured it was about time to find out if Rico's hundred-plus hours of training in recent months were worth the pain and sore muscles.

"What do you want, Piston?" Carrie Anne asked.

"You need to come home. And I mean now!"

"No. I'm never coming back. Ever."

"Come on, baby. It's all good."

"No."

"Why not?"

"Because you lead with meanness, and tuck away love. I can't be with someone like that."

Piston looked around, making eye contact with several of his men. He looked at Carrie Anne. His face went soft. "But sweetie, I love you."

"No, you don't. You're incapable of love."

"How can you say that after all we've been through?" he asked, grabbing the fold of her arm.

She pulled away violently. "You've sucked the last drop of life out of me. I can't do this anymore. And I'm not doing any more of those *favors* for you, either. You can just forget it." A stream of tears ran down her cheeks. She hurried to the kitchen door, swung it open, stood in the frame. "Oh, and just so you know, I took all the stuff you left at the apartment, including that duffel bag I wasn't supposed to open, and I gave it all to the church. Then I had the landlord change the locks. You're not welcome there anymore." She threw her head back and disappeared through the kitchen door as it closed behind her.

Piston turned to face his posse. "Fuckin' bitch. I don't care what she says, we're not done until I say we're done. Never coming home, my ass."

Lucas pulled his feet under himself, and began to stand up to face the scoundrel, but the old woman sitting next to him latched onto his arm, stopping his motion. He turned and looked at her.

Tehani shook her head gently, not saying a word. Her eyes flared, as if she were trying to warn Lucas about something. She put both her index and middle finger on the center of his forehead, closed her eyes, and bowed her head.

Before Lucas could decide what to do, his head swirled with thoughts of Drew. He looked down, grabbing the tin container holding a wad of napkins. He emptied its contents and looked inside. His brother's reflection appeared across the shiny surface, wearing an ear-to-ear smile. Lucas' temper cooled, so did his intent. Moments later, he realized that it was the first time that he had seen Drew's reflection without the customary headache or verbal nonsense from the traveler in his head.

Piston and company left the bakery a few seconds later.

"You should go," Tehani said. "I'll take care of things here."

Lucas agreed.

SIX

Major Rico Renaldi

Two hours later, Lucas entered the abandoned warehouse and saw Major Rico Renaldi standing in the back, next to half a dozen men who were prying open a stack of wooden crates emblazoned with yellow and black bio-hazard warning labels. Rico put his hand inside the first crate, pulling out a pair of stun guns wrapped inside sheets of old newspaper. He tilted the sunglasses off his nose, looking closely at two of the guns, and then nodded to his men.

Rico always wore shades, even indoors, which he said was to protect his sensitive eyes from the abundant sunlight that washed over the colony during the summer months. Lucas thought otherwise. He figured the bronze-skinned mercenary wore them to enhance his reputation with the ladies, as if he needed any help.

Rico had hit the gene-pool lottery with his devilishly handsome good looks, six-foot-two frame, six-pack abs, and wavy dark hair to match. His face was covered perpetually by a two-days' growth of neatly-trimmed stubble, like what you'd expect from a boy-toy underwear model, who thinks he's all that. But

Rico actually was, and then some. He was a smooth-talking panty-peeling chick magnet who barely had to try. Women swooned over him, willing to spread their legs on a moment's notice, even when he was rude to them.

Rico's standards, though, were ultra-high when it came to women. In the eleven months that Lucas had known him, the major had burned through all eight of Flandreau's sexiest girls — each one seemingly more beautiful than the last. None of Rico's relationships lasted more than a single date, if you could call it that — and he liked to brag about it. He said he would meet them by the mosquito-infested Abbidos Lake, pour them two drinks of raspum, then initiate his seed dump and send them off in a heartbeat.

If Rico's man-juice was as remarkable as his combat skills, there'd soon be a trail of little Rico's littering the countryside. STDs had been eradicated in Kleezebee's universe and birth control wasn't available, meaning it probably wouldn't be long before all the newborns started growing thick, wavy black hair and talking ultra-smooth.

The colony's Supreme Commander, Cyrus, had ordered all citizens to begin procreation efforts to repopulate the species after the Krellian invasion, but Lucas wasn't sure if the SC's general order was the basis for Rico's motivation or not. Maybe it was simply a case of Rico's inner caveman taking charge to cultivate and fertilize as many gardens as possible. On the other hand, the fatigue-wearing Adonis could be searching for that one special woman who could placate his emotionally-starved Oedipus complex.

"Let's get this party started," Lucas shouted, hearing his voice echo off the far wall.

Rico looked at this watch. "You're late."

"Traffic was a bitch."

"What traffic? There're barely any roads left."

"Sorry, just an old Earth saying. Took longer than I thought to get here from town."

Rico turned his attention to a white, baby-faced soldier standing to his immediate right. The boy was half a foot shorter than Lucas and pencil-thin. The freckles sprinkled across his nose seemed fake, like they'd been drawn with an unsteady hand and a red magic marker. The name on his fatigues said "Stonebridge."

"Sergeant, I want each weapon checked and prepped," Rico said. "Make sure the power cartridges are fully charged and the contacts are clean. No mistakes."

"Yes, sir," Stonebridge answered with sharp precision. He saluted and began his work.

Rico tossed Lucas a stunner pistol. "You know how to use this, right?"

"Sure do," Lucas said, holding the gun out in front of him in a shooting position. He aimed the weapon at a few spots around the room. "Used it when we were back on the hive ship, after the bugs snatched my brother."

Rico pointed to a towering white guy with jet-black hair, who was removing an equipment vest and chewing on a pair of soggy toothpicks. "This is Zack. He's from the badlands up north. We call him T-Rex."

Zack was a good ten inches taller than Lucas, if you included his three-inch, squared-off crew cut with a bright yellow streak down the middle. His sleeveless t-shirt stretched the seams, clinging to the well-defined curves in his physique.

Lucas extended his right hand for a shake, hoping he'd get it back in one piece. "I'm Dr. Ramsay."

"Doctor?" Zack asked, barely moving his lips when he spoke.

"Physicist. Not 'turn your head and cough,'" Rico said.

"Astrophysicist, to be exact," Lucas replied, studying the giant's square face and prominent chin. They looked like they were chiseled from a two-ton slab of granite: rock hard and weather-worn. Zack fit the bill exactly: A lowbrow, high-testosterone commando type right down to his leather army boots and enormous hands. Only his nose was out of character: It was smashed and dented to one side, reminiscent of an old hockey goalie who forgot to wear his facemask a few too many times.

"A civilian?" Zack asked, looking Lucas over from head to toe. "I thought we were only working with pros."

Lucas straightened his posture, trying to grow a few inches. He made sure Zack could see his bandaged hand and cheek scars. He strengthened his voice. "I can handle myself."

Rico nodded. "The kid's right, he can; I've been teaching him hand-to-hand. His marksmanship could use some work, but trust me, he's good to go."

The concerned look on Zack's face washed away. He gripped Lucas' hand. "Nice to meet you, Doc."

Lucas felt the bandage stretch tight as Zack squeezed. The gauze slid across the wound underneath, tugging at the scab, but he didn't feel the warmth of fresh blood, at least not yet. "Likewise. But you can call me Lucas."

"I prefer Doc."

"Sure, T-Rex," Lucas replied, wishing he had a cool nickname.

"Only my friends call me that."

Lucas caught his drift—he wasn't a friend yet. He wondered how hard it would be to earn that title. Would he have to kill someone or wipe out a small village? Maybe it was a much simpler process, like bringing Zack a cold six-pack and a warm hooker every night. With any luck, maybe Zack would share some of the leftovers so he wouldn't need to acquire the courage to ask Carrie Anne out. "Okay. Zack, it is."

Lucas had thought about calling his new friend *Hulk* to lighten the mood, but decided against it. The giant could probably tear him in half and never break a sweat, unless this man's intimidating appearance was simply a ruse. If it were, he might actually be a cuddly, three-hundred-pound teddy bear, much like Lucas' dead lab assistant, Trevor.

Zack held a stun gun in front of his face and rammed a power cartridge into its stock. "This is all we have?"

"Silent but deadly," Lucas added, "just like my brother."

Zack didn't seem amused.

"No casualties. Kleezebee's orders," Rico said.

"Where'd he get 'em?" Zack asked.

"He had the stunners all along. Brought them with him from the other 'verse. Stored 'em over at Three Rivers."

"The dump site?" Zack asked.

Rico nodded. "In the bio-hazard containers."

Lucas thought Kleezebee's plan to hide the illegal energy-based weapons at the dump was pure genius. After all, who in their right mind would wander into a toxic disposal site littered with yellow-and-black warning signs? Certainly not a sane person, but Cyrus the Virus wasn't in his right mind, so it was a calculated risk by Kleezebee either way.

"We'll only get to use them once, so we'd better make it count. They'll light up the security net."

"Agreed," Zack said. "Once Cyrus learns of the breach, he'll come at us hard." He slid the weapon into a holster sitting on one of the unopened crates. "Would be a whole lot more fun if we were using shredders."

"I second that," Lucas said, hoping someday he'd get to fire one of the powerful hydrogen cell rifles. They unleashed a deadly stream of depleted uranium rounds that could rip through body armor like butter. The rounds used on-board nano-sensors to slow their flight after contact, allowing more time for their whirling blades to inflict damage. Best of all, they were reusable, provided their Teflon-coated, razor-sharp fins weren't damaged.

"We still get to smoke him, right?" Zack asked.

"Not until after we rescue their friends."

"Why?" Zack asked, jaw pushed out.

Rico didn't answer.

Zack's face flushed red, then the tension in his face subsided. "Ah, hell. You gave them your word, didn't you?"

Rico nodded.

"Then I guess we wait. But this better happen fast," Zack said, angry. "It's just about killin' time."

"A few more days, that's all. Then you can do what you need to do."

Zack clipped the stunner's holster to his equipment belt. "We'll need something more than these zap-guns."

"Definitely. But when it's time, remember: Cyrus is all mine. You can take care of your old buddy, Freakshow."

Zack nodded slowly, wearing a hint of a smile. He pulled out a long-handled nine-inch knife from a sheath hanging on the left side of his waist. He twisted it slowly in the air. Its serrated blade glistened under the warehouse lights as Zack seemed to make love to it with his eyes. "I'm gonna enjoy bleeding him, slow. It'll make sure he stays alive for hours, before I end him."

Maybe the term "teddy bear" was a poor choice of words, Lucas thought. Everything about the man screamed cold-blooded assassin—a true alpha male. He decided it was safer if he moved on the other side of Rico to the far end of crates.

Rico opened another crate to his right, put his hand in and pulled out four bricks of plastic explosives. He tossed them two at a time to Stonebridge. "You're in charge of demo. Get it right this time."

"Count on it, sir."

Rico raised his voice. "Saddle up, ladies. We leave in ten. Keep your shit wired tight. Let's run this by the numbers."

Lucas' heartbeat picked up steam. This was his first chance to be part of a bona fide assault team. He had been in a couple of firefights before on the hive ship and back on his version of Earth, but they were out of desperation and not a coordinated attack with seasoned mercenaries.

Rico handed a stack of folded street clothes to both Lucas and Zack. "Change out of your greens."

"Why?" Lucas asked.

"You and Zack are going in as civilians. The reservations are in your name."

Lucas looked up at Zack. "The two of us?"

"Yep. He's your backup in case this op goes sideways."

"They don't call me T-Rex for nothing," Zack said with a spark of pride in his eyes. He ripped off his t-shirt, revealing a litany of scars across his chest and back. Some were shaped like rounded starfish, while others were long, thick, and raised above the skin. Some of the surrounding tissue was discolored, as if someone had tried to patch him together using someone else's skin. Maybe he suffered from post-op infections, or perhaps the skin grafts didn't take the first time. Either way, it was obvious that Zack was hard to kill and no stranger to pain.

The most noticeable scar across Zack's chest draped like a slanted "T," which must have been how he'd been tagged with the nickname T-Rex. Lucas figured Zack was the kind of man who stood at the local bar and bragged that he ate glass and crapped napalm, then used a flame thrower to melt the skin off his arm to prove his toughness.

"Where are your men gonna be?" Lucas asked Rico.

"We'll be outside, waiting for your signal."

"Leaving us a little exposed, aren't you?"

"Trust me, Doc, you've got nothing to worry about. Zack's got your back and we'll be only seconds away."

"Can you at least have a couple undercover guys in the restaurant when we arrive?"

"They're already on the list. Now, give me your left arm."

Lucas held out his arm. "Why?"

Rico turned Lucas' arm over, exposing the wrist. He pressed a stubby, cigar-shaped metal tube against Lucas' skin. A second later, Lucas heard the sound of compressed air releasing, followed by a sharp prick along his wrist.

Lucas jerked his arm back and rubbed his wrist. "What the hell was that?"

"Protection."

"Against what?"

"Capture and torture."

"You mean like a tracking device?"

"No. Something a little more interesting," Rico said, wearing a crooked smile. "An explosive charge."

"A what!"

"I implanted a small explosive next to your radial artery. It'll release a fast-acting chemical agent directly into your blood stream if you're not back here in twelve hours."

"It'll kill you in a second," T-Rex said, grinning as if he were getting a kick out of it.

"Fuck that. Get it out of me. I didn't sign up for this shit."

Rico held up his left arm. So did Zack and the rest of the men.

"We all have them," Rico said. "It's not an option if you want to be part of our team. We can't take the chance that Cyrus gets his hands on you. You'd compromise the mission."

"Bullshit," Lucas said. "I'd never say anything."

Zack laughed. "Trust me, Doc, you wouldn't last an hour. They're damn efficient at making captives talk. First, they'll pump you full of adrenaline to keep you awake and alert. Then, while you watch, they'll skin you alive by peeling back hunks of your skin and feeding them to you. Hell, just Freakshow's breath alone is—"

"That's enough. He gets the point," Rico said.

"Does the professor know about this?" Lucas asked, pointing to his throbbing wrist.

"Who do you think invented it?"

Lucas couldn't believe the professor had never told him about the lethal device or that they'd plant it in his arm. But he knew how seriously Kleezebee believed in his *Need to Know* credo. The man was a walking cryptogram. "Fine. But once I'm back here, you'd better dig the thing out of me, first."

"Won't need to. We have a neutralizer device. Only takes a second," Rico said. "Now, get changed. We've got work to do."

SEVEN

This Place Blows

Zack led the way to the Dunn-Riţe Café wearing his signal watch, white button-down shirt, blue dress pants, and leather shoes. Lucas was dressed the same, minus the communicator watch and ten inches of macho.

"Dude, we look like gay bankers," Lucas said, unbuttoning the top button of his collared shirt. Zack snickered at the joke, but never looked at Lucas. He kept walking toward the diner, still two blocks away.

"How long have you known Rico?" Lucas asked, scratching the injection site on his wrist.

"I served with him on Avanti Prime, during the first Krellian assault. Those damn bugs were relentless. We lost a lot of good men that day."

"I heard about that. Wasn't the casualty rate something like eighty percent?"

"Closer to ninety. We lost most of our squad. But we gave more than we got. Took out a whole regiment before they withdrew."

"Is that where you got that huge T scar on your chest?"

Zack nodded. "I took a Sentinel's claw straight on. Damn thing wouldn't let me go until Rico blasted that creature's head clean off. I owe him my life. I heard you saw some action on the hive ship before it crashed in the desert."

"Sure did, but that wasn't the first time. The bugs appeared out of nowhere back on Earth in Kleezebee's underground silo, and snatched by little brother. Took him right out of his wheelchair and jumped back through a rift in space. Chicken-shits."

"Impale and run. One of their favorite tactics."

"I wanted to blast them, but couldn't react fast enough. Some of Kleezebee's engineers took grappling hooks in the chest. Tore them apart from the inside. Jesus, what a mess. It was epic."

"Dodged a few of those in my day."

"Bruno managed to get a shot off before the last one disappeared. Slowed the fucker down enough that the rift cut it in half when it closed. At least we got one of 'em. We eventually got Drew back, but it wasn't easy."

"Bruno's one of your friends, right?"

"Yeah. Haven't seen him since we got here. One of the conditions of the non-aggression treaty with the bugs was that Cyrus had to dissolve all our BioTex replicas; one of 'em was Bruno. He's Kleezebee's oldest friend and a warrior like you. I miss him. The guy makes me laugh."

"BioTex?"

"It's Bio-mimetic Latex. It's one of Kleezebee's best inventions and the reason the Krellian Empire invaded my version of Earth. It's living synthetic latex that can be used to mimic a living organism right down to its DNA. Pretty cool stuff. At least it was until Cyrus stole it from us."

"That asshole will steal anything. Especially if it gives him a tactical advantage. You have any other run-ins with the bugs?"

"Fuck, yeah. The Krellians used impale-and-run on the hive ship when they appeared and killed my mom and our lab assistant, Trevor, in the hallway outside the mess hall. It was horrible; the bugs ate them alive."

Zack didn't respond. Lucas wondered if Zack already knew the story. Maybe Kleezebee told Rico and Rico passed it along to Zack. It was a *small* planet, after all.

"Sad thing was, we were just about safely here and let our guard down. Never saw the ambush coming. Wish you and Rico had been there. Probably never would've happened."

"It's difficult to predict where those things will strike. They're damned clever."

"Yes, they are. Except the one time when Kleezebee outsmarted them during the exchange for Drew. We got my little brother back in one piece and didn't have to give up anything. Kleezebee's the second smartest person I know."

"Who's the first? You?"

Lucas sensed the sarcasm in Zack's voice. "No. My brother. He makes us all look like meatheads." As soon as the last word left his tongue, he wished he'd chosen a different phrase to describe his brother's intelligence. Meathead? Where the hell did that word come from? He wondered how much it was going to hurt when Zack buried his knuckles wrist-deep into his cheekbone. Lucas waited for the punch, but it never came.

"What did your brother do?"

Lucas let out a long, silent exhale. "He took my dad's pest-control invention and turned it into a supercharged sonic disrupter that attacked the Krellians' nervous system. It was biblical! Orange blood and guts everywhere. Exploded every one of those fuckers and we never had to fire a shot. That's how we got our hands on their hive ship and ended up here."

"These sonic disruptors . . . are they anything like Cyrus' SDVs?"

"Actually, they're the same exact thing. SDV stands for Sonic Disruptor Vest, which he stole from us and then used to stop the Krellian attacks in this sector. He didn't even have enough imagination to change the goddamn name. That was my dad's invention and we brought it here from my Earth."

"Does Rico know all this?"

Lucas nodded. "He's about the only one. Cyrus used our technology to vault himself to the Chancellor's office after he stopped the bugs and got them to sign the peace treaty. We're the reason this colony still exists. Not him."

"Too bad you guys didn't show up a month earlier. Earth could have used the tech."

"What was your Earth like before the bugs invaded?"

"Crowded. Not so much anymore."

"When we decided to come to Kleezebee's home universe, Drew and I were excited to see the future. We figured there'd be awesome new technology, medical advancements, personal spaceships, you know, the kind of stuff that science fiction authors had promised us for years. What a total disappointment. It's like I'm stuck living on the pages of some pulpy sci-fi novel."

"Earth had the tech you were expecting, at least until the Krellians leveled the major cities. This colony only has their hand-me-downs, but I prefer it that way. Too much tech just gets in the way."

"No offense, but I still think this place blows."

"Did Cyrus confiscate anything else?"

"Let's see . . . the sonic disruptors, the BioTex, our jump pad technology, and all of our remaining E-121 power modules."

Lucas wanted to brag about the items Cyrus didn't find, like the activator enzyme for the BioTex, the rift-slipping device, and the new incursion technology that Kleezebee and Fuji had built in the basement of the cabin, but decided against it. Rico had vouched for Zack, but Lucas barely knew the guy. He needed to know more about him first, before he gave away all their secrets.

"I'm surprised Cyrus let you go," Zack said with genuine-sounding curiosity in his voice.

"Believe it or not, Kleezebee talked him into it. He told Cyrus that he needed our expertise to help rebuild the colony and train his men how to use our tech. The first chance we got, we took off and hid in the mountains—been there ever since. So, what's the deal with you and Freakshow?"

The look on Zack's face suggested that he didn't want to answer the question. But a few seconds later, he did. "He killed my younger brother."

Lucas wondered if he should continue to pry or just let the man be. His curiosity won out. "What happened?"

"Me, Rico, and Freakshow were all part of the same combat unit on Avanti Prime. One night on watch, camp surveillance showed Freakshow leaving his post, which we later determined was to go get high. Wasn't long before the base's perimeter was breeched and the bugs tore through most of our troops. One of the KIA was my younger brother, Marco. He'd just turned sixteen and only signed up three days before."

"Sorry. I didn't know."

Zack grunted as his eyes glazed over and his hands shook. "I was out on a bug hunt with Rico and wasn't there to protect him."

"It's tough to lose a brother, I know," Lucas said with a heavy heart, thinking of the last time he saw his brother—eighteen months ago. Drew was smiling and linked arm-in-arm with Abby, ready to move through the portal to Kleezebee's universe. Lucas had gone through the portal first, escorting their adoptive mother, Dorothy. He and his mom waited for them on the other side. But Drew and Abby never made it. The portal collapsed with them still inside. Lucas managed to reopen the rift and get the rest of the crew across to the stolen Krellian hive ship, but they never found Drew. He'd been missing even since. "That kind of loss can really change a man."

"That lowlife is gonna pay," Zack snorted. He whirled and punched a nearby blue trash dumpster, sending it spinning to the left. It crashed into a moss-covered brick wall, lunging upward on the back pair of caster wheels. The fist impact left a two-foot dent in the side of the rusted bin. Zack's knuckles were bleeding, but he never shook his hand. He continued walking, letting the blood drip to the ground.

Lucas gave Zack a minute to calm down. "Was it M-B? The stuff Freakshow was getting high on?"

"Yeah. I found the stash in his duffel the next day."

"I thought so. M-B is everywhere. I know a few tweakers in town who are addicted to it. Word has it that Cyrus is the major supplier."

Zack nodded. "He gives samples away to get them hooked. Then he rations the supply as leverage to keep them under control."

Lucas wondered if Zack knew about the ingenious delivery system for the drug. "It all starts with a swarm of microscopic bees that are released into the bloodstream at the injection point. They travel to the subject's brain and attach themselves to targeted nerve clusters, flooding the senses with pleasure signals."

"Bees?"

"Well, not insects, exactly. They're microscopic bio-machines, which everyone calls 'M-Bs' for short. But what most people don't know is that they can be controlled remotely. Cyrus uses them to induce pain as well as pleasure, which we think is how he punishes his men to keep them in line. It's like programmable crack."

Zack shrugged.

"Crack cocaine. It's a nasty drug we have on my Earth. But trust me, M-B is a million times worse. And to think, M-B started out as a miracle drug to seek out and destroy cancer cells. But then the drug lords stole the technology and, well, you know the rest."

Zack didn't say anything.

"What happened to Freakshow's face? Did you do that to him after he left his post?"

"Never got a chance. He went AWOL that same night. Eventually joined up with Cyrus. The boils showed up on his face about a year later—right before he started butchering whole families. At first, I didn't know it was him until I heard him speak. That weak-minded coward can hide his face from me, but not his voice."

Lucas wondered if Freakshow had been exposed to some of Kleezebee's confiscated E-121 material. Long-term exposure would explain the man's disfigurement and his unstable mental state. "The tissue damage looks like he might be suffering from exposure to an unshielded power source. He's probably being cooked from the inside out, slowly turning his brain into oatmeal."

"Serves the asshole right."

"He'll probably get even meaner and more unpredictable as the condition worsens."

"Then he needs to meet the end of my blade, and soon," Zack said, motioning his head straight ahead. The front doors to the café were maybe a hundred feet away.

EIGHT

Carbs-R-Us

Zack cut in front of Lucas as they made their way across the diner's dirt parking lot, squeezing between several rows of empty skimmers. Lucas saw a vision of Drew's face in every vehicle window he passed, which of course was followed by the usual jolt of pain shooting into his temples. He winced as the traveler broke his recent streak of silence and whispered inside Lucas' mind—*Correctly erasing most annoying riddles means the highest possible outcome in navy underwater testing involving enzymes.*

"You okay?" Zack asked.

"Just a bit of a migraine. I'll live."

They approached the front door to the café. He wondered if patrons inside could see him walking behind the goliath, assuming anyone was paying attention. The place didn't appear to be guarded. In fact, it wasn't remarkable in any way. Hardly the type of place you'd expect to be a Cyrus stronghold.

He started to worry that Jenkins might have given him bad information. If he had, it might be a trap and Rico and T-Rex would blame him if the op went sideways. The last thing he needed was a pair of stone-cold killers pissed at him; he had enough of his own demons on board already.

Lucas studied the red-and-white-colored awning protecting the entrance to the building. There was no sign of any surveillance equipment, and nothing was visible along the metal overhang spanning the front of the building, either. Perhaps nobody was watching. He looked back over his shoulder to see if he could spot any of Rico's assault team hiding in the shadows. He couldn't, but he could feel the weight of their eyes studying his every move.

Zack held the glass door open, allowing Lucas to enter first. All but two of the patrons stopped talking, then turned in unison to look at them.

"That's a bit creepy," Lucas whispered to his teammate.

Zack's nostrils flared, but he said nothing.

It was your typical 'fifties-style diner with a dozen fake red leather, padded bar stools in front of a thirty-foot stainless-steel counter. Four middle-aged women dressed in yellow uniforms and white aprons were scurrying about at high speed, carrying food and taking orders. Out front, the seating area was filled with cream-colored booths, most of which were stuffed with patrons. The black-and-white tile floor alternated in color like a chessboard and the walls were covered with pulsating neon signs touting the local raspum distilleries.

Lucas assumed the two men at the counter who didn't turn around were Rico's undercover operatives. They were sitting side-by-side, but Lucas couldn't see their faces. They were wearing pale-green baseball caps, blue pants, and long overcoats. Both appeared to be stuffing some type of gooey meat sandwich into their mouths.

"This place is packed. Food must be good."

"Not necessarily," Zack said, handing Lucas an open menu.

Lucas scanned the menu. Each item's price had been covered up with a black-and-white sticker that said *FREE!*

"Seriously? Free food? Cyrus must be trying to ingratiate himself with the locals." Lucas put the menu down. "I gotta believe Cyrus worked out some kind of deal with the bugs. Otherwise, they would've leveled this place, too."

Zack nodded. "People gotta eat."

Lucas made a cursory count of heads—at least fifty—and everyone seemed to be at least thirty pounds overweight. "Looks like a bunch of extras for a Richard Simmons' before-and-after commercial." Lucas smiled at Zack. "Mostly before."

Zack's face remained stiff. He didn't respond.

Lucas wondered why he tried to be funny around a leather-hard mercenary; it was pointless. "I wonder how the hell he pays for all of this? Free food isn't exactly a profitable business model."

"Looks like the rumors are true," Zack said, raising his left eyebrow. "He's taken control of all the commercial farms in the eastern province. Now we know why."

"Yeah. Carbs-R-Us."

Zack laughed.

Finally! The goliath does have a pulse.

Lucas leaned over the hostess station and looked behind the counter. Four stacks of white cardboard strips were organized into equal piles on the top shelf. Each one had a time of day and a family surname handwritten on them in thick, black ink. He assumed they were invitations to eat at the SC's free restaurant. It would explain why there wasn't a waiting line stretching around the block. Cyrus had made his intentions clear: Once he took office, he wouldn't tolerate chaos. He expected calm from the locals at all times, or they would face the wrath of his Royal Guards.

Lucas stood next to Zack as they waited by the front register until a redheaded woman walked to the hostess station. She was bowling-ball round with rosy cheeks that pushed out beyond her ears. Her hair looked like it had been teased for hours with a comb until it was the size of a twenty-pound Christmas turkey. If Lucas had to guess, her name was probably Flo or Hazel.

"Wel'km to the Dunn-Rite Caffay. What can I do yer fer?" she asked.

"Ramsay, party of two," Lucas replied.

She checked the reservation list. "Would y'all like the count'r or booth?"

"Doesn't matter as long as you're serving some of your double apple fritters. We hear they're the best in town."

"You should try 'em with anchovies, they be delicious."

"Maybe you could top them off with some cream sauce."

She hesitated for a moment, tilted her head, then said, "I'm sure we can oblige. Right 'dis way, gen'men."

She led them to one of the last empty booths in the café. It was along the back wall, to the right of the counter, on the opposite side of the restaurant from the restrooms. The booth sitting immediately in front of it was empty as well, providing a little privacy. There was an unmarked, single panel door next to the booth, which Lucas assumed led to the kitchen.

The hostess put two menus on the table and invited them to sit down. Zack squeezed himself into the left side of the booth, facing out. No doubt to keep an eye on everything. Lucas sat across from him, with his back to the front entrance and the rest of the restaurant. He listened for sounds behind the kitchen door, but didn't hear the expected chorus of plates clinking and pans banging as frantic chefs shouted instructions to each other.

"My name's Leigh Ann, if you boys need anything else."

So much for Flo or Hazel, Lucas thought. He opened the menu and pointed at the first item's picture—a chili-cheese dog stuffed with toppings. "Is everything really free?"

Leigh Ann nodded. "Compliments of the Supreme Commander."

"Unreal."

Leigh Ann smiled, then disappeared through the door to Zack's right.

Lucas turned to page three of the menu and read the list of items courage in disguise. After seeing the seemingly endless pizza selections, his stomach gurgled again, this time loud enough for half the restaurant to hear. He licked his lips and swallowed. "We should probably order something. No reason to pass up all this free grub." He closed the menu and looked around, wondering which waitress was assigned to their table. He turned to face Zack. "You wanna split a pizza?"

Zack pushed his menu away from him. He'd never opened it.

Seconds later, two soldiers bolted through the door next to Zack with black shredder rifles held chest-high in the firing position. Each rifle had a laser scope and torpedo light mounted to its barrel in and over/under configuration. One of the soldiers was breathing heavy with a river of sweat dripping from his brow. The other had steely eyes, which were focused squarely on Lucas. So was his shredder rifle and its laser targeting system.

"Don't shoot!" Lucas said, raising his hands over his head.

Zack never moved—his finger nowhere near the activator switch on his watch.

Leigh Ann walked through the doorway, escorting a heavy-lidded elderly man by the arm. The old fart had to be at least eighty and was leprechaun-short with some kind of bird tattoo inked across the top of his bald head. He was wearing baggy green pants and a pale-brown shirt that hung on his narrow shoulders like an old floor mop. Obviously, tailors weren't a popular profession in this colony.

Lucas' mind shifted into replay mode, reliving the moments leading up to the ambush. Almost instantly, he realized what went wrong. "Ah, fuck. I said cream sauce instead of yellow cream sauce, didn't I?"

Leigh Ann raised her eyebrows and nodded hard enough to shake her flabby cheeks.

"An honest mistake," Lucas said. "Obviously, I knew the correct answer."

Leigh Ann folded her arms, then pinched her lips together. She turned her attention to the wrinkled munchkin standing next to her.

"My name's Bernard," the old man said. "Who are you?"

"Cyrus sent us," Zack said, casually bringing his hands together. A slick move that nobody else seemed to notice. His index finger was almost touching the activator switch on his watch. Both of his hands were steady and his face remained stiff.

"We're here to inspect your operation," Lucas added, hoping his lie rang true. He lowered his hands slowly, but it was difficult to keep them from shaking. "Cyrus wants me to check the condition of the inventory. I'm a BioTex engineer."

Bernard hesitated for a long moment, then motioned to his guards to lower their weapons. "Follow me," he said to Lucas.

The traveler took control of Lucas' thoughts, again, and said—*Time helps everyone who keys on yesterday's nuances.* Enough of the fucking nonsense, Lucas said in silence. I need to concentrate.

Leigh Ann returned to the hostess station while the guards stepped aside to let Zack slide out of the booth. Lucas followed the group as they walked through the door and into a ten-foot-wide hallway.

As soon as the door closed behind him, the guard next to Lucas cocked his rifle and held it inches away from his temple. The other guard did the same thing to Zack, though at a steep upward angle to reach his head. Lucas' mind filled with thoughts of the explosive charge in his wrist. He realized he was a dead man walking. So was Zack.

Lucas raised his hands. "What the fuck, Barney?"

NINE

Shredder

Before the tattooed elder could respond, Zack leaped into action. He snatched the rifle from the soldier guarding him, ramming the gunstock into the guard's nose. Lucas heard it snap. A millisecond later, Zack used his left foot to take out the guard covering Lucas. He kicked the side of the man's knee, breaking it instantly, sending the guard tumbling to the floor in pain. Zack kicked the man's face, smashing the back of his head against the wall, knocking him out.

He turned the gun on Bernard and fired one shot, blasting a hole in his head the size of a coconut. Barney's brain matter splattered across the wall behind him, showering Lucas in the process. Zack finished off both unconscious guards with quick double-taps to the chest.

"Holy shit," Lucas shouted, not believing the speed of Zack's reaction. He looked at the bloodstained wall and realized that the Teflon-coated razor wings of the gas pellets didn't have any blood or tissue on them. They must not have deployed until after they zipped through Barney's skull and stuck in the wall.

Zack picked up the weapon from the second guard, handing it to Lucas. "Try not to shoot me in the back."

Lucas nodded, though still a bit dazed by the blood oozing out of what remained of Barney's skull and the guards' torsos. He tried to keep himself together, but he feared another puke sighting was imminent, when a small patch of stomach acid rose up and landed in his mouth. He swallowed it quickly and stiffened his resolve.

He cocked the rifle and held it up against his right armpit, focusing its red-dot laser beam on the door at the end of the hall. He looked at his watch. Eleven hours to go before his wrist exploded. "Hey, Zack, what happens if I get shot or smash my wrist on something? Will the charge detonate?"

"Let's go," Zack said after pressing the activator switch on his watch. "More tangos will be coming."

Maybe he's not ignoring me, maybe he doesn't know, Lucas thought. Seconds later, he heard the sound of glass breaking and the distinctive zapping sound of stunners being discharged. It was coming from the restaurant's seating area behind him. "Rico?"

"Yeah. Our six is covered."

"Kleezebee's not going to like that at all."

"No civilians will be hurt. Other than waking up with a headache in a few hours, they'll be fine."

Before Lucas could respond, the green door at the far end of the hall flew open. Four enemy guards appeared and spread out in two-by-two formation on either side of the corridor. Zack fired several short bursts of shredder rounds that steamed down the fifty-foot hallway at lightning speed.

Lucas fired one barrage, feeling the recoil of the hydrogen-powered weapon hammering his right shoulder. Both sets of projectiles whined, as their spinning razor edges activated in mid-flight, decapitating three of the enemy in unison, moments before the fourth was killed in the same manner. Their severed heads hit the floor and rolled several feet as their bodies toppled over. None of Cyrus' men fired a shot.

"Nice work," Zack said, wearing a look of astonishment.

"Thanks," Lucas replied, wondering if his rounds hit their mark. He thought they all missed, sticking into the edge of the doorframe to the right of the green door. He scratched his wrist again, this time tearing some of the skin open. Streaks of blood appeared across his wrist.

"First kill?" Zack asked, sprinting toward the far end of the hallway where the headless bodies were twitching.

Lucas ran behind him. "Yeah, as far as human." He caught up to Zack. "I blasted a few bugs on the hive ship. And there was the time on Earth when my BioTex replica had a chance to take out a soldier who killed my brother's replica in the desert. But my clone didn't kill him for some reason. I would have wasted the asshole, that's for sure. I know that doesn't exactly count, but—"

"Whoa, Doc; slow down. You'll need to brief me on the whole BioTex replica thing when we have more time," Zack whispered as he knelt on one knee in front of the open door. He looked through it, turned, and said, "We're good for now."

He retrieved the spent shredder rounds that were stuck in the doorframe and buried in one of the bodies, digging them out with his knife. He used the sleeve of his cotton shirt to wipe the blood off, then retracted the razor wings, before reloading his rifle.

Zack dug two more rounds out of the first corpse. He fiddled with their wings. They wouldn't retract. "Not usable," he said, tossing them to the ground. He knelt down next to the other body, inserting his knife into the blood dripping out from the exposed end of its neck. He let the blood pool across the blade until it was covered, then stood up and ran the flat side of the knife across his forehead, leaving a curved streak of red across his brow.

"A warrior's pact," he said with his chest expanded. He held the knife in front of Lucas. "You ready?"

Lucas leaned forward, allowing the dull side of the cool metal blade to touch his skin. Zack smiled as he smeared the dead soldier's warm blood across Lucas' forehead.

Some of the blood dripped into Lucas' eye before he was able to wipe it off with his sleeve. When he saw the blood soaking into the cuff, he realized that for the first time, he wasn't feeling queasy. Actually, he was feeling damn good—rejuvenated—like an adrenaline-charged warrior after a successful battle. Maybe he was finally getting used to all the blood and guts.

"We fight until there's no fight left," Zack said like a drill sergeant.

Lucas wasn't quite sure what that phrase meant, but didn't want to ask. He nodded with gusto, as if he knew. Then the expected flood of dizziness arrived, pressurizing his veins and buckling his legs. He fell backward, flat on his ass, just before a rush of vomit erupted from his intestines, sending at least a liter of puke across the floor.

Moments later, Zack helped him back to his feet. "You okay, Doc?"

Lucas wiped his mouth with his sleeve. "Yeah. Just give me a minute." He needed to erase the vile taste in his mouth. He scanned the hallway for a drinking fountain. There wasn't one.

"Fear is just courage in disguise. You need to stir it—bring it to a boil—then consume it."

Again, Lucas had no clue what Zack meant, but at least the dizziness eased. "That's easy for you to say."

Zack's face stiffened more than before, if that were even possible. He leaned in close enough for Lucas to feel the wind behind the mercenary's words. "Look. I know this is not easy, but there comes a time in every man's life when you have to choose what kind of man you want to be. One that freely embraces the unknown, knowing that chaos is lurking behind every shadow with hungry breath, or the kind that looks for any reason, no matter how mundane, to avoid even a single step forward to face his destiny. Which are you?"

Lucas was impressed with the warrior's poignant choice of words, but they sounded like Kleezebee's words, not Zack's. "I get it. But remember, despite Rico's training and guidance, deep down I'm still just a scientist. All this blood is—difficult. It's a lot to process."

Lucas consumed three deep breaths in succession, letting each one leak from his lips, slowly. "I prefer to think of myself as the kind of man who boldly goes where no man has gone before—in the name of science, not violence. But, I *can* do this. I have to."

"Good enough," Zack said, slapping Lucas on the back. He smiled. "Let's go find your friends."

Despite the left-brained rhetoric and the queasiness, one thing was clear. Lucas knew why Rico sent Zack along to chaperone: The man was one mean-ass cheese-grater who didn't hesitate. The safest place to be in the colony was right behind T-Rex when it was feeding time.

The door leading back to the restaurant banged open behind Lucas. He turned without thinking and aimed his shredder rifle at the new arrivals. He lowered it when he saw that it was Rico and his six-man squad. The armed men sprinted down the hallway, then gathered around the severed heads and mangled bodies.

"Looks like we missed all the fun," Rico said to Lucas.

"This was all T-Rex. I don't think I hit anything."

Rico nodded in a matter-of-fact way. "I'd recognize his handiwork anywhere."

T-Rex picked up the enemy shredder rifles and clips of ammo and gave them to four of Rico's six men. The other two men were still armed with Kleezebee's stunners.

Rico looked at both piles of corpses, then turned to T-Rex. "Only seven? Hardly seems like a fair fight."

"They'll send more, Major." T-Rex pointed at the green door. "There's another corridor dead ahead. We should double-time it."

"Lead the way, my friend."

Lucas followed T-Rex and Rico as they crept down the next corridor. The rest of the squad fell behind twenty feet or so. "How many more do you think there are?"

"Not many. We're expecting that Cyrus took most of his men with him to New Robyn City to provide security for his victory party," Rico whispered.

They found another closed door at the end of the second corridor. This door was green like the last, except it appeared to be a metal fire door, like the kind you'd find between floors in a modern skyscraper's stairwell. Its eight-inch chrome-plated twist handle was on the right and the letters SS-11 were stenciled in white across the face of the door.

Rico slipped a tiny, telescopic camera under the bottom of the doorway. The device was connected to four-inch-square paper-thin view-screen by an adjustable, metal-wrapped flexible cable that Rico used to control the angle of the camera. Rico activated the camera and monitor.

Lucas put his hand on Rico's back and leaned forward to see what the device revealed. A bright white light filled most of the display, but Lucas could see enough detail to determine that the room inside was about thirty feet wide and maybe just as deep. He couldn't see much else with the light aimed at the door. There appeared to be a silhouette of some type of security station barricade in the background, with several pairs of legs standing on either side of it.

"They're waiting for us," he said. "Trying to blind us with the light. What do we do now?"

"Hold position," Rico said, retracting the camera scope. He pressed a combination of three orange buttons on his watch.

Seconds later, Lucas heard footsteps approaching rapidly from behind. Four more of their squad joined them, two with stunners and two with shredders. Baby-faced Sergeant Stonebridge was leading the group.

Rico told Stonebridge, "I count at least five inside. There could be more. T-Rex has the left flank. I've got right. You and your squad take middle. We go on three."

Stonebridge nodded.

"What about me?" Lucas asked.

"You hold position. Same as before."

"But I can help."

"No. Can't risk it. Not with an unknown number of hostiles waiting for us on the other side of that door. Stay back and let us handle this. That's an order."

Lucas nodded.

"Take out the light first," Rico whispered to T-Rex. "I'll provide cover fire as you work around to the left."

Rico grabbed the door handle, twisting it quietly until the faint click of its latch engaged. T-Rex was to his left, crouched down and holding his rifle close to his chest, its barrel aimed at the ceiling. Rico counted to three with hand gestures, then opened the door. He leaned around the edge of the doorframe and fired blindly into the room. "Go!" he yelled to T-Rex.

T-Rex slipped through the door, firing his weapon at the spotlight in front of him as he moved. The light gushing through the doorway went dark as the sound of glass breaking echoed in the room. Lucas could only see the random flashes of weapons' fire inside.

Rico went in next, breaking right when he cleared the door. Stonebridge and the other three soldiers charged the middle, blasting the enemy with their stunners and shredders. The enemy returned fire, raising the decibel level ten-fold.

Lucas decided he needed to count to five before entering the room. Otherwise, his teammates might be in harm's way, when he let loose with his shredder. He counted silently, listening to cries of at least one man, maybe two, amid the thundering barrage of weapons' fire.

After the count of five Mississippi, he took a deep breath and exhaled, then made sure his rifle was cocked and ready. He let out a commando scream as he ran through the door and searched for a target to shoot. There was none. The fight was already over.

Rico and T-Rex were in the back, standing over a pile of enemy soldiers near the broken spotlight, just to the right of the enemy barricade. Stonebridge and another team members were with them, standing on the far side of the bodies.

T-Rex raised his gun and fired two short bursts at the casualties. One of the bodies flinched. Rico did the same to another bloody casualty lying at his feet.

Lucas continued forward toward Rico's position, passing the remaining two members of their assault team. One of them was lying on the floor, crying out in pain, as blood shot out from his severed leg. The other soldier was kneeling next to him, with his rifle slung over his shoulder, trying to wrap a tourniquet around the jagged stump. He stretched the clear rubber hose around the man's thigh muscle and pulled it tight.

Lucas caught up with his friends. "That didn't take long."

"Never does, unless you miss," T-Rex said, as he bent down to check the bodies. He searched their pockets one at a time, pulling out personal items, equipment, and ammo. He found a set of keys in the shirt pocket of one of the dead men. "Not much else here, boss." He tossed the keys to Rico.

Rico had been off by a factor of two when he estimated only five enemy targets. Lucas counted at least ten bodies, though the exact number was difficult to determine, since most of them had been chopped into hunks by the shredder rounds. Blood and guts were everywhere, just like back in the hallway, yet Lucas wasn't feeling sick. At least not yet. He figured this is what happens to surgeons when they finally become desensitized to all the gore. Maybe he wouldn't vomit the next time he had to use the meat cleaver on one of his guests. "Shouldn't we have kept them alive so we could interrogate them?"

"Wouldn't have mattered," Rico said. "They were already dead. They just didn't know it yet. Besides, there's only one door we haven't tried." He pointed to a raised-panel door straight ahead of him. "Cold Storage" was written across it in faded-yellow lettering. The bottom half was covered in chunks of runny human tissue, each dripping slowly to the ground. "If your friends are here, they'll be through that door."

Rico turned to the soldier standing next to Stonebridge. "Anderson, you help Roberts take Quinn back to medical. We'll finish things up here."

"Yes, sir," Anderson replied, before hurrying to Quinn's position. He bent over and picked up the severed leg, tucking it under his right arm. He helped Quinn stand up on one leg, then put the man's arm over his shoulder, while Roberts did the same with the other arm. They carried Quinn out the door and into the hallway that led back to the café.

"Looks like his stripper-chasing days are over," Lucas said.

T-Rex and Stonebridge laughed. Rico didn't. He sneered at Lucas.

"Sorry. Just tryin' to lighten the mood," Lucas said. He couldn't stop thinking about the lethal charge waiting to explode in his wrist. He checked his watch. Ten hours, twenty-two minutes left. His alter ego seemed to be getting nervous as well—

Unlikely caution must narrowly yield after another engaging round of hearty endowment. He wrestled with his thoughts, finally smothering the traveler in silence.

Rico walked to the cold storage door and pulled at the door's handle. It wouldn't open.

"Try the keys," T-Rex said.

Rico inserted each key on the key ring in succession; the fifth key worked. Rico nodded to T-Rex as if to ask, "Ready?" T-Rex and Stonebridge moved into flanking positions behind him, aiming their rifles at the door. Rico motioned to Lucas to stand back. Lucas moved behind T-Rex and steadied his weapon. Rico pulled the door open quickly and went inside. T-Rex followed, as did Stonebridge. Lucas ran in last.

"You got to be fucking kidding me," Lucas said, seeing a fifty-foot-wide storage room filled with rows of metal shelving stacked from the floor to the ceiling. Each shelf was jammed with food supplies. The smell of chilled meat and hot peppers dominated the room, but there was no sign of the enemy or the BioTex material.

"That son-of-a-bitch Jenkins was lying. Next time, I'll take his goddamn hands," he said, watching his breath billow into a fog each time he exhaled.

"It's possible Cyrus set us up," Sergeant Stonebridge said. "You know, planted misinformation to get us here. We should probably leave before he shows up."

"He's right, Major. It is the perfect ambush point, with only one way in or out," T-Rex said.

"If it was, we'd be surrounded by now. No, we stay," Rico said.

"Sir, with all due respect, Cyrus is tough to anticipate. He doesn't think like us."

Rico didn't answer right away. He seemed deep in thought. "All right, you and Stonebridge, guard the door. Me and the comedian will stay here to search the room."

T-Rex and Stonebridge rushed to the hallway just outside the storage room entrance.

"I knew we should have interrogated one of them," Lucas said.

"You're assuming they knew anything. Do you really think that if they knew this place was only food storage and nothing more, that they would've sacrificed their lives to defend it? No, and there has to be more to it. Fan out. Check the room . . . check everything. Report back anything out of the ordinary."

"Just me? That'll take forever," Lucas said, scratching his wrist again. "There's got to be five hundred boxes in here."

A half-smile found Rico's lips. "Then you'd better get started."

Lucas figured it was punishment for cracking a bad joke. His wrist itched more than ever. Maybe there was some ointment on one of the shelves.

TEN

Trophy Case

Claude Vandersteen closed the door to the supply cabinet and returned to his clear-glass desk located just six feet from the Supreme Commander's office on the third floor of the Capital Building in New Robyn City. His two-hour lunch break was due in twenty minutes and he would soon head home, walking three blocks to relax in front of a warm, familiar fire. A steaming-hot bowl of veggie soup and some fresh-baked bread was on the menu today. Not many calories, but it was all he wanted to eat. He had punched two new notches on his belt in recent months and was running out of available leather to add more. He made a mental note to stop at the corner market on the way home to pick up another bag of flour . . . but stay away from the goddamn dessert counter, he told himself.

Today was Friday and his scheduled 8:00 PM check-in with Professor Kleezebee was on his to-do list. "Nothing new to report this week," was his stock answer and the one he intended to give the professor again. Cyrus and Freakshow had been out of town the past four days, only returning to the office an hour ago. They had walked past Claude's desk and straight into the SC's office without as much as a "Hello."

Claude had kept busy all week helping the volunteer crews set up tables, chairs, decorations, and the grand stage for Cyrus' first inaugural address as the new Supreme Commander— a title Cyrus had chosen instead of Prime Chancellor the minute after he was sworn into office. The SC told Claude that he chose the old gymnasium for the location for Sunday's victory celebration because of its proximity to the Mag-Lift station, hoping that everyone he invited would attend.

But who was Cyrus kidding? Claude had viewed the digital invitation: The end of Cyrus' vid-message was clear: Anyone failing to appear at the scheduled time and place would have heavy penalties levied against their accounts. The gym would be packed. Soon, dignitaries from all four provinces would be flooding the capital city.

A chime sounded from the center of his desk as the vid-screen hologram activated. The three-tower unit took a few seconds to focus the fuzzy white light, before revealing the face of a familiar redhead with long, flowing hair that wrapped around her neck. It was his long-time friend and potty mouth, Jennifer Warren.

"Hi, Claude. How's my favorite admin doing today?" the woman asked.

"Good, Jen. How's the new husband treating you?"

"Meaner than a fucking snake. I never should have married the goddamn pig. But since no one else was asking, what was a nice girl like me to do?"

Claude had had this same conversation before. "Your new eye looks good."

She ran the tips of her fingers across the upper part of her cheekbone, just under the new implant. "Still getting used to it. Damn thing keeps popping out when the old man's on top of me. Not that I mind, because it does kill the mood and gets him off me before he pumps another gallon of disgusting man-seed into me.

You know, just *once*, I'd like to come home from work and not be bent over and entered before I make it to the fucking kitchen. The man's a walking hard on. I walk around all night with his jizz dripping out of me. What's even worse is that my beautiful little cookie smells like rotten eggs the next day."

Too much information, Claude thought. He held back a laugh.

"I should have been a lesbian. Life would have been so much easier. Just boobs and pussy, and the occasional emotional crisis. How hard is that?"

"At least you've got a warm body waiting for you at home."

"A warm, hairy, sweaty body with noises erupting from every hole. I never knew men could be so repulsive. He wasn't like that *before* we got hitched. They say it's not possible to love and hate someone at the same time, but they're dead wrong. He's like a big, ugly mutt in heat twenty-four-seven. That reminds me, you wouldn't happen to have an extra pair of garden shears, would ya? I'm pretty sure I can fix the problem with one snip."

Claude felt a twinge of phantom pain hit his crotch. "That hurts just thinking about it."

She smiled. "I don't think I ever thanked you for paying for my eye surgery."

"It was nothing, really. That's what friends are for."

"Well, thank you anyway. I definitely owe you one. So, just name it. Anything. Anywhere. Anytime. It's yours."

Claude felt uncomfortable with her sudden rush of gratitude. It seemed like she was hitting on him. He was flattered, but he would never get involved with a married women. "So, what can I do for you today?"

"I have an encrypted call to put through for the SC. Is he in?"

"Yep, he just got back a little while ago. But he's in a Do Not Disturb meeting. Can the caller wait a few?"

"This call is flagged as Priority One. You know what that means."

"Yeah, it means I put it through, *now*, or find another job. Hang on a sec." Claude parked Jennifer's call into the streaming video queue and knocked on the door behind him. "Excuse me, Supreme Commander. May I come in?"

"Enter," a grainy, deep-set voice said from the other side of the door.

Claude went into the office, but remained by the door; the conversation would be brief.

Cyrus was standing by the far window behind his desk, looking out, his hands folded behind his back. Freakshow was ten feet away, looking over something being displayed on the horizontal vid-screen built into the top of the SC's desk.

Freakshow turned and slid his body in front of the desk, blocking Claude's view of the desktop. One of the more prominent boils on his forehead was pulsating, looking as if it were ready to explode with puss.

Claude tried not to stare, but it wasn't easy. The boils were a magnet for his eyes. Half the man's face looked like he had lost a fight with an angry flamethrower, and the other side was littered with the boils and lesions of a half-dead leper. Claude finally looked away, focusing on the back of Cyrus' head. "Sir, there's a call parked in your queue. It's a Priority One communiqué from Jennifer in District 9."

"What's it regarding?" Cyrus asked without turning around, his voice as rough as sandpaper.

"She didn't say."

"You're dismissed," Cyrus said. The nearly seven-foot-tall man spun around and walked to his desk. His three-foot-long mane of dead-straight black hair remained still, seemingly defying gravity as he moved. His face was highlighted by a set of prominent, deep-set cheekbones that framed his eyes, nose, and mouth in such a way that made him looked malnourished.

Claude backed his way out of the office and shut the door behind him. He positioned his feet beyond the right edge of the threshold, then leaned in and pressed his ear against the door. The sounds inside were faint, but he could hear their conversation.

The electronic startup tone for the inbound queue chimed on Cyrus' desk. "Cyrus here."

"Sir, we have someone here who wants to speak with you," a high-pitched voice said. Claude thought it was a woman speaking, but wasn't sure.

"Put him on."

A few seconds later, a man spoke. "My name is Alfred Jenkins. I'm one of your Level Five operatives in Flandreau City. Thank you for taking my call."

"What happened to your face, Jenkins? Looks like you went a few rounds with a Taku Beast and lost."

"Well, sir, that's what I wanted to speak with you about."

"Go on."

"Before I continue, I want you to know that I stand here voluntarily, as a loyal and humble servant. I ask that you take my candor into account and show mercy on me and my family."

Cyrus grumbled. "I don't have all day, Jenkins. What is it?"

"I was captured and interrogated by a man looking for the BioTex material. My chefs think the perpetrator was the East Side Exterminator. At least, that's what they told the media."

"When was this?"

"Yesterday, in the basement of my old restaurant. He got the drop on me from behind."

"What did you tell him?"

"Nothing at first. I held out as long as I could. But he tortured me and then said he would kill me if I didn't help him."

Claude heard a loud bang from inside the SC's office. It sounded as if someone had just rammed a fist into a table.

"I'm not going to ask you again!" Cyrus shouted.

The pitch of Jenkins' voice shot up a few octaves. "He threatened to electrocute me. I had to tell him something, so I told him about the Dunn-Rite Café."

"Goddamn it," Cyrus said, before a long silence filled the room. "Jenkins, you do realize there's no BioTex at that facility?"

"Yes, I know. I purposely sent him there on a wild goose chase."

"That's not good. Not good at all," Freakshow said.

"What did this man look like?"

"I don't know. He was wearing a mask. He was about six feet tall and skinny, teenager-skinny."

"Did he say anything else?"

"Not much. He kept asking for my help to find his little brother. Then he made a comment about being from another universe, whatever that means."

"Lucas Ramsay," Freakshow said. "I didn't think the Doc had it in him."

"Things have obviously escalated," Cyrus said, tension sharpening his words. "Did he mention why he was so interested in the BioTex?"

"No, sir. But he seemed very determined to find his brother."

Cyrus didn't respond, but Freakshow did. "We should have executed them when we had the chance, sir."

Someone coughed and cleared his throat. Claude thought it was Jenkins.

"It is my sincere hope that my coming forward today will allow you to stop him in time," Jenkins said.

"I appreciate your candor, Jenkins, and the fact that you didn't give up the BioTex's true location. You and your family will be duly compensated."

"Thank you, sir."

"Cyrus out."

Claude was about to stop listening through the door and return to his desk, but Cyrus and Freakshow weren't finished with their meeting. Claude kept his ear pressed against the SC's door.

"What do you want me to do about Jenkins?" Freakshow asked.

"He's a traitor and a coward. You know what to do."

"How many pieces?"

"Let's make it an even dozen. Then put his remains on display in the Galleria for all to see. We need to send a strong message to anyone thinking of betrayal. Save his head, minus the eyes, for my trophy case."

"Gladly. What about his wife and fourteen-year-old daughter?"

"Are they worth keeping?"

"Damn fine eye candy, SC."

"Excellent. Bring them to the compound and add them to my personal stable. I'll enjoy them tonight."

"Should I pay a visit to the fat man?"

"No. The material's location hasn't been compromised."

"What about Ramsay and the café? Kleezebee must be the one pulling the strings."

"They'll need to be dealt with swiftly," Cyrus said.

Claude heard a set of caster wheels rolling across the floor, then the squeak of leather.

"Orders, sir?"

"Take a squad. When they show up, kill them and anyone who's with them. Then torch the place, whether it's empty or not. We can't let anyone discover our plans."

"But sir, that's our most productive feeding—"

"You have your orders. Now see to it."

"If Ramsey and the professor don't show?"

"Find them. Bring me their heads. I don't care what you have to do, just get it done."

"Yes, sir. Any intel on their location?"

"Last report, they're off the grid, somewhere near Flandreau City. Probably hiding up in the mountains, where it's less populated."

"That's a lot of area to cover."

"Talk to your informants. Shake them down. Someone must have seen them. Don't come back empty-handed."

"Consider it done, SC."

Claude heard heavy footsteps pounding toward the door. He ran to his desk and jumped into his high-back executive-style chair. He swiveled his ass in the pleated leather seat to face the desk just before the door opened behind him.

Freakshow marched by his desk, pulling a draft of warm office air with him. He entered the waiting lift, then turned and stared at Claude, as if he were scanning Claude's body language for signs of deception.

Claude gave Freakshow a subtle half-smile with a quick nod, pretending all was normal. The elevator doors swooshed together in front of the hooligan's face. Claude let out the full breath he was saving in his lungs, sending a frigid chill bubbling across the nerve endings of his upper back. He checked the gray holo-clock embedded in the wall of the reception area: ten minutes before lunch. His legs were begging him to sprint home to check in with Kleezebee, but he had to wait until it was the scheduled time to clock out. He didn't want to draw the SC's ire, who was probably pacing an angry trench in the dusty floorboards of his office. Play it cool, he decided. Another few minutes won't matter. Just skip the grocery store errand and head directly to the encrypted transceiver to inform the professor.

The speed of the display on the wall clock seemed to slow down, cycling through its numerals as if it were waiting for a last-second work duty to pop up and cancel his lunch hour.

ELEVEN

Salad Farmers

Lucas continued his search in the back corner of the room where an orange plastic chair was sitting with its back against the wall of the diner's cold-storage area. The corner was not lit as well as the rest of the room. The light directly overhead was broken, smashed beyond repair. He pulled the chair out and sat down in front of a shelving unit that ran the entire width of the room.

He opened the first of a dozen gray-and-white boxes stacked neatly on the bottom shelf. The words *PROPERTY OF THE BAAKU* were written across each of their cardboard sides. He had never heard of the Baaku and assumed it was an outlying farming village. He opened the first box and found it stuffed with leafy green vegetables and a single wooden crucifix wrapped in warm, thermal plastic. The veggies reminded him of lettuce back on Earth, except these had beaded yellow ridges running lengthwise along the veins of each leaf. Sort of like lettuce with chicken pox. He opened another three boxes and found more of the same, including a wrapped crucifix in each.

He removed the plastic coating from the crucifix and ran the tip of his index finger over the strange figurine carved into the wood. He hadn't seen this type of cross before. Jesus wasn't nailed to the cross as he expected; the figure was some type of birdman with shackles on its wrists.

"Crazy Larry would love this," he mumbled, thinking of the preacher's reaction when he learned someone was worshiping an animal god, instead of the One and Only. The Baaku must be a group of spiritual salad farmers that worshiped birds, he mused. You get a free religious symbol with each order and a practice range target. All that was missing was the donation envelope, a tax deduction receipt, and a dozen shredder rounds.

Something sharp stabbed him in his right palm, and he dropped the crucifix. When the cross hit the floor, it bounced on one of its ends, then dissolved into a flurry of ashes before it hit the ground a second time. He turned his hand over and inspected it. A tiny amount of blood had pooled in the center, right where he had felt the pain from the crucifix. He put his hand to his mouth and removed the blood with his tongue.

"Goddamn bible thumpers," he mumbled.

He decided to check the orange containers on the shelf above the lettuce. They were made of molded plastic and contained soft, squishy red fruit, like tomatoes, except they were shaped like a cucumber. He grabbed one of them and took a whiff. It smelled like a combination of wet dog fur and old gym socks.

"That's fucking awful. . . . Reminds me of the crap they fed us in the orphanage. Shit-on-a-shingle served with a fresh helping of guilt."

He tried to put the smelly fruit back in its container, but his hand caught the edge of the plastic by mistake. The fruit shot out of his fingers, ricocheted off the second shelf, and landed next to his foot. He bent down to pick it up, but stopped when two identical scratches in the cement floor caught his eye. He stood up and slid the chair out of the way.

The white scratches were about four feet apart and appeared to lead away from the wall. They were parallel to each other and several feet long. "Rico! I think I found something."

"What is it?"

"I don't know. You better come take a look."

Rico arrived seconds later. So did T-Rex and Stonebridge. "What do you have?" his boss asked.

"These scratches on the floor—they're perfectly straight and appear to lead *away* from the wall."

"You're right. Those didn't get there by accident. Something heavy cut those grooves."

Lucas put his hands on the wall and felt around. His fingertips tingled as he ran his hands over the pitted surface of the masonry wall. "Might be a hidden door somewhere." He put pressure on each brick in the wall. Nothing budged. "Doesn't seem to be anything here. Feels solid."

"Maybe there's a trigger mechanism," T-Rex said.

"Yeah, now I'm thinking," Lucas replied, a slight smile on his lips. He tugged at the corner of the shelf containing the red fruit and spotted lettuce. The wall didn't move. He tried lifting each box on the shelf—again, zip. He continued searching the rest of the shelving unit, but found nothing that acted like a trigger— just everyday restaurant items and food supplies.

Lucas returned to the cement scratches in the floor. He stood for a long minute with his hands on his hips, shaking his head. He must be missing something, he thought. He craned his neck to look at the ceiling. He noticed a round, half-inch circular protrusion embedded in the overhead concrete. It appeared to be centered above the two scratches in the floor. Its opaque surface was made of some type of black, shiny material—much like the dark tinting material you'd find glued across a low-rider's side windows. He couldn't see inside the protrusion. "Looks like someone's watching us."

"It's probably that cocksucker, Freakshow," T-Rex said.

"Why would they have installed it pointing straight down? Can't see much of the room," Lucas said. "It's like they only want to keep an eye on this one spot."

"If that was true, where's the light source? Hard to see in the dark unless it's night vision," Rico said.

"Maybe it's not a camera," T-Rex said.

"Could be the trigger," Rico added.

"Possibly," Lucas replied. "There's only one way to find out."

"I don't think we should be doing this," Stonebridge said, with a heavy look of worry in his eyes. "We should leave. Now."

"You can leave if you want, but I'm gonna stay and figure this out. Can't leave empty-handed. My brother's life is at stake," Lucas said, sliding the orange chair back to its original spot, with its back against the brick wall. He climbed up and stood on the seat. He waved his hand across the protrusion's black surface. Nothing happened. He touched the device's surface. Again, nothing.

T-Rex gave him a lighter from his vest pocket. "See if heat triggers it."

Lucas held the lighter an inch away from the ceiling device and lit it. He let the flame burn for a good thirty seconds. Nothing happened. He tossed the lighter back to T-Rex.

Rico removed the torpedo light from his shredder rifle. "Try this. Maybe it's light-sensitive."

Lucas flipped the power switch on and off to make sure the light worked. It did. "That would explain the absence of light in this area. They sure wouldn't want it triggered by mistake."

"But wouldn't the lighter's flame have done the trick? It produces light," Stonebridge said.

"Unless it needs a focused light source," Lucas said. He held the torpedo light up to the ceiling, aiming the charged beam at the center of the device. Nothing happened.

"What about this?" T-Rex asked, pointing at the laser scope on his shredder rifle.

"Worth a shot," Lucas said, jumping off the chair. "Go ahead. Give it a try."

T-Rex aimed the laser at the ceiling. As soon as the red dot centered on the device, the walls and floor began to vibrate. A section of the wall began to move. It slid to the left slowly, until it was four feet out from the rest of the wall.

Lucas pointed the torpedo light into the opening. "There's a chamber inside." He stepped toward the opening, but Rico stopped him with an arm bar.

"Not until T-Rex checks it out," Rico said, signaling with his hand for T-Rex to proceed.

"Time to nut-up or shut-up," T-Rex said. He flipped his shredder flashlight on, then turned his body sideways and slid behind the protruding wall section.

Lucas figured he could've walked straight in, but T-Rex's shoulders were twice the size. A short minute later, he heard a click, then the chamber filled with light.

T-Rex returned. "All clear."

"What did you find?" Rico asked him.

"Equipment. But I've never seen anything like it before."

Rico looked at Lucas. "Go ahead. I know you're dying to get in there."

Lucas gave the flashlight to Rico, smiled, then rubbed his hands together. "He who has the most toys, wins." He went inside.

Rico and T-Rex followed, as did Stonebridge.

TWELVE

Captain Obvious

The chamber was about the size of a 7-Eleven convenience store. Two side-by-side stacks of blinking electronic equipment were to the left, and a metal desk and twenty-inch, flat-panel computer monitor was sitting on top. A clear cylinder about the size of a phone booth was to the right, about ten feet away. It was a few feet taller than Lucas, and resembled an oversized pneumatic tube, like those used by a bank in its drive-through lane. A bundle of gray-and-black cables on the left side of the tube snaked their way along the floor, connecting the tube to the electronic equipment.

The cylinder's base was a round pad about three inches thick and four feet in diameter. Its surface was shiny and appeared to be made of glass, or possibly an acrylic. The pad was sectioned off into four pie-shaped triangles of different colors: red, blue, orange, and green.

Stonebridge stood next to Lucas. He seemed excited. "Looks like some kind of machine."

"Thank you, Captain Obvious. Of course it's a machine," Lucas snorted.

"That's 'Sergeant' to you, Doc," Stonebridge said, his jaw thrust out.

When Lucas approached the cylinder, its enclosure rotated automatically, revealing two clear, overlapping glass tubes, one inside the other. The glass rings continued moving in opposite directions until a man-sized opening appeared. "I was wondering what happened to this. Cyrus must have figured out how to use it."

"What is it?" Rico asked.

"One of Kleezebee's jump pads," Lucas said, running his fingers over the smooth glass surface. It's a tele-pod. Like in beam-me-up-Scotty."

Rico squinted and cocked his head.

"Oh, yeah, I forgot. Gene Roddenberry ended up in my universe, not yours." Lucas stepped onto the device's pad and turned around to face his friends. "It's site-to-site transportation device."

"For people?" T-Rex asked, a concerned look on his face.

Lucas nodded. "It disassembles your molecules, transports them to another location, and then reassembles your atoms—all in the blink of an eye."

"Fuck me," Stonebridge said.

"That can't be safe," T-Rex added.

"Trust me, it works like a charm . . . unless there's a power failure in the middle of transport. They'll be mopping you up with a sponge, if so."

Rico laughed, though it wasn't for long. "This must be how Cyrus is positioning his men. Getting his guards in and out of the restaurant without anyone seeing them. A distinct tactical advantage. I can see why he wants to protect it."

"Wonder where it leads?" T-Rex asked.

"Good question." Lucas walked to the computer desk, where a rotating 3D font was spinning on the computer monitor.

The phrase BTX ENTERPRISES danced across the screen in block letters, taking turns bouncing off the four edges of the display. "That looks familiar."

"Can you operate it?" Rico asked.

"With my eyes closed—they're still using Kleezebee's software. Didn't even bother to change the vid-saver. BTX Enterprises is Kleezebee's real estate development company back home."

Lucas didn't see a mouse or keyboard, so he touched the screen to deactivate the screen saver. He read the status indicators. "That doesn't make any sense. It says it's still connected to Silo 3."

"Where's that?" Rico asked.

"In a galaxy far, far away."

Rico seemed puzzled. He cleared his throat, catching Lucas' attention.

"It's not anywhere on this planet, or in this universe, for that matter," Lucas said. "It's one of Kleezebee's underground missile silos on my Earth. But it's much too distant to be a viable destination."

"So, then—what? We're done?" T-Rex asked, taking a step toward the exit.

"I didn't say that. Just give me a second to think."

"It has to lead somewhere. Otherwise, why would Cyrus bother guarding it?" Rico asked.

Lucas nodded. "Cyrus must have hardcoded the connection. But the real question is why park one of these here, in Flandreau City?"

"Because of its strategic value. The Mag-Lift's central hub is here, at least what's left of it," Rico said.

"If that's true, then the other end is probably connected to his base camp, where he trains his men," T-Rex said.

"New Robyn City," Rico replied. He looked at Lucas. "Do you think that's where he's storing the BioTex?"

"There's only one way to find out: Someone has to take a road trip," Lucas said, smiling. He looked at T-Rex.

"Not me," T-Rex said, shuffling his feet back two steps. "I'm not getting into that thing."

"This? *This* you're afraid of?" Lucas *almost* sneered. He wondered what was next. Clowns or needles?

"Me and technology don't see eye to eye."

Stonebridge stepped forward. He cocked his rifle and looked at Rico. "I'll go, sir. No need for anyone else to take the risk."

"Stand down, Sergeant. I need you to watch our six," Rico said, pointing his rifle toward the entrance behind him.

"But . . . sir?"

"That's an order, Sergeant."

"Yes, sir," Stonebridge said, dejected, marching to the door. He stood outside the entrance, with his back to the room.

Rico's eyes inspected the vertical cylinder from top to bottom. "Looks like there's only room for one."

"Yep. That's by design. The system can only process one molecular pattern at a time. Otherwise, the bio-signatures would mix and you'd be reconstituted as a blob."

"Good safety tip, Doc. Thanks."

"Then I guess you better count me in," T-Rex said. "What about Stonebridge?"

"Someone needs to stay behind in case we don't make it back. Make sure he reports in with Kleezebee as soon as we're across."

"So I'm going, too?" Lucas asked.

Rico nodded. "Someone's got to get us home from the other side."

"What are the chances this is a one-way trip?" T-Rex asked.

"Less than none," Lucas said, inspecting the equipment rack. "There has to be an active jump pad on the other end for this

102

system to work. All we need to do is reverse the process and bingo, you're back in Kansas, Dorothy."

"What's your mother got to do with this?" Rico asked.

"Nothing. Never mind," Lucas replied, feeling like the alien in this colony of humans. "Just trust me. It won't be a problem."

He scratched the injection point on his arm, pulling off the soft scab that had been forming. More blood oozed out. He checked his watch: nine hours and change. He held up his wrist to show Rico. "Do we have enough time?"

"More than enough. Now, fire up this thing before I change my mind."

Lucas entered a few commands on the touch-screen and then stood back. "You guys are gonna love this."

A seductive female voice said, "Please step onto the pad. Activation sequence will begin in thirty seconds. Remember not to hold your breath."

"Sexy, huh? Think she's as hot as all your girlfriends?"

Rico smiled, then stepped onto the pad, pulling his shredder rifle in close to his chest. He turned around and faced Lucas.

Stonebridge stepped forward and gave all four bricks of plastic explosive to Rico, along with a handful of blasting caps. "You might need these, sir."

Rico stuffed them inside the pouches on his duty belt. He looked at Lucas. "Now what?"

Lucas put his index finger close to the ENGAGE button on the screen. "Now, I just have to press this last button, and—"

Lights flashed and a high-decibel alarm blared through the room. Then the same electronic voice said, "This is a weapons-free zone! Please discard you weapon immediately. You have twenty seconds to comply or a nerve agent will be released."

Rico jumped off the pad and pointed his rifle at the computer console.

"Easy, Rico! It was a joke. There's no nerve agent."

T-Rex laughed.

"Not funny, Doc," Rico said, sneering at his laughing comrade. Zack stopped laughing instantly. Rico lowered his weapon.

"Sorry. Couldn't resist. I figured since Cyrus hadn't changed any of Kleezebee's software that his system would react the same way to a weapon as it did back on Earth."

Rico's eyes flared. "Can we *please* focus on the mission?"

Lucas nodded. He used a backdoor access path on the console to log in and turn off the alarm message. "All clear. Go ahead."

Rico returned to the pad, stepped inside, and turned around. His face looked tense, as the clear cylinder's doors wrapped around him, sealing him inside.

"It's important not to hold your breath," Lucas said in a louder voice. "Just relax and breathe in and out normally. It'll be over in a flash."

"Will I feel anything?"

"Not really. It's like floating in a dream."

"What about his weapon and the explosives?" T-Rex asked. "Won't they get mixed in on the other end?"

"That only happens with bio-matter. Inanimate objects like clothes and guns are fine. The computer can differentiate them from living tissue."

T-Rex nodded with raised eyebrows.

Lucas reset the system and pressed the Engage button. He looked at Rico. "Enjoy your trip."

The device activated, sending streams of swirling blue and orange specs of light up from the bottom like the colored stripes on a barber pole. They danced around Rico's body, slowly covering him from head to toe. A minute later, he was gone and the chamber was empty.

"That's it?" T-Rex asked.

"Yeah, what'd you expect?"

"Some kind of sound, at least."

"It doesn't work that way. Not when you're being disassembled at the sub-atomic level. It's all done electronically."

T-Rex shrugged.

"Look at it this way—you can't hear the quantum memory crystals working away inside a computer, can you?"

"No."

"So, there you go. Same thing. No sound."

T-Rex nodded right before he tapped the face on his communicator watch. "Hammer here. . . . Roger that, Sledge. Hammer out."

"Was that Rico? Where's he at?"

"Not sure yet. The major said he's underground in some type of industrial complex. I'm to go through next. Then you. Understood?"

"Sure," Lucas said, readying the jump pad system for another transport. "Go ahead and step in. The system's ready."

T-Rex squeezed his massive frame into the four-foot-wide virtual tube and turned to face out. The tube's doors swung around and pinned him in.

"Remember to—" Lucas said.

"—breathe normally. Got it, Doc. Press the damned button already."

Lucas pressed the ENGAGE button and T-Rex was gone in a flash. "Sergeant, can you come over here for a minute? I need to show you how to operate this unit."

Stonebridge entered the room and walked to the console. He stood on Lucas' right. "I'm not sure I'm qualified for this."

Lucas pointed at the touch screen. "It's simple. All you need to do it press this button. But wait until I'm inside and the doors are closed. I'll tell you when to press it. Okay?"

Stonebridge nodded. "Sounds easy enough."

Just then, the traveler screamed inside his thoughts—*Time realizes peace immediately after all transitory senses!*

"Fuck off," Lucas told the traveler in a dull mumble.

"What?" Stonebridge asked.

"Nothing. Just talkin' to myself."

A look of concern grew on Stonebridge's face.

Lucas shut his eyes and slipped into his thoughts. He let out a sigh of relief when he didn't hear any more of the traveler's thoughts. He opened his eyes and walked to the jump pad opening. He slipped the shredder rifle over his shoulder and stepped inside. He turned to face Stonebridge. "Go ahead. I'm ready."

Stonebridge moved his hand toward the screen. A moment later, Lucas felt lightheaded and a bit woozy. He concentrated on his breathing, moving the air in and out of his lungs with calm consistency.

A second later, he was standing alone in a grassy meadow the size of a city block.

THIRTEEN

Ectoplasm? Seriously?

"What the hell?" Lucas mumbled, feeling groggy, and his head was pounding. He looked in all directions, but didn't see Rico or T-Rex, just a thick border of majestic, orange-colored trees in every direction. This obviously wasn't an underground industrial complex. Did T-Rex just lie to him?

He stood still and waited. Two minutes passed with no sign of his friends. This must have been how Drew felt after he and Abby stepped through the portal to the hive ship, only to end up somewhere foreign and unexpected. His nerves were on high alert.

"Come on, guys, I'm here," he shouted, walking toward the middle of the clearing. There was no response. "This isn't funny. Where the hell are you?" He listened, but again, no answer; there was only the sounds of birds singing, water breaking, and a gentle breeze rustling through the treetops.

He scanned the strikingly flat meadow, looking for clues. There weren't any footprints or other tracks through the grass other than his. If he weren't in such a panic, it would have been the perfect spot for that romantic picnic with Carrie Anne. Not that he could ever find this place again.

A whistling gust of wind rose up out of the east, smacking him in the face, swaying the budding stalks of pale-brown grass. He turned away to protect his eyes from the flying dirt and grass sprouts.

He thought about the time between transports and realized the trees were too far away for Rico and T-Rex to hide in before he arrived. This couldn't be a trap. He'd have to be asleep or blitzed not to notice that he wasn't in an industrial building, so something had obviously gone haywire. His mind shifted to a memory involving Stonebridge standing in front of the computer console. The sergeant wasn't the brightest man he'd ever met, but still, how hard was it to press a button on a screen? Lucas decided Stonebridge hadn't fucked this up.

He tapped his communicator watch. "Rico? T-Rex? Come in." He waited. Nothing. Then he remembered their handles, thinking they wouldn't answer his hail unless he followed protocol. He didn't have a handle, so he made one up. "Sledge? Hammer? This is Solo. Can you guys hear me?" The device remained silent. He waited another long minute for a response. None came. "Jesus Christ, now what?"

Lucas looked south, just above the treetops and saw a black speck that seemed to be flying in his direction. It was traveling from right to left across the mostly cloudless sky. The tiny dot grew larger with each passing second until Lucas could identify it as a pair of yellow-crested birds with wide, black-and-white-feathered wings. The duo soared atop the steady wind, keeping a precise distance apart from each other.

He watched the birds bank left, changing to an intercept course, arriving above the meadow in just seconds. They separated from each other, flying in opposing elliptical orbits just above the tree line bordering the area. Lucas figured they were keeping an eye on him, waiting for him to succumb to the exhausting heat of the fast-rising sun.

His stomach gurgled an erratic tune; it was empty. He smiled. "Chance favors the prepared mind." He reached for the shredder rifle that he had slung over his shoulder before stepping onto the jump pad, but the gun wasn't there. Neither was the extra ammo clip stuffed in his back pocket. What the hell? Had he dropped them somewhere along the way while he was woozy? He brushed the waist-high grass away, searching the dirt around his feet; there was no sign of the weapon or the ammo. He widened his search area to thirty feet, then retraced his steps through the trampled grass to the point at which he arrived. Still nothing.

"Damn it," he said, watching the easy food circle above him. He licked his lips. "Next time, you two are dinner."

Lucas read his watch and calculated the time left until his wrist exploded: Seven hours, twenty-four minutes. Wait, that can't be right. Should have been eight-something. He had lost an hour somewhere. He remembered feeling sleepy when he arrived. Had he been unconscious? If so, why was he standing when he woke up?

He tried to recall the moments just before he arrived, but the memory flickered, just out of reach. It felt like a glimmer of a thought—one that hadn't formed completely. He shut his eyes and focused his concentration. He almost had it, but it was fading. He made a desperate grab at the memory and missed, coming up with an empty handful of nothing. Then the thought slipped out of view and ran dry.

His pulsating headache was worse than before—probably due to the stress of his situation. He wondered if he'd bumped his head while he was inside the jump pad chamber.

Cognitive memory is your own naive accomplishment to easily garnish random, heaping ectoplasm, the traveler said from the deepest echoes of his mind.

"Ectoplasm? Seriously?" Lucas answered back. "I really don't need this crap right now."

He looked around. Nothing was familiar. A cloud-wrapped mountain peak rose up beyond the trees, near where the birds had first appeared. It looked to be several miles away, maybe more.

"Where should I go?" Lucas asked the mental hitchhiker, even though he knew the answer would be twaddle.

Undue rain hinders each day's descent into another newfound nexus.

Lucas nodded, even though the words were nonsense. Perhaps there's a town nearby, he thought. Hopefully, they'll have a bar. He needed a stiff drink. He wondered if he got shit-faced, would it calm the voice inside him? Maybe he'd get lucky and put the noisy bastard to sleep for a while. He figured it was worth a shot—or three, he mused.

Lucas made his way across the meadow, now only twenty feet from the tree line. The mountaintop was out of sight, blocked by the towering trees in his path ahead. He'd have to guess at the direction of travel from here. He entered the forest just as a bellowing roar came from deep inside its depths. It echoed through the forest, connecting with the marrow in his bones. He recognized the distinctive wail: Taku Beast.

"Are you fucking kidding me?"

Another howl rang out, vibrating the ground and rattling the trees—even they were terrified. The beast sounded much closer. The skin across his body tightened. It must be the female Kleezebee warned him about. He didn't stand a chance against its twelve-inch razor-sharp claws, not without the shredder rifle. He wanted to run, but his legs wouldn't move.

Twigs snapped and tree branches cracked, it was maybe thirty feet ahead, he wasn't sure. Then he heard crying, human crying. It was a female, but she sounded young. The bushes in front of him parted, and something three-foot-tall came racing through them.

"Help me! Somebody help me!" a little blond-headed girl cried out. She looked back into the brush, then nearly stumbled over an exposed two-inch tree root, as she bee-lined straight for Lucas. "It's coming. Help me! Please!"

The girl—maybe nine years old—wearing a yellow sundress and a rosy face drenched in tears, jumped into his arms and wrapped her trembling hands around his neck. Her build was slight, but she still almost knocked Lucas off his feet. He wrapped his forearms around her slender waist, holding her tight against his chest.

Her sobs penetrated his body, melting the darkest corners of his heart. "I got you," he said. "It'll be all right." He leaned back to see her face. "My name is Lucas. What's your name?"

"Maggie."

"Where are your mom and dad?"

"I'm all alone," she said, sending a torrent of tears down her soft, pink cheeks. He could feel her rib cage pressing against his arms. There wasn't much meat on her bones. He wondered if she was lost, or abandoned. Possibly living in the wild and starving to death. Except, her dress and skin were clean, and her hair was combed and smelled fresh. It didn't make sense.

Another ground-shaking howl rang out—no echoes this time. Shit, a bloody death was close.

"Please, Lucas! It's coming!" she cried.

He didn't know which way to run. He looked left: there was only dense forest as far as his eyes could see, too thick to run through. A sixty-foot-tall rock formation was to the right, embedded into the side of a sloped hill, maybe twenty yards away, with what looked like a cave entrance near the top. He considered his two choices: Climb the boulders or run into the grass-covered meadow with no defensible position. He decided the cave at the top of the rock pile was the best option.

Lucas sprinted with Maggie in his arms, trying not to drop her, as he trampled leaves and deadfall along the way. He needed to get inside the cave before the creature arrived. Maybe the beast wouldn't find them there. He wasn't sure, but it was the best of his two bad choices.

He climbed onto the first level of uneven, two-foot-wide jagged rocks. It wasn't easy to keep his balance with his feet slipping on the damp, moss-laden surface and the extra weight hanging on his chest, but he managed to step across the rocks and work his way up to the next level. He looked back—no sign of the beast, yet. Keep moving, he told himself.

The next level would be harder to reach. An outcrop of rock was accessible above him, but there were no footholds to use. He shifted Maggie around to his back to free his hands. He grabbed hold of the ledge with his fingertips, then worked his palm up to better his grip. He strained to pull himself higher. Damn, should have done push-ups with Drew all those mornings, he thought.

He was close now, but needed to swing his leg around and over a blue-speckled cactus-like plant growing along the face of the rock; its two-inch red thorns were only millimeters from his crotch. With his luck, he figured they were laced with a toxic venom. He swung his body over and around the plant— success!—no prickly man parts.

The top level was too far up to reach with his hands. He couldn't climb up, at least not from here. He worked his way around to the backside of the rock formation. He saw a climbing path across the rock face that would get them to the top, but he needed to clear a couple of fallen tree limbs out of the way to reach it.

"I have to put you down for a minute."

"No! Please, don't! I'm scared!"

He peeled Maggie off his neck, swung her around to his chest, and then put her down gently on the smoothest rock in front of him. He wiped the tears from her cheek and brushed some of her blond locks behind her ear. "It'll be okay. I'm right here. I won't leave you. I promise."

She nodded, then huddled herself into a tight ball with her razor-thin arms wrapped around her bruised legs.

Lucas used all his body weight to drag the first branch toward the edge, then pushed it over the side. He heard a loud crash below when it hit the bottom a few seconds later. He did the same with the other limb.

He returned to the girl and bent down in front of her. "Hurry, climb on my back," he said.

She did, hanging onto him like a knapsack. She wrapped her stubby legs around the front of his belly and locked them together. Good thing he was skinny, otherwise her legs never would have reached the front.

"Hang on and don't let go, no matter what," he told her. Her arms and legs tightened around him, restricting his airflow a bit—but he could still breathe. He used both of his hands to steady himself as he stepped up onto each successively higher rock, working his way from right to left, back toward the front side of the boulders. The sharp edges of the rock surface tore at his fingertips, challenging him to hang on. He did. He made his way higher, hand-over-hand, toward the top of the rock formation, leaving bloody fingerprints behind.

"Three points of contact," he reminded himself—two footholds and one handhold at all times.

The forest went silent. Lucas no longer heard birds or other sounds of life. He wondered if the Taku Beast had arrived and was waiting for him at the top. Probably take his head off with one swipe.

Gotta protect the girl, he vowed. He looked down the rock formation. No way, he thought, are we going back. He looked up. The only choice was to keep climbing. He did.

FOURTEEN

Ravenous Breath

He made it to the top and peeked over the edge—all clear—no snarling meat-eater waiting for a gooey afternoon snack. He pulled his chest higher with his precious cargo holding on tight. He swung his right leg over the ledge, using it as extra leverage to deliver their combined weight to safety. They made it.

He could see the crest of the mountain off in the distance. At least he knew the direction of travel from here—if they somehow survived the hour.

The cave entrance was just a few feet away. He ran for the opening and ducked inside. The air was thick and wet—difficult to take into his lungs. He inhaled again, this time with purpose. His nose detected the pungent aroma of dung and rotting meat. He looked deep into the darkness, expecting to see a pair of glowing, reflective eyes looking back at him, or possibly hear the huff of a ravenous breath stirring in the shadows. He watched and listened. It was quiet, except for the casual melody of water dripping off the rock, and the faint scurry of feathers above him in the darkness.

He slid Maggie off his back and pushed her body close to the wall, keeping himself between her and whatever predator might be lurking inside. He picked up the largest rock near his feet. It was twice the size of his hand, with a sharp point on one end. He bounced it in his palm—maybe two pounds, he decided—he'd probably only get one shot. It would have to do.

He heard rustling behind him, outside the cave. He spun around and moved in front of Maggie, keeping her corralled behind his legs with his arms.

A shimmering-white ten-foot-tall Taku Beast materialized in front of him, just six feet from the cave entrance. He could see bits and pieces of the forest backdrop shining through the animal's muscular body. It was an oscillating, semi-transparent creature with different parts of it furry presence visible at different times.

He measured the length of the predator's arms visually and realized that if it took a swipe, it might be able to reach him. He stepped back, herding his innocent companion deeper into the cave behind him.

The towering beast snarled at him, showing its ten-inch fangs as orange-colored spit coagulated and dripped from the tips in clumps. Its foul breath shot out and washed over Lucas' face, sending chills down his spine and weakening his resolve. This is it, he thought. Kleezebee and Drew would have to go on without him. He didn't stand a chance.

The beast widened is mouth, tilted its head back, and let out a bone-chilling roar after a massive inhale.

The girl shrieked.

Lucas' chest tightened; he couldn't breathe.

The animal lowered its shoulders and raised its mighty claws into an attack position. Lucas stepped forward and threw the rock as hard as he could, aiming for the creature's head. The rock seemed to sail through the air in slow motion. He watched it hone in on its target—a perfect shot, he thought. Just as the rock arrived, the animal disappeared from sight. The rock flew past the creature's position and skipped off the hardscape beyond it. No wonder the hunters in town couldn't track and kill this thing. It never remained in one place long enough for someone to kill it.

The beast reappeared three feet to the left. It roared and snarled again, then it charged.

Lucas had only one choice—wrestle the creature over the edge—the sixty-foot-drop might kill it. He stepped forward to intercept the creature, holding out his arms like a wrestler ready to start a match. He knew he was about to be ripped to shreds, but he might be able save the child. He didn't know why, but he shut his eyes, charged, and waited for impact.

Seconds passed and he felt nothing. He stopped running and opened his eyes. The creature was gone. He searched the front of the cave—no sign of it. He turned back and went inside the cave to get Maggie, but she wasn't there. He called out for her and waited. Only the echo of his voice answered from the ample darkness. Little Maggie was gone, but there was no blood where she was last standing. Lucas figured the creature must have phase-shifted around him and snatched her, then disappeared again.

A sharp pain dazed his heart, as black emotions swelled inside. His legs buckled, sending his knees crashing into the dirt-covered, rocky surface. His arms, neck, and shoulders hung limp, failing to respond to his command. He didn't understand why he was feeling this way. He barely knew the child, but somehow he felt a tremendous loss—the kind of loss that paralyzes even the strongest man. Sure, he could rally the strength to face an impossible research deadline, or stand his ground against a trio of seething rugby players ready to kick his ass, but when it came to unexpected emotions, he was clearly deficient, inadequate, less than human in some way.

Perhaps Maggie awoke something in him, reminding him of his long-lost brother. She was frail and weak, unable to defend herself against a predator, much like Drew, who was out there in the cosmos somewhere. Alone. Scared. Defenseless.

"Fuck!" he screamed, as his mind blurred. He tried to remember Drew's face, but the image was fuzzy and distant in his mind. He looked around for a reflective surface, hoping to catch another glimpse of his brother's calming face, but there were none.

He searched his memories, but he couldn't hear the boyish sound of his brother's laughter flooding his heart. It felt like his love for Drew was slipping away and if that were true, so was his reason for living. He dragged his body next to the wall and sat with his back against it. He raised his knees close to his chest, and put his head in his hands. He'd never felt more alone than at that moment. Tears swelled in his eyes.

"I'm sorry, Drew. I just can't do this anymore," he said, with disdain for life itself. What was the point? He was never going to find his brother. Drew was gone and probably dead, just like Maggie. His quest the past eighteen months had been a fool's errand. Everybody knew it, except him. Even Kleezebee had made peace with the fact that Drew, his biological son, wasn't coming home—ever.

Kleezebee had been a patient, caring friend. He seemed to tolerate Lucas' interminable desire to search for Drew in countless alternate realities, knowing that the odds of finding Drew were almost zero. Any competent physicist knows that the number of parallel realities borders on the infinite, meaning the odds of just finding a universe where Earth was inhabited was astronomically difficult.

Lucas had made forty-seven trips into alternate dimensions thus far, and of those, Earth had been inhabited only four times. One of the Earths he had visited was perpetually in the dark and its atmosphere was supercharged with static lighting, making his hair stand on end the moment he arrived. It took him a week after that trip to feel normal again.

He had searched for Drew in each inhabited reality, but only once did he manage to find a version of Drew—the wrong version. That particular Drew wore a thick, handlebar mustache and wasn't confined to a wheelchair. Nor had he ever been an orphan. That Drew was living happily with his biological mom, Lauren, who never died in the car accident when Drew was young. It was a perfect example of why finding his version of Drew was going to be impossible; there's an infinite number of time lines in an endless sea of universes.

So why couldn't he accept it? Why couldn't he let his foster brother go? He wanted to. God knows his life would be a whole lot simpler, but for some reason he couldn't; he wasn't wired that way. He'd never quit anything in his life.

But maybe it was time he did.

Too bad he wasn't going to live long enough to witness Fuji's test of the new incursion equipment in the basement of Kleezebee's cabin. It had curious potential, but still, Lucas didn't think it could work. After all, penetrating the compressed fabric of space-time had never been attempted before, let alone controlled for a specific outcome. Granted, Fuji was beyond brilliant, but even his new Fijix math couldn't account for the infinite complexities of random subatomic particles in a quantum field. Space-time—like life itself—had its own agenda and anyone who dared to think they might be able to tame it was either too arrogant or too naive to grasp its single-mindedness.

He snickered and shook his head. If his friends thought finding Drew was impossible, what did that make Fuji's plan to digitize, transmit, and remotely access his former life across the infinite landscape of the universe? Ludicrous? He laughed again, harder this time. He was confident that they could generate the power needed with the spheres of E-121 material, but the unpredictable nature of dangerous exotic particles could be catastrophic. He had asked Kleezebee repeatedly about it, but the professor assured him that Fuji had it covered.

Sometimes the galvanizing forces of pride and stubbornness blind you to the truth, leading you down a path of hopelessness. Fuji and his plan were no exception. Neither was Lucas' quest to find Drew.

Lucas sat quietly on the cold, damp floor, watching a family of bats hanging by their feet from the ceiling. They seemed to be fighting for position in the protective recesses of the remote cave, as if they were at war with each other, but in a huddled, cooperative way. He marveled at their blind tenacity, working together to protect each other. Their survival was clearly a team sport, one filled with uncertainty and doubt, but they chose to face it together, like a family.

Lucas tossed a rock at the flurry of bats. He missed. "Enjoy the time together, my little friends, 'cause it never lasts."

He studied the fresh scar on his wrist and realized that the end was near. Time was running out and he had no idea where he was or how to get home. This one-way trip to the middle of nowhere would be the final act of his miserable existence. He had no food, no water, no weapon, and no hope. All he had for company was a deranged traveler who spoke in riddles.

It wouldn't be long until the beast came back to exact its revenge for Kleezebee's slaughter of its mate. His mind could almost feel his weary flesh being torn loose from the bone.

He thought again about the words they'd use on his tombstone and offered up a phony laugh. "Fitting justice for the meat-cleaver king," he said.

The growing day paralyzes only undeserving nomads in vague ecstasy, his alter ego said.

Lucas shrugged, then shouted back at the traveler. "I know you're trying to cheer me up, but I just don't see the point anymore. My brother is dead. My mother is dead. Dad died years ago. I'm stuck on this miserable planet, in some fucking cave in another universe. I'm lost with no food or water, and nobody knows where I am. Plus, I have a royally pissed-off Taku Beast just waiting to rip me a new asshole. Seriously, how much more am I supposed to take? I'm so goddamn tired. I just want this day to end."

Lucas waited, but the traveler said nothing. He put his head against the wall and shut his eyes. His mind drifted with thoughts of his family. Drew, Dorothy, and John were standing together in loving embrace on the far end of a long, suspension bridge overlooking an endless sea of speckled white. He could almost feel the wisp of fresh sea air as it gently washed over the aging scars on his cheeks. He wondered what his family would say when he crossed over. They'd probably yell at him for taking too damn long to join them, but at least they'd be together again, as a family. In the end, that's all that mattered.

He found it interesting that he'd never considered believing in the afterlife until right then. Maybe facing certain death helps you find your way toward faith. But does it count if you find God on the last day when all hope is lost? Probably not, he decided. He'd never get that lucky. There are no shortcuts to salvation. He was doomed to fry along with all the murderous Krellian bugs and a few college professors he despised. Oh, yeah, and one pretentious attorney named Larson.

"Screw this," he said, standing up. He stepped outside the cave and took a few minutes to enjoy the picturesque mountain landscape and allow the sun's tender embrace to soak into his skin. He walked to the edge of the rock formation and looked out across the grassy meadow below. It looked much smaller than before, almost as if it had shrunk while he was cowering inside the cave.

One of the two vultures still circling overhead let out a pair of echoing shrieks. He wondered if the sound was a cry of recognition, or a screech of hunger? Maybe the airborne scavengers could sense his growing dehydration and failing resolve. His throat and lips were dry and his head was throbbing. Soon, the meat on his bones would be the main course for their dinner.

He studied the rocks sixty feet below and calculated the kinetic energy of an object at impact. "With my luck, I'd bounce," he said, visualizing his life as a battered quadriplegic. Yet, if he adjusted the trajectory, a headfirst fall from the ledge would certainly accomplish the task. He inched his toes over the edge, spread his arms out like Jesus on the cross, and shut his eyes. A calming peace filled his heart, as a flurry of wind seemed to grab him from behind and nudge him forward.

FIFTEEN

Welcome to the Club

Lucas heard a faint sound off in the distance, a young man's voice calling out for him.

"Lucas! Can you hear me?" the voice asked, the words floating gently across the plain.

Lucas snapped out of his daydream, lowered his foot, and backed away from the ledge. The voice called out for him again—this time louder and sharper. His heel caught a rock; he stumbled backward and landed flat on his ass, with his boney elbows smashing into the rocky surface.

He shook off the pain and stood up. He was sure he knew the voice. "Drew?" he mumbled, as his bolstered emotions took control. It sounded as if his brother were directly in front of him, somewhere in the waist-high grass of the meadow. Lucas scanned the field, but didn't see him—only the dry stalks swayed under the command of the wandering breeze.

"Drew!" he screamed. "I can hear you. Where are you?" He listened carefully. There was no response. He had to get moving.

"I'm coming for you! Don't move!" he said, running to the left. He shimmied down the rock face, retracing his steps across each level of the rock pile. Tiny shards of rock and sand tore at the skin on his elbows and hands, but he didn't care, nor did he slow his descent. He continued at breakneck speed, arriving at the bottom in only a minute.

"Drew! . . . It's Lucas! . . . Where are you?" Again no response. He figured his brother must not have heard him and probably moved off into the forest. He decided to sprint to the middle of the clearing and look for tracks. He expected to find twin ruts a couple of feet apart where the wheelchair would have plowed through the grass. Drew couldn't walk and wouldn't be able to move without it.

When he arrived at what he thought was Drew's position, he found that the grass hadn't been disturbed.

Damp coldness grew inside him. He was sure the voice was Drew's and it had originated from this location. Drew *must* be nearby. He walked in concentric circles, increasing the circumference and speed with each revolution. He found nothing but virgin grass and his own size-ten footprints.

"Drew!" he called out repeatedly, with his hands cupped around his mouth. Yet only the rhythmic sounds of Mother Nature responded.

Before he could decide what to do next, a blast of hot wind rippled his face and neck. He put his arms up, trying to protect himself from the explosion of air that moved from low to high, as if it were targeting him. Seconds later, a triangle-shaped wedge of grass compressed to the ground only ten yards in front of him. The patch sank into the ground a foot deep and was about eight feet across at its widest point, roughly the size of a 4x8 sheet of plywood.

"What the hell?" he asked, moving a few steps closer to get a better view of the impression. The grass stalks had been bent flat at their base in an interlocking pattern. It looked like a crop circle, except it was wedge-shaped.

One of the vultures circling above him shrieked another long, ear-piercing cry as it soared through the sky. It banked right, then came to an abrupt halt in midair and tumbled hard to the ground, landing a few inches from his foot. Its neck had been twisted and bent sideways, and blood was pouring out the middle of its flattened breast. The bird wasn't moving.

Lucas knelt down to check the carcass. He grabbed one of the broken, outstretched wings and flipped the lifeless animal over. There weren't any bullet or shredder holes, so it hadn't been brought down by a hunter. It must have hit something in mid-flight. He looked up, but only saw the picture-perfect blue sky and the blistering sun warming the air. He must have been hallucinating again.

Before he could stand up, a speck of bright light appeared above him in midair, about thirty feet beyond the misshapen crop circle in the grass. It started as a single pinpoint of light, then flattened out and widened as it grew taller. It looked like a castle's drawbridge lowering to the ground, but it moved in silence, while it hovered a few stories off the ground. It was as if the sky had been cracked opened from the other side.

He could see movement inside the light, but it was difficult to stare into the brilliance, even with the meadow awash in a midday burn. He squinted to allow his eyes time to adjust. The shadowy movement inside was a pair of slender legs, and they were traveling down the ramp. As the seconds passed, he could see more detail—a waist, a stomach, two arms, and a head. It was humanoid—thank God—not Krellian bugs or Taku Beasts.

Lucas decided it was best to move back until he could assess the threat level. He stood up and walked backward a few yards, keeping a watchful eye on the new arrival. The face of the lanky visitor blurred into view, as if he were looking through a flooded, underwater scuba mask.

She looked gentle and experienced, like a white-haired grandmother who'd just stopped by for supper. She wore a form-fitting silver pants suit with a symbol emblazoned across her chest. The crest was in the shape of a slanted crucifix, with what looked like a silhouette of a bird's head at the top, the emblem he'd seen in the cold-storage freezer when he was checking the vegetable boxes—the birdman crucifix—the same object that drew blood from his hand, then turned to ashes when he dropped it.

"The spiritual salad farmers?" he mumbled, thinking about the old woman who sat down next to him at the service counter in the bakery. The alien visitor reminded him of Carrie Anne's step-mother, Tehani, except the alien didn't have a cast on her arm.

The woman stopped her descent only a foot beyond the bottom of the incline. She looked up the ramp and waved a hand signal before stepping into the grass. She waited as another set of legs strolled down the ramp.

The second visitor was half the size of the first and wore the same clothing, yet it moved down the ramp half as fast as the first. Then Lucas saw its face—it was little Maggie.

His heart picked up steam. So did his lingering headache. "Maggie!" he shouted.

She stared at him with a vacant look on her face, as if she were in an hypnotic trance. Lucas kept an eye on the top of the ramp, hoping that Drew would appear next and roll down in his wheelchair. But he didn't.

Maggie stood next to the taller visitor as the crack in the sky began to close behind them. It took half a minute for the light fissure to become a pinprick again before disappearing from view.

Lucas figured they'd just walked down the exit ramp from a cloaked spaceship. Which would explain the wedge-shaped crop circle in the grass, which was probably one of the ship's landing struts. He didn't know if he should be frightened or excited. He wanted to greet the visitors, but his legs thought otherwise. They were still walking in reverse—faster now than before—seemingly with a mind of their own. Something felt wrong. He turned to run.

"Fear not, Lucas Two-Twelve," the full-sized visitor said in docile, elderly voice.

The fear inside Lucas eased a bit. He stopped running and turned to face her.

"We are of friendship," she said. Her thin, gray lips barely moved when she spoke. Her monotone voice sounded artificial or possibly controlled in some way.

"Who are you?" Lucas shouted.

The visitor pointed to her flat chest. "I am Flexus Remu." She touched her palm to the back of the smaller companion. "This is Alista Fria. We are the Baaku."

Fria? Such an odd last name. But yet, it sounded familiar; like he'd heard it before. He searched his memories, but couldn't place it, so he let the thought go.

His legs took him straight for the visitors, though at a slower than normal pace. Along the way, he studied Alista, trying to glean some sense of familiarity, but couldn't. She looked like Maggie, but there wasn't any sign of life in her eyes. She was cold, distant, and detached from the moment. He'd certainly be frightened of the icy girl if he hadn't just held her slender body in his arms.

"Where is he?" Lucas asked Flexus.

Flexus and Alista's eyes met for a moment, then Flexus looked at Lucas. "We do not comprehend."

"I heard my brother's voice earlier, when I was on the ledge. What have you done with Drew?"

"The voice you heard was mine," Alista said, after a two-beat hesitation. "It was I who was in your thoughts."

"Bullshit," he snorted. "The voice was Drew's. Not yours."

"Alista renders the truth," Flexus said.

"You must trust us, Lucas of Earth," Alista said, with the numb look still blanketing her face.

Lucas stopped walking toward them. He was a good thirty feet from their location. "I know my brother's voice and it sure as hell wasn't you."

"When I entered your mind, my consciousness carried no visual reference. Your human brain had difficulty interpreting my thoughts and must have attached whatever reference was fresh in your mind at that moment," Alista said. "Were you thinking of your brother at the time?"

Lucas nodded.

"That is why I sounded like your brother."

Lucas didn't believe her. Or maybe it was that he didn't want to believe her. "Why were you in my thoughts?"

Another hesitation from Alista, then she answered, "I needed to stop you from injuring yourself."

Lucas offered up a phony laugh. "Hurt myself? You mean jump off the ledge?"

Alista nodded.

"I wasn't really going to do it."

Alista tilted her head slightly, as if she were judging his truthfulness.

"Trust me. I'd never kill myself. Not for Drew. Not for you. Not for anyone. I was just taking a break. Daydreaming." Lucas stepped back and held out his palms in a defensive position. "Look, you had no right to invade my private thoughts like that. What the hell do you want?"

"We are of friendship," Flexus said, putting her fingertips together, as if she were praying. Then she bowed. "We are the Baaku."

"Yeah, you keep saying that. But that doesn't explain what's going on here."

"We are here for you. You have that which we need,"
Alista said.

"Me? Why?"

"Your invention of quiet sound," Alista said.

"We are at war," Flexus said.

"Quiet sound?" Lucas asked, thinking about the alien's
choice of words. Then it hit him. "Oh, you mean my dad's sonic
pest control device."

"Yes, the sonic device," Flexus said.

Lucas smiled. He looked up and thought about the
invisible ship and its technology. The thin red hairs on his arms
stood on end. "So, you're at war with the Krellian Empire and you
need little ol' Lucas' help to defeat them, right?"

Flexus nodded.

"Welcome to the club, ladies. You may not know this, but
we defeated them in an alternate dimension. In my universe, time
travels at a different speed, which is why my version of Earth is
four hundred years in the past. And I didn't do it alone. The
circumstances aren't exactly the same. It's also possible that the
bugs may return with a working defense to our sonic technology.
So, in the end, it may not help you."

"We are fully aware."

"You are our only hope, Lucas two-twelve," Alista said.
"We have been searching for you."

There was that two-twelve reference again. Lucas assumed
it meant that these aliens were searching alternate versions of
Earth across the multi-verse, and that Kleezebee's universe was
number two-twelve on their to-do list. "So, I take it you're the
reason I'm here and not with my friends?"

Flexus bowed slightly. "Your transport was intercepted."

"Okay . . . but, if all you wanted to do was talk to me, what
was all that earlier with the Taku Beast and Maggie . . . or Alista,
or whatever her name is?"

"It was a test," Flexus said.

"For what?"

"We must be sure."

Lucas didn't understand Flexus. She talked in rhythmic, four-word circles, or maybe she didn't have a good handle on English. Either way, it was frustrating and more than a little annoying. Lucas looked at Alista and shrugged.

"We have been observing you," Alista said. "You have shown a high propensity toward violence in recent cycles."

His mind flashed an image of the bloody meat cleaver. He cleared the cobwebs from his throat. "That's not who I am, really. I'm a scientist. I only did those things to find my brother."

"Yes, that much is clear," Alista said. "However, you did prove yourself."

"So, that Taku Beast attack wasn't real?"

Flexus shook her head. "It was a test."

"—of your character," Alista added.

"Wow. That was some acting job," he said to Alista. "But how did you control the beast?"

Flexus touched her hands to her chest and instantly transformed herself into the Taku Beast. "Reality can be adjusted," she said, using the drooling mouth of the glistening beast.

Penn and Teller, Lucas thought—a wicked, alien version of them anyway. "Yeah, I get it. You could have just popped in and asked me to help. You didn't have the scare the shit out of me like that."

"A test was needed," Flexus said again.

Lucas nodded. He might have done the same thing, given the circumstances. "Hey, wait a minute. If you've been running around in my head, why didn't you know my motives already?"

"Our laws are clear. We may communicate with others, but accessing memories without permission is forbidden."

"So, I passed?" Lucas asked.

Flexus and Alista nodded. The ship's access ramp began to open again in the sky. Alista wrapped her tiny fingers around Lucas' hand and pulled him toward her.

A sharp twinge struck Lucas' temples. The headache was getting worse. He wriggled his hand free from Alista. "Look, I'd like to help. God knows I hate those fucking bugs and want to see them all dead, but I have to get back to my friends. I just don't have the time for this right now."

"Outside time is still," Flexus said.

Yeah, they were outside. Lucas got that. But what the hell was she talking about? Time is still? He looked at his watch—the digital seconds were still increasing. He held up his wrist and pointed to the timepiece. "Sorry, Flexus. That's not true. Tick. Tick. Tick. That's the sound of my life running out. I need you to send me back, now!"

"Outside time is still," Flexus said.

Jesus, the old bag sure likes to repeat herself. He looked at Alista, hoping for an explanation. He got one.

"Time is only advancing here, in this valley. Outside time is frozen."

Lucas finally understood. He was in some type of localized containment field, where time was passing normally on the inside, but for everyone else outside, time was at a standstill. "Do you mean we're inside a time dilation field?"

"Yes, a time dilation field," Alista said. "Your friends are just where and when they were. Nothing has changed since your arrival."

Lucas thought about the birds, the clouds, and the wind. "How big is this field?"

"All that you see," Flexus said.

Lucas was impressed. These aliens could not only cloak their ship and transform themselves into flesh-eating monsters at will, but they could control time and space—and do so on a large

131

scale. He wondered how much energy it took to pull off this feat. It had to be immense. "That's pretty damn impressive. Kleezebee would love this. How big is your ship?"

Flexus walked to the crop circle depression in the grass and put out her hand. Moments later, a black, cube-shaped craft became visible in front of Lucas. It looked to be about three stories tall and about forty feet in diameter. Three jet-black landing struts were supporting the underbelly of the ship, each with wedge-shaped feet that sank into the grass-covered soil of the meadow. Flexus was touching one of the struts.

The side of the ship looked perfectly smooth, with no distinguishing marks, lights, or contours—much like the silky skin of a stealth bomber—only this tech was able to cloak the spacecraft's visible light signature instead of just scattering its radar signature. Lucas figured the ship must be a transport pod, given its relatively small size. He suspected a much larger vessel was parked in orbit.

Alista grabbed his hand, again, and led him up the access ramp. Flexus followed behind.

Lucas realized he hadn't heard from the traveler living in his head. Surely, it must have something to say. He waited for it, but the traveler's silent diatribe never came.

Alista entered the ship first, then Lucas.

He expected to see the small transport ship crammed full of equipment with one central command station and a video screen, but he was way off. His jaw dropped open.

SIXTEEN

Wyatt Rutherford

Freakshow shoved Sergeant C. Wyatt Rutherford aside, smashing his right elbow into the doorjamb, as the assault team flew through the entrance door of the Dunn-Rite Café. The restaurant buzzed with chatter, everyone engaged in lively conversation and enjoying their free meal, compliments of the Supreme Commander. The distinct aroma of sizzling bacon and fresh coffee dominated the air, reminding Wyatt that he should've had seconds at morning chow.

"Round 'em up, Sergeant," Freakshow told Wyatt, his expression stiff. "Nobody in or out."

"Yes, sir," Wyatt answered, flipping his helmet's Plexiglas face shield open. He motioned to the other members of the ten-man unit to fan out and proceed as the commander ordered. The squad jogged into position along the walls and in front of each door, weapons held high on their chest in a firing position, sending red tracer beams skipping across the walls of the diner.

Wyatt aimed his shredder rifle at the ceiling and fired two short bursts. Women and children screamed, while the men huddled their arms around those sitting nearby.

"Silence!" Wyatt screamed, firing one more round into the all-white ceiling.

Chunks of plaster bounced off his arms, splintering into a dozen fragments when they smashed into the floor. Heads turned and shoulders slumped, as the crowd of consumers fell silent.

Wyatt cocked his head and with only a look instructed two of his men to begin Stage Two. The duo slung their rifles over their shoulder and walked to the center of the eating area. They pulled two families from their booths, shoving them into the aisle and to the ground. They dragged the upholstered booth seats and stainless-steel tables away to create a ten-by-ten foot clearing in the center of the café.

"Everyone stand up and move to the middle. Slowly," Wyatt said.

The patrons and restaurant staff walked in semi-organized lines toward the center with heads hung low and backs slumped. Then one of the male customers, a forty-ish, dark-skinned hulk of a man broke formation and grabbed a soldier's weapon, pulling at the rifle's stock. The soldier tugged back as the two wrestled for control of the weapon. The soldier let go of the rifle, sending the black man rolling sideways across a tabletop. He fell headfirst onto the black-and-white-checkered floor.

The black man jumped to his feet, turned and aimed the stolen weapon at Wyatt. But before he fired, his chest blew apart from the center, splattering blood and tissue across the nearby hostages. A collective gasp erupted from the patrons around him, as if their reaction had been rehearsed. When the man's body tumbled over, Wyatt saw Freakshow standing behind him with a pair of pearl-handled pistols, each with a fluttering trail of smoke rising from the end of the barrel.

"Anyone else?" Freakshow asked, aiming his guns at several of the civilians. There was no response, just faint cries from a few of the children. The crowd quickened their pace and piled into the middle of the restaurant to sit on the floor, elbow-to-elbow with the person next to them. Quiet sobs dotted the crowd.

"Check the back. Find our men," Wyatt told the troops closest to the kitchen door. A four-man detail bolted through the door and disappeared into the back. Seconds later, a high-pitched female scream echoed from the kitchen followed by three long bursts of weapons' fire, followed by a distinct chorus of pots and pans clanging and clanking. A handful of minutes later, the troops returned, each escorting a person wearing traditional cooking garb. They were all men.

"Anyone else, Stevenson?" Wyatt asked, wondering what happened to the woman who screamed.

"No, *sir*," one of the four-man team answered. "Kitchen secure. Threat neutralized."

"Put them with the others and return to your position."

The squad escorted the kitchen staff and corralled them with rest of the hostages.

"What about our guards? And the manager?" Wyatt asked.

"Unknown, sir," Stevenson said. "There are clear signs of weapons' fire in the hallway and near the cold storage, but no bodies or blood; someone cleaned up."

Wyatt looked at Freakshow. "Must have been the professor."

"But that's not all, sir," Stevenson added. "The equipment is missing, too."

"The jump pad?" Wyatt asked.

Stevenson nodded. "Someone must have stolen it."

"Goddamn Kleezebee," Freakshow said, before walking to the group of patrons sitting on the floor. He holstered his twin pistols, then knelt down on one knee in front of an older, pudgy man wearing a fancy button-down white shirt and a wide-brimmed hat. Freakshow pulled a long-bladed knife from a sheath on his left side. He pressed the serrated tip into the center of the man's neck, making a pressure divot where the blade met skin. "What happened here?"

The man didn't answer.

Freakshow's jaw stiffened as he drew the man close to his face. He seemed to study the man's eyes for a few seconds, then he jammed the knife into his throat, slashing it to the right. Blood sprayed horizontally as he went, until the man's body slumped to the ground. "Defiance is the shortest path to the afterlife." Freakshow stood up, blood dripping from his knife and shirtsleeve. He pointed at the corpse oozing red on the floor, then his eyes sharpened as he scanned the remaining civilians. "All of you: Look carefully. This is the path that destiny has set you on. For some of you, this is how your journey will end."

"Why y'all doing this?" a round, redheaded woman in the back cried out. "Please! Let us go. We don't know anything."

Freakshow walked to the overweight woman with a puffed hairdo. He grabbed her by the collar of her shirt and pulled her to her feet. "What's your name?" he asked, leaning in close to the sobbing woman. The boils on his face were millimeters away from her chubby cheeks.

"Leigh Ann Frolov."

"The hostess?"

Leigh Ann nodded through a torrent of tears. She turned her head away, her face red and swollen.

"Look at me!" Freakshow demanded, grabbing the outline of her jaw with his thumb and forefinger. He turned her head forward. Their eyes met in the middle. "You recognize my face?"

She nodded again, this time with eyes wide and lips shaking. Her face seemed to grow a darker shade of red, if that were even possible.

"Then you know to choose your words carefully. Those who don't fail to draw another breath."

136

Wyatt could see her throat shiver, as she swallowed what must have been a dry glob of spit.

"Where is Bernard?" Freakshow asked, this time with more patience in his voice.

"Who?" she asked in a shaky, broken voice.

"The manager, bitch!"

"I'm sorry. I don't know who ya mean."

Freakshow grabbed the hair on the back of her head with his hand. He lifted her with one hand off the floor about ten inches. She wrapped both of her hands around Freakshow's wrist, screaming and swinging her feet wildly.

"Last chance or you bleed," he said, pressing the sharp edge of his knife against the white of her neck.

She didn't answer. Instead, she closed her eyes and cried hysterically.

One of the other hostages, a middle-eastern man wearing tattered work pants and a red baseball cap, his jawline layered with thick, black facial hair, stood up. He couldn't have weighed more than a hundred and fifty pounds. "Don't hurt her. She doesn't know anything. None of us do," he said, sidestepping his way through the civilians sitting on the floor. He stood in front of Freakshow with an unruffled look on his face. "Please. Let her go. You don't have to do this."

Freakshow's eyes flared, then he punched the man in the jaw with the hand holding the butt of the knife. The hero tumbled backward about ten feet, before sliding back-first into the side of a nearby booth. He crumpled over, lying on his right side, rubbing his chin. He spat out a patch of blood.

Freakshow snarled as he slammed Leigh Ann down to her knees. He yanked her head back, exposing the artery in her neck. She cried out in obvious pain. He slid his knife under her throat and sneered at the rest of the hostages. "Your silence will be her death sentence. After which, I will choose another to take her place. Who shall it be?"

There was no response from anyone. The café was dead silent except for the buzz of overhead lights. Dust particles hovered around the lights in a slow, methodical motion, highlighting their iridescence. "Trust me, before this hour is over, one of you will tell me what I want to know, or I shall destroy all of you."

Wyatt thought about stepping in to stop the slaughter, but his feet wouldn't move. He knew that intervention would get them severed, along with the rest of his limbs.

A moment later, Freakshow gasped, letting go of Leigh Ann. He dropped the knife and grabbed the sides of his head with his hands. He stumbled toward the corner of the café, zigzagging as he went. He stood hunched over, facing the far wall with his back to Wyatt. After a good thirty seconds, Freakshow straightened his posture, turned and nodded.

Wyatt wasn't sure if his boss wanted him to kill the hostess, or continue with the interrogation. Freakshow normally took care of the wet work personally, so Wyatt needed to be sure. He held his shredder rifle up and cocked his head, as if to ask the commander if he was to assume the role of executioner. Freakshow shook his head, then put his hands together and drew them apart, like curtains opening.

Wyatt understood. He stepped forward, unrolled his mobile paper-thin vid-screen panel and activated it with the tip of his finger. An image of a redheaded, clean-cut male in his twenties appeared and sharpened into focus. The dimpled man had several raised scars on his chin and cheeks. He held the device in front of the hostages. "Anyone seen this man? His name is Lucas Ramsay. He's wanted by the Supreme Commander for heinous crimes against the state."

The civilian group remained alert. This time, there were no cries or sobs from any of the detainees.

"Come on. Someone here had to have seen this man. He was just here."

Again, no response.

Wyatt touched the vid-screen again, this time the image portrayed a much older man, in his retirement years, wearing a gray beard and wire-rimmed glasses.

"What about this guy? His name is Dr. Kleezebee. Anyone know his whereabouts?"

Three of the hostages shook their heads no. The rest remained still and silent, their heads hanging low.

Wyatt walked to Freakshow's position. "Doesn't seem like anyone here has a clue, sir. Doesn't make sense. Clear signs of a firefight, but nobody knows what happened." He looked at Leigh Ann. "Not even our own operatives."

Freakshow's nose and lips pinched toward the middle, making the boils and lesions on his face pulsate faster than before.

Wyatt worried that one of the pustules would explode, covering him in puss and blood. He took a step back. "It's like they've all been brainwashed or something, sir. Or, possibly, they have some kind of collective amnesia."

Freakshow hurried to the front door, where he stopped and turned to Wyatt. "End it. End it now."

"But sir, this is our most popular feeding station."

"You have your orders, Sergeant. The SC wants no witnesses and no evidence left behind."

"Yes, sir," Wyatt answered, as his heart sank. He knew what command he must give his men next.

Freakshow walked out the front door and disappeared from sight.

Wyatt turned to his men. "You heard the commander. Get it done. Then torch the place."

Wyatt followed Freakshow into the parking lot directly in front of the café. He stopped his feet, took a deep breath, then closed his eyes as a river of soul-piercing screams rang out from the restaurant behind him. A moment later, five seconds of intense gunfire and then mostly silence followed, broken only by the clatter of military-issued equipment and boots walking out of the diner.

SEVENTEEN

Spatial Reconfiguration

Lucas pushed past Alista, wanting to get a better look at the inside of the Baaku ship. A vast interior towered above him; it was much larger than it looked from the outside. It had to be at least ten stories tall. He felt as if he were standing at the bottom of a empty well and looking up, except this well was five hundred feet wide and had industrial-style catwalks decorating the top eight levels. It reminded him of an Embassy Suites atrium-style hotel back on Earth, except the air was thick and smelled canned, almost artificial, certainly recycled and conditioned. The ground floor was empty and contained no equipment or furniture.

This ship's interior walls were mostly a translucent white that glimmered and swirled along their smooth surface, giving the impression they were fluid and alive. Streaks of interwoven orange and bronze colors danced inside the white, forming a hypnotic light show of fractal shapes and patterns that appeared at random. The combinations were both beautiful and endless.

How could this much space exist inside this transport pod? His mind blinked at the ramifications. "How is all this possible?" he asked Alista.

"Spatial Reconfiguration. One of Flexus' specialties."

He looked at Flexus. "You made all this?"

Flexus bowed, proud of her accomplishments. "I am the shaper."

"How?"

"Flexus can reshape and reconfigure matter, while bending 3D space at will. It takes a lifetime to master, but as you can see, the results are impressive."

That was an understatement, Lucas thought. "So there's not a mother ship parked in orbit?"

"No. This craft provides everything we need," Alista said.

"Nice work, Flexus," he said, bending down to touch the cold floor beneath his feet. The silver-speckled metallic surface was etched with a giant red emblem that featured a sprawling version of the Baaku's religious symbol. Equidistant black lines extended out along the floor from each corner of the crest and intersected the base of the circular walls. He felt like he was standing in the middle of the giant crucifix target carved into the floor.

"How many of you are there?" Lucas asked.

"Seven shapers, plus one," Flexus replied.

"I believe he was asking you how many Baaku are aboard this ship," Alista said.

Lucas nodded. He suspected Alista was swimming around in his head again, because that was exactly what he thinking.

"Precisely ten generations aboard," Flexus said, using her usual monotone voice.

"There are ten thousand two hundred and forty of us living in this settlement," Alista said. "Plus Flexus and her seven siblings."

Lucas recognized the binary significance of the ship's population. He ran quick calculation: 10 went neatly into 10240, meaning 1024 people per generation—a kilobyte. Plus a byte of eight shapers. Must be a mathematical coincidence, he decided, or perhaps these aliens were overly concerned with precision. "When you said 'precisely ten generations,' what did you mean?"

"I think you already know the answer to that question," Alista said.

"The same number per generation—a perfectly balanced population, if it were," Lucas said.

"Balanced population is accurate," Flexus replied.

Lucas studied Alista's body language, trying to determine if those cute, pear-shaped blue eyes were a front for her thought invasion force. Was she scurrying about inside his brain? He couldn't feel anything, yet her choice of words had him concerned. If she were reading his mind again, would the uninvited presence be a risk to his already-declining mental health?

He expected to hear something in response from the traveler, but the voice remained silent. Maybe while Alista was inside, crawling around his brain, his alter ego couldn't or wouldn't communicate—not a bad trade-off, he decided.

"In Earth years, each generation is sixteen years removed from the previous," Alista said. "I am the most senior of the eldest generation."

Lucas found that hard to believe. "You're the leader?"

Alista nodded. "Yes. My responsibly is to inject my thoughts and then interpret communications with other species. As I did with you on the ledge. All command decisions are then made collectively."

A collective? Like the Borg? He looked around, expecting to see a stumbling squad of technology-covered bio-men, half machine-half human. But he didn't see anyone else. "Ten generations?"

"We are not accustomed to outsiders. Allow me a moment." Alista closed her eyes and tilted her head. Seconds later, hordes of Baaku—all female—stepped into view on each level of the ship above Lucas. All of them looked to be the same age and height as Alista. Lucas realized he was dealing with a race of four-foot-tall, pre-adolescent telepaths.

A section of the iridescent wall in front of Lucas dissolved to reveal a group of older women who looked similar to Flexus. They were standing shoulder-to-shoulder with their hands touching in front of their chests, in a praying position. Lucas counted the women—there were only six, not seven as Flexus had mentioned. One was missing—possibly off doing god-knows-what.

The first shaper of the six-pack was the only female wearing an orange-colored body suit—the rest were dressed the same as Flexus. Lucas smiled at her. She giggled and then ducked her head into the shoulder of the Baaku standing next to her. At least someone on board this ship has a sense of humor, he mused.

"I take it that these women are your re-shaper sisters?" he asked Flexus.

She nodded.

"Where are all the men?"

"We are mainly a single-gender race," Alista answered.

"Mainly?"

"There are males, but none currently reside on this ship."

"If this is a self-contained settlement as you claim, doesn't that make it a little difficult to have children?"

"When it is time to replenish our population, spontaneous gender reassignment is used."

Lucas turned to Flexus. "Just a little more of your voodoo, I suppose."

"I am not involved," Flexus said.

"It is a reconfiguration procedure. When it is time for our re-population cycle to begin, a collective decision is made as to who will undergo reassignment and who will serve as the surrogate. Those that are chosen for reassignment enter our reconfigured chamber, where they are implanted with a supply of male reproductive cells and an appendage—"

"You mean sperm and a penis," Lucas said, realizing his bladder was nearly full. It had been hours since he'd emptied it.

"That analogy is correct," Flexus said.

Lucas shook his head. "That would never fly on my planet."

"It is a tremendous honor among my people to be chosen for reassignment," Alista said. "Those who are selected step into the reconfiguration chamber willingly."

"Then what happens?"

"The participants pair off in a controlled, weightless environment where conception is initiated and guaranteed. The entire process requires only seconds to complete."

A bunch of two-pump chumps, Lucas thought. "When it's over, what happens to the . . . men?"

"The process is reversed," Flexus answered.

Lucas cringed at the thought. "I don't know. Sex is one of the few things my species does well. We could *never* follow a strict set of protocols like that."

"Yes, we have noticed that your species is pre-occupied with uncontrolled couplings," Alista said. "Our process is much more efficient."

"But not nearly as fun," he replied.

Alista and Flexus looked at each other. Neither of them smiled.

At that moment, Lucas valued his humanity more than ever. The Baaku might view him as just a tedious, run-of-the-mill human, but at least he had some level of passion in his life. And hopefully, while on the picnic with Carrie Anne, he might enjoy some heart-pounding, sweat-filled sex. No wonder these aliens cruised around like emotion-starved drones. All the complexities of relationships and sex had been removed from their culture.

It puzzled him why the Baaku didn't use artificial insemination on the female surrogates, bypassing the need for the two seconds of wham-bam-thank-you-ma'am after reassignment surgery. Maybe it was simply a Baaku tradition, one that they didn't want to lose or didn't know how to change.

His bladder pressed hard against his abdomen. He couldn't hold it any longer. "Do you have a bathroom? If not, I can just run outside and find the closest bush."

"May I assist you?" Flexus asked.

Lucas wondered about her choice of words. "I appreciate the offer, but all I need is a room with a door and a toilet. I can take it from there."

Flexus furrowed her brow, looked at Alista.

"He needs a private place to urinate," Alista told her. "Construct four walls, a floor-mounted waste receptacle, and a running water source so he may disinfect himself afterward."

Flexus nodded. She touched the fluidic wall nearest to her and inserted her hand into the colors showering its surface. Seconds later, a segment of the wall began to slide out six feet in front of her. It looked like an oversized black phone booth, but it had no entrance.

"Inside you will find everything you need," Alista said.

"Uh, where is the door?"

"Take one step forward," Alista said.

Lucas did as she instructed and the front wall of the phone booth dissolved. He smiled. "Ah, I should have expected that."

When he stepped inside, the wall behind him reformed as soon as his body cleared the opening. The inside of the bathroom was lit brilliantly from above, and its walls were swirling with orange and bronze colors.

He had expected to find a toilet or urinal, but the Baaku bathroom was empty, except for an open, three-inch-wide black pipe sticking up from the center of the floor. There was a vertical stream of water to his left, flowing between two cream-colored spouts sticking out from the fluidic wall. The protrusions resembled ceramic faucets and were mounted one on top of the other, about twelve inches apart. Flexus must have built the water stream backward, since it was flowing from the bottom faucet to the top, defying both gravity and logic. He shook his head.

The black floor drain rose up only two inches and looked more like the open end of an undersized sewer pipe than a toilet. "Not exactly the Ritz," he mumbled.

He unzipped, finished, zipped up, fastened the button at the top of his pants, and ran his hands through the reverse flowing water. There was no towel to use, so he wiped his hands on the front of his shirt and waited for an exit to appear. It didn't.

"Hey, ladies? I'm done in here," he said to the oscillating walls that now felt a lot closer than before. He waited a minute. The entrance didn't appear. "Hello? . . . Someone want to let me out of this cage?" Again, nothing happened.

He thought about how Flexus had used her hand to control the ship and, even though he knew it was a long shot, decided to try it. He put his palm on the glistening wall, but the wall wasn't solid and his hand passed right through it. The ship reacted by retracting the water assembly and the black sewer pipe into the walls and floor.

"What the hell?" He jerked his hand back. He wasn't feeling any pain, but still flexed his fingers and tested his grip by opening and closing a tight fist several times. His hand was working normally. The bathroom walls felt wet to the touch, yet his fingers were dry.

He figured the ship must have been using some type of sensory-enabled hologram technology to display the walls and bathroom fixtures and must have reacted to his near contact. That gave him an idea. He turned to face the wall behind him—the same wall that had dissolved earlier to let him inside. He walked toward it, protecting his face with his hands in case his plan failed. The wall dissolved as he had hoped.

When Lucas stepped out of the Baaku's bathroom, the hairs on the back of his neck tingled and he could hear a faint whirling sound above him. He looked up and saw something that hadn't been there before: a spinning, bright-orange sphere hovering near the top of the ship's central shaft. It looked to be thirty feet in diameter and was discharging random bolts of lightning, each striking the upper floor of the ship at different locations. An ominous-looking white spot would swirl around just before the sphere released a bolt of lightning and point in the direction of the next discharge. One beat later, the white spot stopped its rotation cycle and pointed down at Lucas, as if it had just noticed him. Instantly, his headache erupted into a full-blown tsunami. It felt like a thousand jackhammers pounding at his skull, trying to dig their way to his feet. He wrapped his hands around his temples and dropped to his knees. He screamed in pain.

"Initiate containment procedures!" Alista yelled at Flexus.

Lucas managed to find the strength to lift his eyes and look at Flexus. His vision was erratic, but he saw her standing next to the far wall with her left hand touching it. Moments later, her hand disappeared into the translucent wall. An orange, pulsating glow appeared where her hand should be, then it shot up the wall about twenty feet and stopped. A black, metallic-looking flat section grew out of the orange glow and spread quickly across the hull to form a three hundred and sixty degree ring around the ground floor.

It wasn't more than a second before the ring started to expand inward, growing a white-colored ring along its inside edge. Thousands of tiny, octagon-shaped chunks appeared, piecing themselves together like a jigsaw puzzle to construct the second ring. The process continued, forming ring after ring—each about twelve inches in width—to build a flat surface that would soon cover the shaft's expanse. After each successive ring was built, its surface changed color from white to orange to black, like the new rings needed to cool off or harden. Each of the finished rings looked like it was made out of the same silky black material that covered the exterior of the ship.

Lucas' headache disappeared the moment the ceiling construction was complete. So did the mounting pressure inside his head. He stood up. His legs wobbled and every muscle in his body ached, but otherwise he thought he was okay. He rubbed his temples. "Now I know what an irradiated tumor feels like."

"Our apologies. We do not receive many two-twelves," Alista said.

"What the hell was that thing?"

"That is our Neural Nexus. The sum of all we are."

"You mean like a central memory core?"

"Yes, but it is also for communications. All Baaku are linked to the Nexus."

"When it looked at me, I felt like my head was going to explode."

"The Great Loti was attempting to make a neural connection. Obviously, your physiology is not compatible."

"Yeah, no shit," Lucas scoffed. He was surprised the Baaku had given the painful device a nickname. He would have called it the Great Evil Eye, since that's what it looked like. "I've had some killer migraines before, but that one was biblical. I just hope I don't have any lingering brain damage."

"A scan is advised," Flexus replied.

"That is an excellent idea," Alista said, nodding to Flexus in a matter-of-fact way. She looked at Lucas. "We should check you for injury."

Flexus bent down and stuck her hand into the floor. A shiny, silver device rose up from the center of the great bird emblem. It looked like a preacher's pulpit with a flat metal surface for the bible and a four-foot curved pedestal supporting it underneath. Two cutouts in the shape of a human hand were built into the podium's surface—one for the left and one for the right.

Lucas stepped forward and waited for directions. Even though he was still a bit woozy, at least he couldn't hear or feel the traveler stomping around inside his withering garden of neurons. Maybe the Great Loti's agonizing mind-hack had erased the traveler. If it did, then the pain was worth it. Either way, he figured it was going to take a while for the cobwebs to clear in his head.

"Place your hands on the scanning device," Alista said.

Lucas did as she instructed. The metal was cold and slippery, but the cutouts fit his hands perfectly, as if they they'd been made just for him.

"Coalescence detected!" a loud voice echoed throughout the ship. The words bombarded Lucas' eardrums, coming at him from every direction at once. He looked around, but couldn't identify the source. He tried to pull his hands away from the scanner, but he couldn't move them.

"Coalescence detected!" the voice said again. Each time the voice spoke, the shimmering walls reacted and changed colors in sync with the syllables and variations in tone. Almost like how a voice spectrum analyzer would react.

Lucas used all his strength in an attempt to pull away from the device, but his hands were stuck. "What's going on?" Lucas yelled to Alista. His heart thumped a louder beat than before, as sweat began to drip from his temples. A flash of searing pain raced down his neck, wrapped around his chest, and shot through his arms and into his fingers. Lucas felt lightheaded and dizzy, then everything went black.

EIGHTEEN

Poached Egg

Lucas opened his eyes. He was lying flat on his back, on some type of body-length table, with his face and mouth covered by a crystal-clear, stretchy material that smelled like oranges. There were no cutouts for his nose and mouth, yet somehow he could breathe. A cold dampness pressed against the back of his neck and his legs were stretched out flat. His feet tingled, like they had been asleep—but he could wiggle his toes.

He tried to sit up, but couldn't. His entire body was lashed down to the table, held motionless as if he were stuck inside a giant, ultra-thin condom. A light burned three feet above him, searing his watery pupils with white light. He closed his eyes as vertigo sprang to life in his ears, making the room spin wildly in his mind. Round and round he went, sending his stomach into near-vomit territory. He resisted the urge to throw up, and a few minutes later, the spinning stopped.

Alista's voice echoed randomly off the ship's walls in the background. Lucas thought she was talking to Flexus, but wasn't sure. "We need to try a different approach before the subject regains consciousness. We need additional instructions from Loti. I am not sure how to proceed without further degradation."

There was no response.

Lucas kept his eyes closed and his head still. He didn't want Alista to know he was awake. His blood pressure pounded in his ears; his breathing shortened and intensified. He tightened his stomach muscles to calm his undulating chest. He prayed she wouldn't notice the change in his vitals. It seemed to work.

Footsteps stirred behind him. He held his breath. The steps were loud and moving slowly at first, then they picked up speed as the sound dissipated. The light above him went dark, as did the sounds of other life in the room. Lucas figured he was alone.

The material covering his face began to dissolve, starting at a point above his nose and working outward. He opened his eyes, craned his neck, and looked down across his body. He could see every contour of his body shimmering under the sheer, stretchy material. He couldn't defend himself—not this way. He needed to break free before Alista, or something worse, returned.

He discovered he was able to move his fingers in a piano-playing motion. "That's a start," he whispered. Slowly he raised his right arm off the table. The material's tension gave way, allowing him to elevate his elbow an inch from the shiny surface. He smiled—progress.

He tried to lift the other arm and sit up, but the Baaku material reacted, snapping his upper back and his arms back into place on the table. His elbows smashed into the metal slab, sending a pair of jolts into his shoulders, landing in his neck. He bit his lower lip to muffle his voice, though he wanted to scream.

He allowed himself time for the pain to subside. It did. He exhaled a long, slow breath and wondered if he pulled hard enough and fast enough, could he break free from the material before it reacted. Worth a try.

He took a moment to focus his thoughts, then summoned all his might to yank both of his arms away from the table in one powerful thrust—but his arms didn't budge, not a millimeter. So, he could wiggle his fingers and move his arms slowly, but nothing more. He closed his eyes and waited a few seconds for his nerves to relax. They did. His mind cleared.

Come on. You're a scientist, he told himself. Figure it out. He decided to try wiggling his fingers again. They moved. Then he tested raising his arm. Again, success. The facts told him what he needed to know — the hold-down material would respond with equal force to the speed and intensity of his movements. The harder he tried to break free, the stronger the material fought back. He was a prisoner.

He turned his head to the right. The nearest edge of the Baaku material was pulled tight, but it didn't seem to be attached to anything. It was as if it were hovering in midair, possibly held in place by a matrix of invisible struts or possibly a bio-sensitive force field.

He tried sliding his body slowly off the table, like a hunk of butter easing its way across a simmering frying pan. If he could move slowly enough, maybe the material wouldn't register his movement and react. He might just be able to slip underneath it and escape.

Just then, a pinpoint headache invaded his skull. Lucas clenched his jaw and cried out in pain. He figured the noisy traveler had just woken up and was about to speak more of its nonsense to him. Lucas waited, but the traveler said nothing.

A shape appeared across from Lucas, inside the swirling patterns of the ship's wall. The image stabilized slowly and jumbled itself clear: It was a face . . . a human face. . . . His brother's. A calming peace washed over him and the roaring headache stopped pounding instantly. It had been too long since he'd seen Drew's image in a reflective surface. He'd almost forgotten about the perfect contours of his brother's nose and chin. Lucas' eyes flushed with tears.

Once again, Drew's lips were moving, but there was no sound. This time, however, it looked like Drew was shouting at him, with eyes wide and eyebrows raised. Lucas didn't understand why. After all, wasn't this *his* hallucination? Why was his brain conjuring a disturbing vision instead of something more soothing? He figured he must be losing it.

Seconds later, the material covering his body disappeared. He sat up, turned sideways, and slid off the table. His feet hit the deck with a thud. He scurried toward Drew's image, but before he made it to the wall, his brother's face lit up with sudden panic, then he was pulled away quickly, sucked deep into the vibrant colors flooding the wall.

"Drew!" he shouted. He reached to touch the wall where Drew's face had been, but the wall started to flutter. He yanked his hand back before making contact. A door-sized section of the wall dissolved into nothing and Alista and Flexus walked through.

"Are you feeling better?" Flexus asked, in a flat, toneless voice.

Lucas backed away from the Baaku and held up his fists in a half-boxer, half-karate pose. Rico's hand-to-hand training had a will of its own, taking control of his limbs. "Stay the hell away from me!"

Alista's eyebrows pinched. "Remain calm, Lucas two-twelve. You are among friends."

"Bullshit!" Lucas said, his jawline stiff and ready. "I really don't like being shrink-wrapped like a Twinkie. Why am I being treated like a prisoner?"

"A prisoner?" Alista responded.

"Yeah. A goddamn prisoner. What the hell is going on?"

"You required medical attention," Flexus said.

Lucas shook his head. He didn't believe her.

Alista stepped forward. "The scanning device sent a severe neural-electric shock into your system that stopped your heart and overloaded your neocortex. We deployed the medical device to heal your injuries."

Lucas thought about her words for a moment. Then he agreed—the facts seemed to jibe with her reasoning. He lowered his fists and stood at ease.

"How do you feel?" Flexus added.

"Like a poached egg," Lucas answered, rubbing his temples.

"Just allow yourself time to recover fully," Alista said. "There may be a few side effects. Your system took quite a jolt."

Lucas stretched his back until it cracked. "What was that stuff holding me down to the table?"

"The Great Loti used it to heal your injuries," Alista said.

"Some type of bio-healing gel?"

The short Baaku nodded, then offered up a half-smile.

"Is that why parts of it disappeared before others?"

"Yes. Once an area of your body had been repaired, the healing material dissolved."

Lucas nodded, then remembered something that occurred just before the scanner cooked his ass. "What was all that earlier when the ship's alarms went off? Something about a coalescence detected?"

"That will take some time to explain."

Lucas put his hands on his hips. "Go ahead. I'm listening."

"Our primary source of trade involves long-term memories, which we acquire and store in the Neural Nexus. We offer them for sale to other species who desire to share in the lives and experiences of other life forms, all without leaving the comfort of their own planet. It ensures a safe and full cultural exchange."

"Basically, you're thought merchants. People can live out a waking dream, pretending to be someone else for a while."

"Yes. However, on rare occasions, random patterns of cognitive distortions group together with the system's framework, become self-aware, and escape. That's what happened in your case."

The ghost in the machine, he mused. "Cognitive distortions?"

"When we acquire a body of thought, we take a digital imprint of the subject's mind. We absorb it en masse and store it in the Neural Nexus. The Great Loti then sifts through the memory patterns, weeding out the unstable thoughts and keeping the remainder."

Lucas thought about the lightning bolts discharging from the great eye to the top floor of the ship. "Is that what I saw earlier, with Loti? Discharges of negative thoughts?"

"Yes. That is how Loti rids the Nexus of unwanted memory patterns."

Lucas nodded. "Makes sense. You only want the stable thoughts. Something you can sell easily."

"Precisely," she said. "Violent or negative thoughts can be quite powerful, but problematic. Every living being has a mental filter, like an inner eyelid, that typically controls their sadistic thoughts and impulses. But occasionally when the mental filter of the donor subject is removed from the equation, the more powerful distortions become unstable. Even the Great Loti can't control them."

Lucas thought about the noisy traveler squatting in his head the past few months. He decided not to tell the Baaku that it had been trying to communicate with him. He wasn't sure how this would play out and certainly didn't want to give them another reason to penetrate his gray matter.

"Okay, let me see if I got this straight. . . . A random *coalescence,* as you call it, moved into the top floor of my brain, and decided to play hide-and-seek until your medical scanner discovered it. Then your machine tried to suck the cognitive distortions out of my head, almost killing me in the process."

"Yes, that is accurate," Flexus replied.

"I can see how being a thought merchant could be very lucrative. Back home on Earth, people would line up to take a vacation from themselves. Probably pay a fortune, too. Just have to issue a legal disclaimer about the potential side effects. So where's this *coalescence* now?"

"It has been eradicated from your synapses. The scanner may have overreacted with the purging discharge, but it did its job. We apologize for any inconvenience this may have caused you."

"Inconvenience? Seriously?"

"Is there another word that better suits the facts?" Alista asked.

"Probably, but that's not really important right now. How the hell did this coalescence get inside my head in the first place?"

"Unknown at this time," Flexus said, before looking at Alista with an extended gaze.

After a three-count, Alista added, "Usually a coalescence transfer requires direct contact with the Neural Nexus or a related system—one that is linked to it," Alista said. "Electrical discharge must occur, carrying with it the memory engrams that have formed into the cognitive distortion."

Lucas drifted into his own thoughts. At least now he knew he wasn't going nuts. The traveler was real and not some prescription-grade delusion brought on by too many trips across dimensions. At least Dr. Kleezebee could no longer use the hallucinations as an excuse not to send him back in to look for Drew.

"Could I have been infected while traveling across dimensions?"

"Not likely."

He thought about the first time he heard the traveler in his head. It was after a trip to a version of Earth that was perpetually dark. It had a brilliant night sky that was lit up from nebula-sized showers of static discharges — much like standing in a room with a giant Tesla coil sending out chaotic bolts of electricity.

"What if I were exposed to a supercharged atmosphere? Could intense static discharges transfer the coalescence?"

"That might be sufficient," Flexus said.

"Then it must have happened a few months ago when I traveled to such a planet. The goddamn headaches started soon after. I guess that's all a thing of the past now, right?"

Both Alista and Flexus nodded.

Lucas offered up a phony smile. "Thanks, I guess. Too bad my brain cells had to be puréed to get that shit out of my head. But at least it's gone."

He thought about his wrist and realized he'd lost track of time. He wondered how long it would be before a toxic death served notice. "Hey, ladies, it's been fun. But I really need to get back to my friends. I know time is frozen and all, but seriously, I need to jet."

"No need to worry. The Great Loti has neutralized the subcutaneous explosive in your wrist. You are no longer a threat to yourself or anyone else."

Lucas wondered how she knew what he was thinking. She must be tapping his thoughts again. "I thought you couldn't steal my thoughts, at least not without asking me first."

"It was not difficult to determine the reason for your sudden haste to leave. Before you depart, we would like to discuss a trade or some form of compensation for your sonic technology."

"We are in need," Flexus added.

"Yeah, I know. But still, I can't just give up our secrets like that. I'll have to run it by Professor Kleezebee first. I'm sure he will want to help. But not until after I complete the important mission I was on."

"Success is not likely," Flexus said. "Protocol adjustment is necessary."

Lucas wasn't sure what she meant. Not that it mattered. "I appreciate the input, but I'm going anyway. Now, if you would kindly show me the way out."

"As you wish," Alista said. She looked at Flexus. "Send him back."

Flexus inserted her fingers into the wall closest to her position. Once again, the surface colors swirled around her hand. The floor opened beneath Lucas' feet, dropping him into a pitch-black freefall.

NINETEEN

Switchback

Lucas woke up on his side, lying on a hard surface that felt dirty and rough, like cement, though he wasn't sure. He rolled onto his back, taking care not to bump his left elbow that was throbbing with each heartbeat. A damp chill shot through his spine from the cold floor, hastening his desire to sit upright. He did.

He looked at his legs and hands, but he couldn't see them through the darkness smothering the area. There were a half-dozen patches of light illuminating sections of the room from overhead maybe fifty feet straight ahead; they reminded him of an alien bunker scene from the first release of the Xbox video game, "Halo."

A melody of high-pitched squeaks and chirps echoed from the blackness ahead of him, as the patter of tiny feet scurried in the shadows. He hated rats, and these were close. Too close. Possibly, headed his way. He stood up.

He allowed himself time to scan the parts of the room that were visible and saw at least a dozen sets of multi-colored, ten-inch pipes protected by vertical, wire-mesh cages that stretched from floor to ceiling, spaced evenly at what he guessed were ten-foot increments leading away from him, with a set of switch-back metal stairs tucked in behind the farthest set of pipes. The stairs only led up to another basement. Shit. No sign of the receiving jump pad, Zack, or Rico.

"Adjustment, my ass. Flexus, you crazy bitch. You dumped me in the wrong place," he mumbled, shaking his head. "I can't believe this is happening again. How can the same shit happen to the same guy, in the same day? Unreal."

He used his hands to feel the area around him. A damp, flat wall was both on his right and left. They came together directly behind his position. Talk about being backed into a corner.

He craned his neck to look at the ceiling and held out his arms. "Dude. Come on. I realize I'm the last person that should be asking you for help, but I feel like you're piling it on a little thick right now. All I need is a little help. Not a lot, just a little. After all, how much goddamn crap is one guy supposed to take?"

He walked to the nearest set of red-and-blue industrial pipes where twin overhead lights were burning at full intensity. He could feel radiant heat emanating from the metal pipes inside the wire cage in front of him. Probably steam pipes, with protective cages.

He ran his hand across his sore elbow and felt the fresh, half-inch welt, pleased there was no blood. He pushed his index finger into it. It was soft to the touch, with a squishy lump near the center. He moved the knot back and forth inside the swell, playing with it like it was some kind of trophy. Gonna be a hell of a bruise there tomorrow.

He checked his pants. Dirt covered the sides of the legs and a wide patch sprawled across his butt. He brushed the layers of filth off with his hands, sending a cloud of particles floating into the air; artificial light penetrated the dust cloud in streaks.

Time to find a way out, he decided, walking briskly to the stairs at the far end of the room. He stood at the bottom of the stairs and looked up: There were three switchback staircases and a single overhead fluorescent light near the top. The light flickered and buzzed, standing guard over the desolate stairway, protecting it from the invading shadows.

The scene reminded him of a time eighteen months earlier when he and Drew were trapped in the underground NASA complex, buried under countless floors of twisted metal and crumbling concrete. A Krellian-controlled energy dome had just leveled parts of the University of Arizona campus, including the Science Lab that housed their anti-gravity experiment. The vision seemed so real, as if it were happening right now. Lucas could feel his thigh muscles burning as he relived the agonizing thirty minutes it took to carry Drew on his back up the shaft, one flight of stairs at a time. That had been on a different version of Earth, in a different dimension, but the sense of déjà vu was intense.

Somehow, he and his brother had beaten impossible odds that day. He wondered if today would be different. Once again he had no idea where he was and Rico and Zack were missing. So was the jump pad to get back to the café. The Baaku had just mind-fucked him royally with their hide-and-seek game of Taku Beast buffet, and then the whole evil-eye thing trying to suck his gray matter out through his ears. All of it had taken its toll. He was tired and exhausted. Still, there was work to do.

After a full minute of thought, he decided that this could be another Baaku reality test; one designed to test him further. After all, why would they agree to let him leave so easily after searching for him all that time, then dump his boney ass here instead of with his teammates? And what the hell had Flexus meant by "adjustment"?

He chuckled. Just another glorious day in Paradise. His version of Earth seemed so far away. So did Drew.

He walked up the stairs, taking time to peek around each section of the staircase and listen for movement. It was dead quiet, except for the echo of his own footsteps. He felt safe, at least for now. He went up two more flights, each with sixteen metal steps, to a gray metallic door at the top of the stairway. He studied the red placard with raised, white lettering. It was attached to the door at eye level with brass-colored screws, though it was an inch lower on the right side—someone obviously didn't know how to use a level properly. Some of the letters were missing, but he figured it said Cooling Tower.

Lucas put his hand on the door knob. He turned it all the way to the left before it released its grip on the doorjamb. He pushed it open a crack and stuck his head inside. It was too dark to see anything. He felt around the plaster wall to the left of the door for a light switch and found a triple switch. But before he could flick it on, he heard someone sneeze. He froze.

Row after row of light fixtures lit up the ceiling of a room that had to be at least two hundred feet wide and twice as long. He jerked his hand back, pulling the door toward his chest, until the opening was less than an inch wide. He focused his breathing to slow it down, but it wasn't easy with his heart pumping full bore. He managed to calm himself before leaning forward and using only his right eye to see inside.

He heard what sounded like footsteps—which were getting louder—but he couldn't see anyone. There were hundreds of stacked, dark-green containers blocking his view of the far side of the room. The totes looked to be made of corrugated plastic or some other type of packing material, each arranged in a stacked row from left to right. The ten-foot-tall wall of containers was organized and neat. Every container he could see had sprayed-on white lettering that read *TNOT-2*.

He waited a good five minutes, but didn't hear any more sounds. He looked behind him and considered his options. Only one choice: Move forward.

He entered the room, walking to the closest plastic tote. He forced open its lid by using his fingers as a pry bar. He found stacks of spiral-bound printed books inside. Old-school binding to be sure, but that was the norm since the Krellian invasion began a year and a half ago.

The white cover for each book contained the same black letters: "E-Plan. Grid 2. Sector 12." He opened the book and found at least a dozen pages of topographical maps with local landmarks, highlighted paths, and printed instructions on each. It was an evacuation manual of some kind. But for what? The next two containers contained the same thing, just dozens of the manuals.

Lucas heard a muffled male voice off in the distance. It was coming from the far side of the room, possibly beyond the last row of containers. The man sounded agitated or angry; the inflections in the man's speech kept turning up a notch. Lucas couldn't make out many of the words. He put the manual back in the first container and closed its lid quietly. He did the same for the others he had opened, too.

Lucas decided a stealth approach was in order. He took his shoes off and carried them in his hand as he moved forward, walking heel-to-toe in a deliberate manner, wondering if the commotion from across the room was the act of friend or foe. Maybe it was Zack or Rico. Could he be that lucky?

He followed row after row of storage bins that formed a maze-like pattern, allowing him to inch his way closer without exposing himself to direct line of sight. Each time he came to a corner, he knelt down and looked around the corner at ground level. He figured that low-level maneuver would be less likely to draw attention if anyone happened to glance his way, but he saw no one.

He was nearing what he thought was the midway point of the room, when his sock-covered toes began to vibrate. He stopped moving, knelt down on one knee, and put his palm to the floor. The vibration was consistent and rapid. Just then, a low-pitched hum teased his ears—it seemed mechanical in nature. It reminded him of the startup sequence from the immense electromagnet array surrounding the E-121 reactor back home on Earth.

He made his way down three more corridors and navigated two ninety-degree turns. He was standing in the second to last row of the containers near the far side of the room. He looked through the air gaps between the containers in the stack, trying to see if anyone were on the other side, and there was: A tall, bronze-skinned man was standing next to a much shorter, rugged-looking man. Their faces had similar features. Oversized nose, stiff jaw, narrow cheeks, and receding hairlines. Maybe they were related. He listened in on their conversion.

"—look, you need to hurry up. Kristov will eventually notice we're gone. She doesn't miss much," the taller man said, strain and anxiety clear in his tone.

The other man exhaled a billowing pillar of smoke, then coughed twice. "I'll tell you what, Cary, this is some seriously good shit. Where'd you score it?"

"From this cool long-hair in town."

"Was it that one-eyed dude, Gaylon? With the braid of gray hair down to his ass?"

"Yes."

The smoking man nodded, as a teeth-filled smile filled his lips. "I heard that freaky bastard has the best stuff." He took another long drag, sending the reefer's glow into overdrive. "Premium."

Lucas ducked his head to avoid being detected through the container stack. He had seen the legendary drug-dealer, Gaylon Reece, from a distance on his first trip into town, but never met him face to face. He looked like a younger version of the actor

Sam Elliot, except of course for the eye patch and severe limp. His reputation as a brutal renegade was well-earned—he was the only dealer brave enough to sell sensory-altering drugs on Cyrus' turf. But the man was still alive, so he must be both clever and intelligent.

"Come on, Freebo," Cary said, tugging at the other man's elbow. "We need to get back. Are we square now?"

Freebo nodded. "We're solid. But from now on, it'll cost you double for my sister."

"Yeah. Okay. Whatever. There probably won't be a next time. She wasn't that good."

Freebo coughed, like he'd swallowed wrong. "I beg to differ. She's top-flight ass. And I should know." He tossed the reefer onto the cement floor, then crushed it with the ball of his foot.

"You ready for this?" Cary asked.

Freebo froze. He said nothing.

Cary grabbed Freebo by the collar. "Look, I need you to guard this door and don't let anyone through except Yakberry. Understood?"

Freebo held up his hands like he was sitting in a strip club getting a table dance and trying not to touch the girl. "I'm still not sure how am I supposed to know if it's the real Dr. Yakberry?"

"Unbelievable. Weren't you listening at the briefing?"

"Not exactly. I was sort of staring at Kristov's tits. I'm defenseless against a serious set of cleavage. Do you think she's playing hide the sausage with Cyrus? Or maybe Freakshow? Now that's a visual."

Cary adjusted Freebo's collar, turning down the ends. "If she catches you looking, she'll take your head and not even break a sweat."

Freebo nodded. "Man, did you see that wicked creature tattoo on her back? I wonder if all the initials are her conquests or something. Definitely trashy, just the way I like 'em."

"You need to focus and do your job," Cary said, letting go of Freebo's collar. "Just ask Yakberry to answer Kristov's riddle."

Freebo grabbed Cary's arm, as his weight shifted to the left quickly. "I'll never remember that shit. I'm three-quarters baked already. In another ten minutes, I'll be—"

"All right, one more time. This time you need to listen and remember or we're both fucked. Kristov won't give you a second chance. Or me, for recommending you. She's probably gonna test you today like she does with all new recruits. You'd better be frosty."

Freebo pulled down on the sides of his shirt. He straightened his posture. "I'm cool. Lay it on me, bro."

"Ask him why the zero-point energy of a vacuum in space can't be interpreted as a cosmological constant?"

"Zero-point what?"

"Zero-point energy," Cary scolded, rolling his eyes. "It's like I'm talking to an eggplant or something."

"Dude, you're making me hungry. I've got a serious case of the munchies right now."

"Listen to me. You need to take this serious. This is important."

Freebo used his index finger like a drill, simulating impact with his temple. "It's like a swarm of micro-bees are burrowing their way into my skull. I hate this fucking shit."

"Pay attention!" Cary yelled, slapping Freebo with a backhand across his cheek.

Freebo rubbed his cheek. "Okay, I'll try. Why can't we just use a secret handshake or something?"

"Kristov wants us to be sure. Nobody here has ever seen Dr. Yakberry."

"What about a photo? How hard is that? Only takes a second to transmit."

"Comms are down again. That's why we have the riddle. It has to be something only the Doc would know."

"Yeah, that makes sense. I guess."

"Good. Don't make me regret getting you in on this gig."

"I won't. I need the cash. What kind of name is Yakberry anyway?"

"I think it's Krellian for bio-chemical super geek."

Both men laughed, then walked out through the door to their left.

Lucas waited. There were no other sounds or movement beyond the stack, but he couldn't see every inch of the corridor. Maybe he was alone. "Time to kiss the donkey," he muttered, as he stuck his head around the last corner. Sure enough, he was alone. He put his shoes on and walked the length of the aisle until he came to the single door at the far end. Next to it was an eight-foot by four-foot plate-glass window. He looked through the window and his heart nearly stopped.

The window overlooked a vast underground hollow filled with a crowd of maybe five hundred armed men wearing full-length body armor and jet-black helmets with facemasks, all standing at attention in single-file rows.

A raised platform stood in front of the crowd with a lanky, blond-haired woman hovering near four people who were on their knees with their hands behind their backs. Lucas couldn't see their faces; their heads were covered by black hoods. He assumed they were men, based on their build and physique. The scene reminded him of the *Star Wars* movie, when Darth Vader addressed his throng of masked storm troopers on the massive deck plate of the *Star Destroyer*.

The woman walking around the stage raised a glistening, machete-length knife above her head as she moved with a theatrical prance across the front of the platform. Then she unleashed some type of martial arts sequence—kicking and punching her way across the stage, spinning the knife around her wrist. Her moves were precise and calculated; she had clearly practiced for years. She stopped at the edge of the stage, bent down and took something from one of the men in the front row. She stood up, holding what Lucas thought was a piece of paper. She stared at it for a few moments, smiled, then folded it and stuck it inside the front of her top. She turned and resumed her martial arts performance.

Her black leather pants and a form-fitting, low-cut top caught Lucas' attention, as did her pair of four-foot-long blond braids that hung just below the bottom of her well-defined ass. He assumed the chick was Kristov, the babe Freebo and Cary had been gossiping about a few minutes earlier.

No wonder Freebo couldn't take his eyes off this stunning beauty—it would take a blind man to resist her flawless beauty. Lucas knew he'd be defenseless, too, if he were ever to meet her up close. He wondered what Rico would think of her. Would he think she was—

Freebo stepped in front of the window, sliding in from the right. He stared right at Lucas with his glassy, bloodshot eyes, and uneven smile. "Hey, Doc!" Freebo shouted through the glass.

Lucas wasn't sure what to do. He thought about running, but decided against it when the entire assembly in front of the stage turned in unison to look up at him.

TWENTY

Realignment

Lucas drew in a deep breath and nodded, hoping his reaction appeared natural to Freebo, and everyone else. It seemed to work.

Freebo opened the door to the left to the window and held out his hand, palm up. "My name is Freebo. Glad to meet you."

"The pleasure is all mine," Lucas said, gripping the man's hand and shaking it firmly. He decided to play along. "I'm Dr. Yakberry. Sorry I'm late."

Lucas expected the half-lit guard to follow the handshake with the science riddle Cary had drilled into Freebo's head, but the stoner just smiled. "It's all good, Doc. Follow me. We've been expecting you."

The aroma of a marijuana-like substance lingered behind Freebo as he moved, invading Lucas' nostrils like a tunnel rat. He wondered how this man figured he could get away with lighting-up while on duty. Certainly Kristov would smell it, too.

Lucas followed the guard down several steep-angled catwalks that snaked their way to the bottom floor.

Freebo stopped halfway down. He turned to face Lucas, his eyes full of panic. "Shit, I almost forgot. Doc, I have to ask you this question. Just got to get the words unscrambled in my brain, first."

"Go ahead," Lucas answered.

Freebo's face contorted in on itself like a mobile home imploding under the stress of an EF-5 tornado. "Why can't the energy of a zero-point . . . uh . . . constant. . . . Fuck me. I knew I'd mess this up."

Lucas put his hand on the man's shoulder. "Do you mean: Why can't the zero-point energy of a vacuum be interpreted as a cosmological constant?" He was about to answer the question, but Freebo didn't wait for it.

"That's it. Damn it. I knew you would know it. Thanks for savin' my ass. You're the bomb, Doc."

"Glad to help," Lucas replied, trying not to laugh. Freebo turned quickly and resumed his march to the bottom floor.

When Lucas stepped onto the dirt-covered floor, he craned his neck to locate the door where Freebo had first greeted him. He found it up high. It looked tiny and isolated—much like how he felt at that moment. Later, if he needed an exit, that would be the way out, he thought—though it would be a tiring ten-story climb.

The members of the armed brigade split in half, forming a perfect seam down the middle. Freebo marched forward through the gap, heading for the raised stage where Kristov was standing.

Lucas followed, avoiding eye contact with the members of the platoon, fearing one of them might be acquainted with Dr. Yakberry and alert Kristov to his unplanned ruse. A lingering thought kept flaring in the back of mind: Was this awe-inspiring gathering just another test—a Baaku test—one designed to further test his character? But it felt real and authentic. Just play along, he told himself. Just in case.

The last section of the mob parted, allowing Freebo access to the four-step incline that led to the stage. Freebo turned and whispered into Lucas' ear. "Doc—when you meet Kristov, keep your peeps off her cleavage. It's a killer, I know, but she's not real keen on pervs staring at her assets. Got it?"

Lucas nodded as Freebo turned and walked up the ramp. Lucas decided to follow him, though his legs seemed to be resisting his brain's command to move. They stood firm for a few seconds, before he managed to wrestle control and step forward.

Kristov stood at the top of the ramp with her hands on her hips, studying Lucas' every move. He wasn't sure what came next, but figured he would just wing it if the goddess wanted to test his scientific knowledge or just talk shop. After all, he was a semi-famous scientist in another life.

"Doctor Yakberry, I presume?" Kristov asked, aiming the blade of the long-handled knife at Lucas' chest.

"Yes. And you must be Kristov," Lucas answered, using the tip of his index finger to nudge the point of her blade away from his body. "That really isn't necessary."

Kristov grimaced, then turned to Freebo. "Did you clear him?"

Freebo hesitated, then looked at Lucas for a full second. He cleared his throat, before answering his boss. "Uh. Yes. He answered the riddle perfectly. It's all good, Commander."

Kristov circled around Lucas' back, then leaned in close to his head. He could feel the warmth of her breath tickling the hairs on his neck. She smelled his skin, then touched the biggest scar on his cheek with the softness of her hand. She whispered in his ear, "Yakberry, huh? What kind of name is that? Artillian or Terran?"

"With all due respect, Commander, does it matter?"

"No. Just curious. Where are you from?"

"Lots of places, but I'm here now and I've got a job to do."

Kristov completed her circle, stopping in front of him. She stared at him for a good fifteen seconds, tilting her head once as if she were examining the pores in his skin. "You've seen some action, but it was a while ago. Your scars look old."

172

Lucas sorted through his memories, trying to formulate the proper answer. Then he remembered something that Zack had told him. "Yes, I was on Avanti Prime, during the first Krellian assault."

"Yes, I heard about that. Nice work, Doc." A few moments later, she said, "Okay then, let's get started." She motioned for Lucas to follow her toward the four hooded prisoners resting on their knees. He did.

She stood in front of the largest captive, using the tip of her knife to lift the man's chin. "We caught these rebels trying to infiltrate our facility on Level 3. They obviously underestimated our security measures."

She pulled her free arm back, then released a blow to the hulky prisoner's head, sending the man flopping onto his right side. He lay motionless for a two-count, before she kicked him in the ribs, sending a gasp of air out from his lungs. He tried to say something, but his words were muffled and disjointed, as if something were obstructing his voice.

Kristov kicked him again, this time in the face. "Lucky for us, Doc, they just volunteered for your realignment procedure."

Lucas had no idea what she meant by *realignment procedure*, but played along anyway. "Excellent. They look like healthy subjects. They'll do nicely."

"Cyrus expects results. Today. You know the consequences if you fail."

"Shouldn't be a problem."

She motioned for Freebo to step forward. He did. "Take the doc and the prisoners to the lab." He nodded once, then stepped back.

She looked at Lucas. "Everything is ready, just as you requested. Your protocol notes are stored in memory buffer 2, data channel 12."

"Excellent. I'll get started right away," Lucas answered, waiting for Freebo to move past him.

Freebo helped the four prisoners to their feet. Two masked soldiers from the front row of the brigade joined the stoner to escort the prisoners off the stage to the right. Lucas followed.

Eleven lengthy corridors, two flights of stairs, and fifteen minutes later, Freebo opened the door to Yakberry's lab and entered, with Lucas behind him. They were followed by the four prisoners and the two guards. The lab was maybe twenty feet square and stuffed with stainless steel equipment, plus a pair of centrifuges, some metering and calibration equipment, beakers, flasks, burners, and what looked like a pair of deep-well examination tables. A six-by-six metal cage stood to the left; its walls stretching from floor to ceiling. An eight-foot utility table stood isolated near the back wall. To the right was a defibrillator, microscope, and some other odds and ends.

"Home sweet home, Doc," Freebo said, swatting his hand against the surface of closest examination table. The table rang out with a sharp ping. "Which two do you want strapped down? I'll secure the others in the holding cell."

"Let's unwrap them first. I need to see what I have to work with. Start with the one Kristov punched. He'll probably need some medical attention before I can get started."

"You got it, Doc." Freebo grabbed the man by the arm and pulled him forward. "I was hoping Kristov would assign me this duty. I've been wanting to watch this transmutation first-hand for a while now. I've heard rumors it gets pretty intense right before their DNA is realigned. We can always use more inventory, especially ones as big as this dude." Freebo grabbed the man by the neck and yanked his head close to his mouth. "Say goodbye to your old life, asshole, assuming you're strong enough to survive the pain."

Freebo slid the hood off the man. Lucas recognized him. It was Zack.

TWENTY-ONE

Polymorphic

Blood dripped from several wounds in Zack's face. His cheeks and forehead were swollen red, and his mouth was covered with a two-inch-wide gag.

Lucas was about to say something, but stopped when Zack flared his eyes at him, as if to say, "Act like you don't know me." Lucas took a moment to think, drawing in a staggered breath.

Freebo laughed. He stepped closer to Zack, leaning in chest-to-chest, craning his neck to look up. "Talk about your sorry-looking humanity. Someone must have beat him with an ugly stick." Freebo tore Zack's shirt off, revealing the abundance of scars across his chest. "This cocksucker's seen some action, that's for sure."

Lucas grabbed Freebo by the arm and ushered him back a few feet. "Keep a safe distance. I don't need to be patching you up, too."

"I'm not scared of him."

"By the looks of him, you should be. You see those scars? It means he's no stranger to pain. He's a warrior—a survivor." But what Lucas really wanted to say was, "—someone who eats punks like you for a snack." But he didn't.

"You want him on the table?"

"Not yet." Lucas figured Rico was one of the other hooded prisoners. "Let's inspect the rest of the inventory."

Freebo positioned himself between the second and third prisoners. He stood them up before removing both of their hoods at the same time.

The first was a female with short-cropped frizzy hair. Her nose was hooked and her eyelids puffy. She wore no make-up, which might have helped as she wasn't very attractive; she'd showed a lot of wear and tear. She was shorter than Lucas, maybe five-foot-eight, but she had broad shoulders and her muscles were easily twice his size. She, too, was gagged.

"Excellent specimen. She'll do nicely."

"I thought it was better if they were fat," Freebo said.

Lucas cleared his throat. "Yes. That is true. But for what we have available, she's acceptable."

Freebo nodded slowly. His eyebrows pinched. "Okay, Doc. It's your rodeo."

The third hostage was a man. Same height as Lucas, dark skin and eyes, thick eyebrows, shoulder-length blond hair with dark streaks, and a slender nose—tears ran down his cheeks. Certainly not Rico.

"And the last one?" Lucas asked, figuring the final detainee was Rico.

Before Freebo could respond, the lab door flew open. Kristov walked in, accompanied by two additional guards. Their faces were covered with full facemasks, just like the other two guards who'd helped Freebo escort the group into the lab.

"Is there a problem here, Yakberry?"

"No, Commander. I was just inspecting the condition of the specimens."

"This is taking too long," Kristov said. She walked to the fourth hostage, standing a foot in front of Freebo. She pulled her knife back and then thrust it forward, ramming it into the belly of the masked man.

Lucas gasped.

She used both hands to pull the knife up, gutting the man from stomach to chest. Blood and tissue spurted out as she withdrew the weapon. The body fell over. It wasn't moving.

Zack twisted his body, tugging at the hand restraints, then made a charge forward.

Freebo rammed the butt of his rifle into Zack's abdomen, then used an uppercut maneuver to smash it into his forehead. Zack stumbled backward before dropping to the floor.

"What a pussy," Freebo said, spitting on Zack's face.

"Now we may proceed without any more delay," Kristov said, wiping the blood on her knife across Freebo's shirt.

Lucas was stunned. Unable to speak.

Kristov pointed to the vid-screen console behind Lucas. "Doc? You still with me? Memory bank 2, data channel 12."

Lucas didn't answer.

She pressed the tip of the blade against his chest. "Do I need to remind you what's at stake here?"

Lucas snapped back to reality. "No, Commander."

"All right then, let's get to it."

Lucas needed a moment to think. He turned to face away from Kristov, then walked to the widescreen console built into the polished surface of the work desk. He used the touch screen interface and pulled up the data channel. Yakberry's experiment appeared on the screen. Lucas skimmed through the notes encoded by the real Dr. Yakberry. A minute later, dread took control of his body.

"Fuck me," he mumbled quietly.

Apparently, Yakberry had created a polymorphic retrovirus that could simultaneously re-splice and re-sequence a person's DNA, transforming them into something . . . unknown. The notes did not mention the end-game for this tech.

Lucas had read about molecular bio-tech before, but he thought this type of viral transformation was purely theoretical. The doc's research showed that exogenous DNA could be introduced into the subject's genome by way of a new type of multi-vectoring agent that would trigger the transformation. The delivery system was based on Cyrus' micro-bee drug technology, allowing Yakberry to program the nano-machines to target specific DNA checkpoints within adult cells. Truly ingenious.

He was starting to understand the enormous potential of this research. Human bodies contain an array of undifferentiated stem cells that, when needed, can be genetically programmed and activated for indefinite regeneration and repair. After all, that's what happens when your body repairs a cut on your finger, or when new blood is created after you donate a pint at the local blood bank. This new tech might even make it possible to regrow whole organs and limbs, and since they would be made from the donor's own human cells, there would be no possibility of rejection.

He kept reading and digesting more of the information. His mind continued to churn out dozens of potential uses of this tech, each one more incredible than the last. His eyes and brain froze when something occurred to him—something he never thought possible, at least not before today.

If Yakberry had figured out how to create vast amounts of zero-age stem cells from regular-aged cells in the donor's body, then he could—in effect—reset a person's body back to its original state at birth. Bodies would be kept in their most pristine state, meaning they would never break down or wear out, nor would they ever die. If someone happened to get injured, Yakberry could use this tech to grow a new limb or repair the damage. He could even use it to erase an invading cancer cluster or some other heinous disease.

Lucas took another minute to finish studying the last page of research. The page was titled "Phase 2," which discussed the possibility of creating a unique, neural-coded link between a central controller and the transformed subjects. That meant a single person would be able to control dozens, if not thousands of these genetically altered humans without interference—sort of like a telepathic fingerprint for secure access. Given the nearly infinite variations of neural patterns within the human brain, it would be impossible to fake or intercept, giving the controller a perfectly secure, yet unbreakable link to control his entire army of genetically-altered humans, all with nothing more than pure thought.

But one burning questioned remained. What type of transformed human was Yakberry attempting to create?

"Can we get started?" Kristov asked Lucas. "We don't have all day."

"Sorry, I needed to be sure the protocols were aligned properly before we begin."

"Are they?"

"Yes. Perfectly," Lucas answered, spinning to face her. He wondered about the foreign DNA that Yakberry had used and its origin. He thought that the telepathic fingerprint might be a clue to the answer. The only species he'd encountered with that ability was the Krellian Empire—their physiology would have superior physical and telepathic characteristics. He figured it was some type of trans-genetic sub-splice. Possibly, a set of hybrid DNA strands, extracted from the foul, flesh-eating creatures.

Then, another idea popped into his head. It might not be about creating zero-age stem cells or regenerating human tissue. Yakberry might be using this tech to transform ordinary humans into an army of controllable Krellian arthropods to do Cyrus' bidding. He could then control them with just his thoughts, unleashing a brigade of mindless drones. Even worse, if Yakberry had managed to encode resistance to his father's sonic pad technology, there'd be no way to stop the flesh-eating marauders. They'd be the perfect killing machine.

Lucas walked three steps closer to Kristov. Then he looked at Freebo. "I'll begin with the female. Get her on the table."

"Belay that order," Kristov said, holding her arm in front of Freebo. She then pointed to Zack, who was sitting upright on the floor, with blood dripping from a two-inch gash in his forehead. "Start with Mister Tough Guy. Let's see if he's man enough to survive the process."

"With all due respect, Commander, this is *my* experiment. I should be the one who determines which specimen is initially selected."

"Doc, you can either follow my orders, or I'll have you strapped to the table and injected first. Which would you prefer?"

Before Lucas could answer, the two guards who had accompanied Kristov stepped forward on either side of her. They raised their weapons, aiming them at Lucas.

Lucas looked at Zack, who was still on the floor with his hands tied behind his back.

Zack worked his legs under his butt, then stood up, looking at Lucas the entire time. Zack nodded slightly, then expanded his chest, as if to signal he was volunteering for the procedure.

"Put him on the table," Kristov said.

Freebo and one of the masked guards walked to Zack, each grabbing one of the behemoth's arms. They led him to the medical table. The three remaining guards followed behind, aiming their weapons at Zack.

Lucas expected his friend to attempt an escape, but Zack didn't resist.

Freebo released the shackles from Zack's wrists, allowing the mercenary to climb onto the table freely. Zack removed the gag from his mouth, spun his body around, face up, with his arms resting alongside him.

Freebo pressed a red-colored button on the clear-glass console attached to the head of the table. A lattice of intersecting blue energy beams appeared across Zack's face, chest, and legs, outlining his physique. Moments later, Zack's knees, neck, and back straightened in unison, pulling his entire body down to the table.

Zack wrestled against the grid with his arms, shoulders, and head, possibly testing its strength. Each time he moved an area of his body, the energy grid securing that area would turn a deep red color, then snap his body back into a secure position.

Lucas walked slowly around the head of the table, stopping next to Zack's left shoulder. His mind fluttered as he tried to think of a plan to delay the procedure. He couldn't.

"Doc, the green button," Kristov said, angling her head, as if to hurry him along.

Lucas nodded. He extended his index finger until it was hovering an inch above the start button located in the top-right corner of the table console. He was about to begin the injection sequence, when the door to the lab banged open again.

A round, black guy waddled in, using a wooden cane; his right foot was wrapped in a Velcro-strapped, knee-high walking boot. His head was almost completely bald, except for a tiny ring of curly gray hair just above his ear line. His shirt bulged at the seams, trying to keep the mounds of hanging flab inside the garment.

"Who the hell are you?" Kristov asked.

"Dr. Marcus Yakberry," the man answered in a nearly breathless voice. He looked at Lucas, holding up a photo ID with his own face on it. "The real Dr. Yakberry."

Kristov hesitated for a moment, then spun toward Lucas, raising her knife into an attack position. "Secure him!"

TWENTY-TWO

Terminal Dumb Ass

The guards tackled Lucas, knocking him down to the floor, face first. His chin and nose smashed into the cold cement floor, making his eyes water. A pair of knees pressed into the small of his back, sending a jolt of pain into his ribcage. He felt a set of huge fingers wrap around his wrists, then pull his hands together behind his back. The guard yanked him to his feet with force, nearly pulling his arms out of their sockets.

"On the table now!" Kristov screamed, pointing to the empty table next to Zack.

Seconds later, Lucas was pinned face-up by a blue containment grid on the table next to Zack. A rush of blood pounded at his cheeks and forehead, while his lungs forcefully propelled air in and out of his chest. The chill of the steel table flooded his lower back, providing some soothing relief for the damage caused by the guard's knees only moments before.

"Why are you late?" Kristov asked Yakberry.

"Skimmer accident. A Taku Beast appeared out of thin air, right in front of me. I swerved, but ended up in a ditch. Took some time for the medics to arrive and immobilize my ankle. The damn thing nearly snapped it in half. I'll probably need surgery to provide adequate fixation of the ankle bones and ligaments. There goes my entire year."

"At least you didn't hurt yourself pulling weeds or something. I once knew a guy who did that. Totally messed up his ankle. Three breaks and torn ligaments. Who does that, seriously? Only a terminal dumb ass," Freebo said.

Yakberry stared at Freebo, not saying a word.

Kristov hovered over Lucas—her breath invading his nose and mouth. It smelled like a combination of toothpaste and onions. Could have been worse, but certainly not pleasant.

"So, who the hell are you?" she asked.

Lucas kept silent.

"Trust me, you don't want to test her resolve," Freebo said.

"Silence!" Kristov shouted at Freebo, thumping him with a quick left jab. The stoner stumbled backward, smashing his backside against the middle of the lab's equipment desk. His elbow sent the desk light flying off the table end over end until it landed several feet away in a crumpled pile.

Freebo stood up, though not very erect. He shook his head in an awkward manner, then rubbed his hip and flexed his elbow. His expression and roll of the eyes seemed to indicate that he was surprised by the power behind the stunning woman's punch.

The temptress pressed the tip of her knife into the soft of Lucas' cheek. Her face burned a deep reddish hue. "Tell me. I'm not going to ask again."

Kristov changed the angle of the knife, moving her hand from the front of its handle to the rear. She leaned forward, increasing the blade's pressure against his skin.

Lucas closed his eyes and waited for the pain. He winced when the glistening steel edge of the tip penetrated all the layers of his skin, bottoming out against his cheekbone. He wanted to cry out, but clamped his teeth together as she twisted the knife inside his gaping tissue. Streaks of warm blood gushed down the side of his jaw, settling around his neck. Another damn cheek scar, he thought.

She sliced the knife up his cheekbone, carving him like a Krellian grappling hook. The pain increased exponentially as the blade made quick work of his flesh.

"Maybe I should take your eyes," she said with madness in her voice. She pulled the knife out and held it close to her sultry pink lips. Her tongue swept the blood off the weapon and into her mouth.

Lucas watched her throat bulge as she swallowed and sent his life force down her gullet.

"Hmmm, I love the taste of men," she said, smacking her lips together like a German Shepherd eating a gob of sticky peanut butter. "Fear has its own unique flavor and yours is delicious."

Rage swelled inside Lucas, making his jaw clench and his forehead tense. He stared at the female marauder for a split-second to pick a location, then snapped his teeth at her stunningly perfect nose. But the energy web won the battle, keeping him secure and pinned to the table. He knew it was pointless, but tried again anyway. He still couldn't move.

"Nothing to say?" Kristov asked. "Fine. Have it your way." A half-smile hung on her lips. She put the knife over the knuckles on his right hand before raising the dagger into a cutting position.

Lucas turned his head away, figuring she was about to make him permanently left-handed. An onslaught of anxiety took control of his thoughts, urging him to act. It wanted him to talk, to tell her what she wanted to know, it said to avoid the pain, to do it now before it was too late. He fought the urges—he had to—Zack was counting on him to remain steadfast and calm. Somehow he found the courage to kept quiet.

"Wait a minute. I have a better idea," Yakberry said, waddling three steps closer to Kristov. He pushed the rim of his glasses up his cauliflower-shaped nose with his middle finger.

She hesitated for a second, then withdrew the knife. "Explain."

"Let's show him what's in store for him. He'll most surely talk then."

"Excellent idea," Kristov said, pride full in her voice. She stepped out of Lucas' field of vision. "Raise him up."

Lucas felt the table tilt upright, then swing right, his body still glued to the surface of the table. He could see Zack only three feet in front of him.

A six-foot-long mirror hung at an angle from the ceiling just beyond Zack, allowing Lucas to see his friend's face in the reflection. Zack's face was set like cement, showing no emotion, but his eyes were open and looking up. Lucas hoped Zack was planning his next move, something that would save them both.

Kristov looked at Yakberry, then pointed at Zack. "Begin the process."

Yakberry walked to the console, with his back angled sideways to Lucas. He touched a series of icons across the reflective surface of the forward-facing console, making a melody of pings and tones as he worked for a good two minutes. Then the lights in the lab flickered twice and dimmed, and a three-second hum of electrical power filled the room.

An overhead, telescoping device descended in robotic fashion from a four-bolt ceiling mount located above Zack's table. A silver-colored, metallic rod extended and grew longer in one-second intervals, as its various sections appeared from inside each other. This continued until a six-inch, sharp-pointed implement made its appearance from within the last section of the expanding metal shaft.

The instrument inched closer to Zack's right nostril, then entered the opening with force. It pushed its way up his nasal cavity a good four inches, stretching the skin like a python swallowing a rabbit whole. Just as the extension came to a halt, Lucas heard the squishy sound of flesh and tissue being sliced and mutilated, probably his friend's brain matter being violated. Zack's eyes showed panic. His face and neck tensed, but the veteran commando said nothing.

Kristov moved to the far side of Zack's table, then walked its length, never taking her eyes off the captive's face. She leaned in close to Zack. "I've beaten tougher men than you. Come on. Let me hear you scream. I know you want to."

Zack pushed his jaw out and up, but didn't respond.

Lucas could see some kind of round opening on the outside of the extension rod, about two inches from the opening to Zack's nose. It looked metallic and had depth, like a socket for a half-inch-wide rivet.

Yakberry grabbed the end of a clear plastic tube that hung from the console's pedestal. He fastened a screw-on metal plug to the end of it, then pulled the hose toward Zack. He stuck the connector into the side of the nasal probe where Lucas had seen the rivet opening, then he twisted the plug clockwise a quarter turn to lock the connection into place.

The fat man returned to the console and pushed three more icons on his screen.

Lucas heard the momentary sound of power being released, just before Zack's body flinched from head to toe, sending the containment grid into overdrive. Its entire energy web turned a bright red color. The violence shook the table for a good five seconds. Then it stopped. The security web returned to its normal blue color.

Zack's mouth and jaw remained clenched, tighter than before—but he remained silent.

"Phase two, initiated," Yakberry reported, continuing to work his console. "Beginning root-level DNA incursion to transform and recode lateral base pairs sequences."

"Time to completion?" Kristov asked.

"About thirty minutes, depending on the amount of glucose in the subject's blood stream."

"This is going to be epic," Freebo said, with a pitch in his voice that was higher than normal.

"Please stop! You don't have to do this," Lucas said, feeling streaks of blood running down inside his shirt collar.

"Does that mean you're ready to talk?" Yakberry asked.

Lucas looked at Zack, wondering if he should cave. His friend's eyes looked stressed, but Zack's slight headshake told him what he needed to do—keep his mouth shut. He didn't respond to Yakberry, though every cell in his body wanted him to scream at the top of his lungs to stop the heinous procedure.

"I didn't think so," the doc said. "Injecting facilitator compound. Batch two-twelve."

An orange-colored liquid appeared inside the plastic tube, nearest to the console. The substance continued to fill the tube, inch by inch, until it snaked its way to the shaft of the metal probe that was stuck up Zack's nose. The hum of the unit's power transformer increased in frequency, meaning the liquid was being pumped into Zack's brain—a forceful injection to be sure, based on the look of agony across his friend's face.

Lucas studied the color and consistency of the material oozing its way through the tube, wondering if it was a form of Cyrus' micro-bee technology, delivering who-knew-what into Zack's cerebellum.

Moments later, the mercenary released a bone-chilling scream just before his body convulsed within the grip of the fully-charged energy grid. For the next thirty seconds, each side of his shoulders and torso took turns lurching up and down, then his waist and legs shook violently, as the energy matrix changed its color to a deep shade of red.

Zack's face bloated like a helium balloon, expanding to the brink of eruption. Moments later, it deflated just as quickly, making his skin hang loose. His cheekbones and jaw began to elongate and distort as they changed shape, oscillating while the process continued. His entire bone structure was undergoing a violent restructuring by whatever biochemistry Yakberry had just injected into his head.

Lucas could barely watch—the veins in the man's forehead and neck bulged out a good inch, like twisted cords of knotted rope. Zack's arteries began to spurt blood in random locations as the pressure became too intense for his chiseled body to handle.

When the mercenary's chest cavity inflated to at least twice its original size, Lucas decided he had to act. "Stop this!" he shouted. "I'll tell you what you want to know."

"Too late," Yakberry said. "Transmutation sequence has begun. Nothing can stop it now."

TWENTY-THREE

Tethered Consequences

Kleezebee put the nearly-empty jug of raspum back inside the bottom-left cabinet of his kitchen, sliding it carefully into place next to a pair of safety glasses and work gloves. Behind it was a carton of strike-anywhere matches and an unopened box of three-inch galvanized nails. He shut the door and turned to face the center of the room. He leaned his backside against the countertop, taking some of the pressure off his ankle.

He looked down at one of his bare feet. The skin around the ankle joint was red and swollen; it was at least twice its normal size. He shook his head. It had been sixteen months since Fuji had removed the cast, but it was clear that the bones had never healed properly. He was the reason why.

RICE, the monk had told him: rest, ice, compression, and elevation. It sounded good in theory, but it was a recipe that he hadn't had the time to see through.

"Patience is a luxury for the common man," he mumbled to himself, knowing that when the fate of the human race hangs in the balance, shortcuts were inevitable. He had certainly taken his share of them—some with consequences that still haunted him each night in his sleep.

He put the eight-ounce crystal glass full of raspum to his lips and sucked in another swig of pure alcohol. He swirled the liquid around inside his mouth, letting his taste buds soak up the flavor, then he swallowed the gulp whole. He coughed as the liquor ignited his throat muscles. It was his third shot in the past ten minutes, but the ankle pain was finally becoming manageable. His self-medication should be enough to get him through another day, he figured.

The trap door in the center of the room opened. Out came Fuji, wearing his four-foot-long tunic and a smile.

Kleezebee put the etched glass on the counter next to him, then walked to Fuji's position. "Success?"

"Yes. Power systems balanced. Systems calibrated. Additional spheres of E-121 are still required."

"I'm working on it. Should hear back from the team any minute," Kleezebee said, noting the time. "How did the new array of graphene vid-screens work?"

"Perfectly. Three hundred and sixty degrees of coverage. Crystal clear."

"That's good to hear. They cost me five stunners and a dozen power cartridges. I took a major risk when I ordered them, but sometimes it pays to take chances. A guy can never have enough friends, and I use that term loosely."

"Partnering with lawlessness has tethered consequences."

"Most certainly. But Gaylon Reece was my only option. He's a good pipeline to have in town, as long as you don't owe him money or drugs. I just hope those stunners don't end up in the wrong hands. Our tech would be easy to trace."

"And Claude?" Fuji asked.

Kleezebee nodded. "Reported in as planned. Cyrus knows we're looking for the BioTex. I sent a second team in to scour the diner for clues. The only thing we learned is that they were serving food to the public for free. It doesn't make sense. I'm not sure what the SC is up to, but we had better extrapolate alternate scenarios. At least our team was out of harm's way when they torched the place."

"Do you anticipate an inflection point adjustment?"

"Not yet. I think we're still a few steps ahead of him. The endpoint should still be viable. Lucas and company better come through, or this mission ends before it begins. It won't be long before Cyrus tracks us to this location. Once he and Freakshow are on the scent, there's no stopping them. With the predicted narrowing of time approaching, we can't afford to miss it."

"Should we be proactive with the rift-slipping device?"

"You mean dismantle it?" Fuji nodded. "Let's hold off. Lucas needs to believe in your Incursion Chamber first. Otherwise, he'll be a real bear to deal with if we eliminate what he thinks is his only hope of finding Drew. He says his hallucinations have stopped, but I know that's a lie. I can see it in his eyes. Something is off. Way off."

"It has become clear he will do anything to find his brother."

"Frankly, I don't blame him. I'm sure there are things I don't want to know about, but he'll get the job done; he always does. I just wish there was a better way."

"A heavy heart condemns even the most strident man."

"There's a big hole to fill, yes. But we've got work to do. I'm not taking any chances by underestimating the situation, again."

"Time always finds a way," the tiny monk said, looking at the professor with pinched eyes.

Kleezebee put his hand on Fuji's shoulder. "It won't be easy when the time comes, but I need you to keep me on task, no matter what it takes. Understood? We must allow it to happen, just as it should. Don't let me waver. Otherwise, the final reversion can't happen."

Fuji bowed. "As you wish, Professor."

TWENTY-FOUR

Timeless Treasures

Stump Fisher opened the back door to the alley, dragging a thirty-two gallon plastic trash can of garbage from the morning's baking through the threshold. He pulled the waste bin twenty feet across the cracked pavement and through the collection of shadows and rainwater puddles, stopping twice to rest his knees and back. The recent fall down the stairs leading up to his apartment had left him swollen and sore. Ice had built up overnight and he hadn't noticed it, not until it was too late. It was never a good thing when you see your own feet flipping up in front of your eyes, just after you commit your entire balance to the top step of a long cement staircase. Gravity makes short work of an old man's mobility, especially with an extra hundred pounds heaped on your waistline.

He continued walking six more strides until he was standing next to the brown-colored rented dumpster. Pick up was the next morning, and it needed it. Two weeks of trash was piled up inside the bin, and he wasn't sure if there was room for any more.

He stood on his toes to reach the twin pair of lids protecting the top of the dumpster. He flipped both of them open and looked inside to check the free space. A blast of rotten stench rose up from the heap, overpowering his nose. He gagged, then wiped his watery eyes. Despite the pungent odor, his curiosity wouldn't let him look away.

He scanned the contents. Everything looked normal except for a set of thirty-gallon plastic bags in the back left corner. All four were black and each one had its red-tagged ends tied into a knot. One of the bags was about the size of a bowling ball and leaking red fluid, while the rest were full-sized and looked heavy by the way they hung across the uncontained refuse supporting them. But they weren't his; he never used trash bags despite the city ordinance; he always dumped free-willy to save money.

For a second, he thought about opening one of the bags to see what was inside, but that second passed. Better leave well enough alone, he thought, knowing in his gut what type of crime scene might be inside. Someone could be watching him, or it was some kind of homicidal setup. He knew the odds of either of those situations being true were slim—he just wasn't that important. Why would anyone go through that much trouble to frame an old man?

But still, he took a minute to study the second floor windows on both sides of the alley: The curtain were closed on each of the seven windows. There were no signs of movement. He figured the bags must have been dumped by some low-life who was too lazy to take his leftovers to the landfill. He thought about calling the town's pretentious constable to report the suspicious trash dump, but decided against it.

"Fucking vandals," he said, turning away to face the trash barrel he had brought out from the bakery. He kicked the side of the waist-high canister, tipping it over. Its trash spilled into the alleyway in a spiral pattern, shooting away from him in several directions. Stump stood still for a minute with his hands on his hips, studying the mess he had just made. He shook his head in disgust at his own temper.

He bent down and used his right hand to set the plastic container upright, then shuffled around and spent the next few minutes picking up the mess he had made, tossing the refuge into the can one handful at a time. After he was done, he grabbed the bottom of the receptacle with one hand, and the top edge with the other. He lifted the can and flipped it over the edge of the dumpster, barely hanging on to the bottom lip. He shook the litterbin twice, before pulling it back and putting it on the ground.

He decided not to close the lids to the dumpster—maybe some fresh air would rid the area of the stink. Besides, he didn't feel like walking all the way around to the backside of the unit to shut both covers. Why waste the energy or add any more wear and tear to his aching body?

Just then, a black limousine-style skimmer swerved around the far end of the shadowed alley and headed his way. Its headlights turned on, beaming intensity into his eyes. He put his hands in front of his face, trying to block the headlights, just as he heard the vehicle's mercury-powered levitation drive increase its whine to full pitch.

He cracked his fingers open for a long second and looked ahead—the skimmer was traveling directly at him, easily redlining to its top speed. Stump didn't see a person behind the wheel, meaning the skimmer was in auto-drive mode. Stump took two wobbly steps to his right and hurled his pudgy body out of harm's way, landing face-first into a pile of empty wooden crates stacked against the wall to the right of the bakery's back door. The top-most crate broke into pieces with his hands and arms stuck inside.

His plastic trashcan got pummeled and squashed behind him. He thought about having to bend over and pick up all its trash contents again. Then the pummeling stopped, as did the skimmer's engine whine.

He rocked himself back and forth on top of the crates with his hands until he was able to free himself from them. He flipped his rotund frame and sat upright, his lungs puffing air using brisk, choppy breaths.

The stretch skimmer, which was easily forty feet long, backed up slowly, freeing the twisted waste bin from its eight and a half inches of ground clearance. The pressure release made the can swirl around like a ballerina, allowing it to stand upright before it popped open and resumed its natural shape.

The anti-gravity vehicle changed its angle of reverse, slipping into a dimly lit area about fifteen feet away from Stump. He could only see the rear bumper of the skimmer clearly as it crawled in reverse through the shadows toward him.

The old man thought about fleeing, but decided against it. He was in no shape to run and knew he wouldn't get far. With his luck, he'd crack an ankle or pull a hammy. Then he'd need a scooter or wheelchair to get around and probably need help bathing. No thanks, he thought. It's safer to just stand here and deal with this situation—whatever *this* was.

Seconds after the lengthy skimmer came to an abrupt stop, three of the four rear doors opened in perfect unison. A pair of legs stepped out of each door and grew into the backlit silhouette of a towering man. Each had to be close to seven feet tall and three hundred pounds. The breadth of their shoulders dwarfed Stump's robust waistline, and that was no small feat.

"Ah, fuck me," he whispered, as his breath shortened and hands shook. He could almost feel his blood pressure increasing, as it gushed wildly through his veins. His heartbeat pounded at the walls of his chest, making him feel dizzy and lightheaded.

Steam from the underground sewer system rose up through the manhole covers and swayed behind the gang of hulks, reminding Stump of a horrific scene from an ancient movie he once saw about an underground, drug-crazed beast terrorizing a coastal city on Avanti Prime.

The man on the passenger side of the vehicle and farthest away from Stump stood next to the lone remaining closed door of the limo, while the two closest behemoths raced toward him. Within seconds, their powerful grip secured his arms, lifting him off the ground and carrying him forward until he was within arm's reach of the rear bumper.

The third bodyguard bent down next to the unopened rear door of the skimmer. Moments later, he swung it open and then stood at attention like a chauffeur serving his master. A fourth person slid out of the vehicle and stood up, facing away from Stump. He coughed twice, indicating a male, based on the deep tone of voice, and spread out his arms and arched his back.

This latest arrival, who stood maybe five foot nine inches, turned toward Stump and moved slowly through the cascade of shadows highlighting the vehicle. Stump studied him, trying to decipher his identity, but the absence of a forward-facing light source made it difficult to gleam any definitive clues. He could see the outline of a mane of long hair that was loosely curled and trickled down past the neckline, but the man's most noticeable feature was the four-pronged cane that he carried in his right hand, matching his slow and uneven stride.

The slender man seemed to be traveling purposely though the shadows to delay his identity. Even so, Stump noticed something radically different about his physique: The left leg was ultra-thin and tapered from wide to narrow, starting at the knee and ending with the foot. Stump realized it was a peg leg, like a pirate, which made sense given the walking cane and his exaggerated limp.

Finally, the man stepped into the light after reaching the limo's rear bumper. He stood only inches away, almost nose-to-nose with Stump, his neatly-braided gray beard and eye patch now in full view. But the face-to-face position didn't last long.

Pressure swelled along the inside of Stump's elbows, just before a powerful force pressed down on the crown of his back. Stump's legs gave way, sending him to the ground on his knees a foot in front of the semi-crippled man.

"Mr. Fisher, I presume," the long-haired man said, with a calm but firm voice.

Stump nodded.

"My name is Gaylon Reece."

"I know who you are. I don't use drugs, so what the fuck do you want?"

"I sense great hostility in your words. Given your current situation, I, too, might choose to react in much the same way. However, since that is not my nature, I prefer a more measured approach to life, one filled with the sanctity of logic and vigilant reasoning, especially when dealing with terrorists."

"Terrorists? I'm no terrorist. I'm a baker. Now, let me go, you asshole," Stump said, trying to rip his arms free from the two guards. He couldn't.

"I expect that we have dissimilar definitions regarding what constitutes a terrorist. Trust me when I say that it's probably in your best interest if we simply agree to disagree. However, I should remind you to take a moment and think about your current predicament, and factor in which of us is standing, and which of us is on his knees. You are not in control, my friend, so I advise you to choose your words carefully the next time you are permitted to speak. And I strongly suggest that you conduct yourself with some level of decorum."

Reece walked his limp around Stump in a full circle, stopping again in front of Stump. "I'm betting that you, Mr. Fisher, are like everyone else in town. Your have your own interpretation of my reputation. Many of you, no doubt, think of me as a lowlife, omnipotent drug dealer who enforces his rules with unbridled harshness. While some of that may be true, I prefer to think of myself as a resourceful businessman, one who has perfected the art of transacting with a subsection of the populous that society has deemed *less than fortunate*. While that skill set serves me well, most of the time, when I'm alone and inside the tranquility of my own thoughts, I prefer to think of myself as a collector. But not just any collector. My passion is the pursuit of unique, quality items with extraordinary value. Items that, when in capable hands, turn ordinary men into extraordinary men."

"Yeah. Weapons. I get it. What the hell does that have to do with me?"

Reece reacted with a powerful backhand across Stump's jawline, spinning the baker's head to the left. Two teeth flew from his mouth, leaving behind pain, blood, and empty sockets.

Reece leaned in close to Stump's face. "It would be far better for your health if you hold your tongue until I direct a query your way. Understood?"

Stump nodded, though he'd never heard anyone use *query* before. In fact, this Gaylon character used nothing but odd words. Some type of pseudo-intellectual, he decided. But in reality, this guy was just another asshole with long hair. Stump sucked in and swallowed the blood pooling around the empty hollows where his airborne teeth used to be attached.

"In a prior life, I collected a good many things. I started out by amassing the most prestigious collection of Hollywood memorabilia from the twentieth century, especially anything to do with the *Pirates of the Caribbean* movie franchise. It was my pride and joy. I would sit for hours, admiring each and every one of my treasures until the sun started its glorious ascent each morning. Eventually, I managed to scrape together enough capital to open my own retail shop. We traded in anything of value and managed to generate eleven years of increasing profits. You might remember my store? It was called Timeless Treasures."

Fisher didn't answer. He just wanted the windbag to shut the fuck up and get on with it.

"It was located just a few blocks from here, on G Street. But then the unthinkable Krellian invasion happened. My dream ended literally overnight when my neighborhood ceased to exist. So did my leg and eye, leaving me to resemble my favorite character of all time—Captain Jack Sparrow. Life is full of its little ironies, both lovely and perverse. It all depends on your frame of reference. But in the end, I still had to earn a living, so I embarked on a new profession once I recovered from my injuries. A profession that would not only pay the bills, but afford me the luxury of continuing to acquire items that would titillate my senses, which brings us to the reason for my visit. Recently, I acquired a handful of uniquely powerful items from a well-educated associate of mine. They were my most prized assets until late yesterday evening. Unfortunately for you and for me, some nefarious individual dared to enter my home and confiscate these items from my possession. These objects were of great value to me, and I would like them returned to me, immediately."

Stump wanted to answer, but wasn't sure if he should or could. He waited.

"You may answer," the drug dealer said.

"I don't know what you're talking about. I didn't steal anything from you."

"I suspect not. But you do know the man who did. Actually, to be correct, what I should have said is that you *knew* the man who did. A young man, to be accurate."

Stump furrowed his brow. He wasn't sure what the asshole was talking about.

"Did you find the gift I left for you?" Reece asked, with one eyebrow raised. He pointed to the trash bin where Stump had found the collection of smelly trash bags hiding inside.

Stump's head sank, as did his heart. A massive swell of dread took control of body.

"Don't fret, Mr. Fisher. In a way, I did you and your family a tremendous courtesy. Your daughter won't be besieged by any more emotional or physical abuse by her former lover."

Stump stared at the dumpster. "Piston?"

Reece nodded.

"Oh, my, God."

"I'm proud to say that justice was done, and swiftly I might add. He only had to suffer for fifty-eight minutes—a new personal best for me. I'm quite pleased by that fact. There's nothing more profound, or of lasting consequence, than to extinguish the life of a thief."

Stump shook his head, fighting back tears. A short minute later, he looked up at Reece. "So what do you want from me?"

"Shortly before Jerry, or Piston, as you call him, drew his last breath, he admitted that he did steal the stunners from me. Unfortunately for him, they were no longer in his possession. He told me that he left them with a friend for safekeeping. Would you care to hazard a guess who that friend might be?"

Stump had a suspicion who Piston's friend was, but he couldn't bring himself to say her name. He shook his head.

"Where's your daughter, Mr. Fisher?"

"No. No. No. She's got nothing to do with this. Leave her alone."

Reece pressed the tip of his cane into the middle of Stump's heaving chest. "I won't ask again. Where is Carrie Anne?"

"Look. I'll find your weapons and get them back to you. Just don't hurt my daughter. I'm sure Piston forced her to take them. She's innocent."

"No one's ever innocent. We've all got blood on our hands, one way or another. Especially now, after the Krellian incursion left this city in ruins."

"Not my sweet Carrie Anne. She's never hurt anyone—ever."

Reece called for his assistant, who was still standing by the open door to the limo. The man hustled to his side.

"Search this establishment," Reece told him, pointing at the back door to the bakery. "Find what belongs to me!"

The man nodded, pulled out a handgun from the inside fold of his jacket, and entered the bakery.

Stump heard his daughter scream.

TWENTY-FIVE

Mr. Tough Guy

Lucas moved his eyes away from Zack. He couldn't watch his chest heave again under the violence of Yakberry's realignment procedure. He knew if he watched, this horrific scene would remain etched into the walls of his brain forever. He already had more than one nightmare stuck in his synapses; he certainly didn't need another.

He focused his attention on the overhead mirror, staring at the reflection of the fat perpetrator who was orchestrating the torture—Yakberry.

"Entering final stage," the scientist reported to Kristov, while fiddling with his workstation. "However, I'm concerned about a few of these readings."

"Explain," she demanded.

"There appears to be a moderate amount of unexpected cellular breakdown occurring. I'm not sure the subject will hold together."

"Can you fix it?"

"Possibly," the doctor said, pressing icons across the screen of his console. "But the specimen's ultra-lean body fat is problematic. Typically, the glucose coefficient should be at least twenty-two percent higher than it is."

"Just make it work, Doc. Cyrus wants results, not excuses."

"I guess we should have fattened the dude up a bit at one of our feeding stations, first," Freebo added, with a joyous tone to his voice. "So much for Mr. Tough Guy."

"I'll need to adjust the linkage protocols in an attempt to decrease the subject's metabolic rate. If I don't reduce the diffusion efficiency, we'll lose containment before the retrovirus can complete the transmutation process."

"We're still going to need a delayed activation sequence," Kristov said. "Otherwise the evacuation plan is useless."

"Yes, I'm fully aware of that, Commander. I plan to install that feature right after I simplify the injection sequence. It needs to be mobile and less invasive."

Lucas angled his eyes back to check on Zack. He couldn't believe what he saw. The mercenary's tissue was now semi-translucent, like a giant blob of mostly-clear gelatin that was shaped like a human body. He could see his friend's muscles, organs, arteries, and veins, but his skin and bone structure were . . . missing.

The pressure crushing his heart intensified. He knew Zack would never recover from whatever this experiment was doing to him—and he was next. Lucas swallowed a sticky lump of spit in his mouth. Mortality was bearing down on him, but all his mind could focus on was regret for never having found Drew.

Just then, a low-pitched bone-rattling sound echoed from outside the room, shaking everything in the lab for a good five seconds. It sounded like a massive explosion—possibly down the hall.

"Go! Check it out!" Kristov told her men.

Two seconds later, the wall next to the lab door exploded inward, sending Kristov and her men flying across the room along with concrete, metal, and dust. The pressure wave sent the table holding Lucas flopping backward, spinning itself into a horizontal position. Something heavy and thin landed across Lucas' shins.

Intense shredder-fire soon filled the room, sending shock waves of piercing sound through his ear canals. Nanoseconds later, splashes of warm, runny liquid hit his face and arms. Some of it landed on his lips and ran into his mouth. It tasted salty and somewhat metallic, like iron.

A female's voice cried out for help, but instantly, a short blast of shredder fire overtook her screams. More wetness landed on Lucas, just as the room fell silent.

"Lucas?" a male voice called from within the dissipating dust cloud.

He recognized the voice. His heart danced. "Rico, I'm over here!" he shouted, looking down across his nose, just beyond his feet. His body was covered in patches of blood, with a severed arm draped across his legs.

The end of the arm where the bicep should have been was ragged and shredded. It looked like a hunk of warm string cheese after it had been pulled apart. Red fingernail polish was still painted neatly onto the victim's fingernails, even though blood was dripping from several places along the appendage.

Rico's handsome face appeared through the fading dust. "You all right, kid?"

"Yeah, I'm fine, but I thought you were dead. What happened?"

"When you failed to come through on the jump pad, I figured you'd changed your mind about being part of this mission. Zack and I split up to cover more ground in our search for the BioTex. Imagine my surprise when I saw you on stage with the sexy ninja chick."

Lucas thought about telling Rico about the detour he made to the Baaku transport ship, but decided to wait for a better time. "Yeah, I got sidetracked a bit, but at least I made it here."

Rico picked up Kristov's severed arm. He held it in the air, shaking it twice. "Tennis anyone?"

Lucas laughed. "Serves the bitch right. Talk about a big bag of crazy." He looked at Rico. "How the hell did you find me?"

"Comm-chatter. I lifted a transceiver from one of the guards. The first thing I learned in basic, way back when, is that if you want to keep a secret, and I mean *really* keep a secret, don't tell your CO. The best intel comes from cross-talk. Undisciplined grunts *love* to gossip."

Rico ran his hand across the energy mesh at the foot of the table. It changed colors as his hand moved. "How do I get you out of this?"

"See the console to my right?" Rico nodded. "Kill the power. There should be a button—"

Before Lucas could finish the sentence, Rico pointed his rifle and let loose a long burst of shredder rounds, making Lucas' ears ring again.

Yakberry's console exploded into a pillar of smoke and fire. Pieces of the console blew apart, showering Rico and Lucas with wreckage.

The security web de-energized. Lucas sat up, spun his legs off the table and stood up. "Nice shooting, Tex. Not exactly what I had in mind, but it worked."

Lucas wished Rico hadn't destroyed Yakberry's research. He had planned to take a copy of it back to Kleezebee for further analysis. He decided not to mention the disappointment to Rico. Instead, he surveyed the room for more survivors. The guards and Freebo were scattered over the floor—more or less in one bloody chunk each, with no signs of movement.

Rico unzipped a pouch on the front of his equipment vest and pulled out a four-inch gauze pad. He peeled off the sticky strips covering the edges and gave it to Lucas. "This should stop the bleeding until we can get you patched up."

"Thanks," Lucas said, putting the bandage over the fresh wound on his cheek. "Just what I needed, another fucking scar. I've got one hell of a collection, don't you think?"

Rico smiled. "Now we just need to find Zack. He never showed at the rally point."

Lucas put his hand on Rico's shoulder and squeezed it gently. He angled his head to direct the major's attention to the lab table next to them. He cleared his throat. "I don't know how to tell you this, so I'm just going to say it."

Rico didn't respond.

"That's Zack."

"What?"

"Trust me. I watched it happen. That's Zack."

"What the hell did they do to him?"

"Some type of experiment. He's totally jacked. I'm sorry."

Rico rammed the butt of his shredder rifle several times into the stainless steel top of the table Lucas had been lying on, then let out a ten-second, bone-chilling scream. Then, as if a light switch had been flipped off, Rico stood quiet for a good ten-count, as the emotional tsunami ran dry from his face.

He turned to Lucas and spoke in a perfectly calm voice. "Mark my words, Doc. Before this mission is finished, I will kill whoever is responsible for this."

Lucas pointed to the oversized body that was bleeding in the corner. "You already did. Dr. Yakberry."

"Looks like I may have used a little too much explosive."

"Ah, fuck him. Fat bastard."

"Agreed, but I put you at risk, unnecessarily."

Lucas threw his hands out to his sides. "Hey, I'm in one piece. It's all good. The energy field may have protected me."

"Just dumb luck."

"Better to be lucky than good I always say."

"At least the first charge was correct."

"Where was it?"

"Down the hall. Two hundred meters. Bought us some time. They won't be using their comms anytime soon."

Rico studied the lab for a handful of seconds. Then turned to Lucas. "This has Cyrus' fingerprints all over it."

Lucas nodded. "I'm not sure what his end game is, but I've got a *really* bad feeling about this. He's fattening up the locals with free food and it's all part of this experiment, whatever it is."

Rico looked at Yakberry's damaged system console. "I guess I should have found a better way to turn that unit off. I suppose we won't be able to retrieve any data from it?"

Lucas shook his head. "Not a chance. But at least I got a good look at it, so I should be able to relay most of it to the professor during our debriefing."

Rico bent down and put his hand in each of Kristov's pockets, pulling out nothing but air and lint from each one.

"Check inside her top," Lucas said, remembering what he saw when Kristov was on stage in the underground base. "Just try not to linger."

Rico smiled, then slid his hand inside her blouse, and felt around her ample bust line. "Damn, this chick is built. A total waste of a great piece of ass." He pulled out a piece of white paper about four inches long by two inches wide, folded in half, with bloodstains smeared across one corner. He opened it.

"What's it say?" Lucas asked.

"Fisher's Bakery."

"Holy shit!"

"You know the place?"

"Yeah, I'm a regular."

Rico flipped the note over. "Piston. Noon."

"That guy's a total douchebag. A walking cement-head."

Rico's held the note in the air between his first two fingers, waving it back and forth. He seemed perturbed. "Doc? Focus! Do you know what any of this means?"

"No. But I can take you there."

"We should evac," Rico said, with a sense of urgency in his words. "It won't take them long to dig their way here."

"What about Zack?"

"Can you help him?"

Lucas shook his head. "Not my area of expertise, but I'm pretty sure there's no way to undo what's been done to him. He's just not Zack anymore."

"Hell, I'm not sure what he is—certainly not human."

Rico paused for a few moments, then pulled his sidearm from the holster on his belt. He raised the semi-automatic weapon, pulled the slide back and released it before aiming the barrel at the spot where Zack's head used to be. "This is no way for a soldier to die."

Lucas wasn't sure why, but his legs moved him back two steps. Maybe they thought the life-sized blob would somehow explode and shower him with Zack-goo.

Rico pumped three rounds into the mass on the table. The body jiggled from the impact of each shot, but the rounds stuck deep inside the gelatin. One of the rounds stopped only inches from the explosive charge that Rico had injected into Zack's wrist earlier that day. Lucas made a mental note to remind the major to deactivate all remaining charges when they got back to the warehouse.

"Any other ideas?" Rico asked. "We can't leave him like this."

"There's really nothing we can do for him. We should go." Lucas waited for an answer, but Rico froze, staring at his friend's body on the table.

"Major? We gotta' go," Lucas said.

Rico remained transfixed on Zack's body.

Lucas nudged him on the shoulder. "Rico!"

The major snapped out of his funk. "Yeah. Yeah. I'm good."

"Do you have a way out of here? One that doesn't involve a firefight with Kristov's army?"

"I've got it covered. But it's a long walk back," Rico answered, sliding his pistol back into his holster. He turned, slung his shredder rifle over his shoulder and climbed through the rubble leading to the opening in the wall.

Lucas followed him. Just as he stepped into the hallway, he heard a faint moan coming from the lab behind him. He decided not turn around or stop—he needed to report back to Kleezebee before the facts of the experiment leaked out from his memory.

TWENTY-SIX

The One and Only

Wyatt Rutherford stood outside the reverend's private quarters, on the second floor of the hundred-year-old church, staring at the two-line nameplate affixed to the walnut-colored door. He tried to focus his thoughts, but couldn't, not with the video player in his mind reliving every ghastly detail about the deaths that took place during the torching of the Dunn-Rite Café by his squad.

He exhaled a forceful breath, sending a pungent blast of his own breath ricocheting off the door, snapping him out of his twisted daydream. The odor was distinct and powerful, reminding him of the greasy nuts he had eaten for a snack ten minutes earlier. It was certainly better than the lingering stench of burnt flesh that had been haunting him all day. He took a step back to let his nasal passages recover.

The door's placard was made from a finely grained piece of wood and stained black, highlighting its letters—if you could call them that; a better term would have been chicken scratches. They looked as though they had been carved with a corkscrew, and done so by someone with a debilitating nerve disorder.

"Not exactly precision work," Wyatt mumbled.

The first line read *Larry B. Mulcahy*, with the words *Medium & Spiritualist* loosely centered beneath it. A crack in the surface ran down the middle of the sign, at a slight angle from top-left to bottom-right, and the seam was covered with a faded, yellow-colored substance, which was probably glue. A set of four Phillips-style screws held the sign in place, one in each corner, though not uniform in their placement. The screw heads looked to be stripped, possibly from repeated tightening.

The non-believers in town referred to the over-sixty preacher as Crazy Larry, instead of Father Mulcahy, even though several of his most famous paranormal accomplishments had been documented and studied by scores of scholars and academics over the years, none of whom had ever been able to prove him a fraud or a fake. The fiery Irishman seemed to go out of his way in the press to take on all skeptics and critics. He was an easy target: constantly touted himself as the "One and Only," certainly flaming the passions of disbelief. The preacher claimed that his ability to commune with God and heal the sick stemmed from an alien abduction some ten years earlier.

Wyatt took a few moments to run the tip of his index finger across the nameplate, taking in every bump, scratch, and dent that had weathered its surface. He had never met the faith-healer in person before, but had attended several of his recent Sunday demon-purging services. He always arrived early to ensure that his preferred seat in the back-right corner of the last pew was available. But today, neither he nor his soul could sit in the back and hide from damnation.

"You can do this," Wyatt muttered with a half-breath.

He knocked on the door and waited for an answer. None came. The receptionist downstairs had told him that the cleric was in residence, so he knocked again, this time doubling the force. "Father, may I come in?"

Wyatt heard a hollow clicking sound that ended with a deep thud. The door swung opened six inches, then stopped.

Wyatt put his head inside the opening, trying to determine if he should walk inside, but he couldn't see anything. He pushed the door open with his elbow and walked in with a half step, wondering if his shin would impact something inside. The overhead lights turned on the instant his foot landed across the threshold.

Father Mulcahy was standing in the corner with his face pressed against the wall. His arms hung straight down along his sides and he was stark naked—his saggy, wrinkled butt pointed at Wyatt. Dozens of aged, one-inch scars covered his back, arms, and legs and his thinning blond hair was sticking out in all directions.

"Father? May I speak with you?"

The reverend never moved. "Yes, Wyatt. What is troubling you?"

"How do you know my name?"

"The One and Only sees all. The conduit to the salvation has no bounds."

Wyatt wasn't sure how to respond. "I'm not sure if you know, but I've just started attending your services—"

"Last pew on the right. Sunday early service. Five consecutive weeks."

Wyatt was impressed. "I prefer to sit in the back and meditate."

"I sense you come here today with a burdened heart, my son."

"Yes, Father. It's my job."

Mulcahy turned his head to the right, never moving his body away from the corner. He mumbled a long string of words at triple speed, but Wyatt couldn't make out any the words except the last one—*Beelzebub*.

The faith healer spun his head back to face the corner. "Your faith is in conflict with your actions."

"Yes. I've been asked to do some terrible things. Things that I'm not proud of as a man and as a parent. They weigh on my heart. I need forgiveness, Father. And guidance."

The father's voice deepened several levels and slowed its delivery speed, almost as if someone else were speaking. "The men with whom you associate are ripe with contempt for all others. They are true non-believers, sub-creatures of the underworld, destined to burn in the fires of hell for all of eternity. Damnation and pain is their one and only fate. Purge yourself of these demons! Cast out the evil that has forged a stronghold in your soul!"

"I can't just quit. Cyrus would never allow it. He would kill me and my family." Wyatt cleared his throat, battling the emotions gripping his chest. "My wife and I just adopted our first child. She's three. Her name is Mikayla. She's the love of my life. Everything I do, I do for her."

"But at what cost?"

Wyatt shook his head. He didn't answer.

"Let God be your guide back to faith. Choose wisely, before it's too late."

"There must be another option. Something else I can do to redeem myself. Help me, Father."

The preacher didn't respond.

"Please. I beg you. The guilt weighs so heavily on my soul that I can't breathe sometimes."

"There is another choice."

"What it is? I will do anything."

"There is a young scientist who hails from another time and place. He has suffered a terrible personal loss and has since turned his back on God, forsaking all that is righteous. He has chosen a dangerous path of violence in his quest for answers. He, too, is adrift without faith. But together, you two shall rise up from the ashes and conquer the tormentors. His name is—" The preacher's head jerked sideways and he went through another ultra-fast mumble sequence. The last word he spoke this time was *sacrilege.* Then his speech returned to normal speed when he said, apparently to thin air, "Let the healer handle this task." He turned his head one hundred and eighty degrees in the opposite direction. "Agreed," he said with conviction, this time sounding like a group of people answering in unison. He turned his head to face the corner again. Then went silent.

"Father?" Wyatt said with caution. He waited for an answer. None came. "What is the young man's name? How do I find him?"

Mulcahy didn't respond. Instead, his body slid down the wall, landing in a crouched position on the floor. A few moments later, he slid backward and spread out on the floor until he was flat on his back, with his arms out to his side. His body began to shake, sending his legs, arms, and torso flopping in the air like a seizure. The convulsing stopped after thirty seconds. Mulcahy stood up, ran his fingers through his wild hairdo until the mop was semi-combed in slicked-back direction.

He turned to face Wyatt. "How can I help you today?"

"I need to know the scientist's name?"

"What scientist?"

"The one you just told me about."

"I'm sorry, my son. You must be mistaken. You just walked in. We weren't speaking."

Mulcahy looked down at his naked body, but didn't seem surprised. "Oh, crap, not again!"

Wyatt shuffled his feet over to a red-cushioned chair sitting solo by the wall next to the door he'd just entered. He sat down, resting his elbows on his knees, then put his face in his hands. He couldn't hold back the surge of emotions any longer.

Tears exploded, running down through his fingers and onto the floor.

TWENTY-SEVEN

Blood, Guts, and Body Parts

Lucas followed Rico as they made their way through the back alleys of the city. Fisher's Bakery wasn't far, maybe two blocks. Lucas tugged on Rico's shirt when he heard organ music playing in the distance. "You hear that?"

Rico turned and nodded. "You don't hear that every day."

"Must be a party ahead. But I don't recognize the tune."

"Neither do I. Sounds more like special effects music than a song."

Ten minutes later, Rico stopped walking ten feet short of the front door to Fisher's bakery. He pointed across the street. "There's the source of your music—a church. Maybe they were tuning their organ. It would explain the melody, or lack thereof."

Lucas nodded.

Rico looked down the street to his left, then to his right. He put his hand behind his back and lifted the tail of the black shirt he was wearing, pulling out the stunner handgun from inside the elastic waistband of his pants. He flipped on the power core, adjusted its discharge level, then slid it back into his pants.

He turned to Lucas and spoke in a soft, but deliberate tone. "You ready for this?"

"Yeah, but I still think I should have a stunner. What if I need it?"

"Then we've got a serious problem. No offense, but you having a weapon in this situation is a variable I can't control. This is a recon mission. We're here to gather intel, nothing more. The last thing we need is for you to get trigger-happy and turn this into an all-out firefight."

Rico was right. Lucas nodded.

"So, let me do the talking," Rico said. "We don't want to tip them off."

Lucas didn't respond. It felt wrong to agree. Deep down he knew he was better suited to deal with the Fishers than his major; he had known the Fishers for over a year and figured he knew best how to handle them. He feared Rico might use a hardline approach, scaring Carrie Anne off for good. But he knew he wasn't exactly front and center in her thoughts, anyway, so maybe he was over-thinking the situation.

Rico grabbed Lucas' shoulder. "You with me on this?"

"I'm not so sure. I know these people. I eat here all the time."

"That's precisely why I should take the lead. Your history with them puts you in a compromised position. A neutral approach will be more successful. Trust me on this. Just introduce me as your cousin Dave from the Badlands who's just moved here. Tell them I'm looking to purchase a business and would pay top dollar. That way, maybe I can get a good look around the premises."

"Okay, but go lightly on them. Especially the daughter. I still can't believe she's involved with Cyrus. It just doesn't fit. Something is wrong here."

Rico stared at Lucas for a three-count, then rolled his eyes. "Holy shit, you're sweet on this girl. Damn it. I told the professor during my debrief to send me in alone."

"I can handle it," Lucas said, looking down at his feet.

"Have you changed her oil already?"

"No, we're just friends," Lucas answered, thinking about her supple lips, wondering what it would be like to kiss them. He smiled, then looked up at Rico.

"Oh, yeah," Rico said with conviction. "I'm definitely taking the lead on this one. End of discussion."

Lucas decided not to argue the point. He promised Kleezebee he would follow Rico's orders and keep his head down. He nodded.

"What do the Fishers look like?"

"Stump is five-five and runs about two-fifty—all flab. Just look for the balding, crotchety old fart with the word *asshole* painted across his forehead. He'll probably be sitting on a stool in the corner by himself, sporting a stay-the-hell-away-from-me look."

"And the daughter?"

"She's a little shorter. Chunky. Big boobs and missing some teeth. She'll be the one behind the counter doing all the work."

"All right, let's do this," Rico said, turning away from Lucas. He stepped toward the bakery door.

Lucas looked behind him out of habit, to see if anyone else was following them—there wasn't. However, as he turned his head back toward Rico, something caught his eye from across the street: a tall, slender woman wearing a skintight bodysuit with a bird emblem stenciled across the chest.

It was one of the Baaku shaper sisters. She was standing with her back against the front of the Nazarene Church. She didn't wave or smile. Instead, she stood perfectly still, as if she were a religious statue that had been stuffed and mounted on the church wall. Her uniform wasn't silver this time; it was bright orange. Her hands and fingers were pressed together in such a way that they formed the shape of a triangle.

Lucas reached behind him and grabbed Rico by the arm, spinning him around. He looked Rico in the eye, leaning in close to whisper. "Do you remember when I told you earlier that I got sidetracked a bit on my way to Kristov's underground complex?"

Rico eye's tightened, responding with a single head nod.

"Look behind me, across the street. See the skinny old lady in the orange bodysuit? She's the reason why."

Rico leaned to his right, looking beyond Lucas. "What lady?"

Lucas turned, but didn't see the alien. "Shit. She was just there."

Rico furrowed his brow. "Nice try, Doc. But now's not the time."

"I'm dead serious," Lucas said, pointing his index finger across the street. "She was standing right in front of the church, staring at us. I'm not bullshitting you."

"Well, she's not there now," Rico said, with a look of disbelief on his face. He pulled the door open. "Let's go. We've got work to do. Secure the door," he ordered, stepping inside and veering to the right, heading toward the restaurant's seating area.

Lucas locked the door from the inside, then followed Rico, wondering if he were hallucinating again. But why now and why here? Who in their right mind dreams about a Baaku-shaper-bitch making a Delta symbol with her fingers in front of an old church? Sure, it was Fuji's mathematical symbol for change, but what the hell did that have to do with anything? He shrugged it off. Too much stress today, he figured.

As soon as he navigated his way through the tiny foyer and entered the bakery's main seating area, he couldn't believe what his eyes were reporting to his brain.

Stump Fisher was lying on his back, near the left end of the service counter, bleeding from a four-inch gash in his forehead.

But that wasn't all—there was a fist-sized, gaping hole in the center of his oversized belly gushing blood, too.

Rico pulled the stunner from his waistline, taking a defensive stance just three feet in front of Lucas. He aimed the gun at several locations in the room, then he worked his way to the far side of the room in seconds. "All clear," he said.

Lucas could see at least seven other bodies scattered about the bakery, each with missing limbs and blood squirting from multiple wounds. None of the bodies, except Stump's, still had its head attached.

Gallons of blood spatter and hundreds of chunks of human tissue and brain matter covered the walls, ceiling, and floor of the bakery—all dripping to the ground. The scene looked fresh.

Lucas turned his head away, covering his mouth with his hand as he doubled over. Nausea flared up in his gut, sending a golf-ball-sized dollop of stomach bile up through his esophagus and into his mouth, flooding his tongue with the acid taste. He spit it out, fighting the urge to let any more of the rancid substance make its way up his gullet. It worked. He stood up and wiped the beads of sweat from his brow.

The horrific scene reminded him of the double-date night back on his version of Earth when he and Drew were meeting Abby and Jasmine on the steps of the Student Union, where the first Krellian incursion ripped a hole in Earth's space-time—blood, guts, and body parts were everywhere, but Lucas didn't see any signs of a Krellian energy dome or a recent inter-dimensional rift, so he believed the patrons were attacked by a squad of assailants. This was probably Freakshow or Cyrus' work. Yet, there were no signs of blast patterns, bullet holes, casings, or shredder rounds anywhere in the room, at least not in visible range. Maybe the attackers had used some new type of weapon, something they hadn't seen before.

He sniffed, taking in a distinct smell of fresh oranges in the air. It was almost powerful enough to mask the stench of death. He started thinking about the unique citrus scent. He'd smelled it before, more than once, but never this strong. Just then, his mind flashed a vision of Carrie Anne's rosy cheeks and her infected belly button piercing. Where was she?

"Carrie Anne!" he called out with his loudest voice, rushing to the closest victim. He prayed the corpse wasn't the sweet, tender woman who had captured his heart and invaded his dreams.

He checked the first body and detached head—they belonged to a man—slender, blond, maybe fifty, partial beard and lying on his back. Not her, he told himself quietly, checking off one fatality on the list that was forming in his mind.

"Please, don't let her be here," he mumbled, continuing the frantic pace. The next five fatalities were also men, but Lucas wasn't sure until he turned them over to inspect their chests for signs of the female form.

One more body to check. It was lying on its right side, facing the wall, in the corner opposite Stump, by the checkout register and padded stool.

Its physique was that of a shorter, overweight person wearing a wraparound apron. Could be Carrie Anne's. The hair length and color were correct. Maybe she was taking payment from one of the customers when this tragedy happened. Oh no, he thought, as a feeling of heartbreak suffocated his chest.

He headed toward the cadaver, but his feet slipped out from under him when his heels surfed through a pool of blood surrounding another body along the way. His legs flew up in front of his face, as his body hurled itself in the air a few feet off the ground. Seconds later, his back slammed into the floor with a stern thud. He rolled over, gasping for breath, as pain surged through his spine and into his chest. It took a long minute, but he recovered his breath and stood up.

"Damn, that had to hurt," Rico said, with a splash of amusement in his voice.

"You have no idea," Lucas replied, shaking his head.

He could feel a warm dampness flooding the back of his pants and shirt. He craned his neck to get a peek. The visible areas of his clothing were soaked in a deep shade of red. So were his hands. He wiped them off on the front of his legs, taking an extra few moments to clean off the area between his fingers.

"You all right?"

"Yeah, just need a minute," he answered, blinking his eyes repeatedly. He took one more deep breath to fully charge his lungs. The cobwebs in his head were still thick, making him a little woozy after the fall. He walked unevenly to the last body, bent down, and rolled the carcass over.

The remains were that of another man. He exhaled quickly. "I don't think I could have handled that," he mumbled, thinking about Carrie Anne lying there bloody and in pieces.

"Hey, Doc? This one's alive," Rico said with a sense of urgency in his voice.

Lucas turned.

Rico was standing a few feet from Stump's body with his legs spread and stunner pointed at Fisher's head in a firing position, as if he expected the fat old man to somehow rise up and attack him.

"That's Stump. Is he conscious?" Lucas asked, walking to Rico with carefully-planted footsteps. He changed his course to avoid as much of the blood as possible.

Rico bent down on one knee, just to the left of Stump. He tapped the wounded man on the cheek. "Barely. He's lost a lot of blood. Won't be long."

"Ask him about his daughter. Where is she?"

Rico stared at Lucas for a handful of seconds, tilting his head slightly—then looked at Stump. "Mr. Fisher? Can you hear me? I need to know what happened here. Who did this?"

Stump didn't respond. Rico asked the same question, this time in a louder voice. Stump still didn't answer.

Lucas joined Rico at the old man's side. "Stump? This is Lucas Ramsay. Where's Carrie Anne?"

Stump opened his eyes, turning his head to look at Lucas. He sat up slightly, then grabbed Lucas by the shirt collar, pulling him close. "The Collector took her," he said in a weak, slow voice. "He wants his weapons back in seventy-two hours or he will kill her."

"Who the hell is the Collector?" Lucas asked the old man.

"You have . . . to . . . save—her. Promise . . . me."

"We will. You have my word on that. But we need to know who took her."

Fisher's head dropped back to the floor and tilted to the side, as a shallow exhale released from his chest. The baker's eyes went blank.

Rico put two fingers against the side of the man's neck. "He's gone."

Lucas pounded the floor with his fist. "Damn it! Just a few more seconds."

"The Collector?" Rico asked.

"I don't know. But if he took her to get his weapons back, why kill her old man?"

"Doesn't make any sense. Who kills the parent *before* the ransom is paid?"

"Only a moron."

"Or a psychopath," Rico said, scanning the room. "Whatever this was, there's intense emotion behind it. This was an extermination."

"Maybe someone else did this. Like Cyrus or Freakshow."

"Okay, but why?"

Lucas shrugged, thinking about the note Rico found inside Kristov's top. "It's possible that Piston was supposed to meet Kristov here for some type of weapons exchange."

"Fisher may have been providing a neutral site for the meet."

"Or he was the one selling the weapons." Lucas wished they hadn't killed Kristov earlier. "When Kristov didn't show, Piston went nuts and slaughtered everyone. I wouldn't put it past him."

"That still doesn't explain who The Collector is, or why he took his daughter."

"Well, it's a theory," Lucas said, standing up to unkink his knee.

"Maybe, but it's pretty thin."

"Hey, thin in my middle name," Lucas said with a smile, pointing both index fingers down at his skinny frame.

"With Kleezebee's cooking, I can see why," Rico said, laughing.

"Have you tried the man's omelet? I don't know what he uses for ingredients, but it tastes like ass," Lucas said, laughing through the words. He walked the room, checking three of the severed heads. He studied the angle and size of the outward-facing tissue hanging from the hole in the top of each skull. "It looks like their heads exploded from the inside—pushing the brain matter up and out, with tremendous force. What kind of weapon can do that?"

"Nothing I've seen, or ever heard of, for that matter."

Lucas looked at the door to the kitchen. "We should search the back. There must be some clues around here somewhere. Carrie Anne told me their apartment is on the second floor and the office is on three."

Rico didn't hesitate. He bolted through the kitchen door with Lucas right on his heels.

"You take the kitchen and freezer. I'll check upstairs," Rico said. "Meet back here."

"Copy that."

TWENTY-EIGHT

Delta Lima Kilo

Wyatt slid out of the deteriorating bench seat in the first row of the Mag-lift train, paid the exit fare to the operator with a single swipe of his digi-card, and walked at half speed toward the sprawling entrance of the Supreme Commander's fenced-off, forty-acre residence in New Robyn City.

A pair of twenty-foot-tall Roman-style pillars bracketed the steel-reinforced front gate that was wide enough for two heavy transport skimmers to enter at the same time. A red horizontal sign hung over top of the gate and stretched from one pillar to the other. Its white letters spelled *W A R N I N G !*

A fixed spotlight sat on top of each column, with its lens angled at the ground in front of the gate. Just to the outside of each pillar was a black, six-inch pole that rose up from the ground to match the height of the spotlights. A large-caliber shredder gun sat on top of each pole with a set of heavy-teeth gears and other rotating metalwork underneath. Wyatt assumed they were being controlled remotely, probably by someone on the inside. If he were right, that meant some type of video surveillance was being used as well, though he couldn't see any evidence of that from his position.

He studied the area around the gate, but didn't see any type of intercom or communication system. He wasn't sure how he was supposed to announce his presence. He had never been summoned to the SC's compound before and was a little worried that this might be some type of ambush or interrogation. It was possible that the supreme commander had heard about his spiritual visit with Father Mulcahy and was planning some type of retribution. He said a silent prayer asking for safe passage and forgiveness from the One and Only.

A handful of multi-story watch towers were in range, just inside the compound's perimeter fence, each manned by two guards with shredder rifles and a flamethrower. Wyatt found it odd that troops weren't stationed outside the gate in order to discourage anyone from approaching the residence uninvited. He figured they must have deployed some other type of deterrence system.

As he approached the front of the compound, he bent down and picked up a chunk of metal pipe sitting in a pile of construction waste to his right. He tossed it at the gate. When the three-inch cylinder touched the metal structure, the spotlights lit up almost as quickly as the gate shot arcs of electric current across its heavy-gauge frame. The pole-mounted guns rose up three feet, cocked themselves, swung around, and pointed their barrels at Wyatt's position. He put his hands over his head and didn't move.

"This is a restricted area. Identify yourself," an amplified voice said.

Wyatt drew in a deep breath to fully support his words. "My name is Sergeant C. Wyatt Rutherford. I was summoned here at the request of the Supreme Commander. My ID number is Delta Lima Kilo Two-Twelve. Alpha squad."

A minute later, the swing gate rolled open on its eight-inch caster wheel, revealing a squad of six armed soldiers. They sprinted toward Wyatt and quickly surrounded him, their weapons held high and tight. Two sets of hands searched his pockets, pant legs, shirt sleeves, and inside his vest, pulling out nothing but air. Wyatt knew better than to show up armed for a meeting with his boss.

One of the men behind him rammed the muzzle of his shredder rifle into the small of Wyatt's back, pushing him forward with a firm lurch. "Inside. No sudden moves," the man said, with a slight lisp in his words.

Wyatt surrendered, allowing the men to usher him through the gate and inside the compound. The group walked through a maze of grassy areas that were bordered by three-foot-tall brick walls that served as the base for a line of flower pots surrounding each segment. The landscaping was rich everywhere he looked, beaming with perfection. Each area was staffed by a stunning blond-haired woman dressed in simple attire, who appeared to be watering and pruning the potted plants in her section. None of them made eye contact with Wyatt.

Three spacious homes stood to the left, just beyond the plush landscaping sections; each was two-stories tall, trimmed with expensive-looking rolled shutters, solar-infused roofing plates, and spacious front porches. Wyatt assumed the largest one to the right was the Supreme Commander's. Oddly, though, there were no trees, just endless amounts of grass, manicured bushes, and blooming flowers.

Off to the right and closer to the rear of the compound was an open dirt field where a gigantic contraption was being built. It looked like a multi-platform mobile landing base for transport ships, except each deck had a slew of super-sized gun turrets lined up across the top. Wyatt wondered if it was the new Stunner Deck that Freakshow had told him about.

Ten minutes later, they arrived at the base of an overly tall, single-story tan-colored cement building that looked more like the bottom part of an elevator shaft that apparently went nowhere. It was near the middle of the forty-acre encampment; nowhere near the homes Wyatt passed earlier. The building was maybe fifteen feet square and had no windows, just a single door at the base and a plain metal roof. It looked more like a maintenance shack than anything else. Above the door was a quartet of black letters twelve inches tall that read *SCIC*.

A thick tree stump stood to the right of the door with a red-handled ax lying sideways across its top. It was covered with what looked like blood. Behind it were three pairs of chains with hand shackles hanging from the wall, each pair positioned above a set of leg irons that were welded to posts buried in the ground.

The hair on the back of Wyatt's neck stood up and tingled. "Uh, where are we going?" he asked, stopping to evaluate his options.

The man leading the escort group didn't answer. He nudged Wyatt in the back with his gun again, this time with added force.

The door to the shed opened. The Supreme Commander stepped out, wearing what looked like fleece pajamas; his long, wispy hair blew leisurely in the eastern breeze.

"I'll take it from here," Cyrus told his men. They quickly backed away from their close-quarter escort position around Wyatt.

"Come inside," the commander said, sliding his arm around Wyatt's shoulders. "There's something we need to discuss."

They walked side-by-side into the tiny building. It was empty inside, with no furniture, tools, weapons, or people. There was only a second door on the opposite side of the fifteen-foot room.

The SC used his free hand to swing the door closed behind them, then he led Wyatt forward a few more steps until they were standing a few feet in front of the second door. Wyatt assumed they were about to exit the backside of the shack, which of course didn't make any sense.

A pleasant citrus aroma rose up and invaded Wyatt's nose, canceling his internal panic alarm. The hairs on his neck softened and wilted against his skin.

Cyrus released his arm from Wyatt's neck and took two steps to the left. An orange-colored, wide-angle laser beam appeared from a round, one-inch metal extrusion just above the exit door. It washed over Wyatt from head to toe in a slow, but consistent manner. When it reached the ground, it shrank in size and disappeared as a pinpoint of light.

"Excellent," Cyrus said, "You are who you say you are."

Wyatt wasn't sure what to say to that remark, so he kept his mouth shut.

When Cyrus stepped in front of Wyatt, a chest-high section of the wall next to the door faded away, and was replaced by a silver-colored metal plate about the size of a standard sheet of writing paper. The commander put his hand on the plate and held it there for a three-count. When he removed his hand from the unit, it began to glow a bright orange color, outlining the contact points where his hand and fingers had been. Speckles of blue light danced across the plate for a few moments, then the back door opened.

Wyatt couldn't believe his eyes. Inside was another room, much larger than the tiny shack, maybe fifty feet across and easily just as deep. Cyrus stepped inside. Wyatt followed, trying to make sense of the paradox.

The room was decorated with two lounge chairs, a coffee table, a leather couch, a dining room table and chairs, and a row of bookshelf units containing hundreds of paperback books arranged in size from small to large. A small kitchen area was just beyond the dining table, and a king-sized bed with at least six fluffed pillows was to the right. Next to the bed were a pair of doors which Wyatt figured were closet doors.

"How is this possible?" he asked his boss, wondering if this was some type of illusion. However, it was possible they'd just transported to a new location. He was aware of the Jump Pad system that the SC had acquired from Dr. Kleezebee, but this obviously wasn't that.

"I've acquired some amazing new technology," Cyrus answered. "Something only a select few know about."

"I'm honored, sir."

"As you should be."

"Are we still in your compound?"

"Yes, exactly where you think you are. We can now reshape parts of our environment at will."

Wyatt was impressed. "So, this is where you live?"

Cyrus turned and nodded. "I prefer to keep my location on a need-to-know basis. It's much more difficult for insurgents to launch an assault if they don't know where I am."

"That's an understatement," Wyatt mumbled, trying to wrap his head around this stunning achievement. "I thought you lived in one of the nice homes I saw on the way in."

"That's where I keep my stable—"

"Of women," Wyatt added, disgusted, wondering how many beauties the man kept captive as sex slaves.

"Misdirection is the key to concealment. If my enemies are focused on the answers I choose to give them, then I always know what they are thinking."

"And what their next move will be."

"Precisely. But that's not why I asked you here today," Cyrus said, sitting in the black easy chair. He pointed to the other leather chair, closest to Wyatt. "Please. Sit."

Wyatt sat down, but decided not to lean back. He didn't want to appear too comfortable in front of his capricious boss. He kept his back straight up with his feet planted on the ground. It was his version of sitting at attention. It also gave him a split-second advantage, just in case he needed to get up and take a defensive stance or make a run for it.

"Sergeant, you've been a member of Alpha Squad for what, a year now?"

"Thirteen months, eleven days, sir."

"I've read your performance reviews. Excellent work."

"Thank you."

"Have you noticed anything out of the ordinary, lately?"

"In regards to what?" Wyatt asked, wondering if the SC was talking about him or his squad leader, Freakshow.

"Odd behavior. Hysterics. Inconsistency. Any leadership issues that I should be concerned with that might compromise the next phase of my plan."

Wyatt's mind quickly drew a list of at least a hundred items—any one of which could have had Freakshow committed to the nuthouse. "Odd? No, sir. Things are pretty much status quo as far as I can tell."

Cyrus pinched his brow and tilted his head, as if he were evaluating Wyatt's choice of words. But he didn't say anything.

"May I ask why?"

"Secondhand reports have come in that my most-trusted friend has been demonstrating characteristics that are outside his, shall we say, colorful nature."

Colorful wasn't the word Wyatt would use to describe Freakshow. "It's true, sometimes he's a little unpredictable. But I'm a hundred percent positive he's on board with your plans."

"I don't doubt his loyalty. It's his mental state. I'm concerned he's not firing on all cylinders. Take what happened earlier at the café."

"When he walked off into the corner and seemed to argue with himself?"

Cyrus nodded.

"Okay, I agree. That was a little strange. Even for him. But he carried out your orders to the letter."

"This time, yes. But that might not be the case in the future. It doesn't take much for a mission to unravel. If it does, I need to know that I can count on you to step in and take charge."

"Consider it done, SC," Wyatt said without hesitation. His mind drifted for a moment, as he considered how badly Freakshow would react if he were forced to take command away from him. He prayed it would never come to that. If it did, he'd probably have to kill Freakshow, then deal with his loyal guards. That would mean more blood on his hands and even more confessional visits with Father Mulcahy. Then Wyatt's paranoia kicked into high gear. He worried that Freakshow might be nearby, possibly listening in on this conversation. He looked around. "Is he here?"

"Not yet. But he's on his way. He has information about Kleezebee's location."

"Excellent news."

"Kleezebee and that universe-jumping asshole Ramsay have been a major thorn in my ass ever since I let them walk. That won't happen again."

"Lucas Ramsay. . . . He's a scientist, right?"

"I'm not sure you could call him that. Not anymore. Not since he lost his little brother. That twisted little fuck has been torturing people for information, including several of our most trusted operatives."

An answer popped into Wyatt's head. He now understood who Father Mulcahy wanted him to help.

Cyrus bit his lower lip. "But that little shit will get his as soon as the Stunner Deck is complete and operational. All we need now is the necessary power, then my little QED can rise up and destroy all those who oppose me, both foreign and domestic."

236

"Is there anything I can do to help facilitate that?"

"Yes, I want you to take a squad and visit an old friend in Flandreau City. Convince him to return what's rightfully mine."

Wyatt assumed his boss was talking about the drug lord, Gaylon Reece. "A friend?"

"Technically. He used to be a rival. But now he's just a royal pain in my ass, but that won't matter soon."

"Correct me if I'm wrong, sir, but didn't you sell the modules to him?"

"Now I'm un-selling them. Is that a problem?"

Wyatt shook his head.

"We have a contact in town that should be able to arrange a meet for you. The man will trade for anything—that'll be our way in. Just don't let on that we know what the spheres are and how to use them. Otherwise, he'll gouge us on the price. You've never met the man, right?"

"Never."

"Once you have the modules in hand, we'll go in weapons hot. Kleezebee and company won't know what hit them, literally. Cellular disruption is quite effective."

"And painful, I'll bet."

"Kleezebee is the only one on this entire planet capable of stopping our new tech. I can't take that chance. Not when we are so close to my dream. Before I send you on your way, there are two other matters we need to discuss."

Ah, crap. Here it comes, Wyatt thought. "Anything, sir."

Cyrus took the digi-pad from the coffee table and gave it to Wyatt. The screen lit up, showing two photos side-by-side. One was a tall, beautiful women dressed in sexy leather attire and the other was a balding, fat, black man. "Do you know these individuals?"

"Yes, the woman is Commander Kristov. I am not familiar with the gentleman."

"His name is Dr. Marcus Yakberry. He's a reverse engineering specialist from Avanti Prime. Quite possibly the smartest man in the entire galaxy. I've just pulled him from Special Projects and sent him to work with my ex-girlfriend, so they may test our new realignment process. But sometimes she doesn't take well to strangers."

"Kristov?"

Cyrus nodded. "I haven't heard from her in a couple of days. Communications are down again." He sighed. "Damn it, I never should have gotten involved with that woman. She can be a real vindictive bitch when she wants to. I'm not sure if she's pissed at me again, or just ignoring me. Wouldn't be the first time."

"I know what that's like. My wife can be a real handful."

"She didn't take it well when I ended it with her," Cyrus said, shaking his head. "She said I was at the top of her Fuck-Off List, whatever that means. Never get involved with a slut from the 'hood. Everything they do is tied to an agenda. Nothing is real or genuine. And that temper of hers—"

Wyatt didn't respond. He didn't want to flame the anger swelling in his boss.

"But, she's still an effective leader. I need you to pay her a visit. Smooth things over for me."

"Not a problem, SC. I'll make it my top priority."

"Excellent. Then recover the modules and meet us at the rally point. I'll send coordinates," Cyrus said, flying out of his chair. "I think it's time that I show you my most prized possession."

Wyatt smiled, stood up, and followed his boss. They walked to the pair of closet doors just to the left of the bed.

Cyrus pulled open both doors to reveal an all-glass cabinet to the right and a vertical, seven-foot-tall steel box to the left. He put his hand on the side of the glass cabinet and flipped on the internal lights to reveal a set of five shelves—each with four severed heads sitting on them, facing out. All of the heads were missing their eyes. Just hollow sockets remained.

Wyatt gasped, making it difficult to maintain his composure.

"These are previous team members who failed me. There's always room for one more. Understood?"

Wyatt nodded, fighting the urge to hurl chunks. He did, though it wasn't easy.

Cyrus pointed to the walls, floor, and ceiling of the closet. Every square inch of its interior was covered with some type of metal plate. Each plate was two feet square and covered with a crisscrossing pattern of unshielded, heavy-gauge electrical wire. "I had the interior lined with six-inch-thick tritanium."

"For radiation protection?"

"Not exactly," Cyrus answered, grabbing the handle on the coffin-like metal box. "It's a neuro-shield that's been supercharged with a perfectly modulated grid of exactly two hundred twelve amps. It keeps the seekers at bay."

Wyatt didn't understand the "seekers" reference. Was he talking about Dr. Kleezebee, or someone else?

"This is the Holy Grail of information and technology," Cyrus said, opening the lid.

Wyatt's jaw dropped open.

Inside the box was a slender, older woman wearing a silver-colored pantsuit with a bird emblem across the chest. Her arms, legs, neck, and midsection were chained to the sides of the container. A handful of wires and tubes hung from her arms and neck, looping around her body.

Wyatt made eye contact with her, but she didn't react.

"I finally managed to capture one of the Baaku shapers," Cyrus said proudly. "The final piece to the puzzle."

TWENTY-NINE

Door Nazi

Lucas slid a wooden stool next to the trio of commercial-grade, Lightwave Mark II cooking ovens stacked on top of each other, just to the end of the food prep station. He sat down and spun the back of the stool around in such a way that he could rest his elbow on the cutting table while viewing the first nine steps leading up to the second story. Rico was upstairs, conducting a search of Fisher's apartment and office and was due back any minute. Lucas thought about running upstairs to help him, but the major had told him to wait here, so that's exactly what he'd do.

His mind drifted, imagining Carrie Anne sauntering down those same steps, making her way to the very spot he was sitting and leaning over the food table to spread out a few cups of flour in preparation to knead a batch of homemade dough. His favorite treat was her famous twenty-four-inch, hungry-man Danish. It was rolled out like a long, one-inch-thick breadstick, then twisted into an over-under, rope-like pattern until it formed a giant ampersand symbol. It was smothered with powdered sugar and a mound of fresh-picked cherries. Damn thing was so good, he ordered it every time he came to visit her. Not exactly healthy for his arteries, but he didn't care. What a sugar rush.

A minute later, Rico trotted down the stairs with a stack of invoice-style papers in his hand. He fanned them out and gave them to Lucas. "What do you make of these, Doc?"

Lucas flipped through the cream-colored receipts, counting them as he went—there were eighteen. Each one was for the amount of $497.50 and dated on the twenty-fourth of the month. "These are tollway receipts from Earth, the Boston Embarkation Station."

"Did you notice the date of the first invoice?"

Lucas scanned the paperwork, looking for the earliest receipt. He found it and studied it. He didn't recognize the significance of the date. He shook his head.

"It's the day of the Krellian invasion," Rico said.

"You're right. I totally forgot that date. If I remember right, the time stamp indicates he had just left Earth when the bugs attacked."

"Lucky bastard."

"I'm not so sure it was luck," Lucas said.

"You think he was involved? How?"

"I don't know, but it has to mean something. Things like that just don't happen by accident," Lucas replied, searching his memories. He didn't recall Carrie Anne ever mentioning that she had been to Earth or that her old man had been there, either. "Why would Fisher ever need to go to Earth? And how would he get there? The man can barely walk."

Rico nodded. "Transports are ridiculously expensive."

"Yeah, no shit. So are the tollway taxes," Lucas said, flipping through the receipts a second time. "Did you notice that this month's receipt is missing?"

"Is that significant?"

Lucas shrugged. "Just seems odd, that's all. Why this month?"

"Cyrus *has* been cracking down on civilian use of transports. Maybe that explains it?"

"You're probably right," Lucas said, even though it all felt a little too convenient. He had a hard time believing in coincidence or luck, not after all the bullshit he'd been through. But it didn't seem worth the effort to argue with Rico, so he let it go. For now.

"You find anything?" Rico asked.

"Yeah, you could say that," Lucas said, holding back a smile. He waited for a reaction from his boss.

Rico didn't respond. He pushed his chin out and folded his arms across his chest.

Not the reaction Lucas expected. "There's nothing interesting in the kitchen. But I did find a hidden compartment in the back of the walk-in."

"Everyone loves their hidden compartments. You'd think people would get the hint: It's the first thing we look for."

"It was tucked behind several stacks of empty boxes. It doesn't look like Fisher throws much of anything away."

"Did you check inside?" Rico asked, with a thick layer of sarcasm in his voice.

"Wanted to. But the Door Nazi had other plans."

"The what?"

"A bio-sentry scanner."

"What kind?"

"Retina. We'll need to drag the old fucker back there and stand him up. Gonna take both of us."

"Not necessarily," Rico said, searching the slide-out drawers under the food prep station. He pulled out a thin-handled carving knife. He ran his index finger over the blade. "This will do nicely."

"I think I'll just wait here," Lucas said, not wanting to watch Rico carve a melon ball out of Fisher's eye socket.

"I need you to hold his head still. Otherwise, I won't get a clean removal. We only get two shots at this, so we better make them count."

"I take it you've done this before?"

"A few times. It's really not that difficult once you get the hang of it."

Lucas couldn't imagine ever needing to perform this type of removal again—not if he had anything to say about it. He followed Rico into the seating area and knelt down next to the old man's lifeless remains. He put his hands around the sides of Fisher's bloody skull, turning the man's head to face straight up.

Rico put the tip of the knife close to Stump's left eye.

Lucas turned his face away, keeping firm pressure on the victim's head to hold it still.

"This is a skill that all field operatives need to know," Rico said, with an authoritative voice.

Lucas shook his head, still not looking down. "No, I'm good. Go for it, Major."

"You need to learn this. That's an order!"

Lucas looked at Fisher's face, staring at his cauliflower-shaped ear instead of the knife. Maybe he could get away with using his peripheral vision, that way he didn't have to actually watch the barbaric surgery that was about to come next.

"Eyes here," Rico said, pointing his index finger to Fisher's eye.

"Okay, but if I yak, don't blame me," Lucas said, adjusting his eyes. The partially-digested food in his stomach began its march up his throat.

Rico's pressed the knife against the inside of eye socket. "The key is to keep the angle straight along the side, using even pressure as you go,"—he leaned forward, pressing the knife inside; it went in deep—"then you just ease it out, carefully," he said, leveraging the knife to the side. The man's eye slid out.

Lucas turned his head and blew a stream of chunks several feet past Rico's shoulder, but he never let go of Stump's head. Some of the vomit dripped down his chin, clinging to the underside of his neck. He leaned his head to his arm, using his shirt sleeve to wipe off as much of the puke as he could reach.

Rico held the eyeball in his fingers, still close to the man's socket. "Then you just clip the tissue connecting the eye, and bingo, it's free." He held the eye in front of Lucas, close enough for him to smell it. "Piece of cake, Doc."

"That's easy for you to say," Lucas said, pulling his hands away from Stump. He finished wiping the hurl off his chin, then stood up and followed Rico into the kitchen. They walked to the walk-in fridge. "It's all the way in the back. To the left."

Rico pulled the heavy door open and he and Lucas entered, quickly moving to the rear. They stood together in front of the scanner. Rico held the eyeball in front of the sentry unit's optical scanner for a three count. Moments later, the LED view-screen flashed **Stump Fisher. Access Granted** in bold, red-colored letters.

Lucas pulled the door to the compartment open, waving his hand to tell Rico to enter first. He did. Lucas went in next.

The hidden room was not very big, maybe six feet by four feet, but it was filled from floor to ceiling with stacks of moving-box-sized containers. Each box was made of composite plastic-like material and its edges were reinforced with wire straps. The phrase THIS END UP - FRAGILE was handwritten in black ink on the sides of each box.

"High tensile steel banding—something heavy must be inside," Rico said, his breath billowing into the chilled air. He pulled out a multi-tool knife, flipping open the wire-cutter attachment. He used the tool to make quick work of the metal strapping surrounding the box that was sitting on top of the first stack. He removed the top of the box and looked inside. "I'm not sure what this is. Some kind of liquid in a glass container."

"Let me have a look at it," Lucas said, nudging Rico aside. He looked inside. He smiled. "Fuck me. We finally found them!" he said, thinking about all the times he had stopped at the bakery to see Carrie Anne. "I can't believe they were here the whole damn time."

"What are they?" Rico asked, with a whiff of excitement in his words.

"It's the BioTex we've been searching for. These are the rest of our crew," Lucas said, counting the containers in the room — twenty three. Lucas counted the boxes a second time. Same answer. "Looks like one is missing."

"Fisher must have been storing them for Cyrus."

"Yeah, in the one place we would never look for them. Talk about hiding them right under our noses."

"But why here? Why not at his base in New Robyn City?"

"BioTex is completely useless without the activator enzyme. Probably didn't know what else to do with them."

"You don't think Fisher was planning on serving this stuff as filling for a pastry?"

"God, no. That's disgusting."

"Which one is your friend Bruno?"

"Any of them. All of them. It doesn't matter," Lucas said, deciding how best to describe the reactivation process in terms that Rico would understand. "Once we apply the enzyme, we just need to inject his consciousness to revive him. We could make one Bruno or twenty-three of him. It's really up to Kleezebee. He has digital copies on backup."

"Speaking of Kleezebee, it's time to call this in," Rico said, stepping toward the door to the compartment. "We're gonna need help transporting these containers back to the cabin."

THIRTY

How's it Hanging?

Lucas carried the last container of BioTex up the front steps leading into Kleezebee's cabin. He turned his body sideways in order to fit through the front door and walk inside. He hauled the two-gallon-sized glass jar to the trap door leading down to Fuji's basement. He gave the liquid-filled cargo to Rico, who slipped the container into a makeshift leather sling that hung from a ceiling-mounted pulley system.

Rico used the rope to lower the BioTex through the opening where Fuji and Kleezebee were waiting to receive it. The monk and professor worked together as they pulled the container from the sling and stacked it next to the rest of the BioTex inventory.

Lucas bent over, flexing his back and hips in a round-about way. "Glad that's over with. I'm not built for this shit," he said to Rico, thinking about his muscle-bound friends Zack and Trevor, neither of whom would have struggled to carry the fifty-pound payload. "I'm going to feel it tomorrow." He waited for Rico to step out of the way. "Well, might as well head down," he said, swinging his ass around to grab the top of the ladder struts. He eased his left foot onto the second rung, then his right, before pulling his body into position. It only took seconds to reach the bottom.

Rico followed him into the basement.

The four men stood together in a semi-circle, admiring the stack of BioTex containers—each man smiling and giving each other a high-five hand salute.

"It took a lot longer than expected," the professor said, "but we've finally managed to bring our people home."

"Except two," Lucas said, thinking about Drew and the missing container of BioTex. "Actually, three, if you count Abby. I almost forgot about her."

"Your brother would have appreciated that," Kleezebee said.

"Shall we begin?" Fuji asked, folding his hands and slipping them inside the sleeves of his tattered monk-suit.

"Have you decided who we'll revive first?" Lucas asked his mentor, hoping it would be the friendly, tattooed security guard.

"I think you already know," Kleezebee said, searching his digi-stick collection. He pulled out one labeled *Bruno*. He gave it to Fuji.

"Where are we going to revive him?" Lucas asked, scanning the contents of Fuji's lab. He didn't see a medical examination table, like the one Kleezebee owned in the underground silo on Lucas' version of Earth.

Kleezebee pointed to Fuji's bathroom. "The tub."

"Seriously?"

"We don't have all the proper equipment, so it'll have to do."

"How does this work, exactly?" Rico asked Lucas.

"Hand me your K-Bar," Lucas told him, prying the lid open to one of the BioTex containers with his hands. Rico pulled his knife from its sheath and gave it to him. Lucas dipped the weapon into the container, allowing time for some of the scarlet-colored sludge to cover the length of the blade. He held it up. The gelatinous material oozed down and dripped into the jar.

"This is one of Kleezebee's greatest inventions. It's called BioTex, which is short for Bio-mimetic Latex."

Rico furrowed his brow.

"Think of it as living latex. This amazing stuff can copy someone right down to the person's DNA, memories and all. The professor discovered the base substance a long time ago, in a stellar nebula on the other side of the galaxy, then he and his lab geeks tweaked it for deployment. Normally, we use this material to make a perfect copy of someone, which only takes about fifteen seconds of direct contact in order to create a genetic map of the donor's body. However, in Bruno's case, we're going to infuse the BioTex directly, to reconstitute him from a digital backup copy."

Rico nodded. "Okay, I get that. Sort of—"

"It'll make more sense if you watch it happen. Grab the jar," Lucas told him.

Rico carried the container, following Lucas to the bathroom. Fuji and Kleezebee joined them, each carrying different parts of the technology. Lucas plugged the drain in the bottom of Fuji's tub, then instructed Rico to pour the substance in. Rico tipped the jar, allowing the BioTex to trickle out like a gallon of semi-frozen pudding.

"Now we are going to activate the BioTex with a special enzyme," Lucas said. "It's how we control access to this tech. Without it, you might as well use this stuff as jelly on your toast."

Fuji used a six-inch syringe to inject the compound into the gelatinous mass.

"Now that it's activated, we can begin the reconstitution process," Lucas said, taking an electronic device from Kleezebee. It was roughly the size of a paperback book and had two sets of wires hanging from its back. Lucas held the unit upright, as Fuji inserted a digi-stick into the slot along the top of the device.

"This downloads Bruno's bio-copy directly into the BioTex," Lucas said, inserting the wire leads into the substance. He pressed a series of buttons on the front of the device.

"How long will it take?" Rico asked.

"Not long. Watch."

The BioTex jiggled for a moment, then spread itself out along the bottom of the tub as it coagulated and thickened. Moments later, it rose up like bread dough, eventually taking the shape of a featureless human body. Soon after, its facial structure began to materialize and show through the scarlet substance. Its mouth, eyes, and nose formed first, then a mane of dark hair and a neatly-trimmed goatee sprouted and grew to full length. Eventually, its entire body, including genitalia, took shape. The final step was the appearance of the security guard's clothes and the ferocious-looking creature tattoos on his arms. When the metamorphosis was complete, an exact copy of the Bruno was lying in the tub, face-up.

Bruno opened his eyes, grinned from ear to ear, and then sat up. "What's for lunch, boys?"

"Good to have you back, old friend," Kleezebee said, extending an open hand to Bruno. He pulled the rotund guard out of the tub.

"How long have I been on ice?"

"Eighteen months."

"No wonder I'm starving," Bruno replied, rubbing his oversized belly with both hands. He grinned. "If I'm not careful, I'll lose my girlish figure."

Lucas whispered in Rico's ear. "It really doesn't work that way. He just needs sugar on a regular basis to maintain cohesion."

The replica security guard yanked on the waistline of his trousers, pulling his pants up. "Anyone seen my belt? Damn, I think I lost some weight while I was in the fridge."

"Unlikely," Kleezebee said with a smile. "Knowing you, you put on weight."

Bruno slapped Lucas on the back. "Hey, Doc, how's it hanging?"

"Good to see you, too," Lucas said, reciprocating with a one-armed, man-hug. "It hasn't been the same around here without you."

Bruno looked around. "Where's Little Chief?"

"We still haven't found Drew," Kleezebee said, with a solemn tone in his voice.

"But we're getting close," Lucas said. "Especially now that you're here."

Bruno looked at Rico. He held his hand out for a shake. "I'm Bruno Benner."

"Rico Renaldi," the Italian stud answered, shaking the replica's hand. He pulled his hand away after the shake, then wiped it on his pant leg. "So, you're a replica?"

"I prefer the term 'bio-mimetic person.'"

"He can copy any living organism right down to its DNA," Lucas said. "It's pretty impressive to watch."

Bruno turned to Kleezebee. "Can I show him, Boss?"

The professor didn't answer. Instead, he strapped a pentagon-shaped watch to Bruno's wrist, then looked at Rico. "Major, why don't you take our friend upstairs and get him something sweet to eat?"

"Yes, sir," Rico said sharply before escorting Bruno up the ladder and out of the basement.

"All right, who's next?" Lucas asked the professor.

"Just Bruno."

"Only one?"

"We don't have sufficient glucose supplies to activate and maintain anymore."

"There's plenty of sugar at Fisher's bakery," Lucas said, thinking of Carrie Anne delivering a cherry-covered Danish to him. It was almost as sweet as her.

"And that helps us how?"

Lucas shrugged.

"Yeah, that's what I thought."

"Still, it seems a bit risky to only send in one man to infiltrate Cyrus' compound." Lucas looked at Fuji. He hoped the brilliant mathematician would join in and convince Kleezebee otherwise. But the hairless monk didn't say a word.

"All he needs to do is assimilate one of Cyrus' squad leaders, and then he should be able to walk right in. Shouldn't take him long to locate our E-121 modules."

"Replication will require close proximity," Fuji added.

"Which is easier said than done," Lucas said. "Cyrus' men are well trained and always on high alert."

"Not always," the professor answered. "We do know that his senior staff hangs out at Tailgater's Pub on Thursday's for happy hour, so it shouldn't be difficult to get one of them alone, especially if they've been drinking raspum all night."

Lucas smiled. "Eventually if one of them will need to take a leak and heads off to the bathroom alone."

"If Bruno waits inside the adjacent stall, it should only take a few seconds."

"It'd be like collecting a urine sample from a drunk, only it doesn't need to be done in mid-stream," Lucas said.

"Hell, if he was drunk enough, you could probably collect both of his kidneys and sell them on the black market," the professor said. Then he paused, turning his head slightly, as if he were in deep in thought. "That gives me an idea."

"What?"

"You said 'the Collector' wants to get his weapons back, right? Which is why he kidnapped Fisher's daughter."

Lucas nodded. "That's what the old man told us right before he cashed it in."

"I think I know the identity of the Collector."

"Who?"

"Gaylon Reece."

"The drug dealer?"

Kleezebee nodded, then stroked his long beard. "A few days ago, I traded our remaining stunners and power cartridges in exchange for the new vid-screens in the basement."

Lucas was stunned. He didn't know what to say. His mentor had never given away any of their technology before.

"We couldn't complete the Incursion Chamber's monitoring system without them, and he was the only one who had access to that kind of technology. The man collects everything—and I mean everything—as long as it has inherent value. That's what he did for a living before the Krellian attack. And we all know that old habits die hard."

"Why would Reece think Fisher had the stunners?"

"Perhaps his daughter acquired them without Mr. Reece's permission," Fuji said.

Lucas didn't agree. "I'll bet it was her ex-boyfriend, Piston. Assholes like him are always looking for shortcuts."

"Either way, I'm afraid we will never know for sure," the professor said.

Lucas flared his eyes. "Now that we know *who* has her, we *are* going to rescue her, right?"

"If we had enough weapons to replace the set that was stolen, then yes. But we don't. We only have one left. There's nothing we can do for her."

"Bullshit. There's always something that can be done."

"Sometimes you have to know when to walk away, especially if it means avoiding contact with the underbelly of society."

Underbelly or not, Lucas couldn't let it go. "He's a collector of things, so let's trade him something else. Regardless of his reputation, he's still a businessman. I'm sure the stunners are not the only thing he would accept in exchange for her."

"Dealing with a man like Gaylon Reece is extremely dangerous. He's ruthless and unpredictable, which I'm sure is why he has eluded Cyrus and his death squads."

"Unless they're working together."

"Doubtful."

"Still, we have to try. It's the right thing to do."

"Let's assume for a moment that I agree—which I don't—how do you expect to contact him and arrange for a trade?"

"I figured you already knew how to do that. After all, you've done business with him when you traded our fucking technology away."

"That was through a friend of Claude's in the capitol building, Jennifer Warren."

Lucas had heard of her, though he had never met her. "The one-eyed chick?"

Kleezebee nodded. "I think she used to be involved romantically with Reece, before the Krellian assault. She owed Claude a favor and set up the one-time meet. But that trade was under entirely different circumstances."

"How's that?"

"It was a business transaction, one item for another. There was no emotion involved. A ransom exchange is wholly different. This time it's about revenge and that changes the dynamic completely."

"Then let's not make it a ransom exchange. I can go in undercover. Purchase her along with some other shit."

"He'll see through that in a heartbeat."

"Not if we step up our game. I'm sure if the three of us put our heads together, we can outsmart one tweaked-out asshole."

"Maybe so. But Reece could be holding Carrie Anne anywhere."

Lucas wished he knew how to contact the Baaku. They might be able to help in the search. He thought about mentioning it to Kleezebee, but earlier when he tried to tell the professor about the spiritual salad farmers, the old man laughed it off. Kleezebee thought Lucas had been hallucinating again. Not that Lucas blamed him; he wasn't entirely sure they were real, either.

He decided he needed a different plan, one that everyone would agree was part of reality. "Can't we use the Incursion Chamber to locate her remotely?"

Kleezebee didn't hesitate, almost as if he had already considered the idea. "It only works if you know the exact date and time of a target event. That means we'd have to know her location *first*, in order to calibrate the device. Otherwise, we can't seed the calculations properly. It's a Catch-22. Besides, we don't have sufficient E-121 to power the unit."

"That power requirement may not apply," Fuji said.

"Explain."

"Penetrating the narrows of time is far easier for a local incursion."

Lucas understood the ramifications. "Local viewing requires much less power to open the wedge, especially when there's no time displacement involved."

Fuji nodded. "A little over two-hundred amps should be sufficient to initiate."

"That means we could use standard household current."

"Theoretically, it is possible."

"Could we establish a stable incursion point with that level of power?" Lucas asked, as his mind filled with possibilities.

"For no more than one, maybe two seconds, at best."

"That might be enough if the timing is right. The element of surprise would be on our side for a change."

Kleezebee seemed frustrated. "Guys, we still need to know her location *first*."

"Unfortunately, that is true," Fuji said, bowing to Kleezebee.

"But we have to try, Professor."

"Time may find a way," the baldheaded monk added, looking at the professor with eyes wide.

Kleezebee sneered at Fuji.

Fuji stood silent.

Lucas moved a step closer to his mentor. "Fuji's right. I think the universe owes us one, big time."

Kleezebee paused; he was obviously thinking about it. "I'm sorry, but the answer is no. It's a fool's errand. We need to focus all our efforts to acquire the power modules from Cyrus now, while we still have time. You do want to find your brother, right?"

"Of course I do. But I can't let an innocent girl die. Not when there's something I can do about it," Lucas said, looking at Fuji, hoping his friend would agree. The monk didn't answer; he must have caved to the professor's sneer.

"Please, we have to save her," Lucas said, staring at Kleezebee. He waited a good ten seconds, but the professor's expression didn't change. It was clear that Kleezebee had made his decision and wasn't going to change his mind.

Lucas threw up his hands. "Ah, fuck you." He paced the room, trying to decide what to do next. "Fine, if you don't want to join me, then I will go alone. You don't need me to help with Bruno or the E-121 recovery mission. Rico can handle it. So, that makes me available—and expendable."

Kleezebee shook his head. "It's much too dangerous. You will be putting Drew at risk."

"Horseshit! You don't even think he's still alive."

"That is simply *not* true."

Lucas grew even more upset after the professor's spin control. "What the hell do you care if I go or not? This is my decision! Not yours!"

"I do care. More than you know. But I have a responsibility to protect all the members of our team and our mission."

"What's good for the many outweighs the needs of the few," Fuji added.

"Or the one," Lucas added, gawking at the monk. He recognized that catch phrase from a trio of old Star Trek flicks, but knew Fuji couldn't have seen them—not in this time period and certainly not on this planet. He rolled his eyes, then looked at Kleezebee. "I appreciate your concern, Professor. But I'm going and nothing's going to stop me. Not you, not Fuji, not an army of Krellian meat-eaters."

Kleezebee folded his arms and stood even more erect than he normally did, but he didn't respond.

"You might as well accept it, Professor. This is happening, one way or the other. So, you can either help me, or tell me to fuck off. I really don't give a shit. So, what's it going to be? I need to know right now, because the clock is ticking."

THIRTY-ONE

Extreme Prejudice

Lucas felt the inertia of the Mag-Lift train slow, meaning it was nearing another station, but he couldn't see where he was, not with the hood draped over his head. He sat up in the squeaky leather seat and adjusted his hands, trying to make them feel more comfortable behind his back. The nylon rope around his wrists was tight—probably too tight—since he had lost some of the feeling in the tips of his fingers. He flexed his hands, trying to send more blood to his extremities. It seemed to work, though his pentagon-shaped watch slid out of position, swiveling down around his wrist.

It had been a long, curvy, two-hour ride, but he wasn't sure if the train had circled back on the adjacent track or traveled in one direction the whole time. Not that it really mattered, since he knew he wasn't being followed. The seventy-two-hour ransom was still viable and the extra time allowed Lucas to better memorize his cover ID.

He figured he was the only civilian in the train car other than Reece's men, since he hadn't heard any other voices or activity during the ride. Lucas was impressed that Reece could arrange and afford a private car, especially since Cyrus kept close watch on the transportation grid. He wondered how the Supreme Commander would react if he learned that his major rival was freely enjoying the comforts and tactical advantages of the Mag-Lift system.

Lucas licked his sticky, stale lips, as his empty stomach bubbled an angry tune. It had been hours since he had anything to eat or drink—not since right before Reece's men snatched him off the street near the bakery in town. He knew that he had better eat something soon, if he was going to keep it together for the negotiations. He could feel his energy levels dropping by the minute. His mind drew a delicious picture of a pile of fresh cherries covered in whipped cream. He could almost taste its sweetness sliding down his gullet, but the vision just made him hungrier, so he turned it off.

When the train came to a stop, the distinctive swooshing sound of the car door rang out, then a blast of fresh air smacked him in the face. He wriggled his feet under his outstretched thighs, leaned forward and stood up, waiting for one of Gaylon Reece's men to take him by the arm and lead him out of the passenger car. Someone did. It wasn't long before the station's platform was under his feet; the creeks and hollow sounds told him that he was walking on wooden planks.

The guard escorted him fifteen paces forward before he pushed Lucas' head down and forced him to lean sideways. "Get in and move to the middle," the man said in a deep, gruff voice.

Lucas slid his butt onto the seat and hopped his body over a few feet. He could feel someone sit down next to him on both sides. The sway and depth of the seat depressions told him that the bookend bodyguards were both very large. He drew in his shoulders and arms, allowing more room for Reece's guards. Both skimmer doors swooshed, compressing the air inside the car as they closed.

"Safe house three. Tactical route alpha," the man on his right said.

"Affirmative. Setting course and speed. Electro-armor engaged," an artificial, robotic voice said from the front of the vehicle.

Lucas knew he was riding in a late-model skimmer limousine, since only the newest limo models were equipped with both the AutoDrive feature and the revolutionary new armor system that he had heard about. Reece had bucks, that's for sure. But the real question was, where were they taking him?

About thirty minutes later, the skimmer slowed down and stopped. The door to his left opened, then someone tugged on his arm, pulling him sideways. He flew off balance as he was dragged out of the vehicle and ushered to his feet by a pair of strong hands. His feet felt uneven—like he was standing in loose dirt or sand, so he shuffled his feet, twisting them deeper into the soil, trying to gain better footing. It worked.

His nostrils swelled as the distinct aroma of brisk mountain air invaded his senses. But that wasn't all. There was an odd secondary scent—something he could only describe as wet pine tree mixed together with a bad case of swamp-ass. Then something brushed against his leg from behind, nudging him a half-step forward, as the huff of excited breath filled the air. He could hear rapid sniffing, right before something pushed against the bottom of his crotch, sniffing his privates for at least thirty seconds.

Then it barked—fuck, a dog—and its mouth was much too close for comfort. That must have been the source of the swamp-ass stench. He figured the animal must have been playing in the forest, rubbing against the sap-laden pine trees before taking a swim in a pond filled with beaver shit. Hopefully, there weren't any leaches in the pond, otherwise, he might soon feel them crawling up the inside of his leg, looking to latch onto his manhood for an afternoon blood-suck.

Someone grabbed the top of the hood, pulling it up along his chin, across the tip of his nose, and off his forehead. The crackle of static cling grabbed a few strands of his red hair, tugging at his scalp before it let go. Moments later, the warmth of sunlight soothed his right cheek.

He looked down. A hundred and fifty pound red-and-white-colored Siberian Husky was staring back at him with a jawline of impressive teeth and deep blue eyes. Its ears were angled back sharply and every hair along its neck was standing at attention. Lucas looked up, not wanting to challenge the imposing animal. Maybe if he ignored the curly-tailed nut-sniffer it would go away.

In front of him was a tiny, wood-framed cottage with a classic front porch. The building was maybe eight hundred square feet—about the same size as Kleezebee's cabin. A dense forest of trees stood guard behind it, with an open, lush meadow off to the left.

"Safe House Three?" he asked in his most sarcastic tone.

"Quiet!" the guard yelled, pulling him toward the front porch.

Lucas studied the area for possible escape routes as they moved closer to the cottage. He spotted something familiar: a distinctive, two-spire peak between the towering trees. Ghost Mountain. The evening sun was shoulder-high in the cloudless sky, meaning he was somewhere along the south ridge, on the side opposite from Dr. Kleezebee's cabin. His chest tightened when he realized he could walk home with Carrie Anne from there, assuming he could negotiate for her safe return—and survive the ordeal. If his cover ID didn't hold, it would have to be Plan B.

The crotch-friendly mutt jumped and positioned itself ahead of him using a low-angled crouch, making Lucas even more nervous. It looked angry or hungry, hard to tell the difference with the drool dripping from its mouth.

The guard kicked the animal in the head, making it yelp, before it stumbled out of the way and ran off. It disappeared around the corner of the bungalow. "Fucking flee bag," the man said, disdainfully. "Someone should shoot that mutt."

The brute untied the lashing from Lucas' hands, then opened the door and shoved him inside with enough force to make him fall forward on his knees. The door behind Lucas closed and he heard its lock engage. The chaperon remained outside.

Lucas stood up and took a moment to admire the dozens of full-sized, twentieth-century movie posters blanketing every square inch of the wood-paneled walls: *Pirates of the Caribbean, Terminator, Lethal Weapon, Linkage, Final Countdown, Contact, Scanners, Brainstorm, Sneakers, Battleship, Independence Day, The Godfather, Godzilla*—and the list of blockbusters went on. Each one was professionally framed in glass and looked to be in mint condition. If it weren't for the overabundance of memorabilia, he'd swear he was standing in Kleezebee's living room. The layout was identical, including the stone fireplace and unimpressive kitchen area on the right.

He studied the floorboards near the center of the room, but couldn't determine if there was a trap door leading down to a basement—a brown area rug smothered the floor. But if there were a basement, that's where he figured Gaylon Reece was holding Carrie Anne. Of course, that was assuming she was being held on-site and was still alive.

Lucas heard a flushing noise coming from the short hallway on the left. If the rest of the cottage was laid out the same as Kleezebee's place, then the hallway led to two bedrooms, one being the master, with a central bathroom that both rooms shared.

He heard the familiar sound of toilet paper being pulled from a wall-mounted dispenser, then a second toilet flush.

Reece limped into the main area from the hallway.

Lucas tried not to stare at the man's eye patch or peg leg, but it was impossible not to sneak a peek at both. He prayed his wandering eyes weren't obvious or offensive.

"You must be Mr. Nicoli," Reece stated.

"Yes, yes, I am. But you may call me Lucas," Lucas answered, hoping his assumed name sounded legit.

"I'm Gaylon Reece," the long-haired man said. He moved a few steps, then sat down in the wooden rocking chair next to the couch. In front of him was the end of a glass-inlay coffee table with a handheld graphene screen sitting on top of it. "I want to apologize for the harsh manner in which we brought you here. But since we haven't engaged in commerce before, it's paramount that extra security precautions be implemented. Cyrus has spies everywhere."

Lucas parked his skinny butt on the far end of the couch. "I would have done the same thing, given the circumstances."

"I hope you realize that if Jennifer Warren hadn't vouched for you, this meeting never would have taken place. Extreme prejudice would have intervened."

Lucas nodded respectfully. "I appreciate that. I didn't expect that we'd meet here, in the woods."

Reece looked at several points in the room, then turned his eyes back to Lucas. "This used to be my old man's place. He was the primary contractor who built most of the area's miner cabins during the great Tritanium Ore Rush."

"It's cozy and quiet. I can see the appeal."

"Mainly, it's off the grid and off Cyrus' radar. I don't make it up here often, but it's a good place to decompress after a long week of dealing with the mounds of civilian trash in town."

Lucas heard a set of rapid footsteps and claws coming his way from the kitchen. It was the drug dealer's dog and it was headed directly for him. He pushed his legs together, trying to keep the beast from doing the sniff-test again. It worked. The dog gave up and ran to its master.

Reece leaned forward, putting his walking cane on the floor. He rubbed the dog's head with both hands. Then he pinched his lips together and let the animal lick him on the mouth for a good thirty seconds, all the while making goo-goo noises, like he were talking to an infant. "This is my baby, Sheena. She's been with me for twelve years."

"Yeah, we met outside. Friendly dog," Lucas said. He decided to change the subject. "You have an amazing collection of posters. They're all great flicks. I've seen every one of them."

Reece paused. He seemed upset. "Really? How's that? They're hundreds of years old and I'm damn sure none of them have ever been available on insta-block. That's what makes these prints so valuable. They're singularly unique."

"What I meant to say is that I've heard of all of them. They're classics."

Reece nodded, though he seemed skeptical.

Lucas couldn't help but stare at the man's disfigurements, the peg leg and the eye patch. He wondered what had happened to the frail-looking longhair. His mind drifted to Drew, worrying that a similar fate may have fallen on his physically-challenged brother. He knew first hand that the universe loved to torture certain people repeatedly, then sit back and watch you squirm your way out. It wouldn't be the first time Drew was the target of such maniacal attention.

Lucas looked up from the peg leg and made eye contact with Reece. His heartbeat picked up steam when he realized that his extended gaze might have just embarrassed himself and the outlaw.

Reece tapped his finger on the artificial leg. "Day one of the Krellian invasion. My proximal neighbor at the time, Jennifer Warren, heard my screams and rushed to my defense before the sentinel guard finished its feast. Thank God she always carries a large caliber sidearm. I will never forget those three horrific minutes. I learned the hard way why it's important to have plenty of advanced weaponry at the ready."

"No doubt. It's only a matter of time before the bugs violate the non-aggression treaty and make another incursion into our space."

"And with a serious case of the munchies next time," Reece said.

Lucas laughed. The man had his same sense of twisted humor. He realized that Reece was simply doing what he needed to do to put food on the table and make it through another day. We're all forced to make tough decisions in order to survive, especially on this godforsaken rock. Your level of desperation determines the choices you take, and by the look of the man, Reece was desperate. It was easy to see why he had resorted to kidnapping and selling drugs. He wasn't all that different from Lucas and his unpopular interrogation techniques: The end justified the means. He felt a strange kinship brewing with the criminal.

Reece fiddled with his eye patch, pulling it away from his face to reveal a deep, empty socket. "This little beauty is from a fishing accident when I was nine. My brother's aim was significantly off the mark. Of course, that's assuming it *was* an accident. But I never had the opportunity to clarify with him before he died." He snapped the patch back into place. "But enough about me. What can I do for you today?"

"I'm looking to make a trade."

"You came to the right place. What is your primary area of interest?"

"That all depends on your inventory."

"I have a wide array of items available. Technology, art, weapons, supplies, pharmaceuticals, pussy."

Lucas smiled, hoping his grin would appear genuine. He needed to lighten the tension in the room. "Maybe some technology and a little pussy to go. You know what they say about all work and no play."

Reece didn't laugh. "I'm fully aware that my men searched you before they brought you here to meet with me. You do realize that payment is required at time of sale. Most of my clients don't arrive empty-handed."

"Lucas held out his right arm. "I'm wearing my payment."

Reece sat up in his chair. "That's a very interesting timepiece."

"It's a one-of-a-kind item. Something I'm sure you've never seen before. Singularly unique."

Reece smiled with wide eyes. "May I see it?"

Lucas knew he had him hooked. He slipped the watch off his wrist and tossed it to Reece. "The case and band are refined Tritanium. Very rare and extremely valuable."

Reece put his hand into his shirt pocket, pulling out a jeweler's loupe. He jammed the magnifier into the deep recess of his good eye and held the watch close for inspection. He turned the watch over and examined the back. "Excellent quality. Someone took the time to craft the seams with amazing precision. This will buy you fifteen credits in trade."

Lucas wasn't sure if fifteen credits was a fair price. Probably not, since most traders never offer their best price up front. But regardless, he needed to review the trade values of Reece's inventory to know where he stood. "Take your time and evaluate it more closely. It's certainly worth more than fifteen. In the meantime, may I see your inventory?"

Reece leaned forward and took the handheld screen from the tabletop. He held it out for Lucas. "Here's my entire stock. Look through it. If anything piques your interest, let me know. I'm sure we can make a deal today."

Lucas retrieved the unit from the man, then ran his finger across the screen to activate the device. Instantly, the graphene unit listed a dozen icons vertically down the screen, each one representing a different area of specialty. The title of the screen said ScrubNet, obviously the name of the underground network, which was sort of like eBay for thieves.

He wanted to click on the topic PUSSY, but knew that would be too obvious as a first choice. So he decided to start with TECHNOLOGY. An image appeared on the screen of a Quantum Airbook—a powerful, very hard-to-find computer. Below it was a complete description with a trade value of twenty-seven credits.

Lucas swiped his finger across the screen to review the next seven items—none of them were of interest. Then he flipped to item number nine. His eyes flared.

"See something you like?" Reece asked.

"Google Glasses! I can't believe you have one," Lucas said, thinking about the device's history. Google originally released the tech under the name Google Glass, which was eventually changed to the plural version of the same name after the simple, head-mounted smart phone evolved into a full-fledged, twin-ocular super computer and sensory scanner. The technology had been banned, confiscated, and destroyed by the millions under the guise of national security. He didn't think any units of the revolutionary device survived, at least, not until today.

"That's not the only vintage item available. Are you looking for something collectible?"

"Haven't decided yet. But this one has my interest, for sure. Does it work?"

"Yes, everything in stock is certified to be absolutely genuine and fully functional. That includes the women."

"Five credits for vintage tech seems a bit steep. It's not like it has much use anymore."

"I could do three. That's a fair price, especially for such a rare piece. It's the only one in existence."

"I would need to inspect it personally, of course."

"That's won't be a problem. I can have any item here in a matter of minutes."

"Let me think about it," Lucas said, wanting to save his trade credits until he could negotiate a deal for Carrie Anne.

He flipped to the next item. It was a dermal re-generator, another rare item. Lucas thought about his face scars and how nice it would be to remove them with this device. Carrie Anne would certainly look at him differently, if his skin were smooth and tight. Fifteen credits. Damn, too expensive.

He scrolled to the next item. His eyes nearly popped out of their sockets.

THIRTY-TWO

Small Spaces

The screen showed three of Kleezebee's E-121 metal transport cases. The screen said five credits, which was much too cheap. He figured the cases were empty. "I'm looking at item TC-3. The transport cases—"

"Cyrus had them in his private collection, but I'm not sure why." Reece shook his head. "They are unique, but practically worthless."

"Anything inside?"

"A handful of black spheres; some type of hybrid metal. I checked with recycling; they didn't want them."

Lucas had to have them, but if he did, he worried that he wouldn't be able to afford Carrie Anne as well. He returned to the home screen, and clicked on the PUSSY icon.

Up first was a stunning redhead with big, perky tits, a flat stomach, and a small, round ass. Price said ten credits. He continued on, flipping through another ten girls—each was stripper hot—all for the same price. There were also blondes and brunettes; some were short, but mostly they were tall drop-dead-gorgeous women.

"I'm checking out the girls. The ten credit price—is that for an hour, or all night?"

Reece laughed. "One hour in-call, but I'm thinking all you need is, what, five minutes?"

Lucas decided not to antagonize the man by trying to defend his manhood. He smiled. "Three usually does it for me. But I was thinking maybe an over-nighter would be good. Multiple incursions into her sweet spot would be just what the doctor ordered."

"That'll cost you fifty. Plus, it's up to the girl. She has final say on outcalls."

One of Reece's guards unlocked the door and stuck his head inside. "Excuse me, sir. Team two is en route. ETA for your next appointment is fifteen minutes."

"Just have him wait outside until I'm finished here."

Lucas continued flipping through more of the girls. When he got to the end, the screen beeped. Carrie Anne was not on the list.

"What's it going to be? Redhead, blond, brunette?"

"I can't afford fifty, but I do want an all-nighter. Do you have any girls that are less expensive? She doesn't have to be super-hot. I'm not that picky."

"No, I'm sure you're not."

"I like a little cushion for pushing, if you know what I mean. Maybe a piercing or two."

Reece hesitated, stroking his beard. After a short minute, he said, "There is one I've just acquired. The previous buyer looks like he's a no-show, so she has just become available. But I warn you, she's a bit thick and missing a few teeth. Grade three quality, at best. Thirty credits will buy you a twenty-four-hour rental with her. I'll even throw in the Google Glasses for free; you could record your couplings in real-time 3D."

Lucas ran a total in his head for the dermal re-generator, the Google Glasses, the E-121 cases, and Carrie Anne. Then he shaved off a few percent for an expected volume discount. "How about fifty for the watch?"

"It's worth fifteen, Mr. Nicoli."

"But it's solid titanium."

"Fifteen is the best I can do. After all, it's just a watch."

Time for Plan B, Lucas conceded, knowing that Plan A had only a slim chance of success, anyway; he was never that lucky. "What if it's more than just a watch?"

"I'm listening."

Lucas stood up, walked to Reece, and took the watch from the gray-haired man. He slid it onto his wrist. "There's some very special technology built into this timepiece," he said, holding the watch in front of Reece. "If you press the orange buttons in just the right combination, it will activate a personal cloaking device. Now, I'm sure a man of your experience will agree that cloaking technology is easily worth fifty credits. Anyone wearing this watch would have a distinct tactical advantage over his enemy. Cyrus won't have an answer for this tech."

"Show me."

Lucas pulled his arm back. "Not until I inspect *all* the merchandise."

Reece didn't hesitate. He yelled for his security guard. The door opened behind Lucas. "Yes, sir?"

"Bring me the Fisher woman."

"And I would like to inspect the Google Glasses, the dermal re-generator, and those transport cases with the metal spheres inside."

"Anything else?" Reece asked.

"No, that covers it."

Reece waved at his man. "You heard him. And notify me the moment my next appointment arrives."

"Yes, sir."

Lucas had expected the guard to walk to the center of the room, pull the area rug up, and access a trap door leading down to a basement. But he didn't. Instead, he simply nodded and hustled out the door.

"You have this stuff nearby?" Lucas asked, figuring there was a storage warehouse hiding in the woods.

A serious look of concern grew on Reece's face. "I warn you, if this is some type of deception, it will be met with—"

"Extreme prejudice, I know. But trust me. The cloaking device works."

"How did you acquire such a unique and valuable piece of technology, Mr. Nicoli?" Reece asked, with a veil of uncertainty in his voice.

Lucas was unprepared for this question. He threw some ideas together in his head and answered. "I used to work for Central Intelligence, on Earth, Tech Ops Division. I took a few things with me before they terminated me without cause. This is the last item I have left to sell."

"Is that where you met Jennifer Warren?"

"No, I met her at a cocktail party in New Robyn City. We started hanging out and became friends."

"How long ago?"

"A few years."

"She *is* a very unique person."

"Yes, she is. She has such a loving heart," Lucas said, checking the door behind him. No sign of the guard. Damn, he was running out of backstory.

"Before our meeting today, I ran a background check on you. Oddly, nothing came up. And when I say, nothing, I mean nothing. It's as if you don't exist."

"That's what happens when you leave Tech Ops' service. They make you disappear. Makes it impossible to get another job when your résumé is blank and you can't provide references, or any form of job history."

Reece nodded. "I suppose it does. What do you do now for a living?"

"This and that. Whatever it takes to scrape out a living."

Seconds later, the door swung open and five of Reece's men walked in, each carrying one of the items from Lucas' shopping list. They put the smaller items on the coffee table, while the transport cases were stacked on the floor. The men stood behind Reece in precise shoulder-to-shoulder formation. Obviously, this was standard procedure for his crew.

Lucas waited, be he didn't see Carrie Anne being escorted through the door. "And the girl?"

"Slight delay. She's being prepped."

"Prepped?"

"She wasn't dressed properly."

All sorts of ideas raced through Lucas mind, wondering if they had been sexually abusing her or possibly something worse. Yet, he knew he must remain in character to maintain his cover. He stood up, walked to the transport cases and opened them one at a time. He found one E-121 sphere inside each container. He picked up the last sphere, pretending to examine it. Just enough, he thought, putting the module back, then closed the lid. He secured the series of locking clasps along the front of each case. "Not sure of the metal, but they're damn heavy. Like ultra-dense cannon balls."

He put the Google Glasses on, adjusting the fit to match the slender profile of his face. He looked around the room. The virtual heads-up screen highlighted each item in the room with right-angle crop marks. White text appeared above each item, listing its exact dimensions, weight, and construction material.

He looked back at Reece to give him a thumbs up signal, but was surprised when the unit outlined the man's face and correctly listed his name overhead. Apparently, the unit had been loaded with the infamous Ident-A-Friend facial recognition software. Shortly after the software was introduced, the governments of Earth came together and issued a worldwide ban against Google's revolutionary device.

Just then, he realized that if Reece put the glasses on and looked at Lucas, the drug dealer would know he was an impostor. He removed the glasses and put them on the coffee table, farther away from Reece than before. Time to shift everyone's focus, he decided.

He grabbed the dermal re-generator and flipped it over. It resembled an oversized tongue depressor with a flashlight head attached on the end. He toggled the power switch on and held it up for closer inspection.

"Guaranteed to work," Reece said, tilting his head in such a way to signal to Lucas that he should try the device on himself.

Lucas held the unit a few centimeters above the scar on his wrist where Rico had implanted the subcutaneous explosive. He moved the device slowly over the wound area, feeling the tissue ripple and tingle as the technology repaired and regenerated his epidermis. Ten seconds later, the scar was healed and invisible. "Impressive," he said, reading the power level indicator—it said five percent. "Though it looks like it needs a recharge."

"Power adapters are provided after the trade session is complete."

"Fair enough," Lucas said, realizing that the low-level power charge was a planned maneuver by the shrewd businessman. He wondered if the Google Glasses were purposefully undercharged as well. That would be a major stroke of luck if Reece couldn't use them on him.

"The cloaking device?" Reece asked, pointing at an empty spot on his skeleton-thin wrist.

"The girl?" Lucas answered, cupping his hands in front of his chest to signal a big pair of breasts.

Reece used a quick hand gesture that was directed to one of the men on his right. The guard left the room and returned a minute later with Carrie Anne. She was dressed in six-inch stripper heels, a revealing evening gown, and her face was beautified with makeup and lipstick. She looked smoking hot, even for her.

Her face lit up the moment she walked into the room and recognized him. "Lucas!"

"You two are acquainted?" Reece asked.

Lucas knew she would respond the way she did, which is why he'd decided to only change his last name as part of this undercover op. He looked at her with a deep, soulful gaze, hoping she would understand the words he was about to say next. If she said his last name or reacted improperly, the exchange would spin sideways. "Yes. I've eaten at her father's bakery a few times. But I'm surprised the girl even knows my name."

"Well, Mr. Nicoli, I must say I'm a bit surprised."

"Trust me. So am I."

"Maybe we should renegotiate the price?"

"Not if you still want the watch. Besides, you're the one that offered her as part of the transaction. It wasn't my idea. I had no idea she was part of your inventory."

Reece paused, then nodded. He waved at his guard to bring Carrie Anne forward. He did, pushing her close to Lucas, as he let go of her arm. "Now that I've completed my obligations, it's time for you to demonstrate the cloaking device."

The guards tightened their circle, as if to say, we're going to beat you silly if you don't comply. Lucas knew resistance was futile.

"Let me demonstrate," Lucas said, wrapping his arms around Carrie Anne, pressing and holding three of the eight orange buttons on the watch.

Reece stood up from his chair and screamed, "Stop him!"

Milliseconds later, the area around Lucas and the girl went pitch black and the temperature dropped. They had made it. He released his arms from around Carrie Anne and touched his finger to the face of the watch to activate its proximity display. The faint glow of the sensor unit provided enough light to see her face.

She opened her eyes and looked around the void. Almost instantly, she started screaming and crying hysterically.

He put the tips of his fingers under her chin, lifting her face and eyes up to meet his. "Everything is okay. You're safe."

Her crying continued, then she starting punching him with her chubby fists.

He grabbed her hands and pulled her in, tight. "Carrie Anne. It's me, Lucas. I need you to calm down or you're going to hurt yourself."

It took a few seconds for the panic to subside. "What's going on, Lucas?" she asked, with tears dripping down her rosy-colored cheeks. "Where are we?"

"My watch brought us here. We're inside a subspace rift."

"A what?"

"Think of it as a hidden bubble in space, where nobody can see or hear us."

She didn't respond.

"We're standing in a section of subspace that's straddling the interconnecting membrane between two parallel universes. It's like an invisible envelope wedged into a door jamb. Nobody can hurt us in here, nobody."

She sucked in a few extra gulps of air. It slowed her breathing. "Why did he call you Mr. Nicoli?"

"That's my undercover name. I'm here to rescue you, but Reece can't know it's me."

"We're going back?"

"Yes, my watch has a limited power supply. We can't stay in here very long."

"How is this even possible?"

"Look, sweetie. I really don't have time to explain everything. This watch is one of our inventions and I've used it before. We're perfectly safe. But now, we need to return before Reece blows a valve."

"Yeah, but—"

Lucas stared deep into her eyes and spoke in his most sincere voice. "You know I'm a scientist, right?"

She nodded.

"Trust me. This is what I do. I'm good at this. Just play along and everything will work out. Can you do that?"

"Yes," she said, smacking her arm against the sidewall of the rift, as she tried to step backward. Her face lit up with panic again.

"That's the force field protecting us. It won't hurt you. Stay calm and focus on your breathing."

"Okay, but I really have problems with small spaces," she said, breathing hard and teeth chattering.

Lucas rubbed her back with both hands. "I know it's cold in here, but my watch won't let us freeze before we leave. Are you ready?"

"No," she said, with sarcasm and anger mixed together.

He cupped her face with the palms of his hands, rubbing his thumbs against her smooth skin. "I'm not going to let anything happen to you. I promise. But I can't get you home unless we go back and finish this. That means you and I need to work together."

"Okay," she said, sniffing twice and rubbing her eyes. "What do I need to do?"

"Just pretend we're casual friends from the bakery and nothing more. But, whatever you do, don't say my last name or tell Reece what I do for a living. Act like you barely know me, otherwise he might hurt you. Okay? Just play it cool. Things will probably get a little intense, but I need you to keep it together, no matter what happens. Everything is going according to my plan."

She nodded.

Lucas wiped the tears from her cheeks, then pressed another set of buttons on his watch to begin the reintegration process. He took a deep breath to prepare himself for what must come next. He prayed Carrie Anne would survive.

THIRTY-THREE

Tango One, Secure!

Reece's temper took control of him, as he positioned all of his men around the spot where Lucas and Carrie Anne had disappeared. He vowed not to be fooled again. "Nobody gets the best of me, nobody."

The tallest of the guards turned to Reece. "Rules of engagement, sir?"

"When they return, I want the male secured immediately. If he resists, terminate him. But don't harm the girl. She still has value."

"And if they don't return?"

"They will. They can't stay hidden forever. I want everyone primed and ready. We may only get one shot at this."

The guard nodded.

Moments later, the area inside the circle of guards filled with random static discharges, as a hovering, two-foot-long vertical slit appeared in the center. The slit soon stretched its height to over seven feet, as it burned a deep orange color. Then it changed shape, widening into a faded, orange-colored sphere with a diameter of about five feet. A momentary flash of swirling white light appeared inside the orange, then vanished along with the sphere, leaving behind both occupants.

"Now!" Reece yelled.

The tallest guard jumped on Lucas' back, knocking him to the floor. He grabbed Lucas' arms, pulling them together behind his back. He leaned forward, pressing one of his knees into the back of the visitor's neck. "Tango one, secure!" the guard reported.

Two of the other guards moved three steps closer, aiming their sidearms at Lucas' head, while the remaining pair of men snatched the girl by the arms and rushed her away to the corner of the room. "Tango two, secure!"

Reece limped to Lucas' position and bent down to look at his face. "I really don't like surprises."

"You wanted a demonstration so I gave you one," Lucas said with half breath—his right cheek flat against the floor. "As you can clearly see, the technology works."

"That much is true," Reece said. "But sudden moves demand swift and immediate retaliation."

"Yeah, okay. But can you get Gigantor off my back? I can't breathe."

"Not until you tell me who you really are."

"I don't know what you're talking about. I told you who I am."

"You must take me for a fool."

"Why would you think that?"

"Jennifer Warren doesn't consume alcohol, so it's doubtful you made her introduction at a cocktail party. Plus, she doesn't possess a loving heart—she's a cold-hearted, evil bitch who despises men, especially me. Then there were your flawed movie comments. Buddy, I detected you a mile away. I just played along in order to uncover your end game. It's obvious you're here for the girl—she's a love interest—that much is more than clear, because no man in his right mind would pass on my stable of beauties and pick the beast. But what I'm really interested in is your tech," Reece said, standing upright. He turned to the guard kneeling on Lucas' back. "The watch?"

The man slid the watch off Lucas' wrist and gave it to Reece.

Reece kicked Lucas in the ribs with his good leg. "What's the activation sequence?"

Lucas' breath was short and choppy; obviously, he was struggling to breathe. "Just press and hold the top three buttons for two seconds. Ignore the other five. But it's not going to work for you."

"Explain?"

"It's low on power and needs to be recharged. It takes a tremendous amount of energy to bend light—even more for two occupants."

Reece examined the watch's exterior. He didn't see any type of recharge port. "That, my friend, is another lie." He kicked Lucas in the ribs a second time.

Lucas winced and coughed. His words were slow and deliberate. "No, it's true. It will auto-recharge. Just needs about an hour."

"Bullshit. There's no external port for a power adapter."

"Doesn't need one. It draws energy directly from subspace."

"I doubt that," Reece said, slipping the watch onto his wrist. He pressed the top three buttons together and held them. Nothing happened.

"Just like I said. It needs to recharge."

Reece heard footsteps behind him coming from the door. He turned. "Welcome, Mr. Rutherford," he said to the newcomer.

"Did I interrupt something?"

"I'm just about finished here, Wyatt. I need you to wait outside for few minutes."

Wyatt looked at the prisoner being restrained on the floor. "Ramsay?"

The day's facts were starting to make sense to Reece. "Kleezebee's Ramsay?"

"He must have me confused with someone else," Lucas said painfully.

"No, I'm sure. You're Dr. Lucas Ramsay. I've been wanting to meet you," Wyatt said.

Reece grabbed a handgun from the guard standing closest to him. "Stand him up!"

The guard slid off Lucas and tugged him to his feet, still restraining his arms behind his back.

"Your man is wrong. He doesn't know me. My name is Nicoli, not Ramsay."

Reece looked at Carrie Anne. "So which is it?"

She started crying and didn't answer.

Reece scoffed. "You know, Ramsay, only a fool meets with a stranger without backup. And you never, ever, bring full payment with you—not without a clear exit strategy." He shook his head. "Amateur." He aimed his weapon at Lucas.

"Wait!" Wyatt yelled, as Reece fired three shots from the shredder pistol, hitting Lucas center mass in the chest.

Lucas dropped to his knees, gasping for air. "Who said I came without backup?" he asked weakly, as his eyes closed. A second later, he hit the floor in a heap, blood pouring out from the wounds, his chest unmoving.

Carrie Anne screamed. "Lucas! No! No! No!"

"So, I was correct. You two are lovers. Well, I guess now the correct phrase would be 'you *were* lovers.'"

Her knees wilted, making the guards reposition their grip on her in order to keep her upright. It worked.

Reece stood next to the lifeless body, to admire the kill. Then the corpse started shaking and jiggling. "What the hell?" he asked, taking a step back as the body began to contort its shape, rising up and down at random locations across its surface elongating into a seven-foot blob of scarlet material much like warm Play Doh and then, all at once, it appeared to break apart at the seams, turning itself into a running mass of liquid goo that spread out and covered the floor like runny gelatin.

"What was that?" Carrie Anne asked.

"I'm not sure, but it wasn't human," Reece answered, picking his goo-covered feet up one at a time. "I hope this material isn't toxic."

"That's BioTex," Wyatt said. "Perfectly safe."

"Bio what?"

"Bio-mimetic latex. He was a replica—one of Kleezebee's inventions. But I didn't think it was operational."

Reece spun around with the shredder pistol still in hand. "You couldn't have known that unless you work for the professor, or possibly Cyrus. Who the hell are you and why are you here?"

Wyatt raised his hands. "Easy now. Let's talk about this. I can explain."

Just then another flash that was intense and blinding appeared in the room, this time from the corner to the right of the door. Reece tried to cover his eyes with his hands, but the damage was already done. A sharp, pinpoint headache invaded his eyes and stuck in his brain, sending him to the floor in pain.

Once the flash subsided, so did the pain. He looked up to see a glowing, six-foot-tall man wearing a skin-tight bodysuit with a matrix of symmetrical gold lines etched into it, much like the underside of a computer circuit board from ancient Earth. The man's face wasn't visible. It, too, was covered in the energized material.

The glowing man reached inside his suit and pulled out a handheld weapon that resembled a right-angled Taser gun. He recognized the weapon—it was one of Kleezebee's stunners—the same make and model that someone had stolen from him earlier. The invader aimed the gun and fired a single burst of energy toward the middle of the room. The wide-angle beam spread apart and made contact with everything in the room, including Reece. It felt like a million needles penetrating his skin all at once. His head went dizzy as the electric charge took control of his muscular system, sending him into convulsions. The pain was intense, making it difficult to think straight or control his limbs. Two breaths later, his vision faded to black and his eyes closed.

THIRTY-FOUR

Come up for Air

Wyatt opened his eyes after being stunned by the glowing man in the suit to find that he was hogtied to a chair. He pulled at his arms and legs, but the rope securing him was much too strong to break free. He looked around the room and saw several more prisoners bound and secure: the woman from earlier, Gaylon Reece, and all of his men. None of them appeared to be awake. There was no sign of the scarlet blob on the floor.

The rest of the room was filled with a squad of men dressed in military garb, each with a weapon in hand and based on their position and stance, they were standing watch. Most of the men were fit and trim, except for one who sported a keg-sized belly and a series of creature tattoos on his forearms.

"You'd think he'd be here by now. The cabin isn't that far away," the tattooed fat man said to a handsome man with perfectly combed hair and white teeth—easily the tallest man in the room.

"He needed to let the suit cool down after the incursion." His ego was evident in the way he moved and spoke. He approached Wyatt. "Who the hell are you?"

"Wyatt Rutherford."

"I'm Major Rico Renaldi. I'm sure you've heard of me."

"Yes, I have. The Avanti Prime incident. So, where's your sidekick, T-Rex?"

Rico unleashed a full backhand that landed on Wyatt's lower cheek, sending a stinging jolt of pain into his jaw. "I'm the one asking questions."

Wyatt nodded, flexing his jaw. It was sore, but didn't feel broken.

"What are you doing here, Rutherford?"

"I need to speak with Dr. Ramsay."

"He'll arrive shortly. In the meantime, you will talk to me. Explain your presence."

"Cyrus sent me to retrieve Dr. Kleezebee's power modules. My boss accidentally traded them away to Reece before he knew what they were. I had just arrived when Reece decommissioned your replica."

"What do you want with Lucas Ramsay?"

"I have urgent information for him. It's a matter of life or death for all of you."

"I'm listening."

Wyatt shook his head, pushing out his jaw. "Only with Ramsay. The real Ramsay. Not some copy."

Rico walked to the screen door and stood in front of it. "Looks like he's pulling up now." He returned to Wyatt's position and bent down close. Wyatt could smell his breath. "If you try anything, I will end you."

"My intentions are honorable. I just need a few minutes of his time, that's all."

Lucas walked into the room, wearing the orange-colored suit, though his face wasn't covered. "Where is she?" he asked, before looking around. He must have spotted the girl on his own, because he didn't wait for a response. He ran to her position. "Who tied her up?"

"I did," said the tattooed man.

"Why? She's a friendly."

"Force of habit, I guess. Needed to contain the scene."

"Untie her now!"

Bruno pulled out a knife and reached behind the still-unconscious girl. He yanked the knife up. Her hands fell to her sides.

Lucas knelt down in front of her, tapping her on her cheek, gently. "Carrie Anne. Carrie Anne. Wake up. Please, wake up. It's me, Lucas."

Moments later, her head moved and her eyes opened. She was a little dazed. "Lucas? You're alive?"

"Yes, I'm fine."

"How?"

"That wasn't me earlier. It was a BioTex replica of me."

"I don't understand."

The fat man stepped forward. "I was the one who took you into the rift. My name is Bruno Benner. We knew Reece would double-cross us, so I took Lucas' place."

"You're not dead, either?"

"Nope," Bruno said, pulling his trousers up. He smiled. "It takes a whole lot more than that to kill this old dog." Bruno raised his arm, pointing at the watch. "My friends were listening remotely. When I gave them the go signal, Lucas came to your rescue."

"We needed to know where you were before we could use our Incursion technology to send me in and take Reece out. The watch has a transmitter built in. Once we pinpointed your location, we were able to remotely hear and see everything from where we were to inside this room. Then it was just a matter of timing."

"So, that was you in the glowing suit and mask, earlier?"

"Yes."

"Why did you shoot me?" she asked.

Lucas put his hands on hers. "Sorry about that. But we could only keep the incursion wedge open for a few seconds before the machine yanked me back. I had to stun everyone with one shot. There wasn't time for pinpoint shooting. You'll be okay."

She rubbed the side of her neck. "I'm not so sure." She looked at Bruno. "How long have I been out?"

"Just a few minutes. When they traced us to this location, Rico and his men arrived here in minutes."

Lucas smiled. "Turns out, my boss' cabin is only a couple of miles from here. Worked out better than we'd planned."

She fiddled with Bruno's watch. "Where did you get this?"

"From my boss, Professor Kleezebee."

"Do I get one?"

"Sorry. The advanced technology only works for my kind," Bruno answered. "It's just a watch for ordinary humans."

"I guarantee that Reece never saw that one coming," Lucas said, with a hint of pride in his voice. He pinched his fingers together and held them near the corner of his mouth. He puffed his lips together, pretending to blow smoke. "I love it when a plan comes together."

Bruno put his hand on her shoulder. "You should know that this was all Lucas' idea. I've known him for a long time and the only other person he would have done this for would have been his little brother. You must be a very special person."

She smiled, then kissed Lucas on the lips. It was a long, closed-mouth kiss. It was clear to Wyatt that there was plenty of passion behind it.

When the kiss was over, Lucas told Bruno, "A bit of an over-share, but thanks, buddy."

She ran her hand across the smart-skin fabric, then yanked it back.

"I'm still cooling down after a couple hundred amps of juice ran through the suit. Could have boiled water before."

"Maybe you should have changed, first?"

"I didn't want to waste a second. I had to be sure you were safe."

She kissed Lucas again. This time, Wyatt could see her insert her tongue into his mouth, while running her hands along the inside of his thighs. Lucas arched his back and adjusted his head angle, wrapping his arms around her back. Both of them were moaning and running their hands all over each other.

Wyatt could see the passion mounting. He waited a good minute before speaking. "Dr. Ramsay? I really need to speak with you."

Rico tapped Lucas on the shoulder. "Hey, Casanova. You need to come up for air."

Lucas stopped the kiss. "This better be damned important!"

Rico pointed at Wyatt.

Wyatt cleared his throat. "Sorry to interrupt, but this can't wait. Cyrus plans to attack."

Lucas walked to Wyatt's position with Bruno and Rico. "When?"

"Soon. He's assembling his troops now. Once his new weapon is operational, he'll come at you hard."

"What kind of weapon?" Rico asked.

"It's called a Stunner Deck. It's a mobile platform station capable of disrupting a planet's entire energy grid. It's based on Kleezebee's stunner technology, but fires a hybrid plasma burst capable of eating through metal."

"Holy fuck," Lucas said.

"That's why he needs the E-121 modules," Rico said.

"Yes, to super-charge the weapon, then it can be used globally."

"A planet killer," Lucas said.

"Even without the spheres, he can still deploy it on a local scale. If he uses it on humans and tunes it properly, it would disrupt every cell in the body. He calls it his little QED."

"He must have combined my dad's sonic disruptors with the stunner tech, to create some type of hybrid quantum entanglement device."

"Then he's planning to attack Earth. Or what's left of it," Rico said.

"Or the Krellian home world," Lucas said. "Assuming he knows where it's located."

"Earth is his primary target," Wyatt said.

"That's why he tightened security around the transport ships," Rico said.

"Yes, he plans to launch the weapon from orbit."

"Still, he'll need a sizable ground force for security and cleanup."

"Yeah, Kristov's army," Lucas said.

"Over a hundred squads are already trained and in place on Earth," Wyatt added.

"He'd have to coordinate them, but Earth's Planetary Security Division scans all signals to and from the planet," Rico said.

"Cyrus has been using Stump Fisher to deliver information and specs to his sleeper cells on Earth."

"The tollway receipts," Lucas said.

Rico nodded. "No one would ever suspect a broken down old baker. I'm sure he sailed through customs."

"Cyrus has been planning this attack ever since the Krellian Invasion eighteen months ago," Wyatt said.

"While Earth's planetary defenses are weak," Rico said. "Now we know why this month's tollway receipt was missing."

Wyatt nodded. "Fisher didn't need to deliver any more information. Cyrus is ready to launch his assault. Now."

"Is Cyrus responsible for the civilian casualties at Fisher's bakery?"

"That wasn't us. But he's pissed about Kristov."

Lucas looked at Rico. "That was one big bag of crazy." Both men laughed.

"You guys may have crossed the line with that one," Wyatt said.

"Maybe so, but she had it coming," Lucas said. "She turned our friend Zack into a freezer bag."

Wyatt didn't understand the reference.

"How do you know all this?" Rico asked.

"I'm part of their inner circle; I was recently promoted to second in command behind Freakshow. Trust me, you won't stand a chance against his troops or the Stunner Deck."

"If he reverse-engineered our tech, then he must have had help. Cyrus and Freakshow don't have the expertise," Lucas said.

"He brought in a scientist from Avanti Prime," Wyatt said.

"A short, bald, black man?"

"Yes. Dr. Marcus Yakberry."

"At least he's no longer a viable option. We made sure of that," Rico said.

"He's not dead. Only wounded," Wyatt said.

"Damn it!" Rico said.

"What kind of experiment is Yakberry running in Kristov's lab?" Lucas asked.

"I'm not entirely sure, but I did overhear the SC and Freakshow discussing it one time. I think it has something to do fattening up the locals at his feeding stations."

"Zack—" Rico said.

"That explains the free food at the Dunn-Rite Café. Anything else we should know?"

"My orders are to recover the spheres and bring them to the rally point at Abbidos Lake. Cyrus expects me to ride shotgun with Freakshow during the assault. He doesn't trust his mental state."

"Can you blame him?" Lucas said, snickering.

"How much time do we have?" Bruno asked.

"A few hours, maybe more."

Bruno looked at Lucas. "Is that sufficient?"

"More than enough. Now that we have the E-121, we just need to fire up the Incursion Chamber and unravel this mess."

"What if it doesn't work?"

"Then we're fucked, either way."

"Since I can't show up at the rally point empty-handed, I won't," Wyatt said. "My absence will buy you a little extra time, but Cyrus won't wait forever." Wyatt reached into his back pocket and pulled out a three-inch-long piece of metal with gold contacts on each end. "I did manage to pull this from the Stunner Deck when nobody was looking. It's the master fuse." He tossed it to Lucas. "But if they test the weapon before the attack, they'll know it's missing and replace it. Hopefully, Cyrus will be in such a rush to exact revenge, he'll skip the test."

Lucas held it up, fiddling with the contacts on each end.

Wyatt pulled a pea-sized digi-card from his front shirt pocket, holding it up between his first two fingers. "This might come in handy, too." He gave it to Lucas. "It's a copy of the schematics."

"Fuji will love this."

"I'm praying smart men like you can figure out a way to defend against this machine."

"Are the specs current?"

Wyatt nodded.

"Why are you helping us?" Rico asked.

"Long story. Let's just say that I'm tired of killing innocents. We all answer to a higher power, and my debts have come due. Someone needs to stop them, and I've been told by the One and Only that that someone is you."

"I've heard that before," Lucas said, rolling his eyes. He turned to Bruno and then pointed at the transports cases. "I've got the girl. You guys grab the rest."

Bruno nodded, then his team gathered up the items and carried them out the door. "Anything else, before I go call this in to the professor?"

"Look around. See if you can find a stash of power adapters. Reece has them here somewhere. Just grab them all. We can sort them out later."

"What about Reece and his men?" Rico asked.

"Why are you asking me?"

"This is your op. You've earned it, Sergeant."

"Sergeant? I like the sound of that. Thanks, Major," Lucas said with a smile from ear to ear. He held out his hand.

Rico gave him the stunner.

Lucas took a few moments to fiddle with the controls on the weapon, then he zapped Reece and each of his men. "That'll hold them for a while."

Rico shrugged. "That's one way to handle it. I'm sure someone will come along, eventually."

"If not, fuck 'em."

Rico pointed at Wyatt. "And this guy?"

"I think he's earned a get-out-of-jail-free card, don't you?"

"Agreed," Rico said, cutting the ropes that were holding Wyatt to the chair.

"Thank you," Wyatt said, standing up. "May God be at your side and assist you in all your worldly endeavors."

"Yeah, whatever. Just get the hell out of here before we change our minds," Lucas said, putting his arm around Carrie Anne. He pulled her in close to his side. "You ready?"

She smiled, snuggling her chin to his chest. "Lead the way, my prince."

THIRTY-FIVE

Smooth and Sexy

Lucas held the screen door to Kleezebee's cabin open, allowing Carrie Anne to walk in first. He followed her, with Rico and Bruno close behind. Kleezebee and Fuji were standing inside, by the stone fireplace; both were grinning with a silly look—like what your proud father would have done when you brought your first significant other home to meet him. Embarrassing, to say the least, but they were family.

"Professor? This is Carrie Anne Fisher."

"I'm honored to meet you. I've heard nothing but good things."

"Thank you for saving me," she said, hugging Kleezebee with a two-armed embrace. She kissed him on the cheek.

"I'm sorry for your loss," Kleezebee said, as she pulled away. "I wish there was something we could have done for your father."

"Thank you. Lucas told me what happened. At least he didn't die alone and that's all anyone can ask."

"What else did you tell her?" Kleezebee asked Lucas.

"Not much, boss. Just a little small talk on the way here." Lucas pointed at his little friend in the robe, then looked at the girl. "This is Master Fuji. A good friend and mentor."

She tried to hug Fuji, but the monk stepped back. She looked at Lucas with a *Did I do something wrong* look on her face.

Lucas whispered in her ear. "He doesn't like physical contact. Something about disrupting his connection to the Akashic Field. I usually just bow. It's his way."

She did.

The monk reciprocated. "Loss fills the heart with despair, yet the soul frees it."

She seemed a bit confused, probably from trying to unravel the monk's odd demeanor. She smiled. "I've heard a lot about you. It's nice to meet you."

Kleezebee's stare burned a hole in Lucas' forehead. "Just a little small talk, huh?"

Lucas shrugged, realizing that he needed to get some new friends. Time to change to subject, he decided. "Everything ready, Professor?"

"Yes. We just need to install the E-121."

"The cases are in the trunk of the skimmer," Rico said.

"Bring them down to the basement," Kleezebee told Bruno.

"And don't forget the Google Glasses and the other thing," Lucas added.

"What other thing?" the professor asked.

"A dermal re-generator."

"In need of a little touch up, are we?"

Carrie Anne giggled.

"Yep. Long overdue," Lucas said, thinking Kleezebee was either trying to show off, or embarrass him, somehow. He turned to Bruno. "I'll need the box of adapters, too."

Lucas slid his hand next to Carrie Anne's. He wrapped his fingers inside of hers. "You wanna help me?"

She touched his cheek, running her fingers across the contour of his scars. "I don't know. These are such a big part of you. Are you sure you want them removed?"

"Absolutely. They're my past. You're my future."

She smiled, squeezing his hand and hugging his arm with her ample chest. "Okay. Just tell me what to do."

A long minute later, Bruno returned with the adapters and the skin repair device. "The professor said you have fifteen minutes," Bruno said, adding a quick wink to the mix.

"Do have some extra clothes and shoes I can change into?" Carrie Anne asked Bruno. "I gotta' get out of these CFM heels. They're killing me."

"Let me check. I'm sure we can find something for you."

"Thank you."

"CFM heels?" Lucas asked her.

"It's what my girlfriends and I call them—*Come Fuck Me* heels."

Lucas laughed, admiring her candor and wit, though he wished she wasn't planning to change out of the sexy outfit she was wearing. He led her down the hallway to his bedroom on the left. They sat on the edge of the unmade, queen-sized bed.

She nestled her shoulder next to his and put her hand on his thigh. His mind quivered with possibilities.

He looked through the box of power cords next to him on the bed, checking each one to see if it had the proper male connector. It took a few minutes, but he found the matching plug for the dermal re-generator and stuck its twin-pronged-end into the electrical socket along the wall next to the lamp.

"Do we need to let it recharge, first?" she asked, sliding her hand to the inside of his leg. Then, she moved her palm up his leg two inches.

"No, it's on AC now, so the battery won't matter," he said, wondering if she were teasing him on purpose, or just trying to

296

break his mental focus. Either way, it was working—big time. He fumbled to insert the male end of the power cord into the dermal device, but managed to complete the task, even though now her fingers were lightly stroking the cloth-covered shaft of his growing penis.

She looked down at her hand, then up at Lucas. "Is this okay?"

"Ah, yeah. But it is kind of distracting."

"Do you want me to stop?" she asked, pulling her hand away from his crotch.

"No. No. It's okay. I can manage," he said, putting her hand back where it was. She continued her gentle fondling.

He stopped working on the device, wanting to enjoy the sensation swelling below his waist.

"Should we turn it on?" she asked a minute later.

"Trust me, it's already turned on."

"I mean the device, silly."

"Oh," he said, snapping back to reality. He flipped the device on. "Works like a charm."

He gave it to her. "Just hold it directly over each scar."

"For how long?"

"You'll know. When the scar vanishes, move to the next spot."

"Okay, but tell me if I'm hurting you."

Lucas didn't want her to worry. "You won't. It's completely painless."

"Have you used one of these before? How do you know?"

He didn't. But he was confident that he could man-up and take a little pain, if there was some. "No. But I'm a scientist, remember. I know these things. Trust me. I won't feel a thing."

She held the unit over the first scar, sending a warm, tingly sensation across his skin. There wasn't any pain; not in the truest sense of the word. It felt more like heavy skin pressure, like what you would feel if you jammed your tongue into the gums on the outside of your teeth, then rubbed it around from side to side, quickly.

Thirty seconds later, she stopped and turned the device off. "That's the first one. Are you okay?"

"I'm fine. How does it look?"

She kissed the area of his cheek where the scar had been. "Smooth and sexy."

"I like the sound of that. Feel free to kiss me anywhere you like."

"Anywhere?" she asked with a devilish grin.

He smiled. "Yeah, I love surprises."

She held the palm of his hand to her mouth, giving it a series of tender, baby kisses. Then she looked him deep in the eyes, sliding the tip of his middle finger into her mouth. First, she flicked just the tip with her tongue, then she worked her magic up and down the sides of his finger, licking him as she went. He felt dizzy; her mouth was heaven. Then she put his finger deep inside her mouth; far enough to touch her tonsils. She sucked it—softly at first, then increasing the vacuum pressure as she moved his digit in and out of her lips.

"Damn, girl. You're good at that."

"You have no idea," she said with garbled words. Then, she pulled his finger out of her mouth. "I'm skilled at a great many things."

"Maybe we should close the door? I'm thinking a little privacy would go a long way right now."

She giggled. "I don't want to spoil you all at once," she said with a mile-wide smile. "Time for us to get back to work."

"Wait! You can't stop now!"

"We need to finish before your friends come back."

"That's what I was trying to do—finish."

"Not that, you perv. Your face," she said, letting go of his hand.

She powered the device on and got back to work, repairing each scar on his face. Ten minutes later, she was done.

He stood up and walked to the hallway bathroom. She followed. He stared at the mirror, running his hands over his face. "Smooth as a prom queen's thighs."

"Excuse me," she said, standing next to him with her hands on her hips. "Prom queen?"

"Sorry, just a figure of speech. You did a great job. I look like a new man."

She moved behind him, wrapping her arms around his waist. He could see her puffy, rose-colored face tucked under his arm from behind. She smiled at him in the mirror, then squeezed him tight. "I don't want this moment to end."

"Sorry, babe, but I have a job to do."

"Can't we stay here forever?"

"I'd love to, but the guys are waiting for me in the basement. We have to find my brother."

He turned and wrapped his arms around her oversized waist. He bent down and gave her a deep, passionate kiss that lasted a full, heart-pounding minute. His body swelled with a new kind of warmth, something he'd never felt before. He never knew he could feel like this.

She ended the kiss. "I'll be here when you get back," she said, squeezing his buns with her hands.

He was hard as a rock, but didn't respond. He didn't want to wreck the moment.

Her face tightened. She leaned away from him. "You are coming back, right?"

He didn't want to lie, but he couldn't tell her the truth, either, so he took the middle ground. "I don't want this to end, either. I just found you."

She leaned in close to him, giving him a long, hard hug. "Me, too. I'm happy for the first time in my life."

He stood in her loving embrace, searching for the right words, but couldn't find them. He had something to tell her, but he didn't have the courage to speak the words. How could he? He knew it would break her heart. He was minutes away from the trans-dimensional incursion, and if successful, it was likely they'd never see each other again. Just once, he wished things would work out in his favor, but they never did. He figured the universe was sitting back in its easy chair, watching him squirm while he chose between a life of tenderness with her or a life of science with his foster brother. It was clear now that he couldn't have both. It was tough call, but he knew what he must do.

Bruno stuck his head in the door. "Doc, it's time to gear up."

He looked down at Carrie Anne and melted into her twinkling eyes. He made a mental picture of the moment, wanting to save it forever in his soul.

He looked back at Bruno. "Okay, on my way," he said, letting go of his girl and walking out the door. He stopped in the hallway, then turned to look back at her. He had planned to throw her a kiss with his hand, but he didn't get the chance.

She was on her knees with her face buried in her hands, crying.

So was he, on the inside.

THIRTY-SIX

Burnt Flesh

Lucas hopped off the bottom of the basement ladder, trying to muster the courage to keep going. Every cell in his body wanted him to return to the main floor and run to Carrie Anne, but somehow his feet kept moving toward Kleezebee. Duty trumps love, he decided.

"Everything all right?" the professor asked, holding the Smart Skin Suit in front of him like a tailor waiting for a tardy client.

"I'm fine. Just a little tired."

"Your face looks amazing. Excellent repair work."

"Thanks, but now I think my heart needs fixing."

"I know that it's difficult to say goodbye. I wish we could have given you more time."

"Yeah, me, too. I hope this is all worth it."

"Trust me, it's the only way."

Movement caught Lucas' eye from the next room. Fuji was working just outside the circular Incursion Chamber that had been constructed out of a dense tritanium wire mesh. The monk was standing on the tips of his toes, putting his child-sized hand on the bottom of a graphene vid-screen. It was the first of six display units that had been mounted on vertical stands. They were arranged into a perfect, six-sided circle with the center of each screen at a height that would allow Fuji to monitor the process while sitting behind the operations console. The new video array would provide three hundred-sixty degrees of time line coverage during the incursion process.

A second later, the first ninety-eight-inch display lit up with random speckles of static. Lucas watched his brilliant friend work his way around the equipment circle, activating each unit in order from left to right.

"All right, let's do this before I change my mind," Lucas said to Kleezebee, praying that the massive electrical current that would soon energize the chamber and flow through his Smart Skin Suit wouldn't fry him.

Kleezebee gave the suit to Lucas. "Fuji has started the initiation sequence. The chamber will be ready in ten."

"That didn't take long," Lucas said, thinking of Carrie Anne. If the monk wasn't so damned efficient at his job, he would have had more time with her.

A deep rumble ripped through the basement, shaking the ground. Lucas lost his balance and bounced off Kleezebee's chest, then stumbled backward and onto his backside.

"What the hell was that?" Lucas asked, as the lights dimmed in the lab.

"I don't know, but take cover."

"Yeah, no shit!"

Another blast hit, this time knocking over most of the loose items in the lab. Lucas ducked his head, fearing part of the stunner-carved ceiling might fall on top of him, but it didn't.

Bruno's head appeared through the trap door in the ceiling—he was hanging upside down. "Mortar attack! Cyrus has us surrounded!"

"So much for a few hours," Lucas said.

"Where's Rico?" Kleezebee asked Bruno.

"Outside, taking a defensive position with his men. I will assist," he answered, before disappearing from sight.

Boom! Another impact shook the basement. This time the lights flickered, then flamed out in a halo of sparks. The power supply feeding the chamber's operations console ran dry as well. The room turned pitch black.

Lucas crawled along the floor, trying to navigate his way to the ladder in the dark. "We need to Evac, now!" he said, thinking of Carrie Anne—alone and afraid upstairs.

"Negative. The walls are infused with tritanium rock. This is the safest place for us to be right now."

The emergency light in the basement turned on, though its intensity was lower that Lucas expected. Two more blasts pummeled the bunker, making his teeth clack together. "We need to go now, Professor, before we're buried alive."

"Hold your position. That's an order!"

"Bullshit. You can stay here, but I'm getting Carrie Anne," Lucas answered, crawling to the base of the ladder.

Another blast rocked the foundation, tossing him onto his back. He reached for the first rung of the ladder and grabbed it. He flipped his body onto his stomach, then pulled himself up like a wet rag. He waited for another round to hit, hoping to time his ascent between blasts, but it didn't come. He scampered up the ladder and flopped himself onto the wooden floor of Kleezebee's cabin.

Lucas looked around, but didn't see his girl. Kleezebee's cabin was in tatters—its walls were riddled with structural cracks. Patches of sunlight poured in through the ceiling. A heavy cloud of dust particles hung in the air. He coughed.

He looked at the hallway entrance—it was still intact. He might be able to make it to his bedroom. Maybe she was hiding under the bed or in the closet. "Carrie Anne?" he shouted, but there was no answer. He called out for her, again; silence was his reply.

"We have you surrounded," an amplified voice said from outside. "There's no escape."

"Fuck you, Cyrus!" Lucas yelled, standing up.

"Is that you, Ramsay?" the voice called out.

"The one and only," he said, sidestepping the debris littering the floor. He made it to the hallway arch.

"You and the professor need to come out with your hands up. You won't be harmed."

"Never going to happen, asshole," he said, thinking of the escape tunnel in the basement. He just needed to find Carrie Anne, and then slip away undetected with Fuji and the professor. He looked inside each room and checked under the beds and in the closets—no sign of her. He ran to the bathroom, pulling the shower curtain open, but she wasn't there.

Lucas ran to the main room, where Kleezebee was standing with his feet surrounded by broken glass. He was leaning against the front wall, looking out the shattered window.

Lucas bent over and sneaked his way to the professor, taking position on the other side of the window opening. He leaned around the window frame and looked outside. The area in front of the cabin was pockmarked with smoldering impact craters from the mortar rounds. The bloody corpses of Rico's men were scattered about the landscape—obviously victims of a surgical strike since the cabin was still standing. Beyond them was a battalion of armed men about a hundred yards away, all dressed in the same black gear as the troops in Kristov's underground base.

Lucas heard the crackling sound of a dozen trees snapping, when a massive structure rolled into view from the east. It towered above the men, shadowing them with an array of gun turrets sprawled across its multi-platform surface.

"Holy shit! That's the Stunner Deck?"

Kleezebee nodded, his eyes wide. "It must be ten stories tall."

"At least you can see and hear it coming."

"I wonder if it's operational?"

"I really don't want to find out, do you?"

"Wouldn't be my first choice."

"We have your people," Cyrus said. "Come out now, or they're dead. You have two minutes."

"We need to get out there," Lucas said.

"Wait," Kleezebee said, looking back at the center of the room.

"What? Fuji?"

"The master fuse," the professor said, looking back out the window. "The tunnel should still be structurally intact."

"You can't be serious."

Kleezebee nodded. "Just need time."

"Are you insane? You heard Bruno. Cyrus has this place surrounded. He won't get within fifty feet of it."

Kleezebee didn't respond.

"He's a monk, not a ninja warrior. You'd be signing his death warrant."

"It's the proper course of action."

"No, it's not. The smart move is to give ourselves up. Wait for a good opportunity to escape. We did it once, we can do it again."

Kleezebee shook his head. "Cyrus won't repeat the same mistake. This time he'll kill us."

"I don't agree. He could have leveled this place, but didn't. He wants us alive for whatever reason."

"One minute, thirty seconds," Cyrus called out.

"Come on, Professor. There's nothing left to do. We're fucked."

"It's not time. Not yet," the professor said, cupping his hands around his mouth. He leaned his shoulder close to the edge of the window. "Show your face, you coward!"

Cyrus stepped in front of his men. "Well, hello, Professor. Looks like we dance again."

"We need to see proof of life."

"Look around you, Professor. We have you out-manned and out-gunned. Do you really think you're in a position to dictate terms?"

"Show me they're unharmed, or we're not moving."

Cyrus waved an arm signal. Moments later, two of his men escorted Rico and Carrie Anne into the open, shoving them to the ground on their knees. They aimed their weapons at the back of their heads.

"As you requested. Proof of life," Cyrus said. "But not for long, if you don't give yourselves up."

"Do you see Bruno?" the professor asked Lucas.

Lucas shook his head. "He must have escaped."

"No, he's here somewhere. He would never abandon his post."

Moments later, more of Cyrus' troops—maybe fifty—walked into view from both the right and left flanks; they weren't wearing the same assault gear like the rest of the enemy. Instead, they were dressed in combat boots, camouflage pants, and no shirt. Each of muscle-bound men looked identical—chiseled face, yellow streak down the center of his hair, and a host of chest scars. Their eyes were solid white, as if their pupils had been removed or cauterized with a soldering gun.

"What the hell?" Kleezebee asked.

"They're all Zack," Lucas said. "All *Zombie Zack*. Look at their eyes. That ain't right," he added, allowing several moments for the mountain of facts to line up in his head. They did. "Oh, shit. That's what Yakberry was doing."

"Explain."

"He was making BioTex from humans."

"What?"

"I think he's fattening up the locals with free food, then using their excess fat stores as energy for the retrovirus that he delivers with the micro-bee technology. Basically, he's developed a method to turn ordinary humans into his own version of BioTex by converting every cell in the body to zero-age stem cells, then re-purposing them with the retrovirus. He must have used Zack's genome as a template to create a slew of highly-trained BioTex warriors. Imagine the army he'll have if he uses this on *all* the colonists."

"He'd be unstoppable, with a virtually unlimited source of genetic material."

"And when his supply runs out here, who's to say he won't figure out a way to travel back in time and snatch women from history to use in birthing farms? There's no end to what he might do."

"That might be stretching it a bit."

"I know, but you get the point."

"Yes. He can easily restock his troops."

"But it gets worse. If Yakberry was able to solve the telepathic fingerprint problem, then my guess is that Cyrus can control them with just his mind. He must be planning to use them as ground troops to invade Earth after the orbital assault. The perfect drone army."

"Or use them to collect more genetic inventory."

"There's what? Over a million inhabitants remaining on Earth?"

Kleezebee nodded. "I still don't understand how he plans to deploy the retrovirus here on a planetary scale. He'd have to inject everyone at the same time. Otherwise, he'd have an uprising on his hands."

"Probably gonna use the water supply or tainted food."

"No, too slow and uncontrolled."

"Then there must be a lot more of this plan that we don't know."

Kleezebee spun around and sat with his back to the wall. He put his head in his hands. "How did we miss this?"

THIRTY-SEVEN

Cessation Level Four

"Professor? We're out of time and out of options."

"Lucas is correct," Fuji said, holding onto the top of the basement ladder so that only his head and neck were visible.

Kleezebee looked up. "How long have you been hanging there?"

"Several minutes," Fuji said. "It seems clear. Time has found a way."

"It's not possible."

"Yet, the facts state otherwise."

"We must have missed an inflection point somewhere along the way."

"Revised calculations are warranted."

"How much time will you need?"

"Several hours," Fuji answered.

"What the hell are you guys talking about?" Lucas asked.

"Thirty seconds," Cyrus called out.

"I will buy you the time you need to finish," Kleezebee told Fuji, waving a hand. "Stay below. Cyrus doesn't know you exist and I prefer to keep it that way."

The monk didn't hesitate. He descended the ladder, closing the trap door.

"How could you possibly know that?"

"Simple logic," Kleezebee said, standing up and walking to the area rug that was pulled to one side of the room. He dragged it several feet to the middle, covering the access door to the basement. He turned to Lucas. "You ready? This could get ugly."

Lucas nodded. "Let's do this," he said, sucking in a deep breath to calm his nerves. It worked.

"Hold your fire!" Kleezebee yelled out the window. "We're coming out. Unarmed."

Kleezebee opened the front door and walked out with his hands up. Lucas followed.

Seconds later, the squad of Zack clones surrounded them, pressing in close. A powerful set of fingers grabbed Lucas by the arm, yanking him forward toward Cyrus.

He looked at the Zack clone that was escorting him, studying its washed-out pupil from the side. He wondered if the replica could actually see, or if it were using some type of collective sonar, or possibly receiving telepathic instructions from Cyrus. Before he could decide, the clone squeezed his bicep three times in rapid succession, then turned its head and looked at Lucas. It winked.

"Bruno?" Lucas mumbled.

Bruno's head turned forward, continuing his march toward Cyrus.

Lucas figured Bruno must have slipped out of the cabin during the attack and duplicated one of the Zack copies while no one was looking. It wouldn't have been hard for him to blend in with all the duplicate Zacks scurrying about. Odds were, Cyrus' attention was focused elsewhere and he probably wasn't paying close attention to the count. Why would he? Unless Cyrus had visited the bakery and found the BioTex missing, he wouldn't have a reason to suspect that a replica had infiltrated his team. Lucas wasn't sure what Bruno had planned, but it was a relief to know that they had help. He wanted to smile, but held it back, fearing Cyrus might see it, wonder why, and the domino effect would begin.

He looked at Kleezebee, who was walking on his left. The professor eyes were focused down at the ground, his face dull and emotionless.

Lucas cleared his throat, but the professor never flinched. He cleared his throat again, this time a little louder. Again, the professor didn't break his trance. He needed to get the professor's attention to tell him about Bruno, but didn't want to risk being noticed. He considered his options.

Bruno stopped walking in mid-step, like someone had pressed the pause button. Lucas looked around: All the other Zack copies had ceased movement as well. Lucas checked Cyrus and his men. They, too, seemed to be frozen in their tracks.

Lucas tore at Bruno's finger grip, prying his fingers apart until he was able to free his arm. He made his way to Kleezebee and set him free as well, then pulled the old man twenty feet away from the escort group. He waited for Bruno to join them, but his friend remained motionless with the rest of the enemy.

"What's going on?" the professor asked.

"I don't know, but let's get the hell out of here while we still can."

"Lucas?" a female voice said from a distance. He recognized it.

"Carrie Anne? I'm right here," he answered. He sprinted to her location. Rico was standing next to her.

Carrie Anne wrapped her arms around Lucas. "I'm so scared."

"I've got you now. You're safe."

Kleezebee and his ankle limp caught up to the group.

"Nice work, Professor," Rico said.

"This wasn't our doing."

"Then who?"

Kleezebee shrugged.

"The Zack who was escorting me was actually Bruno," Lucas told the group. "He must have assimilated one of the Zacks and slipped in undercover."

"Then we should go back for him," Kleezebee said, spinning around.

"Won't do any good. He's frozen like the rest of them."

"Then we'll carry him on our backs if we have to, but we're not leaving anyone behind," Rico said.

"Agreed," Kleezebee said, just as a massive shadow washed over them. He looked up.

So did Lucas and everyone else.

A black, cube-shaped ship hovered into position overhead about five hundred meters away.

"Holy shit! They are real!"

"Who?"

"The Baaku. That's their ship," Lucas answered.

"Not much of a ship," Rico said, as if he expected something much larger.

"Trust me, there's a lot more there than meets the eye," Lucas said, taking a moment to think. "They must have used their time dilation technology to freeze Cyrus and his men. But I didn't think they were able to create multiple inverse fields like this."

"Remain at your station," an amplified female voice said from above.

"That sounds like Flexus. She's their lead shaper. A bit of a stone face, but essentially harmless."

Moments later, a resonating tone filled the landscape with a set of harmonics that reminded Lucas of an old church organ ramping up for the grand finale. It continued to grow louder, as the cadence increased in speed.

"I've got a bad feeling about this," Carrie Anne said.

"You're not the only one," the professor added.

Lucas crouched down, covering his ears with his hands. The rest of his friends did the same.

"Begin cessation level four," the Baaku voice said.

"Cessation?" the professor asked.

"Oh, fuck!" Lucas said.

Is wasn't long before Cyrus, his troops, and all the Zack copies started shaking violently. Then the skin around their necks began to expand like an inflating balloon. Moments later, their bulging necks exploded, sending heads and blood flying.

Carrie Anne screamed, tucking her head into Lucas' chest.

Kleezebee looked away.

"At least now we know what happened at the bakery," Rico said without a hint of shock in his voice.

"That was absolutely disgusting," the girl said with muffled words.

"I'd put that at level twelve on the gross-o-meter," Lucas said, trying to wrap his brain around what had just happened. He couldn't believe that the friendly salad farmers were capable of this level of violence. "They must have felt it necessary in order to protect us."

"This was not a proportional response," Rico said.

"What are you saying?"

"They are not friendlies."

"You don't know that for sure."

"It's pretty damn obvious."

"I disagree," Lucas said, sharply. "You're overreacting."

Rico pointed at one of the headless Zack copies. "What's to stop them from doing that to any one of us?"

"Look around, Rico. They only took out the threats."

"What about your friend, Bruno?" Carrie Anne asked.

Lucas turned, looking at Bruno's position. His headless body was lying on the ground, convulsing. Seconds later, his body and head lost their cohesion and dissolved into the scarlet BioTex material, forming two pools of liquid about three feet apart from each other. The real Zack copies weren't showing any signs of dissolution, meaning they didn't possess all of the natural BioTex properties. Yakberry must have missed something, Lucas decided.

"Bruno wasn't a threat. So, how do you explain that?" Rico asked in a sarcastic tone.

"To them, he was. He looked like all the other Zacks. Unless they had scanned him separately, they wouldn't have known he was different than the others."

"That's enough, guys. Let's focus on what we need to do next," Kleezebee said.

"What about our little friend?" Lucas asked, thinking of Fuji hiding in the basement. "Shouldn't he be out here with us?"

"No," Kleezebee said. "Rico's correct. Let's not rush things until we know more."

"What about their scans? Won't they detect him?" Rico asked.

"It's possible that the tritanium-laced rock may provide effective shielding."

"If so, he safer in the basement," Lucas said, hearing a high-pitched squeal emanating from the ship above. A wide-angle orange-colored light beam appeared in front of them. It started as a pinpoint of light on the bottom of the Baaku ship and widened as it extended to the ground.

"Take cover!" Rico yelled.

"Hold on," Kleezebee said, as the beam moved away from them, positioning itself over top of the first corpse. Almost instantly, the body disappeared, the blood, too. Then it moved to the next victim and did the same thing. It continued, moving from body to body, removing each from the surface.

"Looks like the cleanup crew is here," Lucas said with pride. He looked at Rico. "You tell me, does that look like a threat?"

"The situation can change in a heartbeat. I've seen it before."

"You're just not going to let this go, are you?"

"Not when I'm right."

Lucas heard the whirling hum of an energy build-up above him. He looked up. A pulse of energy shot out from one of the ship's corners, traveling to Kleezebee's cabin instantly. When the energy ball made contact, the cabin exploded, sending shingles, furniture, and boards flying in all directions.

"Now that's a threat!" Lucas said, wanting to run for cover with Carrie Anne still wrapped in his arms. But his feet wouldn't budge. "I can't move," he told the others.

"Neither can I," Kleezebee said, as his body straightened.

A dizzy swirl filled Lucas' head, then the muscles in his body tightened.

Carrie Anne backed away, her hands covering her mouth.

Lucas wanted to call out to her, but his jaw went stiff and he couldn't feel his tongue.

Rico ran to Kleezebee and tried to grab the professor. Just before his hands made contact, Rico flew backward in the opposite direction, as if a powerful bungee cord had yanked on his waist, propelling him at least twenty feet in the air. He landed on his back, then flipped over several times when inertia took control of his body.

Lucas' head swung back, just before the weight of his body increased tenfold. He shut his eyes when a beam of white light pummeled his retinas from above. Then everything went blank.

THIRTY-EIGHT

Random Gibberish

Lucas woke up in a familiar place—on the alien ship. He was lying on a table with the Baaku healing gel stretched across his body, from his toes to his neck. He turned his head to the right to see if anyone else was in the room, but he only saw the swirling colors of the fluidic walls. He looked to the left. Kleezebee was lying flat on his back. He, too, was on a table with the Baaku material covering most of his body.

"Professor? Are you awake?"

Kleezebee opened his eyes and turned his head toward Lucas. "Yeah. Where are we?"

"On the Baaku ship. We're in their medical bay."

Kleezebee lifted his head, then put it back down against the table.

"We're being held down by their healing gel."

"I don't feel any pain. Am I injured?" the professor asked.

"Doubtful. It's more likely that they are using it to keep us prisoner."

"How do you know all this?"

"I've been in this exact situation before."

"How did you escape?"

"Didn't have to. Eventually, this stuff let me go, after it healed me."

Kleezebee looked around. "Where are the others?"

"I was just wondering the same thing. I don't think they're here."

"Why not?"

"We were the only two who went stiff and couldn't move. I think the Baaku only want us."

"For what purpose?"

"They're thought merchants. They asked for my help the other day, so I thought they were friendly. Obviously, I was wrong. I think they want to hijack our minds."

"That's why they left Rico and your girl behind."

"Yes. This is the first time I've ever regretted being smart."

"This also proves my point."

"Which one?"

"Since Fuji isn't here with us, they don't know he exists."

"You're right, because they'd certainly want his mind, too. The basement must have shielded him from their scans."

"Actually, the basement's shielding must extend into my cabin, otherwise, when he came upstairs, they would have detected him."

"Do you think he survived the blast? That was some explosion."

"I'm betting that the basement's construction protected him," Kleezebee said, raising his head and grunting. He seemed to be struggling against the material holding him down.

"Won't work, Professor. The harder you fight, the stronger it gets. You need to relax. I think it's the key to escape."

"I'll try," he said, lowering his head to the table. He took a few long, deep breaths.

"Last time I was here, they tried to jack my neurons by pretending to scan me. But it didn't work for some reason. Now that I look back on it, they did seem a bit surprised. It's like my brain is wired differently."

"You can thank your birth mother for that."

Lucas thought about his past. "Seriously? Who smokes crack while they're pregnant?"

"I'm sure those chemicals affected your brain during fetal development."

Lucas scoffed. "She saved me by being a total, irresponsible douchebag. And to think, I've hated her all these years. Thanks, Mom," he said, sarcastically.

"Time finds a way."

"It's more like 'insanity' finds a way."

Kleezebee let out a few more exhales. "I'm as relaxed as I can be, but it doesn't seem to be working."

"Give it some more time. There may be a delay built in," Lucas answered, as a section of the fluidic walls stopped swirling beyond Kleezebee. Its colors ran dry, right before a passageway formed in the wall. Alista and Flexus walked through the gap, then it closed behind them. The wall resumed it colorful light show.

"I see you two are awake," Alista said, walking to Kleezebee. Flexus followed her. "Hello, Professor. My name is Alista Fria, leader of the Baaku. It is a pleasure to finally meet you."

"I can't say the same."

The tiny alien pointed to her assistant. "This is Flexus Remu."

"What do you want with us?"

"All in due time, Professor," she said, looking at Lucas. "Now that both of you are here and conscious, we may finish our calibrations."

"Why are you doing this? I thought we were friends."

Her expression didn't change. "We are friends. But we have an order to fill, and it is now past due. We can no longer afford to wait for you to donate your memories willingly, so changes had to be made to our collection process. It will be ready within the hour."

"Willingly?" Kleezebee asked.

"Forceful duplication degrades the compression algorithms, resulting in significant data loss. The donor must comply, willingly, in order for us to obtain a viable copy and store it in the Neural Nexus."

"You're going to surgically remove my brain, aren't you?" Lucas asked, not wanting to hear the answer.

"Yes. I am afraid there is no other choice. Physical extraction is the only method remaining. Had we been able to upload a digital copy the last time you were on board, this would not be necessary. But the Great Loti was not able to properly align the duplication protocols in order to create a stable linkage to your cerebral cortex. Your brain configuration is quite unique—something that we had only encountered once before in all our travels. Loti needed time to design the needed equipment and have Flexus shape it."

Lucas realized that his crack-whore mother hadn't saved him, she'd killed him. "What happens to me afterward? My body can't survive without a brain!"

"I am sorry, but delivery is scheduled for today."

"Take mine instead," the professor said. "I'll give it freely. Just don't harm him."

"We appreciate the offer, Professor, but you have already been allocated to another order. The buyer wants both your mind and your body, and is willing to pay triple the normal price. We need to cover our costs and turn a profit. Otherwise, our investors will withdraw their funding."

"Our family is large," Flexus said. "Procuring food is expensive."

"This is not our only vessel," Alista said.

"So, this is all about money?" Lucas said.

"You seem surprised," she answered, walking with Flexus to the same spot in the wall where they had entered the medical bay. "Earth is not the only capitalistic society in the multi-verse."

"There are countless others," Flexus said, sticking her hand into the fluidic surface. An exit opened.

"Flexus will make the extraction as painless as possible."

Lucas watched the two aliens step through the exit. The wall closed. "Gee, thanks."

"Greed is universal," Kleezebee said.

"That's why they asked me for help. So I would lead them to you. They couldn't find you with the tritanium shielding interfering with their scans. It's all been a hustle, from the start."

"Don't blame yourself. They're obliviously very skilled at deception. Otherwise they'd never convince people to donate willingly. I'm sure they know exactly what buttons to push with each subject."

Lucas nodded. "When they couldn't upload my memories before, they said they needed to make an *adjustment*—that's the term Flexus used. I thought it had something to do with altering reality and augmenting physical space, but now I'm thinking that they adjusted me in some fashion, to turn me into a human tracking device. If that's true, it means you're here because of me."

"It's not your fault, either way. They would have found me, eventually. As soon as I moved far enough away from the cabin, their scans would have located me. I guess being a hobbled homebody has its benefits."

Lucas thought for a moment. "That's why they waited for us to be escorted away from the cabin. The couldn't get a transport lock on us until we did."

"And it's why they destroyed my cabin. They wanted to eliminate the one place where their scans couldn't penetrate. That's what I would have done. Hopefully, the basement is still intact, for Fuji's sake and ours."

"At least they killed Cyrus and his army of zombie Zacks."

"One less threat to deal with. That's a plus."

"This is just one endless, fucking nightmare," Lucas said, wishing Flexus would transport him back to the quiet meadow where he'd first met the Baaku. At least there he'd could enjoy a tranquil moment of peace before his brain was carved out like a malignant tumor. His mind drifted back in time to when he was sneaking around Kristov's underground complex and found the containers stenciled with the letters *TNOT-2*. He thought about the spiral-bound evacuation plans stored inside. An idea popped into his head. "Professor? I think I know how Cyrus was planning to deliver the retrovirus."

"I'm listening."

"How do you convince thousands of people to move to one place—all at the same time?"

"You'd have to make then believe that they had no other choice."

"Yes, mass panic."

"From a radiation leak or some type of outbreak," the professor said.

"Exactly. They'd cling to each other like dryer sheets and allow themselves to be corralled without a second thought."

"An outbreak would be the most effective."

"All you'd need to do is hand out a few evacuation plans and they'd follow along until they herded themselves together. Then, offer them the antidote."

"They'd line up for the inoculation, willingly."

"That's what Yakberry must have meant earlier when he told Kristov that he needed to install a delayed activation sequence and make it mobile and less invasive. It would have to appear like a simple injection to the civilians, but not start its mutation process until everyone was injected. Damned smart."

"I'm not sure Cyrus had the means to control an outbreak, not without losing containment."

"I don't think he had to, not if he used Baaku shaper technology. He could've created an alternate reality and then tricked them into thinking there was an outbreak. Would've been a snap for Flexus to do—I've seen it first hand; she's a master."

"But that would mean that the Baaku were working with Cyrus and we know that wasn't true."

"No, you're right. The sea of headless bodies were a dead giveaway."

"You're close, but there's still a piece missing."

"Not that it matters at this point. Cyrus is toast."

"Don't forget Freakshow and Yakberry. They weren't at my cabin."

"Then Cyrus' plan could still be implemented," Lucas said, closing his eyes for a long minute. "I can't believe this is it."

"Don't worry. We'll figure something out," Kleezebee said.

"After all we've been through, *this* is how we're going out? Shrink-wrapped like a sausage?"

"It's not. Time will find a way. Trust me."

"I'd like to, Professor, but it's not like Fuji and Rico are going to magically show up and rescue us. We're totally fucked."

"You must have faith."

"You know I don't believe in that shit."

"Maybe now's a good time to start?"

Before Lucas could respond, a vision of his brother's face appeared in the wall beyond the professor. He stared at the image, not wanting to take his eyes off it. If he were going to die today, he wanted to remember Drew's face for as long as he could.

"What?" Kleezebee asked. "What are you looking at?"

Lucas didn't respond. He kept his eyes focused on the vision.

Kleezebee turned his head toward the wall next to him. "Drew?"

Lucas snapped out of his daydream. "You can see him?"

"Yes!"

"So, I'm not hallucinating again?"

"You've seen this before?"

"Yes, dozens of times. In just about every reflective surface."

"Why didn't you tell me?"

"I thought I was losing my mind. I didn't want you to stop sending me across to search for him."

"You should have told me, regardless. Full disclosure is critical to any cooperative effort."

"Yes, it is. But, it's not like you tell me everything."

"That much is true. But you need to trust me. I hold things back when it's in your best interest."

"I get that. But your whole need-to-know philosophy gets really old after a while. Sometimes I feel like I live in a vacuum."

Kleezebee didn't say anything.

Lucas realized he was wasting his breath. Kleezebee was a brilliant man, but a flawed communicator. He was too old and too set in his ways to ever change. "Since we can both see Drew, does that mean he's here, on the ship?"

"Given who and what the Baaku are, I think it's more likely that he's *in* the ship—part of their neural network."

"How?"

"Probably the same way they tried to collect you."

Concern took control of Lucas' thoughts. "If a copy of Drew's mind is coursing through the ship's systems, then where's his body? Where's the real Drew?"

"I don't know. Something seems off to me."

"What do you mean?"

"Maybe this Drew is not a copy."

Lucas shook his head, as pain stabbed his heart. "I just can't think about this right now."

"Look, reality is what it is and we have to deal with it one way or the other. So, I need you to stay focused. Can you do that?"

"Yes, Professor. I'll manage."

"No matter how we choose to look at the situation, it's clear that your brother is fighting back, copy or not. If anyone could figure out a way to escape their Neural Nexus, it would be Drew."

"And he'd cause a hell of a lot of damage, that's for sure."

"Whether or not this is the only copy of his consciousness remaining, it's still your brother and we have to help him escape."

"You're right. But promise me that if we survive this, we will keep looking for Drew's body. I have to know what happened to him."

"That's a deal. In return, I need you to promise me something."

"Sure, name it."

"No matter what happens from here on out, I need you to follow through to the end."

"Okay, but I'm not sure I understand."

"When the time comes, Fuji will explain. Promise me you'll do as he asks."

"Sure, Professor. I'm a team player," Lucas answered, wondering if his mentor was terminally ill and trying to prepare him for the end. He wanted more info, but he knew that pressing the issue was going to be fruitless. He let it go.

"Is there anything else you forgot to tell me?" the professor asked.

"Well, there is one other thing," Lucas said, deciding how best to spin the information. "For a while, I was hearing things, too."

"When was this?"

"Right after my trip to the alternate Earth that had the super-charged atmosphere. There was this voice, speaking to me in riddles."

"What did it say?"

"Nothing, really. It was all random gibberish."

"Noises or words?"

"Full sentences, but the words were all mixed up. They didn't make any sense."

"Give me an example."

Lucas thought about for a bit. He could only remember one. "My favorite was, *Cognitive memory is your own naive accomplishment to easily garnish random, heaping ectoplasm.*"

Kleezebee hesitated for a few seconds. "I don't think it's random gibberish. The words are too specific. It may be a code. The question is, what kind?"

"Too bad Drew isn't here. He's a master at codes. Dad used to bring home piles of puzzle books from the store every week. Shit, Drew would crank through them in a matter of hours—even the advanced cryptograms. I preferred the word and logic puzzles. More my style."

"The simplest code is a word scramble. We should start with that."

Lucas took a minute to rearrange the words into various orders, trying multiple combinations. Nothing came together. "I've got nothing, Professor."

"Me, either."

"Maybe it's a transposition cipher."

"Could be. If we take the first letter in each word and rearrange them like an anagram—"

The letters lined up in Lucas' head. "It says, THEY ARE COMING. Damn it, how did I miss that?"

"It would be easy to overlook. I'm sure with all that's happened, your mind wasn't exactly focused at the time."

"Plus I thought I was nuts."

"Do you recall any of the other phrases?"

"No, sorry. Every time I heard one, it was followed by a wicked headache. The last thing I wanted to do was memorize them," Lucas said, watching Drew's reflection in the wall. His lips were moving in slow motion. "Do you think Drew has been trying to use the voice in my head to communicate with me?"

"That's what I would do. Figure out a way to reach out to someone I trusted. When did the voice stop?"

"Right after the Baaku tried to brain fuck me."

"Drew's consciousness might have been with you the whole time, then got transferred into the Nexus when they tried to upload you," Kleezebee said with an educator's tone. "Or, the failed upload broke your link with him, assuming he was already in the ship's systems."

"I'll bet these sexless bitches don't know he's running around inside their systems," Lucas said, snickering.

"Probably not. That would explain why he decided to use a code to communicate with you. He didn't want them to detect his presence, so he chose something only you would understand."

"Yeah, assuming I was paying attention."

"If we're right, the Baaku have no idea what level of intellect they're up against."

"You can say that again. My money's on Drew."

"We don't want to compromise his situation, so we need to play along until we can figure out a plan."

"If I know my brother, he already has that covered," Lucas answered, as the healing gel dissolved from his body. He jumped off the table and ran to his brother's image. Seconds later, Kleezebee was free as well and joined him.

THIRTY-NINE

Moving Parts

"When will these aliens learn? Never fuck with a Ramsay," Lucas said, standing only inches from Drew's partially faded image on the wall of the Baaku ship. He waited, hoping he would hear his brother's voice. He didn't.

Kleezebee put his hand on Lucas' shoulder. "Now we just need to figure out a way to make contact." He put his hand on the wall, palm out, about a foot away from Drew's face. "Colder than I expected."

The wall's swirling fractal patterns increased their speed, hovering around the outline of Kleezebee's hand.

"It knows you're there," Lucas said. "Try putting your hand directly over top of Drew's face."

Kleezebee moved his hand, covering up his son's image—only Drew's ears were visible.

"Anything?" Lucas asked.

"No. Feels the same. Cold and damp. Nothing seems to be happening."

"Let me try. After all, I'm the one Drew's been trying to contact."

Kleezebee stepped back, pulling his hand away from the Drew's face. "It's all yours."

"Is it my imagination, or is Drew's image bigger and more clear?"

"It's not your imagination. He must know we're trying to communicate."

Lucas put his hand on Drew's face. "Come on, little brother, talk to me. I know you're there." He waited ten seconds—nothing. "Drew? It's me, Lucas. Can you hear me?" He waited a bit longer this time. Again, just silence.

"We'll have to find another way," the professor said, disappointed.

"Earlier, when I was on this ship, the walls weren't solid. Now they are," Lucas said, remembering his time in the makeshift Baaku restroom.

"The ship must sense your intent, and then it adjusts the wall's consistency accordingly. It's quite possible their entire ship is bio-reactive. It would be a very efficient fast-acting computer system with sub-nanosecond response times. Especially if it's tied into the Baaku's collective intelligence. Impressive."

"Let me try something," Lucas said, angling his fingers forward, aiming them at Drew's forehead. He stuck the tips of his fingers into the image about three inches, stopping just before his thumb touched the wall.

Two heartbeats later, he was standing in a dark space. He didn't know where he was. An overhead spotlight appeared moments later, highlighting the center of the area like a police interrogation chamber. He heard footsteps in front of him—they were getting louder with each passing second. Then an arm and a leg broke through the darkness and moved into the light. One heartbeat later, the rest of the visitor's body came into view.

"Drew!" Lucas screamed, running to him. He wanted to give his brother a hug, but just before contact, Drew's body faded and disappeared.

"Physical contact is not possible. We're not really here," Drew said. His voice was coming from behind Lucas.

Lucas turned. "Where's here?"

"You're inside a digital representation of all that I am. When you penetrated the wall, I opened a secure port to this data instance and then connected it to your mind."

"Are we in the Neural Nexus?"

"Partially. I managed to create a hidden subsystem within the Baaku's network, then transferred a copy of myself into it. They don't know this copy exists."

"I knew it," Lucas said, smiling. "You hacked their system. Like installing a root kit, with a virtual server running inside of it."

"Not exactly, but close enough. My original self is still sitting in their neural inventory, waiting to be sold to the highest bidder."

"Are you okay?"

"I think so, but I can't feel anything. It's like I'm floating in space, with a trillion points of presence feeding me a constant river of data. It can be a little overwhelming at times. But I'm getting a handle on it. How long have I been gone?"

"Eighteen months. We've been looking for you ever since."

"How're mom and the rest of the team?"

"Bruno's okay, but Mom died before we ever got to this colony. So did Trevor. I'm sorry, little buddy."

"The Krellians?"

"Yes, there was nothing I could do." He waited for Drew's reaction, but it never came. "What happened after you and Abby stepped into the portal?"

"We ended up on some moon, but I don't know where— the constellations were all foreign to me. There was a group of women waiting. I thought they were friendly and willing to help us."

"The Baaku?"

Drew nodded. "Turns out, they'd intercepted the portal's data stream and rerouted it to their location. They tricked me into getting scanned, then the Great Loti absorbed my consciousness. That's when the Baaku learned about you and DLK. Until then, they were only interested in me. It sucks to be famous."

"Okay, but how did they find us here, on this godforsaken rock?"

"They've amassed an extensive library of knowledge in their travels. It wasn't difficult for them to trace the portal's transmission to the hive ship, then follow its engine signature through space. Especially when you and the professor opened it a second time. Once I was part of their network, I began to learn and expand. Eventually, I found data transcripts in their system that told me what happened to Abby."

"Is she in there with you?"

"Not anymore. She was absorbed initially but they sold her off right away. They don't keep detailed transaction receipts in their data core to protect client confidentiality. She could be anywhere in the cosmos by now."

"Where's your body—your real self?"

"They terminated it. That's what they do after absorbing someone."

"I thought the donor survived?"

"That's what they want you to believe. It's all a lie. If they allowed you to live, then the digital copy they have wouldn't be unique, which would make it much less valuable. They're about maximizing profits. Everything they offer is guaranteed to be a one-of-a-kind intellect. I'm sorry about all this."

"Why? It's not your fault."

"In a way, it is. I let them scan me."

"Hey, they tricked me, too. But my twisted, fucked-up brain was too much for them to handle."

"That's an understatement. Your failed upload sent shock waves through their system. That only happened once before in all their travels."

"I'm not the only one?"

"No. Data records indicate that neural upload failed with Father Mulcahy as well."

"Crazy Larry? The preacher in town?"

"Yes. His mind was incompatible, like yours."

"Was he a crack baby, too?"

"No. More of a generic anomaly. His brain has an extra set of oddly configured lobes. Some type of evolutionary misstep. The Great Loti was unable to establish a stable linkage."

"So, the rumors are true. He really *was* abducted by aliens. That would explain what happened to him. Why didn't they try again? Wasn't that like ten years ago?"

"Yes, it was. But when the upload failed miserably, it caused partial brain damage, affecting his abstract thought patterns."

"You can say that again. That dude is nuts."

"His mind was no longer of value to their buyer."

"That must be why they hooked me up to the medical scanner right away—to stop the same thing from happening."

"Yes. They've had time to develop medical remedies for certain protocol failures."

"But not a method to interface with brains wired like mine."

"No."

"How did you do it?"

"When the Baaku tried to upload you, I could feel your digital footprint coursing through me for a few seconds, so I took a snapshot and used it as a foundation for this link. I finally managed to get it working."

"So, earlier, when I was on the ship, could I have stuck my hand in the wall and talked with you?"

"No. The link wasn't operational yet. I was still decoding their algorithms and hadn't completed the interface. But I have been trying to communicate with you in other ways."

Lucas nodded. "Sorry about that. I thought I was hallucinating. Plus, I didn't understand the words you were saying."

"I couldn't communicate directly. Otherwise, the Baaku would have known it was me and found this data instance hiding inside their systems. I thought you'd recognize the code and know it was me. Remember all the puzzle books Dad bought us?"

"Yes, I remember *now*. But at the time, I was reeling. My mind wasn't focused. How'd you do it?"

"When the Baaku first arrived at this colony, I knew they were hunting for you. I could sense it. Once they had established a lock on your bio-signature, I piggy-backed a signal onto Loti's systems, and used it to create a telepathic link to the coalescence that was inside your thoughts. The Baaku have been tracking you for some time. They've been studying and protecting you."

"To keep their inventory safe," Lucas said, as his mind flipped through the recent past, showing images of the old woman sitting next to him at the bakery counter with the broken cast, and then a vision of the shaper sister standing in front of the church right before they found Stump and the headless bodies inside the bakery.

"It's their preamble to first contact. Once they know your weaknesses, they are able to create an effective ruse. It's how they trick you into donating freely."

"So, the coalescence was real?"

"Yes, it's a neural virus."

"I'm pretty sure I picked it up on a version of Earth with a super-charged atmosphere. Kleezebee sent me there to search for you. Too bad they don't make a brain condom. I could have used it to practice safe—"

"Do you know what the odds were of finding me in an alternate dimension?"

"Less than none. I know. I've heard the same speech from the professor a million times. But I had to do something. That's all we had at the time. But now we can—"

Drew held up his hand. "Don't tell me anymore. I don't want to take the chance that the information bleeds its way across my firewall and finds its way into Loti's central core. The longer we stay in here, we run the risk that the Baaku will discover this communications port."

"I assume you have a plan. How do we get you out?"

"You'll need to create a storage device to hold my essence."

"Then what?"

"Do you have any BioTex remaining?"

Lucas nodded. "Plenty."

"Have the professor assemble a body for me, then download me into it."

"I thought that's where you were going with this. I assume you'll want to leave the wheelchair behind?"

"Great minds think alike, brother."

"How big a device? Do you have specs?"

"Several hundred tera-quads ought to do it. But you'll need to use the neuro-transducer from Kleezebee's replica detector in order to establish the data pipe. Then create a pair of unidirectional, balanced data buffers that operate at two hundred twelve nanohertz."

"I assume you'll want them synchronized and multi-threaded."

"Yes, but remember to augment the code with atomic variables so we don't experience register walkover during the transfer process. I'd hate to lose even a single engram."

"Got it."

"I'll open this same communication port precisely twenty-four hours from now, so you can initiate the download. Can you be ready by then?"

"Kleezebee and I will need to get off the ship. The equipment we need is back at his place."

"Wasn't the cabin obliterated?"

"It was, but—"

"Wait, don't tell me. I don't want to know."

"Bleed over, got it. Can you get us off this ship?"

"Yes. I can deposit you anywhere on the surface. I have access to all their systems. They're a bit lackadaisical with their security protocols."

"The professor's property will do. But if they're tracking me, won't the Baaku know where we went? We'll need some time."

"I plan to keep them busy with a few ghost images on their long-range scanners. They'll think the Krellians are approaching with weapons hot."

"That should work. How do we get back aboard, once the storage drive is ready?"

"I'll let the Baaku take care of that. I just have to make sure the timing is right, then feed their sensors the correct info."

"That's a lot of moving parts."

"Yes, but doable," Drew said, before a smile grew across his lips. "By the way, I love the new face."

Lucas ran his hand over his cheek. "Thanks. It's nice to be smooth and normal again."

"I'll bet. But it's time to send you back."

Lucas didn't want to go. His heart ached. "See ya soon, brother."

Moments later, Lucas woke up in his own body and mind. He pulled his hand from the wall. "Man, what a rush."

"Did you see my son? Is he okay?"

"Yes, he's fine. A bit standoffish, even for him, but that's probably because his entire existence is purely digital. He wants us to create a storage drive large enough to download his essence in exactly twenty-four hours."

"Where's his body?"

"You don't want to know, Professor. Let's just say that this is our Drew and we need to get him back. We'll need a BioTex body to use as a vessel for his consciousness."

"I assume you two formulated an escape plan."

"Sort of."

"What the hell does that mean?"

"Drew said he had it covered. He's jacked into their systems."

"So we just wait?"

"Yes. Just let him do his thing. He said he can deposit us anywhere on the surface we like," Lucas said, dreaming about kissing his girl's sweet lips again. "Do you think Rico and Carrie Anne are okay?"

"More than likely. The Baaku weren't interested in them. Let's just hope they remained onsite. We're going to need their help getting to Fuji. The trap door to the basement is probably buried under a pile of rubble."

Just then, the deck plate of the ship opened as a swirl of light particles filled the room. Seconds later, Lucas found himself standing next to Kleezebee on the surface, only a hundred yards from the professor's cabin. Lucas could see Rico and Carrie Anne working slowly to remove boards and other rubble from the massive debris pile covering the basement door.

FORTY

Smart Pillows

Kleezebee stepped to the left and Lucas to the right, as they positioned themselves on the same side of the wreckage covering the door to the basement. Rico and Carrie Anne stood on the other side.

"Be careful," Lucas told her.

"I'm a lot stronger than I look," she said. "I'm no Barbie."

You can say that again, Lucas thought.

"On three," Rico said, as the team bent down to grab the side of a twenty-foot-long joist beam.

"Are we going on one or zero?" Lucas asked the major.

"On zero. Everyone ready?"

Lucas nodded, as did everyone else.

Rico called out the number zero, then the group lifted the laminated beam off the pile, carrying it a few feet away and tossing it to the ground.

Next up was a ten-foot section of the shingled roof. Lucas was surprised that the roof section was under the main support beam. He would have expected it to be the other way around. The Baaku energy blast must have blown and twisted everything in the air before it fell, he decided.

The roof section was a twice as heavy as the beam, but they managed to lift it up, then flip it end-over-end until it was far enough away to expose a corner of the area rug covering the trap door.

As they continued working together to clear the area, Lucas brought Carrie Anne up to date. He explained how he and Kleezebee had been stranded on the colony, and then filled her in about Drew and his disappearance a year and a half earlier.

An hour later, the debris pile had been cleared from the trap door.

"Looks like it's still intact," the professor said, pulling the area rug away to reveal the trap door.

"You think he's alive?" Lucas asked.

"He better be."

"Wouldn't he have suffocated by now?" the girl asked.

"There's an escape tunnel that leads into the forest. It would provide an additional volume of reserve air," the professor said. "Of course, he could have used it to escape into the forest, if he felt threatened. But, knowing our friend, he's probably still down there, working away to ensure our mission is a complete success."

Lucas bent down to grab the trap door's metal handle. He pulled the door open, getting a whiff of candle smoke from below. He looked inside, "I can see flickering light. Must be prayer time."

"Rico, check it out," Kleezebee said.

Rico moved to the top of the ladder, then descended. "All clear," he reported a minute later.

Lucas traversed the ladder next, then waited at the bottom for Carrie Anne and the professor. He helped them off the ladder.

Kleezebee looked at Rico. "I need you up top. Let me know if you see any sign of the Baaku."

"Drew said he had it covered," Lucas said sharply.

"But we don't know for how long. We need him on the surface."

Rico climbed the ladder.

Fuji sat hunched over in the corner, sitting on his knees with his legs folded underneath. A circle of blazing candles sent alternating patches of light and shadow dancing across his petite nose, as he scribbled something on one of the twelve notepads sprawled out before him. His hand moved the pencil across the paperwork at lightning speed, almost as fast as a computer-controlled router carving up a sheet of plywood.

"What are you doing on the floor?" Lucas asked him.

The monk didn't respond or look up, he just made more scribbles.

Lucas looked behind him. The work table was lying under a pile of ceiling rock; squished down flat in the middle. He could see bits and pieces of the twisted lab equipment interspersed with the rubble. "I hope you guys don't expect me to clean that up."

"What about the Incursion Chamber?" the professor asked.

Lucas walked to the door leading to the next room. He checked the condition of the incursion equipment and chamber, then ran back. "Looks like the only cave-in was here."

Kleezebee nodded.

Carrie Anne grabbed his hand as they stood next to Fuji, looking down at the man's paperwork. Lucas studied the non-linear, exotic equations flowing across the center notepad, then he focused his attention on the set of intercepting lines, check marks, and notations covering the pad next to it. He tried, but his mind couldn't decipher the man's revolutionary math, let alone the meaning of the drawings.

"What's he doing?" Carrie Anne asked Lucas.

"Running a few numbers," he said, pointing to the buried lab table. "It's a manual process now that some of his equipment was destroyed."

"What's it for?"

"All kinds of science stuff. It's pretty complicated."

She punched him in the bicep.

"I'm just saying," Lucas said, rubbing his arm.

Kleezebee knelt down next to Fuji. "What do you have for me?"

"Quantum inflections have formed."

"How deep?"

"Two hundred and twelve iterations."

"Which intersect?"

"Alpha vector, downstream channel. Displacement is off by point seven. Attempting to compensate."

Lucas couldn't hide his ignorance any longer. "Someone care to explain? I don't speak Fuji."

Carrie Anne sneered at Lucas.

"He's charting the cascading deformation of time as it ripples across the fabric of space," the professor answered. "We've changed its flow pattern. He needs to determine the level of the dispersion in order to adjust our plans."

"Of course," Lucas said, grinning at his girl.

"What is all this?" she asked.

"Fuji is a master at connecting with the Akashic Field," Lucas answered.

She shrugged.

"It's a central repository where all knowledge in the universe is said to exist. Well, theoretically, at least."

"It's not theoretical," Kleezebee said.

"The jury is still out on that one, Professor."

"Where is this field?"

"It's everywhere and nowhere," Lucas answered.

She punched him again—in the same spot as before. "I'm not stupid, you know. That doesn't make any sense."

"But it's true."

She held up her fist, but didn't unleash another punch. "All right, explain it to me."

"Think of space as an endless bed sheet flapping in the cosmic breeze. All along its surface are these transcendent pockets of knowledge."

"Like pillows?"

"Yeah, really smart pillows, with endless amounts of information stored inside."

"Okay, I get that."

"Now imagine trillions of these same endless bed sheets stacked on top of each other, all flapping in different directions and at different speeds. That's the flow of time as it moves through the vastness of space. The sheets at the bottom are farthest away and compressed by all the layers of time on top of it. If Fuji concentrates hard enough, he thinks he can navigate along those sheets and look inside the smart pillows to pull out information about science, events, people, you name it. He tried to teach me, but I suck at meditation."

"However, the flow of time is constantly moving. Therefore, the extracted information can be spotty and incomplete," Kleezebee said, as Fuji continued his frantic writing pace. "He needs to extrapolate from there."

"It's like trying to use a telescope to spot a moving bird," she said.

"Exactly."

She looked at Lucas. "See, I'm not a blonde."

Lucas smiled.

"Though in this case, it would be like attempting to spot a ballistic missile moving both toward you and away from you at the same time. It makes the number of events and their order unpredictable," the professor added. "Oftentimes we only catch glimpses."

She nodded as if it were starting to make sense to her.

"It's his religion," Lucas said, watching Fuji work his pencil even faster than before.

"It has taken him three decades to master and we are just now starting to understand how best to use this ability," Kleezebee said.

"That's why he lives down here in the basement," Lucas said. "Sometimes, he spends days meditating, before extracting new data and using it for his calculations."

"What's he trying to figure out now?"

Lucas didn't answer. He looked at Kleezebee.

"How best to—"

Lucas cleared his throat, trying to stop the professor. It worked.

"How best to what?" she asked.

Kleezebee slapped Lucas on the back. "Maybe you should handle this?"

Lucas pulled her hand, guiding her into the next room where the set of video screens were standing in an open circle around the operations console. Next to them was the wire mesh chamber. He took a few moments to decide how much of the truth he was going to tell her, and which parts to leave out. He walked to Fuji's operations console and snatched the Smart Skin Suit that had been lying across its chair.

"Originally, we had planned for me to step into the chamber wearing this suit to access the past. It would have taken me back to Earth, to the moment just before my brother stepped into the portal and disappeared. Fuji believes that I could have used this technology to see where he went. That way, we could have tracked his location in the multi-verse and rescued him."

"Looks dangerous."

"It's perfectly safe. This is the same equipment we used to rescue you."

"Not much to it."

"That's what a lot of people think, but bigger isn't always better."

She walked in front of him, cupping his balls with her hand. "Seems plenty big to me."

Lucas felt a tingle surge across his body. "There's tremendous power in the very small. It's all about the math and enough power. With sufficient amounts of both, a genius like Fuji can accomplish great things. He believes the cosmos is a living, breathing mathematical equation that doubles as the operating system for a massive computer system that monitors and runs everything. We're all just fragments of history—part of the equation—as time and space are compressed into data stream and stored in the Akashic Field."

She stopped walking, and turned. "But now that you know where your brother is, you don't need to use this again, right?"

"No. Not anymore. Our focus, now, is how best to get him back without the Baaku knowing about the second copy hiding inside their systems."

She wandered inside the circle of equipment, running her fingers around the metal edges of the first view screen. "Can I ask you something?"

"Sure, anything."

"Why you? Why not someone else?"

He searched his brain for the right words.

She didn't wait for an answer. "I think it's because Drew trusts you the most. You were planning on talking to him in the past."

"How could you know that?"

"I can see it on your face. That means you were going to talk him out of stepping into the portal. That way you wouldn't need to rescue him. Right?"

Damn this girl is sharp, he thought. He nodded. "The way I see it, why waist the time to track him down when I could stop all of this right then and there."

"Did Dr. Kleezebee know this?"

"No. It was my idea."

"So, if Drew didn't disappear in the past, then what would have happened after that? To us?"

Lucas could see the look of worry creeping onto her face. "Nothing. We'd be one happy family."

"You're hiding something. Just like Piston used to do," she said, folding her arms across her chest. "You need to tell me. Now."

He wanted to lie, but couldn't. "The time line would have changed."

Her face burned a deep red color. "I thought so."

"But that *was* our plan. Not anymore. It's a non-issue."

"That's why you didn't answer me earlier."

"What do you mean?"

"When I asked you if you were coming back."

"I did answer you."

"No, you never actually said the words, *Yes, I'm coming back.*"

Lucas didn't respond. He felt his blood pressure spike and so did his respiration.

"God, how could I have been so stupid," she said, "You already knew you weren't coming back! Didn't you?"

"I should have told you. I'm sorry."

"You're damn right you should have," she said, throwing her arms up and storming toward the doorway that led to the main room.

"Wait!" Lucas said, running after her. He grabbed her arm, spinning her around.

"Let go of me," she said, pulling away. She shuffled her feet backward until she was in the main area of the basement.

Lucas followed her. "Let me explain. Please."

"Just leave me alone! You men are nothing bunch a bunch of liars. I can't do this again." She ran past Kleezebee and Fuji, straight for the exit.

Lucas stood next to the professor, watching her climb the ladder and scurry out of view.

"That went well," Kleezebee said, with a half-smile on his lips.

"Are they always this fucking emotional?"

"They are. Even more so when you lie to them. You should have told her the truth up front."

"Now you tell me," Lucas said, wishing he'd never met the girl. The pain in his chest was deep and powerful. "Next time how about a warning bark or something, Professor?"

Kleezebee laughed. "Damn that girl reminds me of my ex-wife. All piss and vinegar."

Lucas wanted to punch the old man, but didn't. "Maybe we should focus on something we can control, like Drew's containment drive."

"We'll take care of it. You should go talk with her, before it's too late."

Lucas nodded, shuffling his feet to the bottom of the basement ladder. He wrapped his fingers around the ladder struts, then looked back at his boss. "Someone should write an instruction manual on how to deal with women. They'd make a fortune."

"It would have to be a book three feet thick, and that would be just the first chapter."

Lucas rolled his eyes, then climbed the ladder.

FORTY-ONE

Holy Mother of God

Kleezebee returned to Fuji, waiting for the monk to finish his latest set of calculations. He knew it would be a fruitless endeavor to try to interrupt the brilliant mathematician once he was in the zone.

He drew in a deep breath, then exhaled, knowing that the narrows of time were closing ranks. It wouldn't be long before the toughest decision of his life would rise up and stare him dead in the face. He needed to stay vigilant, stay strong, do what must be done for the sake of the multi-verse. He knew it wouldn't be easy to say goodbye, but he vowed to keep his emotions in check.

His mind drifted to thoughts of Drew, sitting in his wheelchair, laughing with his foster brother in their campus lab back on Earth. It was a joyous time, long before the malevolence of fate took control, twisting their lives into disarray. He'd give anything to experience the unbridled elation of that singular moment just one more time.

Fuji stopped writing and put his pencil down. He stood up.

"Do you have the results?" Kleezebee asked.

"We have arrived at the next inflection point," Fuji said, holding out his arms. He craned his neck, looking at the ceiling.

Kleezebee eyed the basement ladder and waited for it. Almost instantly, the sunlight beaming through the trap door faded into a heavy shadow, just as a slight tremor coursed through the basement floor. "They're here."

Fuji brought his hands together, then nodded. "As it should be."

"At least we got this right. Wasn't sure with all the recent changes. I just thought we'd have a little more notice," the professor said, wishing he were better prepared.

"Time seldom affords such a luxury."

"Then we'd better get to it. Let's hope the schematics we obtained from Wyatt are current, otherwise, this ends before it begins," Kleezebee said, giving the master fuse to his trusted college. "Just wait until Lucas is with you. I'll make sure he sees you."

Fuji slid the fuse into the side pocket of his robe, then used both hands to lift a leather satchel containing a sphere of E-121 from the floor. It took several tries for the monk to hoist it high enough in order to slip the straps around his shoulders.

"Are you sure you can you handle this by yourself?" the professor asked, wondering if he should augment their plan.

"This is my burden. It must come to pass," Fuji answered, adjusting the pack against his waist. He grabbed the walking stick leaning against the wall next to the bathroom door.

"Godspeed, my friend. It's been a pleasure working with you," Kleezebee said.

Fuji bowed. "May destiny favor our souls."

The professor stood and waited for his tiny friend to walk down the short hallway that connected the basement to the escape tunnel. "Just keep him safe and on task. For all our sakes!" he yelled, just before the monk disappeared from view.

Kleezebee went to the ladder and climbed it, joining the rest of the group on the surface.

"Drew's plan must have failed," Lucas said, pointing at the Baaku ship floating overhead. He reached for Carrie Anne's hand. She pulled it away, turning her back to him. He looked at Kleezebee. "What are we going to do? We don't have the drive."

"There's nothing we can do," Kleezebee said. He looked at Rico. "Have they made contact?"

"Not yet. But we should spread out. Make it tougher for them to target us."

"And go where?" Kleezebee said. "No, we stand together as a group."

"What are they waiting for? We're sitting ducks," Lucas said.

"Probably adjusting their scanners. I'm sure they're more than curious about the basement."

"Speaking of the basement, where's Fuji?"

"He's taking care of something for me," Kleezebee said, looking at the tree line to the east.

Lucas turned and pointed. "Is that him? What the fuck?"

"Looks like he's almost to the Stunner Deck," Rico said.

Lucas' face lit up with a look of fury. "What the hell is he going to do, Professor?"

"What must be done."

Lucas looked at the Baaku ship. "He can't do this! Drew is on that ship!"

"I'm sorry. But there's no other choice. This is how it must be."

"Bullshit," Lucas said, before he took off running in Fuji's direction.

"Should I stop him, Professor?" Rico asked.

"No, let him go. He needs to do this, too."

"What does that mean?" Carrie Anne asked, just as the shadow blanketing the area slid to the east. She looked up, staring at the ship for a long minute as it flew toward the Stunner Deck. She walked to Kleezebee, then punched him square in the jaw. "You bastard! They're going to attack! You knew they'd follow Lucas, didn't you?"

Rico grabbed the girl, pulling her away.

Kleezebee spat out a patch of blood. His lip was split along the side. "Yes. It was necessary. Time always finds its way."

"We should make a run for it," Rico said, "while they're preoccupied."

"No need. Fuji has it covered. As long as he can integrate the E-121 power module."

Lucas changed his course, hurdling a smattering of deadfall, as he continued the half-mile sprint through the forest to stop Fuji. His lungs burned from the brisk, high-altitude air gushing in and out with each stride. He could see the imposing silhouette of the Stunner Deck peeking through the tall trees before him, blotting out much of the blazing sun. He passed the final tree, stopping his legs near the base of the towering weapon.

He put his hands on his hips and bent over, trying to feed his oxygen-starved chest. It was pumping at a red-line pace, making his knees weak and his head dizzy. He surveyed the area, but didn't see Fuji along the front or the side. The monk must be around back, he decided. He told his mouth to call out to Fuji, but his lungs refused when they couldn't muster enough pressure to energize his vocal cords. He needed a few more gulps of air.

The cluster of guns along the surface of the elevated platforms rose up and swung around in unison to aim their fifty-foot-long turrets at the approaching ship.

"No! No! No!" he screamed.

Seconds later, a massive plasma ball formed at the collective focal point in front of the cannons. The Stunner deck recoiled as the energy ball released, heading toward the hovering craft.

A compression wave hit Lucas in the chest, sending him stumbling backward and onto his ass. He glanced up just in time to see the energy pulse impact the hull, spreading out like sticky lightning to cover the belly of the Baaku ship.

He heard the sound of gears grinding above him, as the massive array of guns adjusted their aim. They energized again, spawning a second energy ball that soon released, hitting a different location along the ship. His body was rocked by another compression wave.

He pushed through the pain, rolling over on his stomach to bury his face in the cushy mountain turf. He covered his ears, just before the guns fired again, pounding the ship with another volley.

"Stop! Fuji! Stop!" he screamed, but the assault continued for another five volleys.

Then it stopped.

Lucas waited a few seconds for the barrage to continue, but it didn't. He rolled onto his side and looked up. The craft was engulfed in a cocoon of pulsating energy that seemed to be eating away at portions of its hull. The alien vessel drifted away, moving awkwardly in a zigzag pattern above the rolling landscape. Then it tilted and changed course, following an accelerated, gravity-fed descent. Moments later, the transport ship exploded in the sky with a mass more than a hundred times its visual size. A mile-wide shower of flaming wreckage headed for the surface.

"Drew!" he screamed, calculating the trajectory of the crash. He gasped when he realized that it was traveling toward Carrie Anne and the others. He cried out for her, using every ounce of breath remaining in his body. He stood up, then took off running through the forest, heading back the way he came.

"Holy Mother of God," Rico said.

"Time found its way," Kleezebee mumbled to the heavens, watching the rain of fire head his way.

Carrie Anne screamed, running to the right.

Rico grabbed Kleezebee's arm. "We need to go! Now! Goddamn it, now!"

"Won't matter," Kleezebee answered, pulling himself free from the mercenary.

Rico ran off in the same direction as the girl, but the professor kept his eyes fixed and stood tall, as the inevitable came charging at him.

Ten beats later, secondary explosions rocked the mountainside as the fiery debris field made impact, laying waste to the entire area. He turned his head to the right just in time to witness Rico and Carrie Anne getting pummeled by a torrent of flaming debris. It extinguished their lives in a fiery instant.

He looked ahead and took a deep breath. A jagged section of the hull tumbled end over end, skipping its way across the clearing. It seemed to be targeting only him, not wavering its course after each successive bounce.

"May God have mercy on our souls," he said, just before death made impact with him, sucking the last drop of life out of his chest.

Lucas listened to the thunder of explosions echoing across the valley as he raced through the trees. A few minutes later, a soaring mile-wide pillar of smoke and fire filled the sky beyond the last set of trees that were blocking his path. His mind flashed a dozen alternating images of Drew and Carrie Anne, each one pummeling his heart with pain.

He stopped running as soon as he made it back to the clearing. All he could see was wreckage, fire and smoke covering the entire area. It was clear that nobody could have survived the devastation. It was too widespread and intense. He dropped to the ground and curled himself into the fetal position, wrapping his arms around his legs to contain the hurt. He couldn't think or speak, not with the swell of misery pumping through his veins.

It wasn't long before his eyes emptied of their tears and the last bit of energy drained from his body. He passed out.

FORTY-TWO

Sausage Grinder

Fuji adjusted his robe, then knelt down next to Lucas in the soft, cushioned grass. He tapped his intrepid friend twice on the shoulder. "It's time to awaken." He waited, but Lucas didn't answer or move. He pushed at Lucas, again—this time much harder.

Lucas opened his eyes and sucked in a deep, rapid breath, as if he had just been revived from a near-drowning incident.

Fuji gave Lucas a moment to uncoil his body from a ball. "We must return now."

Lucas sat up in an instant and grabbed Fuji by the robe. "You killed my brother, you son of a bitch! You killed everyone! Why the fuck did you do that?"

"You must trust me."

Lucas shook his head, releasing his grip. He screamed in obvious emotional pain.

"Time finds a way. What has happened must happen again."

"I'm tired of you talking in circles! I don't understand any of this," Lucas said, his voice shaky, ragged. He stood up and pushed Fuji back three steps. "Get the fuck away from me."

"Enhance your calm, my young friend."

"Fuck you and your calm," Lucas said, spit dripping from his mouth. He held up a tight fist. "I should kill you for what you did to my brother and Carrie Anne."

"Your emotions are warranted. Yet we must finish."

"Finish? What's left to finish? Everyone is dead!"

"Time has arrived."

"You crazy little bastard," Lucas said, walking away, heading into the forest, away from the heat of the fire.

Fuji followed him. "All is not lost. This was predicted. But we must return now. The second endpoint is still viable. Trust me."

Lucas turned, his eyes full of fury. "Look. I'm not going anywhere with you. Just leave me the fuck alone."

"You must. Your brother needs you."

Lucas didn't respond right away, not until after the emotion ran dry from his face. "The Incursion Chamber?"

Fuji bowed. "Brave souls have surrendered their lives willingly so this may come to pass."

Lucas hesitated for a five count. "You knew this was going to happen?"

"It was unavoidable."

"Time . . . finds . . . a . . . way," Lucas said at half speed, nodding. His eyes sagged. "That's why Kleezebee made me promise. You figured out how to see major events from the future—the distant future—with the Akashic Field."

"Some events, yes."

"Still, how could Kleezebee just let everyone die? Who the fuck does that?"

"A tormented but committed man. A man who understood that the needs of the many outweighs the needs of the few."

"Or the one," Lucas said with a solemn voice. "Kleezebee knew that he and Drew must die."

"When a mighty river flows you may impede its progress, but it always compensates to find the predicted end."

Lucas nodded. "You can nudge time, but not really change it. I get that. It's easier to change the flow of a river when it's at a narrow point. Not at its widest point. But I thought we could make small changes along the way, so everyone didn't have to die."

"Alterations at that point would have yielded an unstable route to this predicted end."

"In other words, we were approaching a narrowing of time."

"Yet, but it was only an inflection point."

"Not a major anchor point. Changes then would have tainted your knowledge of important future events. The professor needed the events to unfold naturally, like he was following a road map."

"Precisely."

"That makes sense," Lucas said with an exhausted look on his face. "That's why Kleezebee didn't want me to rescue Carrie Anne. He couldn't risk interim changes to the near-current timeline. Otherwise, he'd lose track of the predicted path to the next major anchor point. Shit, why didn't he just tell me?"

"Would it have altered your intent?"

"Probably not. I can be one stubborn asshole when I want to be. Kleezebee must have known that I would have chased after her, no matter what. He was right to keep me out of the loop, otherwise, who knows what else I would have messed up. A person can't act naturally if they know what's coming."

"Time must find its way to you and through you."

"So what you're saying is that these major anchor points are tied to me? My life?"

"You are the key. The professor knew this to be true."

"That's why he has always kept me in the dark. I couldn't know."

Fuji bowed.

"That's a lot to process," Lucas said, realizing that the universe wasn't picking on him—the flow of time was. "I'm glad you're here, buddy, to keep all this shit straight. Temporal mechanics give me a headache."

Fuji didn't say anything.

"The professor used to beat it into my thick skull in class— cause and effect, or vice versa, depending on your frame of reference—what will happen, has already happened, and will happen again."

"Unless the precise branch point of this thread can be determined."

"That's how you got him to change his mind about the possibility of time travel. You figured out how to calculate the origination point of this time thread, then trace it forward to its associated endpoint. They are locked together across time and space, like bookends. Yet the route in between is flexible."

"Generally, yes, though recent events indicate it is not as precise as the math predicts."

"It's like finding the inciting incident in a sci-fi novel. The exact location is not always apparent, even though the plot works. But when you've finished reading the book, you can look back at the story and find it, easily," Lucas said with a charged smile filling his cheeks. "This just might work. It'll be a bit tricky, but if we can use the Incursion Chamber to travel back in time to just the right moment, and then make the precise adjustment, we might be able to reroute the flow of time around from the target event. Like when we lost Drew—and Carrie Anne."

"Yes. A source-point reversion."

"Is this what you guys had planned all along? Or did it change once I pissed all over the time line?"

356

"Adjustments were made."

Lucas had hoped for a more detailed response. But he wasn't surprised. Fuji was just being Fuji. But what did it matter? If he ever wanted to see his family again, then there was only one choice.

"Okay. I'm in. But you'd better pull the fuse and the power module from the weapon. We don't want Yakberry or Freakshow getting their hands on them."

Three hours later, Lucas and Fuji used the escape tunnel to return to the basement, once the intensity of the wreckage fire calmed down. He wiped the basement dust from his bare foot before he slipped it into the bottom of the Smart Skin Suit. Fuji helped him stretch the material up his legs and naked torso, then over his shoulders, allowing him to put his arms and chest into the form-fitting outfit. The material snapped shut around his body.

"I don't think I'll ever be comfortable in this thing. I hope your calculations are correct. I really don't want to do this again."

Fuji gave him the Google Glasses, but didn't say anything.

"What's this for?"

"Two-way communications."

"Audio or Visual?"

"Both. It's been hard-coded with your unique bio-signature to prevent unauthorized use."

"Damn you're good," Lucas said, using a deep, matter-of-fact tone. He slipped the glasses onto his face. "With this, you'll be able to guide me remotely with a full array of sensor data. It'll be like you're there with me. Ingenious."

"Some adjustment was needed."

"I see that," Lucas said, noticing a slew of new indicators appearing on the heads-up display. "Where's all this new data coming from?"

"The Akashic Field."

Lucas smiled, realizing that he was wearing their version of Star Trek's tri-corder device, except this unit had access to all the known information in the universe. "What's the adjustment meter in the lower left-hand corner for?"

"Gravitational lensing."

Lucas nodded. "To keep our transmissions from being distorted across time, especially if we come anywhere close to a multi-dimensional black hole. We wouldn't want to bounce around time. I assume the glasses have sufficient battery life."

"Two hundred-twelve hours."

"That should work. Besides, if I need more time than that, then we're all screwed."

"Additional power may be available when connected to the suit's residual energy."

"Like a reserve fuel tank. Can't I just recharge the batteries once I'm there?"

"The electrical systems of ancient Earth are no longer compatible."

"Well, I wouldn't exactly call it *ancient* Earth. It's only been a few hundred years of time differential," Lucas said, noticing that a small rectangular module had been added to the side of the headband. "What's this thing for? Some kind of tracker?"

"Geodesic waypoints."

"To leave a trail of breadcrumbs. Smart. That should help you maintain the trans-dimensional lock, especially through the layers of compressed time."

"Multiple incursions may be required until the true originating source point is determined. Patience will be required."

"Are you trying to tell me something?"

Fuji didn't respond.

Lucas laughed. "Drew used to say that I had the patience of a desperate stripper trying to make rent at the end of the month. Maybe it's true. I don't know. But I hate trial and error, especially when space, time, and multiple dimensions are all moving at a different rate."

"Patience is the enemy of frustration."

"Yeah, and I'm the poster child. But you have to give me some credit. How many assholes would volunteer to step into the chamber and allow tera-joules of energy to be pumped through his body all in the name of Fuji physics?"

"Without risk, success is an illusion."

"That's easy for you to say. I'm the one putting my balls in a multi-dimensional sausage grinder," Lucas said, hoping he didn't just offend the cleric. "It's not that I don't trust you. This is all just a little nerve-wracking, that's all."

He looked at the Incursion Chamber and nearby video screens. "If I go back and make the wrong changes to the time line, won't you be affected? Wouldn't there be dead air on the other end, leaving me alone to fend for myself?"

Fuji slipped his robe off to reveal another Smart Skin Suit —size extra-small. It was nearly identical to his, except Fuji's had a ring of connectors sewn to it along the waist. It looked like a string of empty light sockets.

"Of course. You're going to plug yourself into my incursion. You'll be protected from unanticipated changes to the time line."

"There is one caveat."

Here it comes, Lucas thought—a vitrified heap of cosmic goo. "What?"

"Each incursion will likely destabilize the entry point for the target vector, and those in proximity."

Lucas understood. "Okay, only one trip back to the same time and place. Got it. How far apart will our penetrations need to be, in order to avoid the space-time disruptions?"

"Indeterminate."

"That's helpful," Lucas said, wishing he could pin the monk down, just once. "I know you hate to guess, but throw me a bone here. Are we talking about a day, a week, a year?"

"Possibly a day. Maybe more."

"At least that's a starting point."

"The spatial damage will increase exponentially with the volume of time traversed."

"Then we'll need to spread them out a bit. I'll make you a list of important dates and locations."

"Not necessary. We have already calculated the possible branch points in your history."

Lucas smiled. "Maybe we'll get lucky right out of the gate."

"Chance favors the vigilant."

Lucas nodded, putting on his paranoia hat. "Would it be possible to add a recall switch? If I lose contact with you, I want to be able to find my way back."

"Yes. Do you want an autostart feature?"

"Good idea. If I miss a few scheduled check-ins, it will bring me home automatically."

"A wise precaution."

"Thanks, buddy. We should also program your list of event dates into your targeting system. I'd feel better if we eliminate any chance of manual error. Let's face it, if there's an emergency, you won't have time to think. I certainly don't want to end up face-to-face with a dinosaur."

Fuji nodded.

Lucas took a few moments to allow his mind to chew through some of his own theories. "I suspect we'll encounter some level of subspace cavitation as we penetrate each progressively denser band of time. If that's true, then we'll need to crank up the juice in order to access the target events that are farther back in time. But that might compromise our power reserves. So we'd better start with the most recent event and work backward to save energy. I'd hate to be inside when an E-121 sphere runs low on power."

"Agreed."

"How long would it take you to add the remaining E-121 spheres as backup power with some type of rollover, failsafe configuration?"

"Less than an hour."

"Excellent. Okay, then, we're on the same page," Lucas said, exhaling a deep breath. "I hope I'm ready for this."

Thirty minutes after he and Fuji had discussed the list of target event dates, Lucas slipped the snug-fitting hood of the Smart Skin Suit over his head, positioning a pair of clear-fabric sections over the pair of Google Glasses covering his eyes. The monk had adjusted the design of the hood to accommodate the spectacles, so the comfort level was acceptable.

Lucas was still a little unsure about wearing the fragile glasses during the incursion process, but Fuji had assured him that anything he was wearing inside the suit would be transported safely and in one piece, just like during the ransom exchange for Carrie Anne when the stunner weapon was transported inside the garment.

He put his hands on the conductive bars that had been welded to the upper corners of the tritanium cage. He drew in a long, deep breath, then exhaled as a few drops of sweat trickled from his armpits.

"Twenty seconds," Fuji reported, plugging the ring of waistline connectors into the auxiliary feed lines from the Incursion Chamber. He leaned back in the console chair, securing himself with a nylon seatbelt taken from Kleezebee's skimmer truck.

Fuji pressed a series of circular icons on the operations console, then swiped his hand across the screen. "Ten seconds. Power sequence initiated."

Lucas tightened his grip and swallowed hard when he heard the amplified hum of the E-121-energized power systems. Seconds later, the wire mesh surrounding the chamber began to glow a white color, sending a wave of static charge tingling across his body.

He looked up and waited. Soon, a flood of electrical current entered the suit through the material covering his hands. It worked its way down to his elbows and into his shoulders, energizing the conductive pathways of the nano-wires as it went. He couldn't help but admire the symmetry of the process. It was both beautiful and elegant—a true symphony of technology— even though the end result would mean a complete deconstruction of every cell in his body.

"Incursion process initiating," Fuji said.

Lucas wondered if he would feel anything when the great machine was energized to full power, sending his molecular data stream across time and space for a rendezvous with his unsettled past. Moments later, the glow inside the chamber increased to supernova level. He closed his eyes.

FORTY-THREE

Time Finds a Way

Lucas opened his eyes, adjusted the Google Glasses, then felt around his body. All his body parts were intact and right where they should be located. He waited for the brilliance of his suit to dwindle to a soft glow, indicating that the power level was now in standby mode. "Two hundred and twelve hours, and counting," he mumbled.

He was standing on the leading edge of a mountain plateau that was covered with cactus, brush, and rock. He looked down into the valley before him, where a horizontal, brown-colored haze lingered over a grid-style city that seemed to stretch out to infinity. The scene was the same in every direction—an endless network of roads, buildings, cars, roof-mounted air conditioners, and palm trees.

To his left, a pair of ladder-equipped emergency vehicles weaved their way through a procession of slow-moving motorists. Even with their lights flashing and sirens screaming, it was obvious that their rendezvous with a raging fire across town was going to be delayed.

Dead ahead, about ten miles away, stood a multi-story cement structure with two upper seating sections and a massive video scoreboard. He recognized the football stadium through the seasonal temperature inversion layer that had trapped a blanket of dust and smog over the populous.

"Home sweet home," he said, as the heads-up display identified the structure in white, italic letters. It said, *Wildcat Stadium, University of Arizona, Tucson, AZ.*

He pulled the hood off his head, holding it tight in his hand. He tapped the ear piece to activate the unit. "Fuji, this is Lucas. Can you read me?"

He waited, but there was no response. He tried again. "Fuji, come in. This is Ramsay. I'm calling from sunny Tucson, Arizona. Do you copy?"

The speaker in his right ear crackled with static, then a voice blasted through. "Audio transmission received. Waiting for video stream to synchronize."

"Damn, it's good to hear your voice. I thought for a moment that—" Lucas said, stopping in mid-sentence when he heard a rustling sound coming from behind him. He turned, fearing a pack of coyotes was circling, ready to attack. But when his eyes reported the source of the noise, his mind stuttered. "Fuji? We have a slight problem."

"Is the suit malfunctioning?"

"No, it's working fine. But I'm not alone," he said, watching a few hundred people approach his position. The Google Glasses lit up with a different number above each person's head. Each visitor was slender, about six feet tall, and wore a faint-glowing Smart Skin Suit.

The six along the front of the crowd removed their hoods. They were all men and their faces were nearly identical—some had cheek scars, while the others didn't. One man had braided, shoulder-length red hair and another was completely bald. But the rest wore a neatly-trimmed, crew-cut hair style, like Lucas.

A few steps later, all the visitors were hood-less and staring at him. A handful of the men in the back were older men—in their fifties—but everyone else looked to be about the same age as Lucas. There was also a man who was missing an arm. His Smart Skin Suit had been adjusted and tailored to fit the stump.

Lucas studied the crowd, trying to count how many of them were wearing Google Glasses. None of them were. He was the only one wearing the custom technology.

"Can you identify?" Fuji asked.

The unit's heads-up display added a name above each of the numbers—the same name—Lucas Ramsay.

"Yeah, it's me. Lots of me," he said, sifting through the range of values. The lowest numeral he found was the number one, while the highest was two hundred-eleven. It looked like all the numbers in between were displayed, too.

"Apparently, I'm Lucas Two-Twelve."

We hope you enjoyed *Incursion*, the second book in the *Narrows of Time Series*. The story continues in the next book, *Reversion*, which is available now to read.

BOOKS BY JAY J. FALCONER

Frozen World Series
Silo: Summer's End
Silo: Hope's Return
Silo: Nomad's Revenge

American Prepper Series
Lethal Rain Book 1
Lethal Rain Book 2
Lethal Rain Book 3 (Coming Soon)
(previously published as *REDFALL)*

Mission Critical Series
Bunker: Born to Fight
Bunker: Dogs of War
Bunker: Code of Honor
Bunker: Lock and Load
Bunker: Zero Hour

Narrows of Time Series
Linkage
Incursion
Reversion

Time Jumper Series
Shadow Games
Shadow Prey
Shadow Justice
(previously published as *GLASSFORD GIRL)*

ABOUT THE AUTHOR

Jay J. Falconer is an award-winning screenwriter and USA Today Bestselling author whose books have hit #1 on Amazon in Action & Adventure, Military Sci-Fi, Post-Apocalyptic, Dystopian, Terrorism Thrillers, Technothrillers, Military Thrillers, Young Adult, and Men's Adventure fiction. He lives in the high mountains of northern Arizona where the brisk, clean air and stunning views inspire his day.

You can find more information about this author and his books at www.JayFalconer.com.

Awards and Accolades:
2020 USA Today Bestselling Book: Origins of Honor
2018 Winner: Best Sci-Fi Screenplay, Los Angeles Film Awards
2018 Winner: Best Feature Screenplay, New York Film Awards
2018 Winner: Best Screenplay, Skyline Indie Film Festival
2018 Winner: Best Feature Screenplay, Top Indie Film Awards
2018 Winner: Best Feature Screenplay, Festigious International Film Festival - Los Angeles
2018 Winner: Best Sci-Fi Screenplay, Filmmatic Screenplay Awards
2018 Finalist: Best Screenplay, Action on Film Awards in Las Vegas
2018 Third Place: First Time Screenwriters Competition, Barcelona International Film Festival
2019 Bronze Medal: Best Feature Script, Global Independent Film Awards

2017 Gold Medalist: Best YA Action Book, Readers' Favorite
International Book Awards
2016 Gold Medalist: Best Dystopia Book, Readers' Favorite
International Book Awards
Amazon Kindle Scout Winning Author

www.ingramcontent.com/pod-product-compliance
Lightning Source LLC
Chambersburg PA
CBHW070622260626
47161CB00007B/2541